W9-BDL-178

From the Nebula Award-winning author of
NO ENEMY BUT TIME,
a new masterpiece of science fiction:

THE SECRET ASCENSION
or
Philip K. Dick Is Dead, Alas

"Intensely thoughtful and highly recommended."
—*Library Journal*

"Bound to be one of the most talked-about and admired books of the year." —Pat Cadigan

"Bishop continues to deliver solid, memorable novels that move the emotions, intrigue the mind, and still keep your hands turning the pages."
—Gregory Benford

"I loved *The Secret Ascension.*" —Paul Williams

"It never ceases to amaze me just how fine a writer Michael Bishop is, and he continues to top himself with each successive work." —*Best Sellers*

"If the science fiction field has a saint it is likely the late Philip K. Dick, the writer who brought spiritual uncertainty and political consciousness to a literary genre innocent of both. Bishop . . . has fashioned a loving homage that explodes with energy and invention." —New York *Daily News*

"Fans of Dick will be fascintated by [*The Secret Ascension*], while those unfortunate enough to be unfamiliar with his work will find that the lapse . . . offers only a minor impediment to enjoying Bishop's superlative storytelling ability."
—Austin *American-Statesman*

THE SECRET ASCENSION

or
Philip K. Dick Is Dead, Alas

MICHAEL BISHOP

TOR

A TOM DOHERTY ASSOCIATES BOOK
NEW YORK

THE SECRET ASCENSION OR, PHILIP K. DICK IS DEAD, ALAS

Copyright © 1987 by Michael Bishop

First printing: November 1987
First mass market printing: July 1989

A TOR BOOK

Published by Tom Doherty Associates, Inc.
49 West 24 Street
New York, N.Y. 10010

Jacket design by Carol Russo

ISBN: 0-812-53157-4   Can. ISBN: 0-812-53158-2

Library of Congress Catalog Card Number: 87-50483

PRINTED IN THE UNITED STATES OF AMERICA

0 9 8 7 6 5 4 3 2 1

This book is for the heirs,
biological and literary,
of
Philip K. Dick

It is the essence of moral responsibility to determine *beforehand* the consequences of our action or inaction.

—Richard Nixon,
No More Vietnams

ACKNOWLEDGMENTS

This novel grew out of my respect and affection for the novels of the late Philip K. Dick. The best, to my mind, remains *The Man in the High Castle*, but I also admire *Time Out of Joint, Martian Time-Slip, Do Androids Dream of Electric Sheep?, Ubik, A Scanner Darkly, Valis,* and *The Transmigration of Timothy Archer*. I think it important— even if more or less redundant—to note that the influence of these novels, and of many other Dick titles, pervades this literary homage.

On the other hand, I do not mean *The Secret Ascension; or, Philip K. Dick Is Dead, Alas* as a slavish pastiche of Dick's work. Yes, I use many of Dick's favorite literary techniques (for instance, multiple third-person point-of-view narration) and some of those quintessentially Dickian science fictional "elements" (for instance, the reality breakdown) to structure the novel, but I do not always deploy them as Dick would have. My failure to do so may or may not be lamentable, but it is *not* an accident.

These books proved particularly helpful in the writing of my novel: *Only Apparently Real* by Paul Williams, *Philip K. Dick: The Last Testament* by Gregg Rickman, *The Novels of Philip K. Dick* by Kim Stanley Robinson, *Real Peace* and *No More Vietnams* by Richard Nixon, *People of the Lie* by M. Scott Peck, M.D., *The Demonologist* by Gerard Brittle, *Engines of Creation* by K. Eric Drexler, and two titles that satirically depict the political personality of Richard Nixon, *Our Gang* by Philip Roth and *The Public Burning* by Robert Coover. I thank the authors.

Finally, I acknowledge the signal contribution of Geoffrey A. Landis, whom I met in July 1985 while teaching a week of the Clarion SF & Fantasy Writing Workshop at Michigan State University in East Lansing. Through a subsequent correspondence, Geoff gave me pages of good material—drawings, tables, personal speculations, etc.—about the likely evolution of the American space program if our country had achieved a military victory in Vietnam in 1974. I have never been known as a writer of "hard"—that is, technologically and/or scientifically knowledgeable—science fiction, and Geoff is largely responsible for whatever accuracy and/or verisimilitude the Von Braunville segments of my narrative may possess. On the other hand, no one should blame him for my surrealistic lapses in these same passages. Once again, Geoff, my gratitude.

Michael Bishop
Pine Mountain, Georgia
January 14 to May 19, 1986

PRELUDE

The alien pink Moon peers into Philip K. Dick's apartment in Santa Ana, California. The year is 1982 (although maybe not the 1982 of most history books), and Dick himself has just suffered a debilitating stroke.

The Moon pins him to the floor in a circle of pink light. It projects—weirdly—an arc of lunar surface onto his back. Craters, maria, and bays ripple across the jacket that he was wearing when the stroke felled him. He is still wearing it as, subconsciously conscious, he lies waiting for someone—a friend, a neighbor, the police—to find him and dispatch him to the hospital.

A hefty tomcat stalks into this ring of pink light, sits down beside the stricken man. The cat meows once, nuzzles Dick's brow, grates his cheek with a tongue like wet Velcro. After a while, the cat gingerly mounts its owner's jacket, pads across the shadowy map of the Moon, and settles down in the clammy swale of the small of Dick's back for a winter snooze.

February, thinks the quasi-conscious stroke victim, is a fucking horrible time to die. . . .

Soon, tiny machines in the fallen writer's blood begin to build a half-substantive, half-astral simulacrum to warehouse his mind and memories.

Half-assed's more like it, thinks Dick, noting the buzz in his veins. This is weird. This is all-fired fucking *weird*.

His second self is a sort of material ghost, which rises buck-naked and shimmering from the mortal body of the stricken man. So swiftly, silently, and imperceptibly is Philip K. Dick₂ lifted out of Philip K. Dick₁ that Harvey Wallbanger, the cat, doesn't even stir. The other cats in the apartment are equally unaffected.

It feels to $Dick_2$ as if someone has left a freezer door open somewhere, and he looks upon his fallen self with astonished pity. "You poor bastard," he says. "Crazy shit like this always happens to you. It's happened again."

A tangible ghost, $Dick_2$ knows that intangible nano-computers in the circulatory system of $Dick_1$ used that body as a template for his own miraculous form.

Goosebumps begin to prickle $Dick_2$'s resurrected flesh, and he begins trembling with compassion as well as the cold. $Dick_1$ has not arisen—he will never arise again—and $Dick_2$, bereaved, loves him as fully as $Dick_1$ loved each of his friends in life.

A life, $Dick_2$ realizes, that is soon to end. A life that the evil policies of King Richard twisted into a parody of the real thing in $Dick_1$'s middle age, and a life for which $Dick_2$ mourns as he stands shivering in the frigid lunar pinkness.

This is another secret ascension, reflects $Dick_2$. My *second* fucking secret ascension. I understand—again—that this world is irreal, and that above or beyond it dwells some benign but hidden Entity who wants to remove our blinders. Although we're occluded, this Entity wants us to see through our occlusion to the reality that eternally appertains. . . .

Time and space are illusions, $Dick_2$ tells himself, walking to a closet to find something with which to cover his naked-ness. For at the moment it is warmth that $Dick_2$ wants, not profound ontological insights. When he opens the closet door, he finds that his half-astral body can indeed impinge upon the "solid" forms of this world. And why not? If $Dick_1$'s world is actually irreal, then why shouldn't a ghost —to some, the very essence of irreality—be able to function within it?

And I *can* function here, thinks $Dick_2$, the *pre*-ghost of the yet living Philip K. Dick. At least for a time. Until the Entity behind our occlusion withdraws its support. . . .

The pre-ghost rifles the stuff in the closet like a prop lady going through the trunk of a theater company. He just wants to get warm. To bundle himself in comfortable clothes that don't make any kind of premeditated statement—except, possibly, that he isn't a proponent of empty style-consciousness.

At last he finds some worn trousers, a loose denim work shirt, and a silver jacket. This last is a name-brand jobbie, with an affected little designer tag, but he—Dick₁—bought it on a whim because he needed a jacket and liked the sportiness of its cut, and he—Dick₂—is delighted to snug into it as soon as he's pulled on the pants and shirt.

No underwear.

Why do I need underwear? wonders the Dickian pre-ghost. Isn't it clear that I don't? Biology's behind me. Us half-astral beings are no longer slaves to secretions and exudates. . . .

Dick₂ falls into an easy chair, tugs on some slouchy, low-cut tennis shoes, glances again at Dick₁.

You're doomed, he thinks. You were always doomed. You managed to get as far as you did only because you were too fucking proud to succumb to the lie of consensus reality. You wouldn't pull in your antennae. And look where it got you, Phil. Just look.

Dick₂ rises, shuffles around the apartment, eventually sits down at the desk in the room where Dick₁'s typewriter resides. He begins to type. Silently but maniacally, his fingers tap-dance the keys. The type arms blur in their cage, a hundred hummingbirds hammering at the mendaciousness of the night. Time is telescoped, reality turned upside down.

Neighbors, barging in, find Dick₁ sprawled unconscious on the living-room rug. Harvey Wallbanger meows, and friends arrive to ferry the comatose writer to a nearby medical facility. Every once in a while, someone enters the apartment to take away a cat or a paperback novel or a toothbrush, but, through all of this, Dick₂ continues to type.

February falls, March marches in, and the pre-ghost becomes a true ghost when a new series of merciless strokes, triggering heart failure, abstracts Philip K. Dick₁ from the alternative irreality of the time stream in which he lived.

You poor fucking bastard, mourns the feverish consciousness at his typewriter, fingers still furiously tapping. Godspeed.

Bizarre images elbow the brain of Dick₂. Writing on erasable parchment, invisible bond, he takes himself to the

Moon. A tunnel opens in the spot where the Moon should be, and he goes through it to the Omicron Ceti binary, seventy parsecs distant, there to meet the Entity sustaining this entire irreal Cosmos. They rap, God and the ghost at the machine, and at the end of their colloquy $Dick_2$ is sent spiraling back through the hoops of his consciousness to an apartment in Santa Ana, California.

The ghost stops typing. He has been mind-wiped. Somewhere in King Richard's Amerika—apparently one of the mountain states—he catches a disturbing glimpse of his primary's burial, but he can no longer remember the identity of this person—which is to say, he can no longer recall his *own* identity.

If he could read, a skill that he has forgotten, he could put a name to himself by pulling out X_1's driver's license, or scanning his book plates, or trying to dig up some of his canceled checks. Unfortunately, just back from his chat with the Deity, all he knows about himself now is that he has fallen prey to an unforgiving kind of amnesia.

I need help, thinks X_2. God knows, I need help.

Although the apartment holds him several more days, he works up his courage by doing snuff and brewing hot black coffee. Finally, he ventures out of doors. Mysteriously, greenbacks bulge in X_1's wallet, and he—X_2—is able to extract them from the billfold at will, a karmic gift of startling proportion. On the sidewalks, out in the wan March sunlight, he, the ghost, acquires full substance. He suddenly possesses both a shadow and a voice.

Impressed by this second shot at life, X_2 hails a cab.

It comes squealing up. "Where to, buddy?" asks the driver. He is a real human being, the erstwhile ghost observes. A dude with a brilliant bald spot. A dude whose breath reeks of jalapeño peppers and bravura cheddar.

"The airport," X_2 says. "Take me to the airport."

1

In order to clean their cage, Cal Pickford picked up two of the varmints known as Brezhnev bears. Although they didn't stink (at least no worse than did most of the critters in the Happy Puppy Pet Emporium), or gobble live mice, or scream like banshees, or secrete venom or musk, or need a lot of arduous grooming, or go belly up if he once forgot to feed them, or parrot his every thoughtless cuss word, Cal wrinkled his nose and unceremoniously dropped the "bears" into a deep cardboard box full of cedar chips.

The fall didn't hurt them, but it was a less than delicate way to treat the creatures, easily the pet shop's most profitable item since his arrival.

Cal knew why he disliked them, of course, but as he worked at the rear of the shop in West Georgia Commons mall dumping out the pee-soaked carpeting of cedar chips from his fifth glass cage of the morning and replacing it with a fresh layer of newsprint and a clean floor of chips, he tried not to think about the popular, but grotesque, beasties. Let the ugly-cute varmints scurry, and let the with-it young professionals (UpMos) who regarded them as status symbols plop down *their* cash to buy 'em.

Today, Lia monopolized Cal's thoughts. She was in only the third week of her private practice as a psychotherapist over in Warm Springs, but if clients didn't soon start signing up with her for sessions, his pay as a pet-shop hand would fall far short of what the Bonner-Pickfords needed to meet the payments on either Lia's new "preowned" car or the rent on their apartment in Pine Mountain. Cal had a paid-for '68 Dodge Dart for his commute to LaGrange, but Lia had mortgaged her success as a shrink to a '79 Mercury Cougar. Together they were just scraping by.

That they both lived seventeen-plus miles from their jobs made no sense, but after moving to Georgia from Colorado, where they had met at a Red Rocks folk-rock concert in '76, Lia had insisted on living as near her surviving relatives—her invalid mother, Emily, and her brother, Jeff, and his family— as possible. Because Jeff managed a horse farm northwest of Pine Mountain, Pine Mountain had snared them, but Cal still wondered how he—a superannuated hippie cowboy—had ever ended up in King Richard's Solid South, land of cotton, cloggers, and Co' Cola.

Suddenly, Cal was aware of another presence at the back of the shop. He looked up and saw a man of immense size walking between the aisles, scrutinizing everything around him. Occasionally, this well-dressed man—his three-piece suit was conspicuously at odds with his middle linebacker's physique—would pick an item off a shelf (a currying comb or a container of flea powder), examine it briefly, and then set it back down. He peered at the ceiling and into the corners of the shop, as well as at the merchandise, and he carried himself with menacing authority.

"Anything I can do for you?" Cal asked, squatting beside a bag of cedar chips.

The man stopped and stared down at him. "Just looking."

"Well, go right ahead. We're glad to have browsers."

"I didn't say I was browsing," the big man replied, stepping closer to Cal's row of glass cages. "I said I was *looking*."

"Looking's okay, too. Go ahead and look."

The interloper scrutinized Cal as if he were a currying comb or a box of flea powder. "One thing I don't do is browse. Guess I'll never be your typical goddamn 'browser.' "

A bruiser's more like it, Cal thought, decidedly uncomfortable with this line of talk. Why was the guy still looking at *him*, for God's sake, and why would he come into the Happy Puppy and put his hands all over everything if he weren't in the market for some kind of animal or pet product?

"If there's anything I can help you with," Cal said, "let me know."

"You'll be the *first* to know, buddy," the man said, the line of his lips vaguely resembling a smirk. But the smirk faded, and the man ambled slowly back toward the front of the shop, picking up or squinting at various items as he walked. Eventually, he swaggered past the cash computer into the main concourse of the mall.

Cal, shaken, tried to recall what he had been thinking about before the interruption.

"Pickford!" Mr. Kemmings, the owner of this franchise of the Pet Emporium, shouted. "Pickford, come up here, please!"

Cal was up to his elbows in cedar chips, fragrant red shavings sticking to his arms like flower petals. He brushed them back down into the sack, shouted "Coming!" at his employer, and then hurried to wash up at a sink in the shop's restroom. When he finally got to the front, Mr. Kemmings, who was trying to sell a couple of ring doves to an old woman in a tweed suit, told him to wait on a second customer.

This woman had just entered. Although she was decades younger than the Agatha Christie character harkening to Mr. Kemmings, she hovered much closer to forty than did Cal, who was still six years shy of that scary personal benchmark. Thirty-nine, Cal estimated. Maybe as much as forty-one. She wore a black cape, sunglasses, and scarlet riding britches tucked into tall leather boots.

Incognito, Cal thought. She's sauntering around incognito.

Mr. Kemmings said, "This lady says she'd like to buy a pet, Pickford. She wants recommendations. Help her."

"Yes, sir." In Colorado, you said, "Yeah" or "All right" or "You bet." In Georgia, you said, "Yes, sir" or "Yes, ma'am."

The woman in sunglasses was peering through her mirror lenses at a tank of tropical fish.

"Do you like fish?" Cal asked her.

"Only when they're baked and served with lemon and a sprig of parsley. Preferably on rice."

"You'd have to bake a whole *school* of these to make a meal," Cal said. "And even one red snapper'd be cheaper."

The woman straightened. Her mirrors tracked him down. "I'm not terribly concerned about costs."

"I wish we'd known that. We could've stocked a few animals from endangered species." Immediately, Cal regretted the sarcasm. If Mr. Kemmings heard crap like that, the old guy'd can him, and then what would he and Lia do?

Surprisingly, the woman was smiling. "That's pretty witty for a pet-store flunky, Mr. Pickford."

"I'm sorry. Really. I shouldn't've said it."

"Why not? It's a free country."

Cal's mind gave him a troubling flash of the big guy who had preceded this woman into the shop. "If you're rich, white, and Republican, maybe. Otherwise you'd better hope whoever you're talking to isn't wired." Cal couldn't believe he'd said that. Out of the frying pan. Into the inferno. Lia would have to buy him an asbestos mitten for his tongue, his most inflammatory appendage.

A wry smile replaced the woman's warm one. "No, it's free even for people like you, Mr. Pickford. In these United States, one out of three's a passing grade. You can flag 'em all and still prosper if you're not an avowed *anti*patriot."

"Yes, ma'am."

"I'd like it better if you said, 'Yes, miss.'"

"Yes, miss."

"I'm assuming you're saying that freely—with no sense of being yanked about."

"Yes, ma'am. I mean, Yes, miss."

"I came in here to buy a pet, a friend to keep me company when there's no one else who'll do."

How often can that happen? Cal thought, for this woman, whether pushing forty or glancing back over her shoulder at it, had a nice figure and a well-proportioned face. Her sunglasses couldn't hide the pleasing symmetry of her features.

Aloud he said, "Are you a dog person or a cat person? Maybe that would help me get a fix on you."

"I hope I'm not either, Mr. Pickford. You make both sobriquets sound like titles."

"Titles?"

"His Royal Highness, the Prince of Wales, *Dog Person*.

All-Star Center Fielder Murph Dailey, *Cat Person*. Can you imagine those words engraved on dinner invitations?"

Suddenly, Cal was frightened. Who was he talking to? Was this person maybe—in actual fact—wired? What about the guy who'd come in ahead of her? Most of Mr. K.'s customers had an easy-going, unpretentious, down-home manner about them. You didn't see that many upper-crusters bopping around West Georgia Commons. Even if they had money, or breeding, or both, they also had enough of one or both to act like everyday Americans instead of the highfalutin characters in a play by Oscar Wilde. Cal was now certain that his "rich, white, and Republican" remark had been a *big* mistake. This woman was letting him know. She wanted him to sweat. And that was the only "fix" on her that she intended him to arrive at.

Maybe she'd like to buy a snake, Cal thought. A rattler. Or possibly our boa constrictor.

"I've heard a good deal about Brezhnev bears," she said. "You have some, don't you? I believe I'd like to see them."

"Take her back there," Mr. Kemmings encouraged Cal. The boss had lost the battle with his own customer, but apparently didn't want to steal Cal's potential sale. "We've got a good stock of 'em right now, miss, but they're going like hot cakes. Pick one or two out before the weekend crowd gets in here."

Hot cakes. Cal imagined drenching the naked backs of Brezhnev bears with Log Cabin syrup.

Shaking this image from his head, he led his customer to the benches at the shop's rear. Here were six aquariums, each housing—on cedar chips, not in water—two or more of the popular pets. One of the aquariums still needed its chips dumped and replaced, but Cal squared his back to it, shielding it from the woman's view, and she began scrutinizing the "bears" in the other cages.

"My, they're odd little animals, aren't they?"

Cal said nothing.

"How long have you been selling them?"

"Me personally or Mr. Kemmings's shop? I've only been here since the middle of January. About eight weeks."

"I meant the shop, of course."

"Well, the Happy Puppy Pet Emporium's had them ever since the first shipments arrived from the Soviet Union. Maybe six months. That's because Nixon's secretary of agriculture, Hiram Berthelot, hails from Woodbury, not that far from here, and I guess he wanted local pet stores to be among the first in the country to offer the critters for sale."

"The efficacy of friends in high places."

"I guess so. Anyway, New Yorkers had to wait a month or two longer than Atlantans to buy theirs."

Gracefully lifting the wings of her cape, the woman squatted before an aquarium. She put the tip of one finger to the glass, an inch away from the tawny-maned head of one of the animals. "They're not really bears, I know that. So what are they?"

"They're cavies, ma'am." Cal swallowed. "I mean, *miss.*" He felt again that this woman was toying with him. A person totally ignorant of Brezhnev bears was a person who had been marooned on an uncharted island for the past half year.

"Cavies?"

"Guinea pigs. Most scientists don't like to call them that anymore, though. 'Guinea pig' has some bad connotations."

"But they're naked. Except for their bushy little manes, that is. Guinea pigs have hair. Some of them have quite a lot of hair. When I was a girl, a friend of mine owned two *Peruvian* guinea pigs, and they looked like tangled balls of chocolate- or soot-colored yarn. She had to clip them every month or so just to be able to tell their heads from their heinies."

"These guinea pigs—cavies—were bred especially for laboratory research by Soviet scientists, miss. That's why they're nicknamed Brezhnev bears. Sort of a tip of the hat to détente and President Nixon's foreign-policy successes."

Cal hated himself for choosing his words with such craven care, but this lady—and the strange guy who'd come in ahead of her—had him spooked. If he blew his job at the mall, Lia might finally stop trying to rescue him from his suicidal impulses. She wanted their move to Georgia to be a fresh start, not a rehash of past problems.

The woman stood up, simultaneously releasing her cape. "But why are they hairless?"

"To reduce the need for hands-on care. That's what makes

them such good pets for busy young people with jobs. Also, it pretty much cuts out the gamy odor that you get with regular guinea pigs, and that's another plus. With all the cultural and technological exchanges we've got going with the Soviets nowadays, it was almost inevitable that Secretary Berthelot would arrange to import some of these bald commie cavies for American laboratories."

"And the manes?"

"I think they're just for cuteness. The Kremlin has a strain that's completely naked. Unfortunately, they give most people the willies. But Brezhnev bears, well, *their* looks mostly make you giggle and feel protective and want to take a couple home for pets or conversation pieces."

"Or status symbols?"

"That, too."

"Do you think, Mr. Pickford, I'm the sort of woman who requires status symbols to bolster her ego?"

"No, miss. You asked to see them."

"I know I did. And I'm going to buy a pair. Not for status, though. For their cuteness. For their company."

She selected two cavies, and Cal showed her some unoccupied aquariums so that she could buy one of those, too—along with a bag of guinea-pig pellets, a water bottle, and a large sack of cedar chips. Her total bill came to $122.00, plus tax, and Mr. Kemmings, beaming, let Cal ring it all up himself.

Maybe now I'll learn your name, Cal thought. He was ready to receive from their customer a check or credit card. He wanted to know her name partly because he felt that knowing it would make her less intimidating and partly because he had the odd suspicion that he ought to know it already.

But rather than a check or a credit card, the woman handed over cash. A one-hundred-dollar bill, a twenty, and a ten.

Feeling stymied, or possibly even subtly mocked, Cal gave her three dollars and twelve cents in change. The two pennies (he noted, as he always did) bore in profile the graven likeness of Richard Nixon, the only living president ever to secure this honor. Moreover, King Richard's men had achieved this coup not after his retirement but during the first year of his third term. Both pennies, in fact, were from that year, 1977, with the word *Liberty* to the left of RN's visage and a *D* (for the Denver mint) stamped a quarter inch beneath his ski-slope nose.

"Is there anything else I should know about their care?" the woman asked, pocketing her change.

"Keep them warm. Sixty-five degrees, or about that, or they'll catch cold and cash in their chips." (Pun half-assedly intended.)

"Can do. However, it's only about fifty outside today. How do I get them to my car?"

Cal remembered that a nippy March headwind had fought his Dart all the way to the mall this morning. The "bears" could stand a few minutes in such conditions, of course, but if one of them were a trifle puny when it left the shop, even brief exposure to the cold could be life-threatening. And because Mr. K. guaranteed the health of his animals for a week after purchase, any Brezhnev bear that died during that time meant lost profits.

But the boss had overheard. "Pickford'll help you, miss," he said, walking toward them from the hamsters and gerbils. "Drive your car around back. Park it where you see our name on one of the service doors. We'll load your purchases for you."

We'll? What's this "we'll" business? Mr. K. was fifty-eight, going on eighty-five, with a damaged ticker and chronic shortness of breath. Cal didn't expect him to tote heavy pet supplies to customers' automobiles, but he resented his use of the royal "we" almost as much as he resented having a living man's kisser on legal coins of the realm.

Outside, after squeezing through the door with an aquarium in which two scared Brezhnev bears were running amok, Cal encountered a big, cordovan-colored Cadillac. He tried to hold a nonchalant look on his face as he eased the cage onto the leather-upholstered seat and put everything else in the Fleetwood's trunk.

"You like my car?"

"I couldn't afford gas for it, much less the insurance."

"Why hasn't a smart fellow your age—over thirty?—found more challenging, and better-paying work?" A significant gesture at the pet store. "Were you ever in trouble with the authorities?"

The wind whipping past Cal's sweated work shirt chilled him. "No, ma'am—*miss,* I mean. It's just that I love animals."

"Oh."

"But my wife's a psychotherapist," he blurted.

"That must be handy for you. Where does she practice?"

"Warm Springs. Her brother owns the office, thank God, so we don't have to pay rent. Her name's Lia. Dr. Lia Bonner."

"That's good to know." Smiling, the woman took off her silver shades. Bright blue eyes whose irises had a cool lack of depth. Tinted contacts? "That's *really* good to know."

She replaced her sunglasses, gave Cal a five-dollar tip, slid into her Cadillac, and drove off around the back of the mall into an encroaching twilight zone of mist or fog. Only a moment later, another car—a late-model Plymouth—followed the Cadillac into this same spooky murk.

At least she has her Brezhnev bears, Cal thought. Because all I've got is my unfocused terror. . . .

2

D r. Lia Bonner sat in her Warm Springs office, waiting for clients to walk in. She had ten or twelve already, including a few referrals from doctors at the county hospital and the Roosevelt/Warms Springs rehab center, but unless she got some consulting work from area industries— Millikin, Goody, Georgia-Pacific—she might not be able to keep her shingle out.

After all, you met with your clients only once a week, if that often, for only an hour or so a session. With only twelve clients, you could hardly expect to stay busy shrinking heads every hour of every day, and for the past three weeks Lia had spent most of her time making telephone calls, paying visits to the merchants and manufacturers who might one day let her session with their troubled employees, and shooing away the salespeople who wanted her to buy couches, filing cabinets, or computer systems.

I can hardly afford dog food for Viking, she wanted to shout. How could I justify seventy-five dollars for a plastic floor protector?

Cal had insisted that it was a mistake to leave Colorado. He'd had steady, if not spectacularly lucrative, work with Arvill Rudd, on his ranch near Gardner, above Walsenburg, and Lia had been doing okay sessioning with clients in a rented house near Walsenburg's hospital. But when her father died in a collision with a logging truck on the West Point Highway in Harris County, Georgia, a wreck that had also severely crippled her mother, Lia—more homesick than she had ever been—had told Cal that it was time to move south.

"What the hell're we gonna do in Georgia, Lia?"

"I'll set up a new practice, and you'll find a job. There's really nothing but legal technicalities to keep us here now."

"This is where I was *born*, gal. It's the country I was meant for. I *have* a job."

"Right. But I was born in Georgia, and that's the place *I* was meant for. We've lived out here in Marlboro Country ever since we got married. Given the Travel Restrictions Act, it would've been stupid to object, but now it's your turn to go where I go."

"But you came out here of your own free will, and I've never so much as set foot in Dixie."

"Cal, my daddy's dead, and my mama's going to be a cripple from now on. I want to be down there for her. You ought to understand my feelings. You know what it's like to lose your folks."

Wearily, Cal had said, "You get over it, Lia."

"Ha! That's really ironic. That's one of the things you most emphatically *haven't* gotten over."

"Lia . . ." (Warning her.)

"Cal, you should take advantage of my expertise. You should sit down and talk to me about that. I could help you."

But he had deflected her argument. "I'll never make a Georgia Boy. I'm a cowboy, not a cracker."

Cowboy or no, he was a cracker today, and Lia felt a twinge of guilt every time she drove to West Georgia Commons to meet him and saw him puttering around inside the Happy Puppy Pet Emporium with a sack of cedar chips or a blow dryer for his poofy Brezhnev bears. It was a far cry from bucking hay for Arvill Rudd or delivering calves on cold February nights with his arms halfway up the birth canal of an exhausted heifer.

The dust of forage; the steaming slime of new life.

Cal had loved those things, and seeing her husband kowtowing to customers and feeding parakeets sometimes made her wonder if she were being selfish. Then she remembered that she had lived in Gardner for five years and that her mother was in the Warm Springs nursing home, confined either to bed or a wheelchair, and she knew that she'd done only what simple decency required.

Exactly, Lia thought. And Cal's getting acclimatized.

What had finally enabled her to convince Cal, though, was the fact that the Internal Travel Restrictions Act—passed in 1971 mostly as a means of controlling antiwar protesters, but still in effect eight years after victory in Vietnam—allowed residents of one state to travel to another, or to make a permanent change of state residency, only under strictly policed conditions.

Those freest to move about were politicians with national reputations; well-connected business types (especially if they kept Republican campaign coffers brimming); professional athletes on major-league franchises; registered truckers; federal employees in the military, the postal service, or domestic intelligence; and Congressionally certified entertainers. Rock musicians and folk singers often had trouble getting certified; and when Pete Seeger, Bob Dylan, and Joan Baez, along with several other big-name figures in the folk-rock counterculture, dropped permanently from sight during a single eight-month period in 1973, only complete airheads and paid administration flunkies tried to attribute their separate disappearances to "coincidence."

In any case, you had to have an "in" with the Powers That Be to travel freely in King Richard's United States, and most "little people"—ordinary folks with civilian employment—could go from one state to another only if they met the criteria qualifying them for an exemption from the Internal Travel Restrictions Act.

These criteria were mercantile, educational, or "humanitarian" in character, and Lia, on scholarship in Colorado Springs at a school recommended by a paternal uncle, knew all the categories by heart. After all, by wedding Cal and settling with him in Gardner, Colorado, she had cut herself off from Georgia forever—unless, of course, a humanitarian exemption presented itself.

Well, the death of someone in your immediate family was grounds for exemption, but it was good for only two weeks after that death, and you had to act quickly to get it. If, by chance, you wanted to file for residence in the state where the funeral was being held, you had to show the authorities cause. Inheriting a farm or a business was almost always sufficient, but you could also prevail if you proved to them that a spouse or child of the decedent now required your care. Lia thanked God that she met this criterion even as she rebuked Him for taking her father and incapacitating her mother.

So here she was in Georgia, with Cal dutifully in tow. It had meant a jumble of red tape getting here and then a puppet theater full of pulled strings establishing her practice. That was why Cal had been able to go to work before she did. Having earned all her professional credentials out of state, she'd had to buttonhole her state representative in LaGrange, write letters to the governor, and impose on her brother Jeff's acquaintance with a federal judge to get set up. Had it all been worth it? A shingle was only a shingle, and the act of hanging it out by no means guaranteed you either a clientele or a livelihood.

I can't believe this, Lia thought. I scratched and clawed to get back home, and now—irony of ironies—I'm homesick for Huerfano County and my tumbledown office in Walsenburg.

Don't tell Cal, she advised herself. He'll say, "My lord, Lia, you wouldn't be happy in heaven," as if *any* place in this country even remotely approximated that metaphysical Happy Hunting Ground.

And if you've *really* begun to think of Cal's Rockies as home again—which you haven't, not at all—then Thomas Wolfe was right: "You *can't* go home again." No, you can't. Just try to reverse an exemption to the ITR Act already acted upon. . . .

Lia got up from her desk and went to the window overlooking the truncated main thoroughfare of Warm Springs. Hard to believe that President Roosevelt once visited this town on a regular basis. He came for the springs, of course, seeking relief from the pain of his paralysis. And today, not a half mile away, there's the Little White House, his residence while he was here. You can pay a park ranger three dollars and tour the place, eyeing FDR's photographs, cigarette holders, and cane collection. I did that as a little girl, when it didn't cost so much, and in the summer there'd almost always be a crowd.

That's what I need today. A crowd. Tourists with neuroses and psychoses—a few problems to analyze and exorcise.

Lia laughed. Nearly all tourism today was in-state stuff, small potatoes. A body would have to have *real* mental problems to try to get an ITR exemption—just to come from New England or the West Coast to visit FDR's Little White House, even with planned side trips to West Point Lake and Callaway Gardens. Maybe if you were rich and powerful or if you knew people. Otherwise, forget it. You might as well plan a trip to the Censorinus crater on the next NASA t-ship flight. Your chances of vacationing out of state were about as good as your chances of cadging a spot on that ship to Von Braunville, the U.S. moonbase.

Lia returned to her desk, took a pack of playing cards from her drawer, and dealt herself a hand of solitaire.

"Dr. Bonner," Miss Bledsoe, Lia's young black secretary, said, "you got somebody here to see you."

Lia scraped her fanned playing cards out of view. "You scared me, Shawanda. I thought you'd gone out for the mail."

"I been back awhile. You want to see this person?"

"Who is it? Somebody who's been here before?"

"No, ma'am. I don't know who it is, rightly. He wants to talk to a doctor, though. That much he say."

"Does he know what *kind* of doctor I am, Shawanda?" Lia was being cautious because Shawanda would let just about anybody in who claimed to have business with Lia: office-supply salesmen, advance people for religious cults, and, twice, curious members of her own family.

"He say he needs a 'head doctor,' ma'am."

"Have you had him fill out the forms? I know we need clients, but maybe we don't need to usher people in right off the street."

"Yes, ma'am."

"'Yes, ma'am, he's filled out the forms'? Or just 'Yes, ma'am, I agree with you'?"

"He hasn't touched no forms."

"Shawanda, why not?" Lia tried not to sound exasperated. She knew that she ought to call her secretary "Miss Bledsoe" rather than "Shawanda," but the young woman—actually, an adolescent of eighteen or nineteen—had such a coltish look and such immature gestures and work habits that Lia couldn't sustain the masquerade of formality.

Besides, Shawanda sometimes spontaneously confided in her, and Lia had hired her not only because she could pay her only minimum wage—a necessity right now—but also because Shawanda was the grandchild of the woman who had been Lia's parents' cook from the late 1940s to the mid-1960s. Shawanda had been graduated from Harris County High School last June, and she was well versed in social science, math, and clarinet playing. Her spelling wanted improvement, and her command of English had a lot to do with her mood and her audience. Because the University of Georgia currently admitted blacks on a quota system, using the percentage of black Americans nationwide as its baseline figure, the girl could not go on to college. If Lia hadn't offered her a secretarial job, she would have never found work that wasn't domestic in nature.

"Ma'am?"

"I said why hasn't this person filled out our forms?"

"Dr. Bonner, I don't think he can write."

Lia stood up. "Is this an adult person, Shawanda?" She feared that their would-be client was either a child or a poor black. Lia hoped not—not because she disdained to treat children or blacks, but because the visitor would have limited resources and she wasn't going to be able to dispense charity forever.

"This is most definitely a grown person, Dr. Bonner. This is, in fac', a grown man. A grown *white* man. With a beard."

"Does he look like a bum?"

"He's not sportin' his Sunday best, but I don't know if that means he's a bum."

"And he can't write?"

"I don't know. He *won't* write, that's for sure. He pushed the papers away and said, 'Lemme see the doctor.'"

Jesus, Lia thought. I ought to go to the door and take a peek at him, but even if he looks like the Penultimate Vagrant, reeking of the sidewalk and unwashed winter clothes, he could still be as rich as that crazy Howard Hughes. Dare I turn away Howard Hughes? For that matter, dare I turn away a guy with *un*resoled shoes? No. Not if I want to eat.

"Send him in, Shawanda."

Shawanda—attractively lanky—went out to tell only the day's second client that, yes, the doctor would see him.

The man peeked playfully around the edge of the door, as if he might not have any greater wish to remain in Lia's office than she had to meet with a bum who could not pay. This was reassuring. If *he* had doubts about *her,* then he was clearly not someone trying to mooch therapy just to be mooching therapy. He had standards. Lia had a glimmer of hope.

"How do you do?" she said, seated again at her desk. "What can I do for you?"

"I wanted to know if you had a coffee maker."

"A coffee maker?"

Her caller chuckled. "Yeah. One of those jobbies that you use filter paper with. Or even an old-fashioned percolator. But I see you've got a filter-paper outfit, the new-fangled sort."

Uh-oh. Maybe he only cadged free therapy from psychotherapists with acceptable coffee makers. Did hers pass?

Lia pointed him to the lounger opposite her desk, a well-padded piece of art that she was buying on time. The man was casually but not sloppily dressed. He looked a few years past middle age. He had a high forehead, a fairly neat pepper-and-salt beard, and eyes either melancholy or menacingly hooded, depending on how the light struck them. Mostly, Lia decided, they were sad-seeming, with incongruous laugh lines at their corners and an equally incongruous mirthfulness etched around his slightly heavy mouth. How to get a handle on the guy?

Seedily distinguished, Lia thought. That's it. He's seedily distinguished.

"I'll do the coffee," he said, crossing to the table with the automatic coffee maker. "I see you've got all the ingredients right here. A pitcher of H_2O, a bag of Brim—dear God, woman, the damn decaffeinated kind!—and a box of these filters." He shook a filter at her. It reminded her of a wimple for an elfin nun. Pretty soon, the coffee maker—once Jeff's, it needed a good vinegar rinse—was steaming away, making eerie puffing noises and dripping aromatic brown fluid into the Silex beaker.

"Hope you don't mind," he said, sitting down in the

lounger. The hollows under his eyes and his precise body movements suggested that he had once carried more weight than he did now. "You know, miss, decaffeinated coffee makes about as much sense as zero-proof Scotch."

"I like the taste. I don't like the kick."

"I like the kick. I don't like the taste. And if you applied the same logic to sex, you'd be just as well off doing sit-ups solo in front of a mirror."

Lia blinked. Who is this character? she wondered. He wasn't your typical manic-depressive. And if he *was* manic-depressive, she had caught him on the upswing, spouting one-liners and baiting her with saturnine charm. An *atypical* manic-depressive.

Composing herself, Lia said, "A couple of questions. What's your name? And what can I help you with?"

"To answer your first question, I don't know what my name is, and I'm not sure who I am."

"What?"

"I think I'm having a keenly severe bout of amnesia—radical amnesia. Only this time it's like I'm dead to the person that I ordinarily am. Or used to be."

My God, Lia thought. You hope for a customer and you get a guy who's so messed up he scares you. Amnesia, he says, and you were waiting for somebody with a minor personality quirk.

Lia shifted her weight. She could hear Cal telling her, "My lord, gal, you wouldn't be happy in heaven."

Now the man was saying, "And so I dropped in on you, see? To get help. And to give it, by answering a prayer that you probably considered only a half-assed sort of wish." He looked at the coffee maker. "Listen to that thing. Swear to God, it sounds like an emphysema victim." He took a balled-up handkerchief from the pocket of his Members Only jacket and wiped his brow. "I love that stuff, coffee—*real* coffee. I have to have it. Making it, though, that can terrify me. All the goddamn gasping and steaming."

"It's a borrowed coffee maker, that's all. An old one. It's certainly nothing to precipitate anxiety."

"Just coffee, huh? Listen, most reputable therapists know that almost anything can precipitate anxiety."

Beneath the desk, Lia closed her knees on her hands.

"Forgive me. You're right. But it's just a coffee maker, and you're safe here." *The question is, Am I safe here? You look respectable enough, even kindly, but your opening gambit—*amnesia!*—caught me off-guard. Any other doozies like that in your natty beard?*

Aloud, Lia told him, "If you really have amnesia, you need a thorough medical examination. There's a hospital within a short drive of here."

"Doctor, you don't pray—half-assedly *wish*—for a client and then try to shunt him off on somebody else when he shows up."

"I'm a psychologist, not a psychiatrist. You need to consult someone who's had medical training. Amnesia often has a physical cause—usually, in fact."

"Mine doesn't. Mine's a mechanism for putting truly painful shit behind me and not having to deal with it."

"I appreciate your wanting me to take you on. You probably guessed by the swarms of folks in my waiting room that I'm just covered up with work. But I *do* adhere to certain standards."

The man in the lounger, his hands folded across his middle, simply stared at her. With amusement, Lia thought.

"And if you know that your amnesia's a mechanism for avoiding emotional pain," she accused, "it's probably not radical amnesia. You recall *that* much about your past persona."

"If it were total amnesia, Doctor, I wouldn't be here. I'd be lying in the fetal position on some street corner."

"So you've come here, knowing that you're subject to spells of amnesia, with exactly what in mind?"

He laughed. "Thank you. You're conceding that I've got one—a mind, that is—and I'm grateful."

"No praise, no blame," Lia said, startling herself. *Where had that gnomic utterance come from?*

"But what I had in mind was this, Doctor—answering your prayer and helping myself. You can help me do both by showing me the way to anamnesis."

"Anamnesis?" *Curiouser and curiouser,* Lia thought.

"Literally, the loss of amnesia. Salvation through knowledge, or gnosis. You'll recall, I hope, that Plato considered learning nothing more than a form of remembering."

"And you want me to help you remember your life so that you can learn who you are? Is that it?"

"Half of it, I guess. The other half's harder."

"Harder than curing you of amnesia? Or, in your terminology, leading you to anamnesis?"

"Exactamente, señorita hermosa."

Perhaps I *can* help him, Lia reflected, taking her hands from between her knees and putting them on the blotter on her desk, as if to declare her sympathy for this odd person. Maybe I can. And I need to do just that if I'm going to call myself a psychologist and make a living at it. I can't force him to go to the hospital if he doesn't want to go, and it would be unethical to turn him away if he really wants me to treat him. But does he have any money? Is it bitchy of me to wonder if he can pay?

Steeling herself, Lia said, "I hope you won't think ill of me, but I need to know if you can *afford* therapy."

"I don't think ill of you. Money's a fact of life. It's also a fact of death, I guess."

Lia waited. I haven't offended him, she thought, but what am I to make of his aphoristic little reply?

"Once," he said, shifting on the lounger so that he could reach his hip pocket, "money was definitely a problem in my life. *That* I can't forget. Today, though, I seem to be flush."

He tossed his wallet at Lia. It skidded across her blotter, bulging with notes of various denominations. She didn't even have to pick it up to tell that her client—putting a possessive in front of "client" no longer seemed foolish—was more than "flush": he was the nearest thing to Daddy Warbucks she'd ever bumped into. Still, it was demeaning to have a billfold tossed at you as if you were a dog waiting for a leftover pork chop.

Then, picking up the wallet, she had an idea. "Wait a minute. Don't you have some identification in here? A driver's license? Credit cards? Something to induce, uh, anamnesis?"

"No, miss. Only money. But go ahead and look."

Curiouser and curiouser is a total understatement, Lia told herself, finding that the wallet contained no plastic, no pictures, not even a library card. Only money.

"Where did all this come from?" she asked.

"I'm not sure. I didn't filch it from the petty-cash fund at General Dynamics, though. I have this weird idea that it's, well, *karmic money*; that it's what I would've made in a perfect world if God or some other truly just observer had translated my spiritual struggles into—what?—coin of the realm, I guess. But it isn't coins, is it? Just the quiet stuff." He laughed.

Lia put his billfold down and wiped her hands on her skirt. What's happening here? What the hell is going on in my office this morning?

"Well?" the man said.

"Well what?"

"Do you think there's enough there to buy me a cup of coffee? Even if it's castrated—decaffeinated, I mean—it seems to've dripped itself to drinkability." He laughed again, a tight, almost maniacal chuckle.

"There's plenty," Lia said. "I'll be glad to take you on."

3

"Why not clean your last cage and treat yourself to an early lunch?" Mr. Kemmings said when Cal came back inside.

It was already eleven-thirty. It took Cal about twenty minutes an aquarium, if he scrubbed it out good, bathed the "bears" in warm soap and water, and dried the varmints with a blow dryer. Thank God, they required this treatment just once a week. Still, today's "early" lunch would net him only ten extra minutes. Sockdolager! Mr. Kemmings's generosity was breathtaking.

But Mr. K. knew what time it was. "Take a whole hour," he said. "You deserve it. You handled that lady, Pickford. I fobbed her off on you, you know. There was something about her that made me afraid to wait on her. But you took her on and made a nice sale. A very nice sale."

"Yes, sir. And I thought I'd be lucky to sell her a couple of white mice."

"White mice?"

"Sure. I had her sized up to take them home and eat them like My Main Squeeze."

Mr. Kemmings laughed. My Main Squeeze was the Happy Puppy Pet Emporium's boa constrictor. It was gratifying to hear Mr. K. get out a genuine chuckle. He wasn't a bad old geezer—just the kind of dyed-in-the-wool Calvinist that Cal himself, his Christian name aside, would never make. Protestant Work Ethic straight down the line, that was Mr. K. A fair day's sweat for a fair day's wage.

"What made you jittery?" Cal asked. "Do you know who she is?"

"I don't know her name, but she seemed familiar. I believe that's what had me shook."

"She's some kind of moneyed swell, Mr. Kemmings. You should've seen her car." Silently, he added, To say nothing of the humongous goon who came in ahead of her.

"Did you get a look at her auto tag?"

"No, I was too—" Cal stopped. Hadn't he put a ten-pound sack of cedar chips into the Caddie's trunk? Of course. Slowly, then, it broke on his mind's eye, an image of the woman's license plate. "It was a federal tag," he said, interpreting this vision. "Not a Georgia tag, but a tag with, uh, some kind of big-shot U.S. government seal or emblem." His own fear came back, intenser than before, raised exponentially by the fact that he and Mr. K. had found an empirical basis for their dis-ease.

"You think she was FBI?" Cal asked. "A Nixonian No-Knock?"

"Agents don't advertise. They'd be fools to label themselves."

"What, then?"

"I don't know. Maybe the wife of some high muckamuck. Maybe somebody connected with Fort Benning down in Columbus. Even high muckamucks and their families have lives to live. Sometimes they probably go shopping like regular people. It isn't necessarily a visit to get ourselves all lathered up over."

"It isn't necessarily *not* that kind of visit, either. Why are we so damned spooked?"

"Maybe she's with some federal agency. Maybe she was making an undercover inspection—to see if we were meeting federal standards for psittacosis control or something."

"Mr. Kemmings, she didn't even *look* at the parakeets. Or the macaws. Or any of the other birds. Her visit had nothing to do with psittacosis."

"Maybe it didn't. If it was official, and if we flunked, we'll hear about it, and there's nothing we can do about it until we do."

"Yes, sir."

"I'm going to feed My Main Squeeze. It's been a couple of days since he last ate, and he's moving around again."

Cal wondered how this sweet old guy could stomach watching the Pet Emporium's boa constrictor take into its elongate craw the cute white mice that sustained it. It ate them alive, of course, and the paranoid anxiety that he and Mr. K. felt in the wake of their visitor's leavetaking could hardly compare to the terror of the mice that Mr. K. put into Squeeze's cage. Cal closed his eyes and clenched his fists.

"I wish you'd wait until my lunch break," he said.

"I guess I could," Mr. K. acknowledged, "but whether you're here or somewhere else, the same thing'll happen."

Mr. Kemmings was already scooping the first of the serpent's intended victims out of its cage, a pink-eyed little mouse with fur the color of a baby harp seal's. Cal had a flash of his boss in caribou-leather boots and a hooded parka smashing a Louisville Slugger on the skull of one of these dewy-eyed seals. Meanwhile, its mother barked a protest, and gouts of blood from this and nearby bludgeonings incarnadined the ice. So vivid was this image that an arctic chill swept through the shop, scouring Cal's bones and turning his knuckles white.

Calm down, he thought. Today, Calvin, your every reaction is out of all proportion to its stimulus. He unballed his fists and tried to shake the tightness out of his fingers.

Mr. Kemmings would never bash a harp seal. As a young man (Cal had learned from some of his boss's off-hand reminiscences), Mr. K. had opened a small factory in Pine Mountain—this was at the end of World War II, in which a heart murmur had kept him from serving—producing argyle socks by hand and employing eight or twelve local people. The business had prospered until a man in Athens, Georgia, invented an automated process for making the stockings and Mr. K.'s workers could not equal their competitor's output. And so in 1956 or 1957 the factory in Pine Mountain had closed.

"What I hated about that," he told Cal, "wasn't getting whipped by a fella smarter than me but having to let go all the good people who depended on me for jobs."

"What'd they do?"

"They looked elsewhere. So did I. And I finally landed a job administering some social programs here in Troup County —from '58 to '76—and that was what kept food on our table. I could've gone for thirty years and got an even bigger pension, but when Nixon won his third term, I opted for an early retirement from government work. Sheer luck gave me the Happy Puppy franchise when they built West Georgia Commons, but I'm glad I got it."

So you can feed baby harp seals—I mean, white mice—to My Main Squeeze, Cal thought. But he was being unfair. How could you get down on a man who worried so much about other people and who wore to the pet shop every day another pair of the argyle socks made in his long-defunct factory? They were poignantly out-of-style socks, but so lovingly wrought that a man could still wear them to work three decades after their manufacture.

Now Mr. Kemmings was putting the mouse into My Main Squeeze's glass prison. Cal started to return to the cavies, but his boss stopped him. Cal glanced sidelong at the rodent, which was already scurrying from side to side at one end of the cage. The boa lifted its big head, flicked its tongue, uncoiled the foremost foot of its eight-foot body, and loosened the hinge of its jaw so that it could engulf its bewhiskered lunch. In the boa's simple movements was so much easy menace that Cal began imagining the situation from the mouse's point of view. Fright to the second power. Terror cubed.

"Jesus. I don't know how you can do that, Mr. Kemmings."

"My Main Squeeze depends on me to do it. If I didn't do it, he'd die."

"Couldn't Squeeze get by on yogurt or field peas or something?"

"I seriously doubt it."

"Even canned dog food'd be better than this."

"For you, Pickford. Not for Squeeze."

Mr. K. was actually blocking Cal's route to the back, and now the rodent, its little body aquiver from snout to tail tip, stood before the boa on three legs, one forepaw lifted and its flinty red eyes glittering like struck match heads. Squeeze, coolly swaying the forepart of its length, was hypnotizing

Mickey. Either that or a built-in defense mechanism—an ancient crisis-activated kindness of the genes—was hypnotizing the mouse.

Cal's own fear was palpable now. "Mr. Kemmings—"

"Why can't we pity critters that crawl? We stigmatize them as evil. We allegorize them as satanic tools. Then we revile them for behaving as nature has made them behave."

"There's no odor as sickening as snake, Mr. Kemmings."

"You can get used to a smell, Pickford."

"Maybe so. But put me in a monkey house any day. That's a strong smell, but at least it's mammalian."

"And that's provincial prejudice speaking, not reason."

"I think my nostrils and my gut have more to do with it than my brain, Mr. Kemmings."

Cal was looking at the floor, the random lay of the tiles. He knew that My Main Squeeze had caught and engorged Mickey—the bumps on the glass had told him so—and he had no wish to see the serpent peristaltically mangle the mouse as it worked the paralyzed lump down its digestive tract.

"Squeeze is only behaving according to plan. He needs fresh meat. Otherwise he gets puny, curls up, and dies. To hate an animal because it behaves as it's been born to do is idiotic. You demean yourself as well as the object of your scorn. You have to transcend those kinds of feelings and develop empathy for natural behavior that you once saw as base or hateful. Squeeze doesn't arbitrarily inflict hurt on the world. In some ways, he's a model inmate of our mortal penitentiary. He moves only when hunger goads him to move. The remainder of the time he slumbers, doing no evil to anyone and dreaming about . . . well, who can say?"

"And the mice that he murders when he's awake?"

"At least they're put to good use. They die to make more life—that's the only way to look at it."

"If you're a fan of life squamous and snaky."

Mr. K. chuckled in spite of himself. "You're an incorrigible snake hater, Pickford. I've talked your head off campaigning for them, and you've missed your early lunch. Go on now. You can get that final 'bear' cage after you've eaten. Take an hour."

But Cal refused, declaring that he'd enjoy his mouse sandwich—well, his Chick-Fil-A—a whole lot more if he finished what he'd started. That said, he went to do what he had to do, leaving Mr. K. to fish out another victim for My Main Squeeze and the boa to flick its tongue in benign anticipation of dessert.

The pellet-littered and pee-soaked cedar chips had to go into a Dempsy Dumpster behind the pet store. Cal carried them out in an old chip sack, which he heaved up and over the side of the khaki-colored dumpster. Then he returned to peel the sodden sheets of newspaper off the glass floor of the aquarium. He hated peeling away the newspaper. The stench of urine was more concentrated in the paper than in the chips, and the newsprint almost always came off on his hands, marking him with blurred headlines and fractured photos of sports figures and politicians.

But Cal bent to the task anyway, and as he was easing back the topmost layer of darkened newsprint, he realized that it bore upon it obituaries better than two weeks old. Death notices. The irony—the incongruity—of discovering death notices preserved in cavy pee gave him pause. Human beings exited the womb in the throes of their mothers' birth pangs, struggled through infancy and childhood to become adults, and suffered how many daily indignities to define themselves as humane persons? And at the end, what? A funeral and oblivion. It seemed God's final obscene raspberry to consign their obituary notices to the bottom of a cage for Brezhnev bears.

On his knees, gripping the plastic cap around the edge of the aquarium, Cal peered down at the obituaries. What he had to do was simple: He had to read them. He would show these people who had died, suffering this final cosmic, not to say comic, indignity, that much honor. What had the *Atlanta Constitution*'s obit reporter written about them? He might lose some of the extra half hour that Mr. K. had given him for lunch, but you made that sort of sacrifice for members of the species to which you belonged. Simple decency demanded it.

So Cal, stooped forward over the reeking newsprint, read, and from each of the notices he learned the date of birth, educational and employment history, noteworthy accomplishments, and surviving relatives. A woman, 28, a ballerina, dead of bone cancer. A man 71, the retired vice president of a meat-packing firm, the victim of congestive heart failure. A 17-year-old boy, not yet out of high school, shot in the head at a fast-food place near I-85 by "person or persons unknown," who may have been shooting at random from a car speeding by on the overpass. Jesus.

Cal lifted the sodden sheet, flipped it, and found an obituary on the other side that hit him like an open-handed slap:

PHILIP K. DICK, NOTED AMERICAN WRITER, DIES AT 53 IN AFTERMATH OF DISABLING STROKE IN SANTA ANA, CALIFORNIA

Philip Kindred Dick, who suffered a stroke in Santa Ana, California, on Feb. 18, died yesterday at 8:10 A.M. in the Western Medical Center there. He was 53.

Dick forged a reputation as a significant post-War figure in American letters with an outpouring of highly original novels from the mid 1950s to the early 1970s.

His first novel, "Voices from the Streets" in 1953, won little immediate approval, being disjointed and overlong, but the critic Orville Prescott nevertheless hailed it for its "unique sense of vision and stinging critique of middle-class American values."

Seven important books followed: "Mary and the Giant" (1956), "A Time for George Stavros" (1957), "Pilgrim on the Hill" (1957), "The Broken Bubble of Thisbe Holt" (1958), "Puttering About in a Small Land" (1958), and "In Milton Lumky Territory" (1959), which Time magazine praised as "the most devastating mimetic deconstruction of capitalism since Arthur Miller's 'Death of a Salesman.'"

Dick's productivity declined during the 1960s. Some argued that he had burned himself out writing seven major novels in as many years.

But in the eight years prior to Richard Nixon's

presidency, he still managed to release three note-worthy works: "Confessions of a Crap Artist" (1962), which many consider his finest novel; "The Man Whose Teeth Were All Exactly Alike" (1963), combining oblique social comment with Dick's idiosyncratic interest in paleoanthropology; and, strangest of all, "Nicholas and the Higs" (1967).

Most of Dick's bibliographers believe that "Nicholas and the Higs" was written in the late 1950s, set aside by the author as "unsalvageable," and completely revised in the three years following John F. Kennedy's assassination on Nov. 22, 1963, in Dallas, Texas.

This odd book was almost universally panned. One reviewer called it an "undisciplined prank" and "concrete proof" of Dick's failing powers as a novelist. Others faulted Dick for attempting to out-Pynchon Pynchon (the apocalyptic American novelist Thomas Pynchon, best known at that time for "V.").

Most objections to "Nicholas and the Higs," in fact, stemmed from Dick's quirky incorporation of fantasy or science-fictional elements into an other-wise naturalistic narrative. . . .

"Pickford, are you all right?" Cal heard this question as if from a great distance. But then he realized that Mr. K.—finding him peering into the bottom of a guinea-pig cage—must be thinking that he had pulled a muscle or suddenly become ill. Maybe his boss thought that he was going to throw up into the aquarium. Both numb and alarmed, Cal realized that this was a definite possibility.

"Pickford!" Mr. K.'s voice had skyed to a falsetto.

"I'm okay," Cal hastened to assure him. "Really, I'm okay." But he made no move to stand up, fascinated by both the fact of Philip K. Dick's obituary—the man had died nearly three weeks ago, without his learning of it until now—and its clinical summing up of Dick's place in Ameri-can letters. So Cal continued to stare at, and struggled to finish reading, the sodden death notice.

"Can't you move? Do you need me to get a paramedic?"

"I've just found out that someone I love has died," Cal said, tears spontaneously misting his vision.

"Your mother? Your father?"

"No, no. Nothing like that, Mr. Kemmings. I'm okay, really. Just give me a couple of minutes. Please."

. . . Successful work by Pynchon, Joseph Heller, James Barth, and Kurt Vonnegut, Jr., may have prompted Dick's own ventures into "literary surrealism," but most critics agree that it was not his forte.

After "Nicholas and the Higs," Dick published no new book for fourteen years. In 1981, however, "Valis," his last novel, appeared from Banshee Books, a small New York paperback house specializing in crime, martial arts, and science-fiction titles. Labeled science fiction, "Valis" strikes most partisans of Dick's work as a sordid record of the total unraveling of his personality.

"This book has no literary merit at all," wrote Luke Santini in a Harper's magazine article entitled "A Crap Artist Craps Out" (Nov. 1981). "It may have value as a case history for students of psychiatry and abnormal human behavior, but as a work of art, it falls somewhere between subway graffiti and the fanatic propaganda of the Watchtower Bible and Tract Society."

Banshee Books earned intense industry criticism for publishing "Valis." The firm received these criticisms for exploiting the past reputation of the author rather than for the garbled content of the novel itself.

Then, charging a seditious libel of Pres. Nixon, the Board of Media Censorship in Washington, D.C., formed during the chief executive's first term, seized a second 60,000-copy printing of "Valis" before Banshee Books could distribute it. . . .

"Cal!" Mr. Kemmings cried, and seldom did he use anyone's first name. "I can't leave you doubled over like this, son."

"I'm okay, I'm okay. Just a couple more minutes."

Rumors have long circulated that Dick wrote at least twenty unpublished novels during his 14-year "silence." Most reliable scholars discount these rumors, but some concede that Dick may have done two or three "absurdist," "surrealist," or "quasi-speculative" novels in the vein of "Nicholas and the Higs" and "Valis."

If so, they had literary or political shortcomings that kept them from print. Representatives of Dick's major publisher—Hartford, Brice—claim that no one at their firm ever saw these rumored non-realist novels. In 1979, the company had rejected "Valis."

Wilhelm Pauls, a professor of Contemporary American Literature at California State University at Fullerton, calls Dick's death "a tragedy for American letters."

"He wasn't a Hemingway or a Faulkner," Pauls says, "but he was still a first-rate, if oddballish, talent. I think you'd have to rank him with writers like Nathanael West, John Purdy, and D. Keith Mano.

"The truly tragic thing about Dick was those lost years between the 'Higs' book and that final schizo mess ["Valis"] that any decent publisher would've let the poor man's heirs bury with him. Had he stayed sane and kept working, he might've become the foremost American writer of the Nixon Era. Unhappily, he did neither."

Three children and five former wives survive Dick. The family intends to bury him in Fort Morgan, Colorado, next to a twin sister, Jane C. Dick, who died not long after their birth on Dec. 16, 1928.

"Who, Pickford? Who in your family died? Are you finding this out from an old newspaper?"

"I'm sorry. Not a family member. I didn't mean to—"

"Just leave the cage be, son. I'll finish it." The old man was pulling him up by the elbow. "I want you to take the day off, Pickford. Tomorrow, too. A person shouldn't have to find out from an old newspaper that one of his loved ones has died."

"It's Philip K. Dick," Cal said. "The writer. He's been dead nearly three weeks, and I didn't know."

"That's a shame. That's cruel. They should've told you."

"But he's not family. They couldn't've known to tell me. He had thousands of admirers, Mr. Kemmings." Cal was on his feet now, his hands gray with printer's ink and his heart thudding.

"Philip Craddock?"

"Philip K. Dick, Mr. Kemmings. The writer."

"Never heard of him. I always liked Murray Spillane—tough-guy stuff. Just to pass the time with, though."

"Remember that movie *Confessions of a Crap Artist*? With Jack Lemmon as Jack Isidore? Dick wrote the book they based it on."

"That's old. Twenty years."

"Only fifteen. Anyway, you *do* know who Philip K. Dick is. You really do. That film won awards."

"I guess it did. And Mr. Dick was a friend of yours?"

Cal felt dizzy. Maybe from standing up too fast, maybe from trying to comprehend the writer's obituary before digesting the fact of his death. Back in Colorado, I'd've known a day or two after it happened. I had friends there who cared about such things and who would've told me. The man's buried there. But down here, I'm isolated. No real friends yet. Nobody that I know into Dick's stuff quite the way I am.

"Take the afternoon, Cal. I won't dock you. Go on."

"I will," he said. "I think I'd better." But over Mr. K.'s heartfelt protests, he finished cleaning the aquarium and making its Brezhnev bears comfortable. Only then did he feel he could grab his windbreaker and exit the Happy Puppy Pet Emporium onto the main corridor of West Georgia Commons mall.

Half a day's sweat for a whole day's wage, he thought. And I'm bereft. The death of a man I never met, an entire continent away, has bereaved me.

And, God, how it hurts!

4

Cal's walk took him toward the Chick-Fil-A franchise, where the smells of french fries and chicken overpowered him. Ordinarily, he liked these smells. Today, they sickened him. That three-week-old obituary in the *Constitution* had stolen his hunger, and he wasn't about to stand in line with the lunch-hour line breakers and elbow throwers to buy a sandwich that his grief for the late Phil Dick would probably prevent him from keeping down.

Therefore, he angled away from the food counter to the other side of the corridor. Here he strolled against the prevailing flow of pedestrians until he was opposite the entrance to Gangway Books, where James T. Michener's *The Boers* and Bishop Joshua Marlin's *Dead Sea, Living Faith* had places of honor in a storefront display. He struggled to see who was at the register, found that Le Boi Loan held that post, and so cut back across the trickle of foot traffic to tell the slender Vietnamese his news.

"Lone Boy," Cal declared even before crossing the store's open threshold, "Lone Boy, Philip K. Dick is dead."

"Lots of people're dead," Lone Boy replied, turning to face him inside the waist-high minifort of the sales counter.

"I just found out about Dick, though. I want to know if you've got any of his books."

"If you want it, we probably don't have it. What you want is almost always weird, and Gangway's big boss has a policy against stocking weird."

Cal liked Le Boi Loan, whom everyone naturally called The Lone Boy, or simply Lone Boy, although Cal had still not figured out why the young Asian—he was a year or two younger than Cal—had chosen to work in a bookstore. Lone Boy was a video game and VCR addict, with a pathological mistrust of the written word unless it reposed in the dialogue balloons of the comic book *Daredevil*, starring his favorite Marvel superhero. He also apparently worked night shifts at a convenience store on the southern outskirts of LaGrange, and money was of course the reason for his employment there, just as it must be at Gangway Books. He had a wife and kids to support, and if he talked like a teenage rebel from a cheapjack Hollywood film, well, that was the sort of celluloid primer from which Le Boi Loan had partly learned his English.

"What's weirder than Dungeons and Dragons or calendars of guys in Day-Glo jockstraps? You've got tons of that stuff, Lone Boy."

"That's movable weird. But you want weird that only a place with you for a customer could *ever* get rid of."

"Philip K. Dick was an important American writer."

"I'll make a note."

"Now he's dead, and I'd just like to know if any of his work's still in print."

"Ain't that the way? A guy has to die, or win a Nobel Prize, before anybody'll crack a knuckle to read him."

"I read him *before* he died, Lone Boy. I've been reading him for fifteen years. I've got copies of Dickian opuses that big-time editors and critics would *kill* to lay their hands on."

"Oh, yeah. Dickian opuses."

Cal stopped jabbering. Hey-diddle-diddle, he was letting his mouth run away with his brain. He had to calm down before someone overheard and started badgering him for incriminating details. As, for instance, the dude who'd cased out the pet shop that morning?

"Lone Boy," Cal said more deliberately, "do you happen to know if you've got any of Dick's books on the premises?"

"He's a fiction writer?"

"Sure. Of course. What'd you think he'd be?"

"Not much of anything. Me, I try not to think. But if he's a fiction writer, go look through the D's over there where all the paperback novels hang out."

"It hasn't been there before."

"Then it's possible we ain't got it now, either."

Cal walked to the fiction section, row upon row of paperbacks emblazoned with Nazi swastikis, ghoulishly complexioned children, embracing lovers, and the cannon-barreled bores of .38-caliber pistols. He could find not a single title by Dick. He returned to the skeptically squinting Le Boi Loan.

"Nothing."

Lone Boy shrugged and spread his hands.

"Look him up in *Books in Print* for me."

"Not that thing. You want me to break my arms trying to lift it up here? Have a heart, Cal."

"I'll do it. Let me do it." Overcome with both impatience and irritation, Cal started to yank up the countertop giving access to the sales area, but now Lone Boy was waving his hands energetically at shoulder height, urging him to halt.

"Wait," the naturalized Vietnamese said. "I've just remembered something." He bent down by the garish nudie publications that store policy did not permit him to shelve with the other magazines and rummaged through a box of slick-papered posters and advertising flyers from various New York publishing houses. He pulled one of these impossibly creased posters free, stood up, and shook it out so that Cal could see it.

"Look here, my bookwormish buddy, Pouch House is going to be reprinting Dick's stuff in paperback as part of a 'Contemporary Rediscovery Series.' All with color-coordinated, hi-tech covers, matching typography, fancy-talkin' lit-crit material, and so on. You'll be able to buy lots of best-forgotten, minor Amerikanski writers in these packages —P. K. Dick, A. Nin, and J. Kerouac, as off-the-top-of-my-head for instances."

Cal examined the poster. The Dick titles that Pouch House was going to be releasing in uniform paperback editions included *Mary and the Giant, The Broken Bubble of Thisbe Holt, Puttering About in a Small Land, In Milton Lumky Territory, Confessions of a Crap Artist,* and *The Man Whose Teeth Were All Exactly Alike.* Pouch had set the price of these volumes at $3.95 a copy.

"I thought you said you'd never heard of Dick."

"You said he was an important American writer. I said I'd make a note."

"You asked if he was a fiction writer."

"Am I supposed to know this kind of trivial Americana from the git-go? *You* can't even name the great Vietnamese emperor that I'm descended from."

"Le Thanh Tong, the founder of the Le dynasty."

"I told you that before," Lone Boy accused.

"Yes, you did. And I remembered." Cal felt that Lone Boy was jerking him around. "So why'd you play ignorant of Dick? And just where the hell do you get off calling him—how did you put it?—a 'minor Amerikanski writer'?"

"When your government brought me over here from Hanoi, not long after the Christmas bombardment of the irrigation dikes that made Le Duc Tho sign the 1974 surrender agreement at Gif-sur-Yvette in Paris, I went into the Grace Rinehart school at Fort Benning to be Americulturated. A two-year program. I read until I was sick. We got force-fed everybody from Louisa May Apricot to James Ghoul Cozzens. *Puttering About in a Small Land* was the Dick title I had to choke down. Flat as day-old beer left uncorked in the fridge, buddy mine. Very deadly boring social criticism. The dude should've grown up in a totalitarian state like the so-called Democratic Republic of North Vietnam."

"*Boring?*" Cal was flabbergasted.

"He picked a good title, though. Little people doing little stuff. One guy in it is a squirty nerd bigoted against blacks. If this is a 'Classic of American Lit,' give me *Daredevil* any day. I OD'd on reading, and your P. K. Dick fella is one supergood reason I still ain't gone back to it."

"One book isn't a fair test. Besides, the world hasn't had a chance to read the *real* masterpieces Dick wrote."

"Lucky world." Lone Boy had grown weary of the conversation. Two customers holding books stood behind Cal waiting for Lone Boy to take their money, and Cal could tell that the Vietnamese wanted him to step aside. Loan refolded the Pouch House poster—not all that neatly—and crammed it emphatically back into the pasteboard carton next to the skin slicks. "These 'Contemporary Rediscovery' titles will get here around the first of April. No PKD available until then, Cal."

"I want you to reserve me a set."

"Reserve you a set? Hey, buddy mine, you might as well reserve you some sand grains at a beach. Nobody's gonna walk off with this stuff before you get a shot at it. Just bring your money in, plunk it down, and go home with your, uh, goodies. April first."

(April first. Right. April Fool's Day.)

Cal took his checkbook from the back pocket of his jeans and wrote a check to Gangway Books for $12.50. Why? he wondered, even as he watched his ballpoint glide. Except for *The Broken Bubble of Thisbe Holt,* he already owned this set in other paperback editions, some dating back to the mid 1960s, and Lia and he really couldn't afford to spend their money on inessentials. Books, given their present financial situation, were inessentials, and Lia would tell him so when she found out what he'd done.

But, damn it, Phil Dick had died, and he had to do *some*thing to commemorate the man's achievement. The Atlanta paper, after all, had buried his obituary—as lengthy and complete as it had been—in the last pages of the business section when news of his death had deserved a banner headline on page one. That canny snub was owing, of course, to King Richard's ill opinion of the writer, a wound reopened and then exacerbated by the publication of *Valis* in 1981. Actually, it was a small miracle that the newspaper had run Dick's obituary at all, and Cal understood that the *Constitution* had dared to do so only because Nixon—in his sixty-ninth year, one year into his fourth term—had mellowed. During his fourth inaugural, the President had smugly declared an amnesty for any draft dodger who would publicly recant his opposition to the war.

Cal ripped the draft for $12.50 out of his checkbook and slid it onto the register. "There. My reservation. Half what I'll owe this place when the books come in."

"Sleeping pills're cheaper, Cal, but it's your moolah. Use it for toilet paper if you like."

That was a knee-jerk anticommunist for you; they revered King Richard and despised any literary or political figure who expressed even the mildest doubts about the superiority of capitalism to all other economic systems. Cal's resentment of Le Boi Loan, however, was mitigated by the knowledge that the Vietnamese had spent his whole childhood and youth resisting the relentless state propaganda apotheosizing Ho Chi Minh, "He Who Enlightens," as the conqueror of the French colonialists and the ultimate Indochinese patriot. That behavior had made Le Boi Loan the oddest of anomalies in the North, a youth who cheered every bomb released on Hanoi and Haiphong by the unseen B-52s overhead, but who prudently took shelter to ride out the earthshaking blasts of those same bombs. Let him dislike Phil Dick. He had earned the right to prize *Daredevil* over Ho and the video game Phun Ky Cong over the Vietcong. Arguing about books with Loan was a fool's game, for he was too idiosyncratically "Americulturated"—in all the worst as well as best connotations of that frightful neologism—to give a damn about literature. He had life to amuse him and his memories of the Bad Old Days to sabotage the artsy-fartsy bitchings of American novelists and playwrights. In Lone Boy's eyes, they were all spoiled leftists anyway, with no hard-knock understanding of tyranny, only *beaucoups* of highfalutin theory and a shared distaste for Richard Nixon—the Great Man who had saved the South and then reunited the entire country under the *truly* democratic government of President Tran Van Don.

But I've had some hard-knock training of my own, Cal thought, leaving the bookstore, and I damn well know that tyranny comes in at least two flavors. . . .

He was out in the main walkway of West Georgia Commons again when he saw Mr. Kemmings coming toward him from the Pet Emporium, cupping something to his chest as he approached.

"I *thought* maybe you'd detoured over this way," his boss said. "How're you feeling, Pickford?"

"Okay." You're not going to ask me to come back to work, are you? Cal worried. I know I should've gone straight home from the shop, but I *had* to make a side trip to Gangway Books. I just had to. Nevertheless, if Mr. Kemmings insisted, Cal was prepared to surrender to guilt and return to the pet store.

"I wanted to give you this as a consolation for the loss you've sustained," Mr. Kemmings said. He pushed the thing in his hands at Cal, who instinctively retreated from the gesture.

A Brezhnev bear nestled in the old guy's hands—a trembling, tawny-maned, pink-gray creature whose naked skin made Cal think of newborn mice or ratlings. The varmint was making noises remarkably similar to those that some computer toys made.

"That's a fifty-dollar animal, Mr. Kemmings. I can't accept that." He didn't *want* to accept it. Just about the last thing he and Lia needed—they already had a pet—was a Soviet-bred guinea pig symbolizing the long rapprochement between the Nixon Gang and Leonid Brezhnev & His Kremlin Kronies.

"Fifty's what we're charging now," Mr. Kemmings replied, "but the cost is coming down all the time. It's no longer necessary to import them from the Soviet Union. So don't let the cost keep you from accepting the animal, Pickford."

"What about the upkeep cost? That worries me, too."

"It shouldn't. You can take a bag of pellets home with you any time you need it. I can't give you an aquarium, but these critters do just as well in a cardboard box. They're good company, and you don't want to sit around all alone when you get home today."

"I've got a dog to keep me company, Mr. Kemmings."

"Take it, anyway." (The squealing cavy had suddenly stopped squealing, and Cal realized that that was because it had begun to chew on his windbreaker's zipper.) "Your wife will love it. Women always love 'em. They remind the ladies of babies."

"Sir—"

"I insist. Make me happy. Make you and your wife happy."

Cal thought, I can't handle this. I can't stand being leaned on this way. Aloud he said, "I don't *want* it, Mr. Kemmings. I just don't want the damn thing. You're very kind to offer, but you can't always make the other guy feel better by making yourself feel better, and that's really what you're trying to do."

Mr. Kemmings's face betrayed stunned confusion.

"Sorry, sir." Cal pushed the cavy back into his boss's hands. "Bright and early tomorrow. To make up for today."

That said, he brushed past the old man and headed for the rear exit—a row of glass doors disclosing the misty March afternoon—giving on the parking lot and his '68 Dart. He tried not to think about what he had just done to his sweet old boss. An impossible assignment. He felt angry and sad. He felt that he was as out of place in this mall—in this state—as a deballed jackrabbit leaping across the Sea of Fertility on the Moon.

In short, he felt lousy.

An overbearing tough guy had given him several bad moments just by making a distinction between "looking" and "browsing."

A mystery woman had scared the bejesus out of him, hinting that she knew more about him than he wanted her to. And he had docilely given that woman the location of Lia's office in Warm Springs.

Philip K. Dick had died of a stroke in California, three weeks ago, and he had found out only by reading the death notice through the newsprint-graying stain of stale rodent piss.

Le Boi Loan had told him that Dick's work was both "minor" and "boring," and yet he had committed himself to a needless purchase of six Pouch House reissues by Dick as a means of dealing with his bathetic grief.

And he had hurt Mr. Kemmings's feelings by rejecting the man's well-intentioned would-be gift of a Brezhnev bear.

But maybe worst of all was the fact that he had bad-mouthed King Richard to that intimidating woman in the pet shop and then made a stupidly self-incriminating remark about his collection of "Dickian opuses" to Lone Boy, a true Nixonian. Had he forgotten that Fourth of July Parade down Denver's Colfax Avenue in 1971?

Of course he had. He had *worked* to forget it.

Oh, what a beautiful morning. Oh, what a beautiful day.

5

The man had called her decaffeinated coffee an ersatz drink, but he was already on his second cup. Sipping it, he reminded Lia of a defrocked priest.

Seedily distinguished.

Miss Bledsoe entered Lia's office with the forms that he had refused to sign in the waiting room. Lia told her new patient that she wanted him to fill them out to the best of his ability, even if that meant leaving three quarters of the questions blank. If he really wanted to session with her, he also had to sign her standard agreement form to legalize their counselor-client relationship.

"You're not afraid I'll sue your ass for malpractice, are you, Dr. Bonner?"

Lia glanced up at him. He was wearing a poker face, but his eyes were grinning. Mocking her. Not maliciously but lightly, as if she were an upstart daughter presuming to lesson her old man on the ways of the world. Yeah, the guy's got a saturnine charm, Lia thought. A funny-prickly sense of humor.

"You wouldn't get much if you did," she said. "It's simply a professional formality."

The man lowered the footrest of his lounger and leaned forward so that he could read Lia's forms. After looking for a moment or two at the first page, however, he shook his head and glanced up at her in unabashed bewilderment. "It's like a foreign language to me," he said. "The letters are recognizable letters, but the words they've fallen into and the paragraphs they make, well, hell, it might as well be Greek. You know, *koine* Greek from the Hellenistic and Roman periods. In fact, that's exactly what it is to me: *koine* Greek."

"You're kidding."

"Never more serious. Unfortunately." He chuckled glumly. "I can't even read the money in my billfold—except, somehow, for the denominations of the bills."

"Then it wouldn't help you much even if you *had* identification in there, would it?" Lia nodded at his billfold. "Social Security card, driver's license—they'd be useless to you."

"Unless someone read them to me, I guess they would."

"Shawanda, read the signature agreement to him, and I'll ask him everything else aloud."

"Yes, ma'am," Shawanda said. She picked up the specified form and read the pertinent paragraphs. He listened to her attentively, reminding Lia of Viking when Vike sat near the dinner table, hoping for scraps and trying to get a fix on how generous they were likely to be. Yeah, that was it. Her new patient had the sad eyes and the guileless intelligence of her Siberian husky, Viking.

"Is that okay with you?" Lia asked when Shawanda had finished reading. "Do you think you can sign that?"

"I don't object to the terms, if that's what you mean."

"Good. Just put your name there." Lia reached across her desk to tap the appropriate spot with one shiny red fingernail.

"Signing is another matter, Dr. Bonner," the man said. He took the pen that Shawanda proferred and wrinkled his forehead in concentration. "Whose name would you like me to sign, and in what alphabet would you like me to sign it?"

Oh, shit, Lia silently exclaimed. The poor guy doesn't know who he is, he's forgotten how to read, and so he's also forgotten how to write. Still, he identified the words on my questionnaire as being—for him—unreadable examples of *koine* Greek. Well, how can he make so specific an identification of the Roman alphabet if he's unable to read the *koine* Greek that he *thinks* it is? I could mind-wipe myself trying to plumb this guy's . . . amnesia.

"He could put an ex on the forms," Shawanda suggested. "My gran'mama used to buy her insurance policies jus' by putting her ex on the policy papers."

"Was it legal?" Lia asked.

"It was legal enough she had to pay her premiums."

"I'll do it," the man said. "I can make an ex with the best of 'em. Just you watch." He put a big capital X at the bottom of the form, studied it as if it might turn into a flaming character with messianic implications, a symbol sacred and daunting. "That's a chi," he said. "The first letter of Christ."

Lia ignored the messianic implications of his comment. "May I call you Kai, then?" she asked him. "It has a genuine Welsh sound, and it'll be a lot less shuddersome than calling you Mr. X."

"Call me anything you like. Just smile when you do it."

"Okay, Kai it is, and we're ready to get going." Lia dismissed Shawanda, and Kai—the name somehow fit him—scooted his butt back into the lounger, tipped its footrest up to support his legs, and folded his hands on his midriff. To his right, a cup of ersatz coffee sat on a TV tray, easily within his reach.

"How did you get here?"

"Taxi from Atlanta. Said to my driver, 'Warm Springs,' and he was happy to bring me, his meter tick-ticking all the way."

"You don't live in Atlanta, do you?" Lia couldn't credit this idea. Kai had an accent more like Cal's than her brother Jeff's. If he *did* live in Atlanta, he'd come there from another part of the country, either the Rocky Mountains or the Far West.

"Caught my cab at the airport. I'd just gotten off a plane."

"Where from, Kai?"

"I don't recall. That's where my amnesia seems to start. How far back it goes"—he gave a shrug—"well, your guess is as good as mine. Better, probably."

"Did you have any luggage?"

"Don't remember that, either. If I did, the handlers must be having a damn good time with it right now."

"What made you say Warm Springs?" You could've saved a tidy sum, thought Lia, if you'd ridden a Greyhound or rented a car.

"I knew that FDR used to come here. I wanted to see the place where he'd visited the springs. I thought it would be profoundly meaningful—for me, you understand?—to look around here."

"You admired Roosevelt?"

"Sure. Who is it who's in there now?"

"The President? Richard Nixon."

"That's right. And it's no comparison. No comparison between Nixon and FDR. One fought—admittedly, out of ambition—for the little person, and the other fights—also out of ambition—for his own greater glory. Equal in ambition but completely different when you come to their impact on the world."

Lia had a small tape recorder going. She had turned it on with her patient's consent—Kai's *X* had been his okay—but this turn in their talk frightened her. The walls had ears. If not ears, then bugs. Too often the walls had bugs, and an enigmatic person like Kai—with the naïve brashness to bad-mouth King Richard—well, Kai was the sort of fellow who could mysteriously go *poof!*, taking with him anyone unlucky enough to have overheard the slanders provoking his removal. Possibly, in fact, he had already had hostile action taken against him, action resulting in his radical, if incomplete, amnesia. On the other hand, why, given a hostile administration, would he still have a billfold full of money?

"What brought you to me?"

"Coming back from the Little White House, my cab driver started reading signs out loud. He read yours. I made him stop."

My shingle, Lia thought. I've actually corralled a customer by my sign. It pays to advertise.

"I meant, did your amnesia bring you to me? You seem sort of blasé about your lack of memory. So I'm wondering if something else is wrong—a guilt, a hang-up, a whole complex of problems."

"All my problems are complex, Dr. Bonner." Kai picked up his cup and sipped some coffee. "But, hey, you're pretty astute, you know that? I didn't come because of the amnesia. I came because even in this lovely town, I feel awful—just awful—about my place, and everyone else's, in this ugly, unreal, fuckin' reality."

"I'm not following you."

"I'm out of place here, doctor. But that's okay. So are you. Everyone's out of place here. What isn't okay is we're sitting on our asses abiding it, letting it go on."

"Abiding what? Letting what go on?"

"I'll try to explain. I'm seeing this reality under the aspect of another reality. One's sitting on top of the other. I call it stereographia, bringing two different pictures together to make a single picture, a new picture. *You* only see the picture that the second one's trying to merge with and eventually nudge aside, but *I* see the one that's trying to do the nudging. I'm *in* your picture, *in* your reality, but I'm seeing—stereographically—the world that wants to displace and redeem it."

Well, Lia thought, I've had strange ones before, a woman who believed she could deflect evil X rays from Soviet satellites with a silver-plated soup spoon and a teenager who imagined that he had traveled to Antarctica with Shackleton. Kai's got them beat. He sounds almost sane, but he's constructed a fantasy that allows him to operate simultaneously in both dimensions, the mundane and the illusional, as if he had some godlike ability to straddle and even reconcile them. Add to that his amnesia, and you have a case study for the books.

"Kai, you're suffering from a kind of estrangement. That may be owing to your amnesia. Don't assume that everyone else feels as distanced and as alien from this 'reality' as you do."

"Who says I assume that? I assume the opposite. And I'm angry that everyone over here seems to be asleep to the need to let the better world take over from the bad world—the one that's squatting on us like a venomous toad."

"Others may not even see this so-called better world, Kai."

"They *won't* see it. Which is exactly what makes me want to hop a barricade and put a grenade in somebody's bonnet."

Anger on top of amnesia; strong violent feelings that accompany and intensify his illusory binocular vision of the world. You'll have to recommend again that he see a physician, Lia. He may have an elevated blood pressure, he may be courting an epileptic episode or a cerebral stroke. You don't want him to die on you, do you? You wouldn't even be able to help the authorities put a name on his corpse. "Kai" probably wouldn't impress them. . . .

"What's better about your better world, Kai?" Accentuate the positive, Lia thought. Maybe that'll calm him down.

"For starters, Richard Milrose Nixon has been neutralized. I don't think he's died or been exiled or anything, but he's not out there running amok, either, like a robot that's got away from its operators and that nobody knows how to deactivate."

"And that makes things better?"

"Yeah. It's crucial, but it isn't—how do I say this?—it doesn't *all* hinge on Nixon. It's the elimination of a mind-set that won't grant the legitimacy of other mind-sets."

Thank God he didn't say that he saw the President dead. If he had, anyone listening to this tape later on would assume that he'd threatened to assassinate the President.

At Lia's fingertips, a disconcerting coldness. "Kai—"

"Once upon a time, we had checks and balances. It was written into the Constitution. What happened to those things?"

"Please tell me something, Kai. Do you want me to help you *cope* with this stereographic phenomenon you've described?"

"Fuck no," the man said angrily. "I want you to help me cure my amnesia. Then help me bring the better world into obliterating focus on top of the bad one."

"You didn't come here looking for a psychotherapist," Lia said accusingly. She could hear a tremor in her voice.

"I didn't?" Kai wore a look of intelligent puzzlement.

"You want a hotshot social reformer or a revolutionary. I'm neither of those things."

"Who is?" Kai slid his cup—the coffee had to be cold by now—onto the TV tray and hugged himself as if freezing. "Really, I didn't come looking for you at all, Dr. Bonner. Or FDR's Little White House. I came looking for an emanation. A focus. Your sign seemed to resonate with what I was looking for. So I came in. I don't understand this any better than you do."

"An emanation?" Lia was baffled.

"You're married, aren't you?"

"I am. But I don't see—"

"Do you have a snapshot of your husband with you?"

Humor him, Lia thought. She had a wallet-sized photo of Cal in her purse, which hung from its strap on her hat tree. She went to the hat tree and a moment later handed the snapshot to Kai.

"This is it," he told her. "Your husband's the reason I came. He may even be the lens that'll focus my stereographia."

"Cal?" What did Cal have to do with Kai, or Kai with him? The man's explanations obscured rather than illuminated. His delusions had taken on the whacky coloring of those plaguing Anita Arrazi, Lia's spoon-wielding X-ray deflector in Walsenburg. Lia took the snapshot away from Kai and returned to her desk.

"Tell me about your husband," Kai suggested.

"That's off-limits," Lia said. "My family life—the members of my family—none of that's relevant to our consultations."

"What if I were in love with you or hated your hubby or thought your brother was trying to kill me? Wouldn't that be relevant?"

"Not necessarily. You're grasping at straws, and if we can't get back to—"

"It'd be relevant to my self-concept. To my perception of my own mental health."

This is outrageous, Lia thought mildly. I can't do anything with this person. What made me think that I could? Desperation, I guess. Anyway, he needs to be hospitalized. I may be dealing with somebody dangerous to both himself and others, and, right now, if I had to make a deposition about his state of mind, I'd tilt to such a judgment—a judgment to commit.

Or would I? she wondered. Even in his rage and irrationality, he somehow projects a disarming, funny-prickly reasonableness.

Abruptly, Lia changed tacks. "To the best of your knowledge, have you ever tried to kill yourself?"

"I'm an amnesiac, Doctor. I don't remember."

"You must have some intuition about the matter. I'd like you to try your damnedest to recall if you've ever attempted suicide."

The coffee maker gave a shuddering, steamy sigh. A noise

like a death rattle. Kai jumped, then laughed self-deprecatingly and wiped his mouth and forehead with his handkerchief.

"Yeah, I probably did," he said, looking at his hands. "More than once. I think."

"Why?"

"I could tell you lots of things, couldn't I? I could say it was failure—a *perceived* failure—in my work. Or disillusionment with the way we've conspired to spoil the goddamn American dream. Or health problems owing to my stupid, flipped-out life-style. I could say any or all of that stuff, foxy lady, and you'd have no way of knowing if I was talking straight or jiving you. Problem is, I don't know myself if any of that shit's on the up-and-up."

"What *is* on the up-and-up? Why kill yourself?"

"Because I was bereft. Something had left me. It had left me like steam sighing up and escaping a coffee maker. It was awful, being bereft. Worse than anything else I can think of, and so I made this heavy concerted effort to cease being."

"What left you, Kai?"

"I don't know. That's something I wish I knew. I'm wondering, sitting here, if maybe it hasn't come back. Or started to."

"Why didn't you die?"

"It must've been medical intervention. Yeah. It was medical intervention. I had friends."

"Tell me what you think has maybe started coming back to you. What you lost and what you're finding again."

"Power," Kai said. "Spirit. I'm dead to the person I used to be, but this Power—an efficacious Voice—seems to be trying to use me again. I think that's one reason I have money in my billfold—it's sort of an ironic promise of my returning Power. But the real Power comes and goes. Sometimes it fades out—stretches so thin—that I nearly cease being without raising a hand against myself. I drink coffee to stop that from happening."

"Coffee?"

Kai laughed. "The real stuff. Not this emasculated brew. Of course, it's a delusion—the idea that thick, black, hot coffee can keep me from fading away. But who said delusions were supposed to make any sense, anyway?"

How can a man who admits the nonsensicality of his delusions be dangerous? Lia asked herself. How can you fear a guy who purports to believe that coffee drinking is his salvation, but who in the next breath ridicules that silly idea? Well, you can't. Kai's a harmless sweetie. As sweet as Viking—all bluff and bluster and ambiguous growl.

But there's the rub. The ambiguity of his personality. Sane or insane? Dangerous or innocuous?

"Your time is about up," Lia said, glancing at her watch. It was nearly noon. "Come back next week—at the same time—and we'll pick up from your coffee fixation." She laughed to show Kai that this was a joke, but an expression of concern—alarm, in fact—claimed his features, and she feared that she had hurt him, either by breaking off the session or by dubbing a "fixation" his fantasy about the redemptive attributes of coffee and caffeine.

Hurriedly, she said, "You'll be staying somewhere in the Warm Springs/Manchester area, I take it."

"Staying somewhere," Kai echoed her vaguely.

"You will come back, won't you?" Did she sound panicked by the possibility that he would desert her after only one session?

"How many rooms are there in this area?" Kai asked. "Who'll get one ready for me?" He sounded abstracted, distant.

"Let me buzz Miss Bledsoe," Lia said. "I'll have her look into some attractive potential lodgings for you. Would that be okay?" Over the intercom she told Shawanda to do just that.

"Ma'am," came Shawanda's voice, "we've got us a small problem."

"What sort of problem?"

Lia glanced at Kai. He seemed to be losing color, as if some unnamed time-lapse ailment were remorselessly leaching the melanin from his flesh. He had heard Shawanda's intercom announcement, of course, and maybe word of an indeterminate "problem" had made him go pale, but, struggling to encompass the reality of the Wellsian Invisible Man routine that Kai was pulling, Lia understood that her patient was fading, not merely because an external threat to him had arisen but because the existential reality of his identity lay outside the bounds of downtown Warm Springs and the thirteenth year of Richard Milrose Nixon's presidency.

"There's a cab driver out here who wants to know how long his fare's gonna be in there, Dr. Bonner," Shawanda said. "Seems Mr. Kai told him jus' to keep his meter runnin'."

"Wait!" Lia commanded Kai, without depressing the talk lever on the intercom. You can't leave like this. It's not an Emily Post–approved exit. Besides, how have you managed to get your clothes to fade the same way your face and hands are fading? Amazingly, her barked command—"Wait!"—seemed to have halted the otherwise steady progress of Kai's decay. He had stabilized on the interface between mundane corporality and story-book ghostliness.

Lia spoke into the intercom. "Shawanda, come in here, please."

"I was tryin' not to interrupt, ma'am. Should I tell this Acme cabbie to go back to his cab for a few minutes?"

"I'd appreciate that, Shawanda. But get in here fast."

"Yes, ma'am."

When Shawanda came in, Kai was hovering between substance and shadow, the image of a defrocked priest modulating in and out of viewability. Like a TV picture in a bad thunderstorm.

"Lawdamercy," Shawanda stage-whispered. "What's goin' on?"

"You see it, too, then? I'm not hallucinating?"

"No, ma'am. It *does* appear to be happenin', whatever it is."

I have a witness, Lia told herself. If I'm going crazy, then I'm not going alone. But I'd better talk to Kai. Maybe another command—voiced authoritatively enough—will rescue him from his impossible in-betweenness. Already I've kept the poor sucker from disappearing into Cheshire Cat gehenna, haven't I?

"Kai, stay! Damn it, *stay!*" It was like trying to rein in Viking when Viking wanted to run. "What's happening to you?"

Dimly flickering, Kai stabilized again. His voice, when he

spoke, was tinny and static-riven, like the sound emanating from an old Victrola horn. "God knows," he said. "You and your damn Brim. Maybe now you'll buy a coffee with some zing to it."

"Like what?" Lia said, desperate to keep him from vanishing.

"Deedle-deedle-queep," Kai said. (Or, at least, it sounded like "Deedle-deedle-queep." If that was the brand name of a coffee, it was a brand name from some other continuum.) And then he said, "I mean, Luzianne, the black kind with chicory."

"That's nasty," Shawanda said. "Makes your mouth pucker."

"It'll hold you to the planet," Kai replied. "I don't like it myself—but it'll fuckin' well hold you to the planet."

We're talking about coffee, Lia thought with astonishment. The guy's flickering between living substance and the intangible gas of nonexistence, and we're arguing the merits of Brim, Luzianne, and Deedle-deedle-queep. Coffees, for God's sake.

"Listen," Kai suddenly demanded, gripping the arm rests of the lounger for dear life. "I think I'm damaged. I'm not going to be able to hang on here. Take your fee out of my wallet, Dr. Bonner, and toss it to me. Do it. Do it now."

Lia obeyed, counting out her usual session fee and tossing the heavy wallet into his lap. He slid it, with considerable trouble, into the pocket of his translucent Members Only jacket. To what Continuum Club does Kai belong? Lia thought. It may be for Members Only, but he seems to be returning to it against his will.

"One final thing," he managed, his voice tinnier than ever.

Shawanda, apparently on impulse, assumed an easy hunker beside him, cocking her head to watch his ghostly departure and stretching her hand toward his arm.

"Don't," he said shortly. Then he added, as if to soften the prohibition, "I'm not totally gone yet, Miss Bledsoe. I'm neither here nor there."

"What final thing?" Lia asked. "What?"

"That pin you're wearing—the one your husband gave you—it's an icon that spiritually disadvantaged persons might risk lynching to get their hands on. Call it a linchpin." Kai guffawed, the deranged cacophony of a nonswimmer balancing on the deep end of a huge swimming pool. "Jesus. Forgive me. All I meant to say was that I like it. It's beautiful. Don't lose it."

Lia glanced down at her blazer. There, on its lapel, shone a golden pin—very simple—featuring the intaglio figure of a fish in profile. Where had it come from? I don't have a pin like this, she thought. I certainly don't *remember* having a pin like this. It's not the sort of item that Cal would go out of his way to buy for me. It's Christian, a Christian symbol antedating even the cross, and Cal's never gone in for religious iconography. He'd be more likely to buy me a wide-brimmed leather hat or a new pair of all-weather boots. . . .

Kai had faded utterly. The lounger, its footrest still in the up position, held nothing but the warm impress of the being—man, ghost, transdimensional visitor—who, a moment ago, had sat there talking about suicide and coffee. Shawanda looked at Lia, and Lia at Shawanda, and the early-spring chill in the office penetrated their bodies like a rain of tiny iron darts.

"I won't say nothin' to anybody about this," Shawanda said, "if you won't."

"Are we hallucinating? We must be hallucinating."

"Look at that chair. There's a fanny dent in it. And look at that coffee cup on the TV tray. It's near drunk up."

"A ghost?"

"Ghosts don't leave fanny dents and down-gulp coffee. And you got his money, too." Then Shawanda said, *"Oh!"* and quickly added, "Even if he did forget to pay his poor cabbie."

Lia went to the lounger, touched it. She tingled up and down her vertebrae, all along her wrists and forearms. A hair-raising experience, she told herself. I've heard about them, but this is the first time I've actually *had* one that wasn't just a kiddy's Halloween nape-tickler. And it's going to change my life.

She turned to Shawanda. "Was I wearing this pin when I came in this morning? Do you remember?"

"I don't remember," Shawanda said. "Sure is pretty, though."

"You don't remember it, and I don't recall ever even owning it. Kai and me, we're both amnesiacs."

"Yes, ma'am."

"What do you think happened here this morning, Shawanda?"

"I don't know. I can tell you what it *remind* me of, though."

"What?"

"Jesus goin' to Emmaus with those two lightweight disciples and them not recognizin' him till he'd broke bread with 'em."

Lia stared abashedly at her secretary. "You think Kai is Jesus Christ?" Mr. X, she thought. *X* is the Greek letter chi, and chi, as he told us, is the ancient symbol for Christ.

"What? Jesus in a Members Only jacket?" Shawanda walked to the window overlooking the town's main drag. "What I think is that that man's got the same kind of body Jesus had when he'd been glorified. A resurrection body. He wouldn't let me touch him, no more 'n Jesus would let Mary Magdalene touch him at the tomb."

"A resurrection body?"

"Seems so, ma'am. Jesus ate him some broiled fish in front of the eleven in Jerusalem—ghosts can't do that—and Mr. Kai, well, he down-gulped him some automatic coffee. Only a resurrection body could eat and then run off up to heaven that way."

It almost makes sense, Lia thought, what Shawanda's saying. As plausible as any other explanation we may be able to mount.

"Kai seemed a pretty shabby messiah stand-in, Shawanda."

"Things go rubbishly after a coupla thousand years. What can we expec'? Mr. Landis, my science teacher, he called it entropy."

"'Things fall apart,'" Lia quoted. "'The center cannot hold.'"

"That cabbie's comin' back, ma'am," Shawanda announced from the window. "Lookin' for his fare."

Lia went to the window and saw that a bulky black man with a cab driver's cap perched on his burnt-umber Afro was crossing the street from his hack and entering the downstairs entrance to her office. He looked angry. Well, he had a right to be angry, Lia supposed. They'd chased him off with a spur-of-the-moment dodge, and now Kai had vanished—evaporated like steam—and the cabbie was swaggering back to collect both his passenger and his fare.

"Shawanda, what'll we do?" Ashamed of herself for desiring her husband's presence and support, she wished that Cal were here.

The cabbie came stomping up the wooden stairs; twenty seconds later he knocked aside the door to Lia's office and stood beyond its threshold glaring at the two women.

"Where is he?" the man demanded.

"He jumped up and ran out," Shawanda said.

"How'd he do that? Y'all got you another door?"

"He jus' sneaked, that's all. He jus' sneaked out of here."

"I been watchin' your downstairs door seem like forever and I never seen a goddamn soul scoot out through it."

"Well, he's *very* sneaky," Shawanda said, hands on hips.

"That cheatin' honky!" the cabbie exclaimed, throwing his cap to the floor. "That cheatin' honky bastid!"

What a mess, Lia thought. Kai's disappeared like Jesus Christ himself, and this poor cabbie's out a two-hundred-dollar fare. And no fare is unfair. It's an unjust reality. . . .

6

The drive from LaGrange to Pine Mountain, south down Highway 27, always semiastonished Cal. He had spent most of his life in or around the Rockies and had seen plenty of breathtaking scenery. Mountains, *real* mountains: rugged steeps with bright ropes of water cascading down them, braiding and unbraiding. But this stretch of highway wasn't like that. It didn't steal your breath; it pulled it from you gently, the way the piano interlude in the Beatles's "In My Life" from the *Revolver* album always did.

Here and there, fog still drifted across the highway, but the sun was stabbing through it. The pines standing sentinel along the two-lane road in easy waves made Cal think of Celtic warriors, green in their garb, ever watchful. He was calming down. And it was the drive through this worn Piedmont topography that had him breathing easy. Even if his Dart did spit and chug on the upslopes.

On one such upslope, Cal saw a gnomish black man sitting on an upper branch of a pine tree at roadside, grinning down at him from the wispy fog. My God, thought Cal, it's Horsy Stout, for that was the name of the stablehand employed by Lia's brother, Jeff, at Brown Thrasher Barony. Because Stout, a muscular dwarf in his fifties, could have no rational motive for sitting where he was sitting, Cal squinted incredulously at the apparition.

Pickford, he told himself, you're seeing things.

Stout's grin broadened. He lifted his hand and waved. Then, like Alice's Cheshire Cat, the dwarf vanished, convincing Cal that the March fog and the upsetting events of the morning had prompted him to hallucinate. If he dwelled on what he had just "seen," he'd go crazy, and because his Dart was now on the slope's downside, he determined to put the image of the little man altogether out of his mind and to go on breathing easy.

That didn't really happen, he thought, and you're never going to mention it to anyone. . . .

Twenty minutes from the mall, Cal sighted Pine Mountain's water tower. The town's name strode around its chalk-white tank in neat green letters taller than any human being, and at the first red light (the town had only two), he turned left and drove two blocks down Chipley Street to the duplex apartment that he and Lia were renting from the McVanes. Immediately, he saw the stunning animal chained in its front yard. "Hello, Vike," he murmured.

Viking was a male Siberian husky—black, silver, and cream—that Lia's brother, Jeff, had given to them about three days after their arrival in Georgia. At Christmas, the dog had showed up at Brown Thrasher Barony, the horse farm that Jeff managed. Although Jeff's kids had begged him to let them keep the dog, Jeff hadn't trusted it enough to let it roam the pastures where his employer's horses grazed. And so Viking had come into town to live with Lia and Cal. An adult husky in a duplex apartment supposedly occupied by them alone.

This ruse soon fell through. You couldn't hide a dog Viking's size for long, and once Cal and Lia began commuting, they couldn't keep him indoors until they came home from work. He'd chew up Cal's books and shed on Lia's furniture. And so they'd had one of their first rip-snorting knock-down-drag-outs in Georgia over a Siberian sled dog that Cal didn't really want, as much as he loved animals, and that Lia wouldn't let go.

Fortunately, Mr. McVane saw no reason to evict them for keeping a dog. Fortunately, because Lia's desire to keep Viking triumphed over Cal's fear that confining him to town, indoors or out, would be to do him (huskies needed room, and Pine Mountain wasn't exactly the Yukon) a terrible injustice.

Viking lay on the porch on a thirty-foot chain attached to a spike driven into the ground under a redbud tree. Cal parked his Dart parallel to Chipley Street, on the edge of the yard. The dog lifted his big head and stared at the car from under cream-colored patches of fur that reminded Cal of eerie eyebrows.

Cal rolled his window down and said, "Hey, Vike, how'd you like off that chain?"

The husky stood up and dragged the chain with him to the car. Cal could hear him making strangled-sounding moans, a disconcerting variety of growling—not in anger, but in anticipation—that made the dog very effective as a watchdog. Most passersby, noting how big and fierce Viking looked, assumed that this intimidating noise was meant to warn them off. Actually, it was his peculiar way of informing visitors that he wanted attention. The little black kids who trailed up and down Chipley before and after school were afraid of Viking and made a practice of crossing to the other side of the street and carrying sticks or rocks with them. You couldn't really blame them, though. Vike looked a lot like a wolf.

Out of the Dart, Cal grabbed the dog's head and thrust him from side to side. Viking liked this. He reared and shoved his muddy forepaws against Cal's chest, meanwhile amplifying the Growl that so frightened folks unfamiliar with him. Cal pushed the dog aside, and Viking came rushing back for more, growling the Growl.

"He's a sweetheart," Lia always said. "All bluff and bluster."

Maybe. Maybe not. Either way, Cal had never owned—or partly owned—so fascinating an animal, and at first he hadn't even wanted him. You could never really be sure, after all, that the Growl was all "bluff and bluster," but you hoped and trusted that it was.

"Hey, Vike, you hungry? How would you've liked a Brezhnev bear for lunch?"

The dog sat back on his haunches, expectantly regarding Cal.

Yeah, I should've brought you that Brezhnev bear, Cal thought. You'd've taken care of it a lot faster than My Main Squeeze puts away Mr. K.'s mice, wouldn't you?

Cal checked the water and food dishes on the porch. The food was gone, of course, but the water bowl still contained water. In February, when he and Lia had first started chaining Viking out in the yard, the temperature had several times fallen below freezing, and the dog's water had turned to clear stone in the bowl. By the time that he or Lia arrived home from work, Viking was so thirsty that he slurped up three or four cooking pots of water as soon as they brought him inside.

About the only disadvantage to keeping the husky in front of their half of the duplex—once, that is, you got past the boredom it posed for him—was the effect that he had on the yard. He had dug a wallow under the scrawny redbud tree, and he had dragged his chain back and forth through the shrubs next to the duplex so many times that he had uprooted some of them. But the McVanes, their landlords, never complained about Viking's brutal landscaping techniques. Lia said that Mrs. McVane tolerated the destruction because she felt safer with the dog on guard.

Cal keyed open the front door and went inside, letting Viking slip in beside him. He turned up the heat, washed his hands at the sink in the kitchen, and sat down with a plastic cup of yogurt at the kitchen table. Lunch. A belated lunch. He wasn't crazy about yogurt, but Lia always had a bunch in the refrigerator, and having no desire to fix anything even mildly elaborate or time-consuming, Cal took the route of least resistance. Blueberry yogurt. It was more palatable than fried mice or raw cavy, and because he'd begun to feel weak—maybe roughhousing with Viking had taken the starch out of him—he felt that he had an obligation to himself to choke down something. Anything.

"Choke down." That was the phrase Lone Boy had used to describe his only experience of reading Philip K. Dick.

Stupid, Cal thought. Unjust.

He couldn't handle another bite of the yogurt. It looked to him like Elmer's Glue with a dollop of ink stirred into it. He stood up, found a cereal bowl in a cabinet, plopped the yogurt into the bowl, and set the bowl on the floor for Viking. Viking downed the stuff in one noisy gulp, then pushed the bowl up against the stove trying to lick it clean.

Cal left him there and walked down the hall to the tiny room that he and Lia had declared the "library." Lia had a desk, a filing cabinet, and an expensive error-correcting typewriter, as well as a cheap store-bought hutch containing many of her textbooks from Colorado College. Cal had a tower of pine-board shelves on cinder blocks for his paper-back westerns, mysteries, and fantasy fiction. Another such tower held "serious" work: Great English and American Fiction, Eloquent Poetry, Learnéd History, and Profound Philosophy. Cal's worn copies of P. K. Dick's contemporary novels occupied a shelf near the top of this second tower.

Also in the room, with a cushion on it so that it could serve as a place to sit, squatted a dilapidated olive-green trunk held shut with a padlock. Cal removed the embroidered cushion from the trunk and flipped it into the hall. Then he knelt in front of the old army locker, sprang the padlock with his key, and raised the battered lid. Amid a scramble of musty letters from his parents (many of them with scissored cutouts or concealing smears of black ink, courtesy of the Board of Citizen Censorship) lay the spiral binders in which Cal kept his illegal copies of Philip K. Dick's unpublished science-fiction novels.

In the Soviet Union, both before and after détente, dissident writers had circulated their works among friends in self-published manuscripts that were often only carbons or photocopies of the original typescript. The system was known as *samizdat*, a term meaning "to self-publish" that dated back at least as far as 1970, but that may have had antecedents even in czarist times.

Well (Cal remembered), with the advent of the dreaded No-Knocks soon after Nixon's defeat of Herbert Humphrey in 1968, and with the crackdowns on free expression during his pursuit of victory in Vietnam, *samizdat* had come to the United States of Amerika.

As an antiwar student at the University of Colorado in the late 1960s and then as a ranch hand during Nixon's first two terms, Cal had acquired a small but incriminating library of "self-published" manuscripts. Despite the surrender of North Vietnam in 1974 and the President's supposed mellowing since his landslide win over the Democrats' quadrennial sacrificial lamb in 1980, Cal knew that he could still go to jail for owning the photocopies. Lia and he had often argued about them—much more violently than they had argued about keeping Viking.

Before their move to Georgia, Lia had even suggested that Cal gather up all his illicit Dickiana and burn them on a bonfire on Arvill Rudd's ranch. She wanted them to make a fresh start, and as attractive as that notion had been to him, he hadn't been able to destroy Dick's work. That driven genius had written his novels as an indignant cry against the sleazy bomb-'em-till-they-holler mind-sets of King Richard and his megalomaniac henchmen. Besides, it would have been a betrayal of the memory of his mom and dad to have torched the books.

Viking, a blueberry-yogurt smear on his nose, came padding into the library. He nuzzled Cal and growled the Growl.

"All right. Don't be nosy. I'll show you."

The husky sat down at Cal's shoulder.

"This one's my favorite, *The Doctor in High Dudgeon*." Cal set the binder down in front of Viking. "It's a far-future history in which the Richard Nixon figure—Dick calls him Abendsen Ferris—sends a combat expedition to a distant star system, only to lose every member. Then he takes out his frustrations on the citizens who protested the mission by turning them into cyber-servants for himself and his imperial aides. Sounds sort of silly, summarized that way, I'll admit. The thing you have to remember is that Dick wrote this right after *Nicholas and the Higs*—but *before* the 1968 election. That's a pretty startling accomplishment, Vike. Not just prescient, more like precognitive. The result was that Dick couldn't sell the book. Publishers were frightened. They realized that it was satire as well as science fiction, a caustic comment on a complex American personality. They rejected it—not by admitting their fear that the new president would disapprove but by telling the author that a novel in this vein would confuse the readership that knew him as a realist social critic. After the debacle of *Nicholas and the Higs* (his editors at Hartford, Brice said), they had to be careful to preserve the tattered rags of respectability still clinging to his reputation."

Viking cocked his head interrogatively.

"You know what Dick's response to that editorial argle-bargle was, my wolfish friend?"

Attentively, Vike waited to hear.

"He said, 'That's bullshit, guys.' Then he told them, 'Up your tender wazoos. Who needs you timid establishmentarians, anyway?' Unfortunately, he was soon to find out that *he* apparently did. No one else would take *The Doctor in High*

Dudgeon, either, and until *Valis* came out from Banshee a year or so back, Dick wasn't able to publish anything at all—that wasn't simply a reissue—for the next fourteen years. A crime. A shame and a crime."

And now the poor man's dead, Cal thought. He fished around on a bookcase shelf, found his stash, and made himself a reefer. (It was one measure of his old-fashionedness, he knew, that he didn't do coke. That was for Upwardly Mobiles, and he wasn't a goddamn UpMo.) Smoking his marijuana cigarette, Vike tolerantly observing, Cal rummaged again through his forbidden Dickiana.

He picked out and set down before Viking the binders containing *Do Androids Dream of Ambitious Veeps?; Flow My Tears, the Policeman Said; Now Wait for Last Year; They Scan Us Darkly, Don't They?; No-Knock Nocturne;* and four or five others, including *Yubiq* and *The Dream Impeachment of Harper Mocton*. Viking stared at the stack of binders for a long time. So did Cal, who remembered, as he did, the circumstances surrounding his acquisition of each photocopy.

"Would you like to know how I got these, Vike?"

"Sure," the dog replied.

"All right, listen. A friend of mine in Boulder, way back in '69, knew a guy who'd known Dick in Santa Venetia, California, and Dick had given this fella a Xerox of the typescript of *The Doctor in High Dudgeon*. Just *given* it to him. My friend made a copy from Dick's friend's copy and sent Dick a check for ten bucks through Dick's friend. . . . This too complicated for you, Vike?"

"If you can tell it, no way it's gonna be too hard for me to follow."

"Right. I'm sorry." Cal took a deep drag. "We felt we had a moral obligation to pay any writer whose work we made keeper copies of. *If* we could afford to, that is. Lots of junk was going around that way *before* Nixon's election— underground comics, poetry, posters, songs, etcetera. As if we were anticipating the crackdown to come. Not many student artists wanted pay for their stuff, but when you ran across somebody with a national reputation who was putting that reputation on the line to protest the coming fascism, the way Philip K. Dick was, well, you didn't feel right keeping a copy of their work without giving something back. I mean, some of these people were *professionals*. Who counted for their *livelihoods* on writing or painting or performing, and when they couldn't hawk their wares to establishment outlets, it *hurt* them."

"So Dick gave the typescript of *High Dudgeon* to his friend so the friend could show it around and make Dick some money?"

"No, no, no! Damn it, Vike, you're a prisoner of a bourgeois dog-eat-dog mentality. What the hell's wrong with you?"

Viking licked his chops, sheepishly.

"It wasn't what *Dick* wanted or expected. He'd given that novel to his friend simply to share it. It was what the friend's friends expected of *themselves* when they made keeper copies. We wanted to show our gratitude by giving something back to the artists—in appreciation of their skill and courage and as a counterweight to the income they'd lost when mainstream corporations declined to sponsor them. And so my friend sent Dick ten bucks when he Xeroxed Dick's friend's typescript, and that's why, hard up as I was at the time, I did the same thing when I made my keeper of *High Dudgeon*. I'd've felt like an utter shit if I *hadn't*. You do understand me, don't you, Vike?"

"I guess so. But since the art *I* like best usually comes out of a can, I'm no authority on the subject, *am* I?" The husky put a paw on the binder holding *Flow My Tears, the Policeman Said*. "Did you send Dick a check for all these other novels, too?"

"If not right when I made my copy from the master, then later, when I had some cash. It would've been tacky not to've, and just look what I got in return."

Viking cocked his head at the binders on the rug.

"Eleven masterpieces of American fiction," Cal said. "Eleven *unacknowledged* masterpieces. Unacknowledged because unpublished by any establishment company. But *I* own copies of them, Vike, and that's a high honor. It's also a charge to resist the tyranny that kept these works from reaching print in the first place."

"How are you doing that, Cal? By working at a pet shop?"

This unexpected question enraged Cal. "I'm *not* doing it,

not at all, and, listen, I'm sick because I *know* I'm not!" He stubbed his spent roach in an ashtray and stood up.

You fuckin' dog, he thought. Why're you questioning *me* when the only goddamn thing *you* do is dig holes in the fuckin' yard and snooze for three quarters of every goddamn day?

But Viking was relentlessly Socratic. "I know you're not, Cal, and I don't understand something. Why do you hinge your resistance to the Nixonian tyranny on these unpublished novels?"

"I'm not following you, bung-sniffer."

"I mean, that's bad. But you have a far more pressing motive, don't you? A motive that hits closer to home?"

Don't you dare say it, Cal thought. Listen, you leg-lifting, flea-ridden, bung-sniffing growler, *don't say it.*

"What about your parents?" Viking persisted. "Isn't what they had to suffer far more painful—to *you,* I mean—than King Richard's career-trashing of a writer unrelated to you?"

The word *parents* does it. Cal grabs Viking by the collar and yanks him out of the library, down the hall, and through the living room to the front door. Viking is happy to get outdoors again, probably because he believes that Cal is going to take him for a walk, but Cal has other plans. He hooks the cold chain to Vike's collar and hurries back inside before the husky realizes that, instead of exercise, he has only another long stretch of tethered boredom ahead of him.

'S what you get for being a goddamn busybody, Cal thinks. He returns to the library, sits down next to the open locker, amid his illegal Dickiana, and proceeds to mourn the man.

In 1974, after meeting his contact in Snowy Falls, Colorado, a little town in the mountains above Walsenburg, and receiving from this guy a copy of *They Scan Us Darkly, Don't They?,* Cal sent Dick a check for fifteen dollars—more than he could really afford. Two months later, he wrote Dick a letter about *They Scan Us Darkly,* entrusting it to the dude who'd been his contact. This fellow hand-delivered it to Dick in Fullerton, California, violating the Internal Travel Restrictions Act regulating all interstate movements. Two weeks later, the smuggler met Cal at a chop-suey joint in Manitou Springs and gave him a typewritten note from the author.

Recalling how he fumbled open the note, Cal finds it taped to the inside cover of his photocopy of *They Scan Us Darkly* and frees it so that he can read it again. Nearly eight years old, it has not even yellowed, but Cal can smell the Chinese cooking odors—eggroll, sweet-and-sour pork—still clinging to it from that grimy café up in Manitou:

Dear Mr. Pickford,

Thank you for sending me your comments on *They Scan Us Darkly, Don't They?* and on my work in general. I have reread your letter ten times and I say at last to myself, "I think you did it; I think you wrote what you set out to write. I can tell by what Cal Pickford says in this letter about your novel."

It took me five years to write *They Scan Us Darkly,* and as you so clearly realize, my heart and body and life are in it. That's a lot to risk by putting it on paper; you hand the world your soul.

Of course, the risk may seem less when no publisher will issue the book for general distribution, but really it isn't. The risk lies in intervening in the wretched little lives that I try to mark in my unpublished books. It lies in trying to make a permanent record of their sad comings and goings. It lies in the writing.

I would say more, or would write again saying more, but I don't want to put you at risk, too. Your response to my work and your financial support proves that you are a genuine human being. Too many of those with power over our lives today are artificial human beings.

So I am cordially yours for a better day, later on, when people will understand.

The name "Philip K. Dick" was typed at the bottom of this note, of course, but above the typing the man had penned "Phil" in an easy, forward-slanting cursive that warmed Cal's heart.

He returned the letter to its taped pocket on the inside of

the spiral notebook. Then *They Scan Us Darkly* and all his other bound typescripts went back into the trunk, after which Cal dropped the lid, reaffixed the padlock, and put the cushion from the hall back on top of the trunk so that, if necessary, some weary, forlorn soul could sit down on it.

Cal sat down, his hands dangling between his knees. Outside, Viking began to howl—a weird, lugubrious keening.

That's just how I feel, Cal thought. You've got it perfectly.

He had to do something to mitigate his grief. If not mitigate, then articulate. He had tried to do it by talking to Viking, but Viking had hit him with that lousy non sequitur about his folks, ruining the effort. What, then? What should he do to speak his grief until Lia got home and he could take his wife into his arms as a buffer against the heartlessness of the world?

A poem, Cal thought. An elegy. You should sit down and write an elegy for Philip K. Dick.

This idea excited Cal. (On the porch, Viking was howling ever more pathetically.) He went to Lia's desk and pulled a pad of yellow legal paper from the drawer. He took a pen from the drawer and arranged himself so that his elegy to Dick could flow out onto the long sheets as easily as tears from a grief-stricken child.

Nothing happened.

Cal waited, meanwhile assiduously thinking, but the poem would not come. *Stirrings* of inspiration came, but only stirrings, and Viking's continuing howls did nothing to goad him to creativity. He shut them out by thinking again on Dick's lovely note and all the unacknowledged masterpieces in the trunk.

And at last he had a sound opening line and a good second line to go with it:

> *Philip K. Dick is dead, alas.*
> *Let's all queue up to kick God's ass.*

But after recording these lines, Cal got stuck again and could find no way of proceeding. "*It's clear that in a world so crass*," he mused, testing the words aloud. And soon after: "*The President deplored your sass.*" They rhymed, these additions, but they didn't get it. Cal would have deleted them, had he bothered to write them down, but he hadn't bothered. They sucked. He knew they sucked.

And so he decided that the two lines he *had* recorded— "*Philip K. Dick is dead, alas. / Let's all queue up to kick God's ass*"—perfectly encapsulated everything he wanted to say about the death of Phil Dick. They had rhythm, rhyme, assonance, and alliteration, and they spoke both his bereavement and his bitterness. What more could anyone ask? Cal stood up, holding the elegy, and declaimed it to the room in a voice as deep and melodious as the sea's.

On the porch, Viking howled.

"Shut up, you bargain-basement wolf!" Cal shouted. "Goddamn it, shut your whinin' trap!"

But Viking did not shut up, and standing there in the middle of his and Lia's library, Cal realized that tears were cascading down his cheeks, waterfalling helplessly from some inner source that he would never be able to pinpoint.

7

You mean you've been home since one o'clock and you left poor Vike on the porch all afternoon?"

"Philip K. Dick died, Lia. Mr. Kemmings let me off. He didn't have to, but he did. He's a pretty decent guy."

"Too bad his decency isn't contagious."

"For God's sake, Viking's a husky. Leaving him on the porch a few hours isn't like sticking him in the freezer."

"You're stoned, aren't you? Your eyes are glazed over, and you're listing to the left. Ridiculously."

"It'd be even more ridiculous to list to the right. In this day and time, it'd be *redundant*."

"You promised me you'd lay off that stuff down here. This is a small town. Besides, pot makes you heavy-lidded and slow, and I'm not sure you need any help there. Worse, it made you indifferent to a fellow creature's need for company."

Viking sat on the living-room rug, only a few feet away, taking in their argument and bemusedly thumping his tail.

"A few tokes to soften the hammer blow of Phil Dick's death—that's all it was. And Vike's fine. Look at him."

Lia knelt by the dog. Then, burying her face in his fur, she began to weep.

"You poor baby," she consoled the dog. "You poor, poor baby."

"Jesus. *He's* got a so-so case of I-been-stuck-on-the-porch-for-a-few-hours blues while *I'm* the victim of genuine bereavement, and you're cooing over him and cutting me dead."

Lia continued to cry and Vike to thump his tail on the rug.

"Bad day at the office?" Cal put his hands into his pockets.

Lia caught her breath and lifted her head. A new sob started to overtake her, but she mastered it by patting her chest. "Like you wouldn't believe."

"Try me."

"Like *I* can't believe, for that matter."

"Then we're a pair. Bad days at the office for the empathetic Bonner-Pickfords."

"Cal, I'm sorry that your writer friend died."

"Thanks. I'm sorry about whatever happened to you today in the psychotherapy business."

"Are you sorry you left Viking on the porch?"

"I am now. Maybe you'd've understood if you'd been here. The bung-sniffer was being obnoxious."

Vike's ears erected. He growled the Growl.

Lia went to Cal and embraced him. "Maybe I would've."

She and her husband held each other. The dog padded into the kitchen to push his empty yogurt bowl around.

"Let's shower," Cal said. "Let's get naked, literally and then emotionally. Show and tell. The latest fad in home psychotherapy, doctor." Still holding his wife, he began to unbutton his shirt.

"When did you give me this?" Lia asked. She touched the pin on her blazer, the pin with the intaglio side view of a fish.

"Did I give you that?"

"Didn't you?"

"I don't *remember* giving it. Not exactly my style, is it? I'd be more likely to give you a hat or a pair of boots."

"So where did I get it?"

Cal shook his head. "No idea. Nice, though. Very nice." He nuzzled her ear. "Come on, Lia, let's show and tell. Therapeutic ablutions for the blue and the world-battered."

Hot spray bludgeons them, and steam billows in the stall as if it were a gigantic coffee maker releasing aromatic vapor into the air. Bad metaphor, Lia thinks. But the steam puts her in mind of the coffee maker in her office, and of Kai's obsessive talk about coffee, and—how can it fail to remind her of this?—of Kai's own impossible vaporization from the lounger in which he was sitting. He turned to steam—or mist, or undulant spirit—right before her and Shawanda's eyes, and so they vowed never to speak of this fact to anyone. Lovers and husbands excepted, of course, and Lia has just told Cal.

"Dick," Cal says.

The word startles her. He stands at her back, his arms around her in the hot pelting spray, and the part of him that a romance novelist would call his "manhood" slides provocatively toward and then away from the cleft of her fanny. Almost as funny as erotic, it engorged at Cal's first sight of her nakedness and grew tauter and tauter—nigh to bursting, like an overinflated balloon—with every touch; her back and bottom, and his belly and thighs, slide slide slide against each other in the lubricating downpour.

Lia says, "I *know* what it is, but that's not my favorite name for it. And I wonder why you can't relax a few minutes."

"I can't help this one upright part of me. Of course, there *is* a sure-fire way to relax me. For a while, anyhow."

"Uh-huh."

"If I *could* help it, Lia, and if I were you—which would put us both in an embarrassing bind—I think I'd be insulted."

"You're not thinking straight, hubby. An involuntary response like that isn't a compliment—it's a witless reflex. A gatefold in a magazine can prompt the same idiot snap to attention."

"Lia—"

"And it hacks me off when you start using adolescent nicknames to talk about your penis. You sound like a schoolyard tough. A *would-be* schoolyard tough."

I really do hate that kind of crap, Lia thinks, enjoying the feel of Cal's freshly shaven face on her nape. Men have more names for their goddamn penises than Eskimos have words for snow, and they seem to think that pulling out one of these nicknames—not to mention the eager dojiggy so dubbed—is going to act on us as an absolutely masterful turn-on. It's enough to—

"Lia—"

"What, damn it!"

"I meant Philip K. Dick, not angry ol' Captain Standish here. Listen, don't accuse me of talking punksterese. I *wasn't* talking dirty, and if I *had* been, I'd've hit you with esoteric dirty. The member from Cockshire. Quimstake. Mister Pl—"

Lia swivels around, pressing her breasts to Cal's chest and opening her mouth on his throat. The member from Cockshire grazes her mossy pubes, and the water thundering down threatens to blind Cal's cyclopean friend. She glances down to see it eyeing her and puts her mouth again to her husband's mouth, letting her tongue go spelunking there as her fingers caress the rain-slickened rungs of his vertebrae.

This is one way to make you shut up, she thinks. One foolproof method.

After this kiss, Lia says, "What does the man with the priapic surname have to do with us, Cal? With anything that's happened to us, me today?" The demanifestation of Mr. X from her office lounger seems—now—a fever-dream. All that is significantly real is Cal, her husband-lover.

Cal grips her by her upper arms. "I meant that your client today—this 'Kai' fella—and Philip K. Dick are one and the same. You were visited by the very person I've been grieving over."

Lia suddenly remembers. "He asked to see a picture of you. He said *you* were the reason he'd come to Warm Springs. That maybe you were . . . how did he put it? The gist was that you could help him overcome his problems. Amnesia, binocular perception—like that."

"Me?"

"But I told him my family life was none of his business."

Lia sees that, even in the reddening spray, Cal's face has gone pale. Her tale of Kai's metamorphosis into see-through nothingness didn't much perturb him, but letting him know that Kai thinks him the focus of a telling emanation . . . ah, *that* news has brought the reality of the whole irreal situation home to him.

"Look. Your Captain Standish is at half mast."

"Don't be flip. Something incredible has happened."

"I know that. And you've just told me that I was visited by a dead man. A ghost, I assume." But no, not a ghost. Lia remembers what Shawanda said, that Kai must have appeared to them wearing a "resurrection body." Otherwise, how could he've drunk coffee? And why would he've warned Shawanda not to touch him?

"Phil Dick visited you, and he said I was the reason. You've got it all on tape, don't you?"

"Captain Standish has been demoted. You may have to start calling him Private Limpley."

"Lia!"

"Cool it. My story didn't hit home until you realized Kai had asked about you. *Then* your eyes light up and your rudder relaxes."

What egos men have. They can't empathize with anybody unless that other person's problem directly involves them, too. Abstract sympathy, long-distance compassion . . . sooner expect a piranha to ask the blessing before meals than a male human being to show such selfless kindness, ever. Another example of the me-first mentality that sent Viking to the porch.

"Lia, I asked you if you had it all on tape."

"In my briefcase. Hearing what Kai—Philip K. Dick— had to say about King Richard, I wasn't about to leave it at the office."

Dripping wet, Cal pushes aside the shower curtain, steps over the edge of the tub, and exits the bathroom bare-assed.

"Cal!" Damn you, Lia thinks. You'll get everything wet. She shuts off the spigots, gropes for a towel, and, finding one, dries her upper body and wraps it around herself toga-fashion.

Cal returns, puts her cassette player on the sink stand, sits down on the pink commode-lid cover, and turns the player on.

"You're going to electrocute yourself. You probably sopped all my notes and reference material."

"They're all right—I was very careful. And this thing runs on batteries. Just let me listen to it, okay?"

"Let's get dressed and eat something. You didn't happen to fix us something during your long afternoon's journey into the dinner hour, did you?"

Fat chance, Lia decides. You're obsessive today, a one-track engine chugging hell-for-smelter toward . . . what? A head-on crash with a self-annulling illogicality. You're certainly not thinking about scrambling eggs or frying hamburgers.

Waiting for the tape to play, Lia shivers more violently than the cool of the apartment would require. Because what you really fear, she admits, is the possibility that outside your office, it won't play at all. If not, Cal will say you've flipped out. He'll razz you about getting stoned on curried chicken in the Victorian Tea Room. You gave him a hard time for doing grass, but he hasn't conjured from his tetrahydrocannabinol-assisted trip a vision half as loony as your tale about this morning's drop-in amnesiac.

Almost holding her breath, Lia waits.

Then the tape begins to play, and the first voice she hears is her own—*"How did you get here?"*—followed almost immediately by Kai's response: *"Taxi from Atlanta."* The miniature reels in the cartridge keep turning, and more words issue from the player's tiny speakers. A powerful feeling of gratitude grips Lia, who murmurs, "It's real. We've got corroboration."

"That's definitely Phil Dick," Cal says.

"How do you know?"

"Once upon a time, in Snowy Falls, I heard him on tape. The guy who had the master of *They Scan Us Darkly, Don't They?* smuggled it out of Fullerton and played it for me in his pickup's cab. Dick was talking about Jung, stuff like that. This is the same voice. This is definitely the man famous for *Confessions of a Crap Artist* and other masterpieces of American literature."

I've talked to a dead man, Lia thinks. Or maybe to the soul of Cal's dead writer clad in its resurrection body—like Christ's body after its crucifixion and entombment. In addition to the money Kai paid me, I have his voice on tape. Irrefutable corroboration of my interview with him.

"Cal—"

"Let me listen."

"I'm cold. I'm getting dressed. Why don't you—"

"Go ahead."

A pox on you, Lia thinks. From *Homo erectus* to *Homo deflectus* in less than five minutes.

Angry, Lia brushes past her husband, goes to the bedroom, and clothes herself in fresh underwear, blue jeans, heavy socks, and a bulky fish-net sweater. She gathers up keys, change, a paperclip, some other things to put in her pockets. When she returns to the bathroom and looks in on Cal, he's sitting there like Rodin's *The Thinker*, lankier maybe but just as abstracted, totally engrossed in her session with the Man Who Faded Away.

Time passes. Tape unreels.

Wide-eyed, Cal raises his head and mutters, "He called me the reason he came to you. He said that I may even be the 'lens' that will focus his stereographia."

"I *know* that. Do you have any idea why?"

"None. Absolutely none."

Lia fixed tomato soup and cheese toast for dinner, and although Cal wanted to complain that he'd had nothing to eat today but some blueberry yogurt, he knew that he'd better not.

"What're we going to do about this?" he asked.

"Don't say another word to me about it, not one more word. I'm not up to it."

I should've taken her to bed, Cal thought. I should've soaped her back and kissed her and dried her off and carried her into the bedroom and screwed her until neither of us could think straight. At least we'd've had that much pleasure out of this dippy day. My big mistake was abandoning her when she was telling me, with those ever-lovin' kisses and body bumps, Take me, just like a heroine in a trashy bestseller. She wanted comforting as much as she did sex, but you gave her no comfort and got no release yourself. Now we're both as tight as clams. And nothing's been resolved.

"'Philip K. Dick is dead, alas,'" Cal impulsively recited.

"What?"

"That's the first line of an elegy I wrote for him today."

"You wrote Phil Dick an elegy?"

"Well, sort of. I mean, it isn't . . ." (Calvin, you've set yourself up for a tumble at the hands of your harshest critic.)

"What's the rest of it? Do you remember?"

Go on, Cal encouraged himself. Recite it and get it over with, or she'll badger you all evening. Aloud, he said, "'Philip K. Dick is dead, alas. / Let's all queue up to kick God's ass.'"

Lia just stared at him, a spoonful of soup midway between her bowl and her mouth. Then she said, "Go on."

"That's it. That's the whole thing."

"First line's okay, but the second's contemptible. Irreverent for the sake of irreverence. Which is crap typical of teenagers or maladjusted adults."

"That's a psychological interpretation."

"What did you want?"

"How about an unbiased aesthetic judgment?"

"There's no such animal, Cal."

"A decade in Colorado couldn't completely wipe out your uptight Southern Baptist biases, could it?"

"What you'll never figure out, Pickford, is that I'm not upset because your stupid 'kick God's ass' line rubs me wrong. I'm upset because it demeans you."

"Jesus. What you'll never understand is that I wrote it not to be irreverent but to voice my anger and frustration over an unjust death. Existential outrage, not irreverence, powers that line."

"La di da."

"But you give me a psychological judgment instead of a literary one. A judgment tainted by small-town religiosity."

Whereupon Lia said, "We really *should* go to church here, Cal. I've wanted us to since the first day we arrived."

"Dear God." Me? thought Cal. Squeezed into a pew of the First Baptist Church? I'd have to put my Indian braid down my shirt collar. It even bugs Mr. Kemmings, and the folks at First Baptitst are going to find it harder to take than he does. But maybe you might really meet God over there. In Georgia, He has to hang out *somewhere* around Baptist churches. Too many of the goddamn things to ignore.

"Dear God," Lia echoed him. She slurped her tomato soup.

"Lia, I'm not going to try to *publish* my elegy."

"Good. You'd wouldn't find anyone to take it, anyway. If you did, you'd be humiliated by the reviews."

"Thanks." He slurped his own scummy soup. Presently, he said, "Listen, I sold a pair of Brezhnev bears this morning. To a lady who asked me if I'd ever been in trouble with the authorities."

Lia straightened. "What did you tell her?"

"I lied and said no. Scared the shit out of me, though. She was wondering what a fellow my age was doing working in a pet shop, and all I could think to say, loading up her car, was that I was married to a psychologist who worked in Warm Springs. I even gave her your name."

"Okay. So?"

"Maybe she'll drop in on you."

"Probably she won't."

"I'm afraid she'll drop in at the pet store again, though."

"Why?"

"Because she looked familiar. I should've known who she was. And after all this crazy Phil Dick business, we can't let anything out of the ordinary go unexamined." (Like the fact that some sort of troubleshooting goon cased out Mr. K.'s shop before the lady even entered.)

"You need to chuck those damn photocopies of his novels."

"You need to throw away your tape."

"No."

"Then I'm not chucking my photocopies."

Lia stood up and began clearing away dishes.

Viking, hearing the clink and clatter, came in from the living room; he sat down at her heels to wait for a handout.

"I'll get the dishes," Cal said, standing. It's the least you can do, cowboy, he told himself.

"We're leaving them until we get back."

"Get back? From where?"

"Visiting my mother."

"Didn't you visit her before you left?"

"I couldn't. I was too shaken. I spent the afternoon calling local businesses. To keep my mind off . . . you know. If we go now, we'll be back by nine-thirty."

Christ, Cal thought. Duty calls. And we drag ourselves around endlessly in weary answer to its summons. . . .

Emily Bonner, Lia's mother, had a semiprivate room in the east wing of the Eleanor Roosevelt Nursing Home in Warm Springs. The accident that had killed Jim Bonner, Lia's father, had left Emily badly crippled. She could cruise the corridors of the home in her wheelchair, but she didn't always gladly greet those who visited her. Cal's experiences with

Emily since relocating in Georgia had been far from pleasant, probably because before the accident she had known him only through photos and telephone conversations. When he said, "Hi, Mom, how're you doing?" she would shrink away, goggle her eyes, and reply, "I'm fine. I'm not ready to go yet. Why don't you fly back to God and tell Him I'm happy *here*?" The only conclusion that Cal had been able to reach was that Miss Emily identified him with the Angel of Death—a paranoid response that made him reluctant to visit her.

At the nursing home, Cal and Lia parked, leaving Vike to pace the upholstery in the dark rear seat.

Doing the necessary, the Bonner-Pickfords entered the building in lockstep and proceeded down the hall to Emily's room. Cal was wondering why Lia couldn't have made a quick swing by here before coming home, and Lia was wondering why her brother hadn't made arrangements to keep their mother at Brown Thrasher Barony. Still, Lia enjoyed visiting her mama on her good days, and Cal was glad to get out after brooding all afternoon over Phil Dick's death.

Emily was lying in bed watching TV. Lia sat down next to her. Cal, his hands behind him, smiled half-heartedly and said, "Hey, Mom, how you doing?" The show was a PBS documentary—Channel 28—about the mutual benefits of Soviet-American détente: cooperation in space, less military spending, stepped-up trade and cultural exchanges, etcetera. Emily was thoroughly absorbed.

"Mama," Lia said. "Are you okay?"

"How could she be okay?" said Emily's roommate, Phoebe Flack, an octogenerian who made Lia think of the droll little dolls carved from dried apples. "*I* want to see *The Sinatra Hour* on CBS, but *she* won't let me. She's making me watch this boring crud about us and the Rooshuns." Phoebe jerked her hand at the TV set.

A lucid light appeared in Emily's eyes. "You've already seen *your* boring programs, Phoebe. Every evening, right after dear old Ronnie on the news, the same silly thing, *Death Valley Days* or a *General Electric Theater* rerun. It was my turn to choose."

"She's watching that out of spite," Phoebe complained to Lia.

Lia wondered if maybe Phoebe had a case. Only rarely

had Miss Emily displayed much interest in television. And never, to Lia's knowledge, in news, sports, or documentaries. This was weird. It was like finding a polar bear taking a voluntary stroll through the Sahara. But her mama's gaze was firmly riveted to the screen.

"Mama, I think Phoebe's right. Why not let her watch Sinatra? Besides, you've got company—Cal and me."

"This is important. I'm tired of watching junk. This shows us what the President's done to bring sanity back to the world."

Ouch, thought Cal. The doctors say it isn't Alzheimer's, that she's capable of thinking in clear, logical progressions . . . but she's obviously lost her grip on the reality that's here for her to think about now.

Emily looked directly at him. "Do you believe that an unending state of tension between us and the Soviets is healthy, Calvin?"

Cal was taken aback, not simply because she had spoken to him—a rarity—but also because she had challenged his latest thought.

He stammered, "N-no, ma'am. It's just that—"

"Why don't y'all be quiet and let me finish watching this? It won't be on much longer."

"Long enough that I won't get to see Old Blue Eyes," Phoebe griped. She reached her hand toward Lia. "Take me to the chapel, won't you, darlin'? I haven't been down there all day."

"I'll take her," Cal said, anxious to escape. He brought his mother-in-law's roommate's wheelchair out of the closet and began to unfold it. Lia caught his wrists.

"Mama just spoke to you," she whispered. "A red-letter date. Stay here with her. *I'll* take Phoebe to the chapel." Maybe, once the PBS program was over, Emily would speak to Cal again, and the two of them—the people who meant more to Lia than anybody else in the world—would finally begin to develop a relationship based on understanding and love.

This was not what Cal wanted. "Lia—" he began.

"Help me get Phoebe in the chair," his wife said aloud. "Then sit down and keep Mama company."

A moment later, pleased with herself, Lia was propelling Phoebe Flack down the long corridor, going past room after room in which a pair of pathetic oldsters lay TV-drugged or chemically sedated; the inmates' tortoiselike beaks pointed boob-tube- or ceilingward, and the numb resignation of their boxed-up lives quickly stole from Lia the pleasure she had taken from outmaneuvering Cal.

The chapel of the Eleanor Roosevelt Nursing Home was not much bigger than a broom closet. It had wheelchair space, six folding chairs, a tiny altar, and a miniature stained-glass window (lit from behind by a small yellow emergency bulb) above and behind the crucifix at the altar. Lia parked Phoebe in one of the wheelchair slots and sat down on a nearby folding chair.

Maybe I had another reason—besides leaving Cal and Mama alone together—for coming down here with Phoebe, Lia thought. Maybe, like Phoebe, I came down here to pray, to get close to myself by getting close to God. Wasn't that why I told Cal that we ought to start going to church? Or am I simply feeling poleaxed by what Shawanda and I witnessed this morning in my office?

Phoebe Flack was staring at the spooky sheen above the altar cross and moving her wrinkled lips. Lia tried to pray, too. God help me, she silently intoned. God help me. It became her mantra, an incantation, until she felt something in the pocket of her jeans sticking her, destroying her prayerfulness, and she shifted on the chair to dig out this object.

In her hand, the fish pin that she had found on her blazer that morning. It glinted briefly off Phoebe's astonished eye.

Lia's first response was to fling the pin away from her, as if it were a spider that had crawled onto her palm. But she stopped and stared in consternation—even fear—at the well-wrought piece of jewelry. She set the pin between her denim-encased thighs on the olive-drab metal of the chair. She put her hands on her thighs and fixedly regarded the intaglio fish.

As the fish grew brighter, more sharply etched, the chapel's walls and furnishings blurred. Lia's eyes magnified the object, like a microscope bringing a slide specimen into focus. As for Phoebe Flack, she faded away; so, in fact, did the entire Eleanor Roosevelt Nursing Home. Only the golden fish continued to exist, a touchstone on the disappearing chair.

Where am I? Lia wonders. Where have I gone? She tries to shut her eyes. It's hard, almost an impossibility. Finally, though, she manages. Opening them again, she finds herself caparisoned in a wedding gown.

The broom-closet chapel has become the grotto of an outdoor sanctuary walled about by sandstone pillars, towering arabesques of ocher and Navajo red.

Lia realizes that the marriage ceremony now going forward—hers—is doing so in the blue-sky splendor of the Garden of the Gods in Colorado. Hundreds of people attend, and, giving her away, is her dead father. Not a corpse, thank God, but the man he must have been in the mid-1970s, flushed with pride and vigorous. Miss Emily, her brother, Jeff, and her sister-in-law, and dozens of aunts, uncles, and cousins stand behind her and her daddy, looking on.

The presiding cleric has a beard and an ivory collar, but no distinct face, as if the sunlight has blanched it of its features. Already Lia suspects that the hidden visage belongs to the man who visited her office today. Apparently, he is a member of a secret, albeit kindly, priesthood.

"Give her the pin," this man instructs the groom.

It didn't happen this way, Lia recalls, turning toward Cal, who materializes at the sandstone altar in a white leather coat fringed like that of a dream-sequence movie cowboy.

She likes the way he looks, but this isn't how it happened. They were married in the den of Arvill Rudd's ranch house by a justice of the peace (her parents couldn't attend), with Rudd's wife, Bernadine, as her matron of honor and Arvill himself as best man. Their honeymoon was a white-water-rafting trip on a stretch of the Arkansas River in miserable September weather.

"With this pin, I thee wed," Cal tells her in the shadow of the lofty rocks. And he affixes it to her gown.

"Love, honor, cherish, and connect," the cleric enjoins them. "You may kiss." (His voice is the voice is the voice. . . .)

They do kiss, miniature figures in the diorama of the

Garden of the Gods. They kiss beneath the profile of Kissing Camels Rock, to the hubba-hubba murmuring of the wedding guests.

"How appropriate," Jeff says from the crowd, a smirk in his voice. "Now they can go home and hump."

Letting the kiss go on and on, Lia discovers herself grinning against Cal's mouth, grinning at Jeff's remark, at the blessedness of the memory that this ceremony will hardwire into them for all the ever-after days of their lives. . . .

Except, of course, that it didn't happen like that. History and circumstance intervened to evict the gods from the garden and to drown the kissing camels in spotlights. There was no pin. Like everyone else, they used a ring. In their case, a ring that had once belonged to Cal's mother's mother.

Lia heard a violent snort. Suddenly, the chapel and all its furnishings reappeared. The snort had come from Phoebe Flack, who, sitting in her wheelchair, praying or pretending to, had fallen asleep. Lia smiled at the woman. Then, looking between her legs, she saw that her fish pin had disappeared.

Where is it? Lia wanted to scream. Instead, she lifted her bottom and felt the warm metal basin into which the pin might have slid. No luck. She eased herself to her knees and began groping for it on the Lysol-scented floor. Still no luck. So she began crawling, palpating the featureless tiles for an excrescence that they did not possess. Then she bumped into a chair.

"What a target," Phoebe Flack said, snorting herself awake. "A man in boots would have a fine time kicking your fanny."

When Emily's documentary ended, she turned to Cal. "Look in my robe," she said. "The pocket."

Cal got up from the uncomfortable hospital chair and felt in the pocket of her robe, which was hanging from a hook on the inside of the bathroom door. His fingers closed on something round and squat; his first thought was that they had wandered onto a tin of shoe polish. But that didn't seem quite right.

The size and weight are wrong, Cal reflected. Plus there's no lip on the top to get a coin or a wingnut under.

"That's right," Miss Emily encouraged him. "Bring it here."

He brought out the object—a small, yellow tin of Dean Swift's snuff. Which astonished him. So did the fact that when he turned back around, Miss Emily, sitting up, gave him the weird impression of a person in costume. She looked like Emily Bonner . . . and she didn't. Cal, eyeing her, imagined that he must feel, now, somewhat the way Little Red Riding Hood had felt peering at the Big Bad Wolf in its brummagem Grandma getup.

"Calvin, I said, 'Bring it here.' " A peculiar husk to Lia's mother's gentlewomanly voice.

Her face seemed to waver—tremble—in the room's fluorescents. Her scalp hair was retracting, pulling in, like flower stalks in reverse time-lapse photography. Meanwhile, bristles began to sprout on her jawline and chin, stubbling her matronly face. And yet the effect was reminiscent of a double exposure. Cal could still see, behind these changes, the unchanged countenance of the woman whom Lia and he had come to visit.

Laminations, he thought. It's more like an identikit rendering than a double exposure. Put one plastic layer down on another, and if you squint, the original layer remains visible.

"I didn't know you did snuff, Mrs. Bonner."

"I can't do it if you stand there gawking, can I? Bring it to me, please."

Cal obeyed. Miss Emily took the tin and held it over her blanket; she screwed the top off and shook a sprinkle of fine brown powder onto the back of her hand. Then she snorted the grains like a blitzed-out coker doing a crooked line. Cal, cocking his head, felt like a boy standing in queue at a freak show and raptly gazing up—well, *down*—at the Bearded Lady. In a moment, if he didn't wet his pants or barf from a combination of embarrassment and nausea, she would stand up and show the crowd her virilia.

My God, a hermaphrodite. My mama-in-law's a hermaphrodite.

But she doesn't stand up and open her nightgown. She taps out more snuff, noisily snorkles it, blows her nose into a monogrammed handkerchief, taps out more powder, snuffles, and so on. Maybe she isn't an hermaphrodite, Cal thinks, but she's certainly an addict. A chain-snuffer. He watches Miss Emily furiously chain-snuffing, breathing tobacco dust faster than any cowhand, and he's finding it harder and harder not to sneeze. Finally, he does sneeze.

Kuh-CHOOOF!

"Shut the door," Emily commands him. "If a night nurse catches wind of this, she'll be in here with a vengeance."

Cal closes the door, wiping his nose on his sleeve. Lia's mama sounds like a man. To wit, the man who regaled Lia's tape recorder with stories of stereographia and the need for anamnesis.

"Damn!" the person in the bed exclaims. "This crap isn't any goddamn better than coffee!"

"I beg your pardon."

The veil over Miss Emily's face replies, "'I beg your pardon.' Christ, what an expression." More snuffling. "All I'm saying is that this lousy nozzle dust probably won't hold me to the planet any better than your wife's coffee did."

"It was decaffeinated."

"Yeah, yeah. But even unadulterated Maxwell House couldn't do the trick. And this isn't working, either."

"Philip K. Dick," Cal says. "Lia told me that you visited her this morning. You're actually—I mean, *actually*—Philip K. Dick." (Even if you've mysteriously usurped the body of Lia's mother.)

"Means nothing to me," the blur says. "You could tell me I was someone famous—Einstein, for example—but if I were really someone famous, I'd already know, and since I don't, I must not be. Philip K. Dick is therefore a nonentity—"

"No!"

"—or a man with so restricted a celebrity that ninety-seven out of a hundred Americans would never have heard of him." Snort-snuffle-snort. "Damn!" A powerful sneeze. "'Scuse me. Like the umpteen millionth customer at McDonald's or the first Vietnamese to open an argyle-hosiery mill."

"But you're a—"

"Pooh-pah. I'm off. This isn't working. I aimed at a victim of senectitude for a couple of reasons. One, to ease my takeover attempt. And, two, to zero in on you, Mr. Pickford."

"But why?"

The Philip K. Dick aura around the body of Lia's mama trembles, brightens, dims. "If I weren't trying so goddamn hard to talk with you, coming unglued like this might be fun. It's my secret love of chaos that gets me off on the depredations of entropy. But it's my love of justice that makes me kick and scream against them."

Briefly, the walls go clear; Cal can see through them into the chilly March night. The overheads dim as Dick's aura dims. When his aura pulses back, so do the lights. "I came to you because you're my beacon. Something to home on, a strobe in the ectoplasm into which I'm continually drifting, then kicking back. Pickford, you know better than I do why I've picked you out."

Like hell, Cal thinks as Miss Emily emerges from the watery lamination. He has no idea what to say, what to ask.

"Watch and wait," the Dick voice croaks. "I'll try to help."

Emily Bonner sat up out of the Phil Dick aura, knocking the tin of Dean Swift's snuff to the floor. Motes of gauzy dust whirled in amber slow-motion around her. Cal hurried to capture the tin and to brush the telltale paprika specks from her blanket.

"Tobacco," Miss Emily said. "All over."

"I'm getting it. Don't worry." Cal took her blanket, shook it out over the bathtub, ran water into the tub, returned the blanket to her bed, and scrubbed the floor with a wet towel.

"Funny, that smell. It's a hayloft smell."

"Yes, ma'am."

Lia returned with Phoebe Flack. Cal and his wife traded looks, each trying to decide what had been going on with the other. They were going to have more—a great deal more—to talk about on their drive home from Warm Springs.

8

Behind the counter of the Save-Our-Way convenience store, Le Boi Loan made change for a night student from the nearby vo-tek school, where the zombied-out gal was probably training to be a cosmetologist. She had a beehive hairdo that Sandra Dee would have swatted killer bees to possess, lips as red as a sucking chest wound, and enough violet goo on her eyes to drive a male mandrill mad. Lone Boy felt sorry for her. Despite her 1950-ish 'do and garish face paint, she seemed a sweet enough kid. She was buying a carton of milk and some cold cuts, and when he gave her her change, she smiled, said, "Thanks," and, on her way out the door, reverted to fatigue-ridden zombihood.

Chasing the American dream, Lone Boy decided. Works her ass off all day waiting tables or slinging hash, then goes to school at night to "better" herself. Eventually, she'll be able to buy good clothes, a neat car, and a single-family dwelling. Eventually, if the restrictions are repealed, she may get to travel. . . . Hell, she's a lot like me.

Lone Boy, who had been running this place since six, only an hour after going off duty at Gangway Books, checked his watch. He had twenty minutes before his shift ended and Norman Fraley, the midnight-to-morning clerk, arrived to relieve him. He ached in every sinew. An annoying tic rippled his right eyelid. If only I had some of that vo-tek gal's blue goo, he thought, I could stop the ticking . . . weight my damn eyelid down.

Now, at least, he had a quiet moment before Tuyet drove up in their secondhand Datsun. Tuyet always brought Triny and Tracy so that they could all go eat at whatever place was still open, Burger King or a pancake house. Sometimes this was the only meal that they got to take together, and when the girls started school, even this "tradition" would end. Tuyet was a lounge hostess, who did not have to report for work until early afternoon. So Triny and Tracy had long mornings in which to sleep. First grade, however, would dictate earlier bedtimes.

Lone Boy sat back on his stool, perusing a copy of *Daredevil*. Gangway Books didn't carry comics, but Save-Our-Way had all the major brands—Marvel, DC, Stupendo. You could stay abreast of almost any superhero's monthly adventures just by whirling the upright comic rack around, thumbing through the flimsy multicolored booklets, and yanking your favorite titles. Frank Miller's revitalization of *Daredevil*—a comic devoted to the crime-fighting exploits of the red-suited alter-ego of the blind attorney Matt Murdock—so delighted Loan that he had been buying and collecting it for over a year now.

Tonight, he was eyebrow-deep in the May issue, the poignant tale of Murdock's obsessive grief for his ex-girlfriend Elektra. In the April issue, Elektra, a with-it antiheroine in a skimpy scarlet costume, took a blade from a bad guy named Bullseye right through the heart, and now Matt, aka Daredevil, is trying to convince himself that—somehow, some way—Elektra has survived this brutal shish-kebabbing and secretly fled to a far corner of the earth, there to hide out until Daredevil can track her down and punish her for plunging him into needless mourning.

Many of the comic's tall, skinny panels feature characters in mysterious silhouette, and many colorful onomatopoeic expressions—KLUDD, KRESSH, CHOK, CLUGGG, and KRAK—heighten the excitement of the fight scenes between Daredevil and the pathetic stooges of his archenemy, Kingpin.

Lone Boy, turning the pulpy pages of the comic, is sucked into the action. He becomes a participant in Murdock's painful search, and the whole world encompassing the Save-Our-Way convenience store fades off into utter irreality and complete inconsequence.

"You're crazy, Matt," Lone Boy said. "She's dead, fella. You can't go digging up her grave. . . ."

But, of course, that is exactly what Matt intends to do and is doing now. KREEE goes Elektra's coffin lid as the blind man prises it up and leans down into the stench of her icy grave to lay hands on her face. Foggy, Matt's friend, enters the cemetery to rescue Matt from the horror of what he is about to learn: that Elektra does indeed slumber the forever sleep of death.

"My God!" Lone Boy exclaimed. "What a helluva story!"

He flipped back to the beginning of the comic and started going through it again, just as engrossed as the first time.

A shadow fell across the page. Terror clutched Lone Boy, and he looked up expecting to see a Saturday-night special in his face.

"It's only me—me and the girls," Tuyet said.

"You scared me, baby."

"The bell tingled. You didn't hear. Another *Daredevil*?"

Loan looked past his wife at the twins. Four years old and as cute as koalas, bundled as if for a snowstorm. They stood beneath the counter looking up at him expectantly.

Before he could even wink at his daughters, Tuyet handed him a letter, her expression clearly fretful. Something was wrong. Now Lone Boy saw that she had torn one end off the envelope, to get at its contents, and his own lack of ease mounted.

"It's from the Liberty Americulturation Centers of the Greater Southeast."

Lone Boy relaxed a bit. "An update on alumni, I bet. Progress reports on the successes of various graduates."

Tuyet was shaking her head. "They want you to report to the Fort Benning LAC for a refresher course. You've been out on your own since '76. It's time for your biennial reindoctrination."

"I was exempted from that in the spring of '78," protested Lone Boy. "I've got a fuckin' certificate, and I'm—"

"Shhh, Loan. The girls."

"—an *official* certificate, and I'm fully Americulturated, from the taps on my shoes to the tip of my ducktail." Shaking, Lone Boy pulled the LAC/GSE letter from its envelope and studied it. Tuyet had not misrepresented its message.

This is harassment, Lone Boy thought. I'm as American as hot dogs, baseball, apple pie, and Chevrolets. Quickly, he directed a worried glance at the Datsun that Tuyet had parked in front of the Save-Our-Way. But even buying foreign was American. Surely, they couldn't hold *that* old clunker against him; he was still struggling to establish himself as an enterprising capitalist. After all, it takes longer for some than others. I've voted for Nixon in two presidential biggies, and I'm moonlighting like a sonuvabitch to prove myself. What more can the lovely people at LAC/GSE expect of gutsy Le Boi Loan?

"I want a Whopper," Triny piped.

"Not me," countered Tracy. "I want pancakes."

Tuyet touched her husband's wrist. "But this evening something else happened."

"Something else?" Lone Boy asked suspiciously.

"Grace Rinehart phoned. You're to meet her at twelve-fifteen at the Chattahoochee Valley Art, Film, and Photography Salon."

"She's here in town? She wants to see me?"

"So it appears."

Lone Boy slid the May issue of *Daredevil*—he had already paid for it—into a sack containing a bottle of cranberry juice and a bag of popcorn. Grace Rinehart, Oscar-winning film actress and a Freedom Medal recipient for her work Americulturating political relocatees from Southeast Asia and elsewhere, wanted to meet with him on Hines Street in the Art, Film, and Photography Salon—long after its stated closing time. What a whopping big honor. Maybe she would countermand the LAC order that he show up at Fort Benning every night next week—losing income and maybe even risking his second job—for reindoctrination. Possibly, she hadn't caught wind of this letter until after one of her workers had typed and mailed it. Although a celebrity nine times over, she took a real interest in Little People. She went out of her way to rectify the mistakes of overzealous Americulturators.

"It's five-after now!" Lone Boy shouted. "We've only got ten minutes to make it! Where's that drag-butt Fraley?"

"Here I am, chink," said Norman Fraley, entering. "And here's a goddamn quarter." He slapped it on the counter. "Five minutes' wages, prorated from our hourly pay."

Lone Boy pocketed the quarter, shed his apron, and got

out from behind the counter so that Fraley could take over. "You may be a drag-butt, but you're a decent drag-butt."

Tuyet hurriedly told Fraley hello and tried to get the twins to greet him, too—but Lone Boy, pulling on a jacket, herded the three females out the door and into the Datsun, thinking, Two jobs down, an interview with Miss Rinehart ahead of me, and miles to go before I sleep. . . .

Twelve minutes later, Loan's family's Datsun pulled up in front of the Chattahoochee Valley Art, Film, and Photography Salon. This odd remodeled building, with tinted windows at various heights and sheets of intricately stamped tin covering its many roofs, sat at the bottom of a hill, with a concrete wall surmounted by flower boxes around its tiny access court.

Loan set the emergency brake to keep the car from rolling onto the railroad tracks going shadowily past the salon's east side. He had to fight the sensation that this building—the most striking piece of architecture on Hines Street—was itself about to topple over onto the tracks. Lights were on inside the salon—cold white lights. Lone Boy shooed Tuyet and the twins through the front gate, up the steps, through the unlocked doors, and into one of the bright first-floor galleries of the multichambered hall.

Why has Miss Rinehart asked me here? he thought. And why at this hour? But that's easy. Because at nearly every other hour I either work or sleep. She's taking care not to be inconsiderate. But what she sacrifices to be kind, she gets all the way back in the area of mysteriousness.

They were in a gallery devoted to Popular Americana. Coca-Cola signs, serving trays, magazine advertisements. Movie posters from six decades. A display case full of belt buckles, some shaped like stock-car racers, some like bucking broncs or jumping trout. One bore the brass legend BORN AGAIN. A rack of baseball bats; a rack of shotguns and rifles; a display of *TV Guide* covers; a diorama of events—depicted with the aid of tiny, well-dressed dolls—from the presidency of Richard Milrose Nixon.

Triny and Tracy had their noses pressed to the front of this diorama. The ingenious miniatures of the President and other world leaders had entranced them.

Lone Boy looked, too.

Here was a chipper Richard Nixon doll talking with a portly Mao Zedong doll in Beijing. Here was an amiable Nixon hugging a bearish Leonid Brezhnev in Moscow. Here was a dour Harry Kissinger doll presiding at the War Crimes trials of North Vietnamese army officers and communist party shills, all shown in the diorama as hangdog mannequins wearing khaki prison garb. Over here was a sad Jimmy Carter effigy conceding the 1976 presidential election to his opponent. (The Carter figure was an ambiguous sop to the pride of native Georgians.) Over here was the new Shah of Iran receiving from Vice President Westmoreland a delivery of fighter aircraft and tanks, symbolized in the display by tiny metal toys. . . .

"It's good to see you again, Loan," a female voice said, and he turned to find himself facing a woman in a black cape, sunglasses, and scarlet riding britches. "It's good of you to come here after work to see me." She nodded at Tuyet and the girls. Apparently, she had just come down to them from the wide stairs twisting up to the second floor.

"Miss Rinehart?" Lone Boy was suspicious.

"No recognition? Well, I'm glad you have your doubts." She took off her sunglasses and put them away. She peeled off her bottom lip, revealing a lip decidedly more familiar. Then she removed her wig, shaking out her own hair, an auburn cascade in contrast to the brunette tidiness of the hairpiece. She dropped the wig on the floor. "I hope I haven't startled the girls," she said. "It's just that I can't go about this town freely without a few dramatic precautions." She smiled. "Once an actress, always an actress, I guess. And please call me Miss Grace."

"I don't need to be reindoctrinated," Lone Boy declared.

"We're just beginning to get ahead," Tuyet added, and Loan was grateful to her for making this point. Real Americans succeeded, and together he and Tuyet were pushing hard against the remaining barriers confining them to the lower middle class. If he lost his job at Save-Our-Way to be re-Americulturated over several evenings at Fort Benning's Liberty Center, they'd be losing ground in their daily quest for an inheritable estate.

"That's what I'm here to talk to you about, Loan." She turned to Tuyet. "Upstairs you and the kids will find a table laid out with various refreshments. Then you can watch the nonstop showing of Looney Tunes in our screening room. Okay?"

Although Tuyet did not seem anxious to comply, she thanked Miss Grace and took the twins upstairs. After which the actress led Lone Boy into a gallery with a modern sofa, a glass coffee table, and dozens of *objets d'art*—mobiles, he supposed—hanging from the ceiling on wires. Lone Boy sat down, placing on the coffee table the sack that he had inadvertently brought in from his car.

Miss Grace lowered herself into an excruciatingly modern chair a small distance from the sofa. The woman's famous bottom lip—the pout that had launched a thousand B-52s—looked wan and chafed, but she had hidden it all day under a strip of sculpted rubber.

"We last saw each other four years ago, didn't we? When I gave you your LAC exemption certificate."

"But I've seen *you* dozens of times since then, Miss Grace. On television. In the movies. I watched the President give you the Freedom Medal, along with Clint Eastwood, Commissioner of Baseball Agnew, country-western troubadour Berle Haggard, and the fine spy novelist E. Howard Hurt. And the sequel to *The Green Berets—Going After Ho's Guys*—that you directed and starred in . . . my God, Miss Grace, I must've seen it at least five times!"

The actress stared—embarrassedly?—at the floor and then said, "I knew about the letter that Headquarters LAC/GSE sent out to you, Loan, and I approved it."

"You approved it? Why? I'm fully Americulturated. I can rap with the coolest, I can—"

"Please, Loan."

"But I can, miss. I can tell you the averages of all the major league batting champions since 1945. The birthdays of President Nixon's grandchildren. I can recite from memory Ronald Reagan's splendid castigation of the discredited liberal media when he took over from Cronkite as anchor on the *CBS Evening News*. I can tell you all about the inventors of bubble gum, the microwave oven, and the revolutionary process of xerography."

"Don't fret yourself about xerography, Loan, and all that other junk is just window dressing. True Americanism is an attitude, a philosophy, a pattern of behavior. Surely, you know that by now."

"I do know that!" Lone Boy insisted, panicked by Miss Grace's implacability. "I only learned all that other crap to show you and everyone else how fuckin' committed I am."

"You can't skimp on essentials and expect superficialities to save you."

"But where have I screwed up?"

"LAC recently had the Internal Revenue Service's computers give us rundowns on every Americulturated citizen in the Southeast. The computers spat out the names of certificate holders who hadn't made more money last year than the year before or who seemed to be stuck in dead-end or downscale employment."

"Am I the *only* one who's made no measurable progress?"

"Then you admit that you haven't."

That was not what Lone Boy had meant to imply. He backed up. "No, no. In '78, when you gave me my exemption certificate, Tuyet and I had just had the twins. Until then we'd been zipping along. Then the medical bills. Also, feverish saving for their college. Now I moonlight at Save-Our-Way after working at Gangway. And so we still have that foreign clunker out front. And so we *seem* to be walking a treadmill. An illusion, actually. We're full of hope. We'll be self-made millionaires in five years, tops. The twins will go to Agnes Scott and become renowned ballerinas or fantastic foreign-policy consultants."

Pity and impatience from Miss Grace: "Your tax returns and job profiles don't present so sanguine a picture."

"But—"

"A barmaid and a bookstore clerk. She takes in sewing in the mornings, and every evening you oversee a place designed to attract holdup men. And you think you're in J. Pohl Getty territory?"

"We're making money for day care, we're fattening our savings, we're working our asses off."

"Do you have any investments? Any CDs or municipal bonds? An individual retirement account? What about starting a business—a service enterprise—of your own? Our IRS report says you've done none of these things—unless you've been so foolish as to fail to record either your investments or your write-offs."

Why is life so complicated? Lone Boy asked himself. All we're trying to do is become millionaires. The rest of this gobbledygook is just that—bankers' and stockbrokers' lingo. If you can only get rich talking such shit, maybe Tuyet and I really *are* doomed to lower-middle-class quasi-poverty.

Miss Grace lectured him a while. She said that she had come to see him because he and his wife Tuyet had been among the first thousand refugees from the Hanoi-Haiphong area of North Vietnam to enter the Liberty Americulturation Center at Fort Benning. Before their arrival, the center had processed primarily South Vietnamese nationals and rehabilitable North American dissidents. She had a personal stake in the subsequent free-market performance of every member of that trailblazing class, and, to date, three quarters of those passing out of her program had exalted American capitalism by achieving measurable wealth and/or status. A few hadn't done well, of course, but they had probably developed slothful habits or a cynical defeatism aggravated by their inability to meet opportunity head on. Loan didn't fall into these categories, thank God, but it did appear that he had forgotten certain LAC lessons about taking intelligent risks and playing the entrepreneur. He worked hard, but he got nowhere. He saved money, but he didn't use it to build an investment power base. In many ways, he was like the servant in Jesus' parable who accepted a gold coin from the nobleman, hid it in a handkerchief, and, when the master returned from his journey, gave this same coin back to him.

"And do you know what the nobleman said to his servant?" asked Miss Grace.

Lone Boy had heard this passage preached from a Catholic pulpit here in LaGrange—but the end of the parable escaped him.

Miss Grace remembered for him. "He said, 'To everyone who has, more will be given; but the one who does not have, even the little that he has will be taken away from him.'"

My God, Lone Boy thought, does she intend to ship us back to the reunified Republic of Vietnam, along with the twins, to wade about in rice paddies behind fly-bitten seladangs?

Miss Grace said, "No, we don't intend to take away what you have now, Loan. Good capitalists are kinder than Jesus' nobleman, and it's my desire to help you. However, God helps those who help themselves, and so does the American free-enterprise system."

At this point, Triny and Tracy came squealing down the steps. Each was clutching close a wrinkled ball of pink flesh—circled by a wreath of fur—that Loan could not quite identify. The girls were squealing delightedly, but the creatures pressed against their coats were squeaking in alarm. Tuyet followed the twins wearing a look of bemused exasperation.

"Brezhnev bears?" Lone Boy asked.

Miss Grace nodded.

"I'm calling mine Skinhead," Triny announced.

"I'm calling mine Piggy," Tracy told everyone.

"They're not yours," Tuyet reminded the girls. "You can't name what doesn't belong to you."

"But they *do* belong to your daughters," Miss Grace said. "I bought the 'bears' for them today at West Georgia Commons."

Tuyet said, "The girls are too young to take care of them."

But Triny and Tracy had found the cavies in a glass box in the screening room, and Miss Grace insisted on giving them not only Skinhead and Piggy but also the aquarium and a supply of guinea-pig food. Once the twins realized that the actress meant them to have the Brezhnev bears, it was impossible to deny the girls. Tuyet, Loan glumly noted, looked nonplussed and put out.

"I couldn't make them watch the Looney Tunes after they'd seen these things," she said. "It's hard to handle a pair of determined little ones all by yourself, Miss Grace."

"It's all right. They're sturdy little animals."

Lone Boy wondered briefly if Miss Grace meant the twins or the Brezhnev bears. Tuyet acquiesced in the gift—what else could she do?—but, now that the girls had seen their daddy and eaten, took them home to bed. Miss Grace would chauffeur Loan and the Brezhnev bears to their rented house as soon as she had finished talking to him. An hour more, at most.

The galleries cold and echoey about them, Miss Grace told Loan, "It might help if you all changed your names."

Lone Boy stared in bewilderment at the woman.

"Don't you see? You've resisted Americulturation further than you realize. Le Boi Loan is a Vietnamese name from first syllable to last, and Tuyet, Triny, and Tracy are more of the same. It's okay to hang on to part of your cultural heritage—"

"Le Thanh Tong was one helluvan emperor, Miss Grace!"

"—but you can't live in the past. Most successful LAC people chose—somewhere along the line—to adopt an Anglo-Saxon first name."

"We have made a beginning in that way, Miss Grace. How can you call Triny and Tracy Vietnamese monickers?"

"Oh, come on, Loan. Triny's a transparent Americanization of Trinh and Tracy's a similarly transparent version of Trac."

"But I was *born* Vietnamese. We're acknowledging our roots."

"Yes, but if you *insist* upon emphasizing your 'roots' in these sneaky ways, maybe you should return to them. We have a precedent, you know, and it was remarkably successful."

Lone Boy heard the blood beating in his temples. The precedent to which she referred was the wholesale relocation of major segments of the black population of the United States to sub-Saharan Africa, nations such as Nigeria, Liberia, Kenya, Senegambia, etc. Parts of this huge exodus had occurred voluntarily, but many relocatees had loudly protested their expulsion and some of the nations accepting them had done so only out of fear. A Defense Department spokesman had publicly announced that the strategy of bombing North Vietnam's irrigation dikes during the late unpleasantness with that (former) country was one that had workable, albeit top-secret, counterparts for other potential battlefronts. Further, an assistant secretary in the State Department had declared that uncooperative governments would surely undergo reevaluations of both their trade status and their eligibility for U.S. foreign-aid programs. Blacks had not completely disappeared from the United States, of course, but they were distributed across the country so as to achieve—in the words of the chairman of the Urban Affairs Council—"a benign demographic picturesqueness."

"I don't mean to threaten you," Miss Grace said. "But

you and yours are resisting—subtly—complete Americulturation."

Angrily, Lone Boy shook his head. "That's a crock. Look here, Miss Grace." From the paper sack on the coffee table, he extracted the May issue of *Daredevil*. "I'm a fan and a collector. I'd've never been either one if I were old-style Vietnamese. And look at this, too." He pulled a floppy cellophane bag of popcorn from the sack. "One of my favorite snacks. I eat it every chance I get. I drink Lite beer from Miller or Coca-Cola when I eat, and if there's a Hawks game or a tennis match on the tube, I watch it while I'm chowing down. During the commercials I've already memorized, I may even re-go through my comics. How American may I get? Before Le Boi Loan, you ought to reindoctrinate Peter Rose!"

Miss Grace was smiling. "It does seem that you've learned a charming American feistiness."

"Damn straight."

They sat for a time in silence. Then Grace Rinehart said, "Do you know the young man who works in the Happy Puppy Pet Emporium?"

Lone Boy, crossing his arms, leaned into the sofa back. She's switching directions, he thought, trying to cross me up.

"Calvin Pickford," he replied cautiously. "Didn't you buy your Brezhnev bears from him?"

"I did. It's my opinion—based on our single meeting today—that he's a closet dissident. What do you think?"

"I don't know. He's an okay guy. Weird taste in books."

"Weird how, Loan?"

"Oh, you know, a Philip K. Dick freak. That guy's death shook him up. Cal came into Gangway today and ordered a whole set of Dick in paperback." Lone Boy halted. There was more he could say, but he wondered if he should. But to prove his loyalty, to prove he didn't need to be reindoctrinated, maybe he could—maybe he'd *better*—proffer the actress an informational tidbit. "He told me he had copies of, uh, 'Dickian opuses' that some people would kill to get hold of, Miss Grace. Bragging, probably."

"Not necessarily."

Lone Boy felt cold; he shuddered and rubbed his upper arms.

"He may be telling the truth. Why don't you find out?"

"Ma'am?"

"Please, not 'ma'am'—'miss.'" She shifted in her chair and tossed one wing of her cape across her body. "If you'll keep an eye on this Calvin Pickford for a month or two, I'll temporarily suspend the order to report for reindoctrination. If you can determine that he really has illegal copies of some unpublished Dick novels, and if you bring them to me, I give you my solemn word that you'll *never* receive another such order again, no matter how long you live or how modest your annual income. Understand?"

"Bring them to you? Steal them?"

"They'd have to be *samizdat* publications, Loan. It violates the amended Bill of Rights to possess *any* kind of literature in that proscribed form. QED, you wouldn't be stealing—you'd be impounding the material for evidence."

"Evidence for what?"

"Prosecution in federal court."

My God, Lone Boy reflected, that's heavy stuff. And all the poor dude's doing these days is working in a pet shop.

"Is this Calvin Pickford person a friend of yours?"

"No," Loan hurriedly said. "Usually, I only see him when he comes in to browse, every coupla days or so."

"He trusts you?"

"Trust doesn't have anything to do with us. Our relationship, I mean. He probably thinks I'm a lousy bookstore clerk. But we don't have any major gripes against each other. He does his stuff and I do mine."

"And will some of the 'stuff' that you do include, from now on, keeping an eye on Mr. Pickford?"

"Okay," Lone Boy managed.

"And trying to lay your hands on these seditious photocopies?"

"I guess so."

"Good. Keep me posted. Call me here any night after eleven."

The interview was over. Lone Boy toted the aquarium and its two naked denizens out to Miss Grace's car (one gorgeous piece of upscale machinery), and then sat as close to the passenger door as he could as she drove him home. I'm a spy, he thought. A domestic espionage agent. My reward will be a forever exemption from reindoctrination. If this crazy Cal Pickford's in contempt of the law, he deserves whatever he gets. And if it weren't me spying, it'd be somebody else. . . .

"I think Philip K. Dick's stuff sucks," he said, just to make conversation in the smoothly purring Caddy.

"Some of the published novels are okay. Back in '59 I was even in a movie based on one of them. My second major role. *The Broken Bubble of Thisbe Holt.*"

"I've never seen it," Lone Boy confessed. "Not even on TV."

"And you won't, either. It was a flop. Not Phil Dick's fault, though—the screenwriter's and the casting director's. As soon as I could afford to, I bought up all the prints. I think Dick was always grateful to me for that. Too bad he went off the deep end during the '60s and started writing hateful, spaced-out crap."

"I had to read *Puttering About in a Small Land*—you know, for my Americulturation. Did you like that one?"

"Never read it. Of course, I didn't devise the curriculum for the centers. I had professionals do that. My film career was going pretty well back then, and I was too busy to see to all the specifics. I'm much more involved nowadays."

She let him off, in the dark, in front of his apartment, in a section of town given over to dilapidated housing for former mill workers. Loan duck-walked up the shattered sidewalk carrying the Brezhnev bears in their aquarium. Triny and Tracy, to his chagrin, were still awake, waiting for him. For the next hour, they played with the Brezhnev bears while Lone Boy explained to his wife that he wouldn't have to report for reindoctrination because Miss Grace had decided that they were teetering on the brink of affluence.

"That's ridiculous," Tuyet said.

Lone Boy knew that it was ridiculous, but that was his story. He could think of no other credible lie to disguise the fact that he would soon be spying on a man who, apparently, was trying to do the same thing that he was—make a living and build a better life. Later, lying fretfully beside the exhausted Tuyet, Lone Boy tried his damnedest to forget that another name for "domestic espionage agents" was No-Knocks.

9

Augustus "Gus" Kemmings had had a strange night. Much trouble sleeping. Luckily, he lived alone and couldn't disturb anyone with his insomniac wanderings around the house. His wife had died the year after he began to manage the Happy Puppy Pet Emporium, and now the little brick house that the two of them had shared seemed as big as a half-empty museum.

It *is* a kind of museum, Gus reflected, standing in his robe and slippers in the living room. On the wall beside him, as in nearly every other room in the house, hung a framed sample of one of the argyle socks that the workers in his mill in Pine Mountain had made on his special hosiery looms. Also, piles of folded argyle socks lay in every chest of drawers on the premises.

Mrs. K. had never minded. In fact, it was Vera who'd insisted on turning the house in LaGrange into a modest monument to Gus's previous occupation. All her life, she had been the victim of poor circulation. Gus would never forget their honeymoon and the first time she'd put her bare feet on him. What a shock. After that, she'd begun wearing his socks to bed.

"Vera," Gus said aloud. Maybe I'd've been able to sleep if you'd been lying beside me running those furry argyles up and down my legs. Maybe.

Right after *The Sinatra Hour*, Gus had gone to bed. Then he had lain awake worrying about Cal Pickford, Cal's grief over the death of that writer Philip Craddock, and the angry way Cal had refused to accept a couple of Brezhnev bears.

It was a spontaneous offer, Gus ruminated. A well-intentioned offer. But, boy-howdy, did that kid light into you. Grief must've been eating him up. Well, you know what he felt like, don't you, Augustus? It wasn't that long ago that you went through those same emotions. You've been through 'em several times.

His son, Keith, had died in 1965 in the jungle near Pleiku with three hundred other kids from his airborne division. Seven years later, despite countless warnings, Kirsten had traveled to the Republican National Convention in Kansas City to protest Nixon's policies in Vietnam. She never came home. In fact, she simply disappeared. No forwarding address. No farewell phone call. No messages from friends, foes, or law-enforcement officers. And, disturbingly, no body. At least, in the aftermath of that Ia Drang Valley business, he and Vera had been able to bury their hero son.

Kirsten, by contrast, was dismissed by those in authority as a "runaway," a 22-year-old runaway. Might as well call a 12-year-old a toddler, Gus had griped, but when nothing came of his and Vera's inquiries and subsequent bitter grumblings but a visit from a pair of No-Knocks advising them to cool it—"You're endangering the war effort"—the red, white, and blue Kemmingses had cooled it, accepting on faith the No-Knocks' argument that Kirsten had gone underground to escape prosecution and imprisonment; hence she was a "runaway." Besides, to keep bellyaching publicly about her disappearance would have tempted the FBI to reclassify her as a "fugitive from justice" and to bruit this news around as a counterweight to the Kemmingses' unpatriotic gripes.

Not quite ten years later, Kirsten still hadn't come home from wherever she'd disappeared to. Keith lay beside Vera in the little graveyard in Pine Mountain, and the Kemmingses' small brick house near the Callaway Educational Association complex in LaGrange was a private memorial to the making of socks and a haphazard menagerie of different animals from the pet shop: tropical fish, ring doves, hamsters, green snakes, and so on. The framed socks kept Augustus from forgetting who he had been; the host of animals kept him from surrendering to loneliness.

Absentmindedly, Gus tapped some fish food into one of

the tanks and watched his darlings fin their way upward for the goodies. He looked at his wrist watch: 6:57. Dawn was past. It had been light for almost an hour. He ditched the box of fish food, turned on the TV, and sat down to catch the news on *The Today Show*.

Ah, NBC. Charlton Heston hosting and King Richard's son-in-law David Eisenhower anchoring the news.

"Our top story this morning," Eisenhower says, his narrow face looking sallow and aggrieved, "is the apparent suicide of another of our mission specialists in the oxygen-production facilities at Von Braunville, the American moon-base nestling in the Censorinus crater of the Lunar Highlands. To commemorate this great country's bicentennial, the first spadeful of dirt at Von Braunville was turned on July Fourth, 1976. Since that time, nearly three hundred different Americans and dozens of persons from both our NATO allies and our Soviet mission collaborators have occupied this base for periods ranging from two weeks to a year. Only about fifty highly trained astronauts, scientists, technicians, and civilian observers live and work at Von Braunville at a time. Suicide, we stress, is not epidemic among them.

"However, five persons have killed themselves since the O_2 plant at Von Braunville came on line early in '77, a rate of almost one a year. NASA officials and key members of the administration agree that five suicides *is* disproportionate, given the intense training and the positive motivation of those assigned to the base and the small number of people living there at any one time. Cold statistics show that slightly more than 1.4 percent of moonbase personnel have killed themselves while on duty there.

"A few others—the number is classified for security reasons—have committed suicide *after* returning from moon-base assignment. Most physicians and psychotherapists agree that these postdeparture suicides, however, are *non*significant in the figuring of any space-related depression or malaise. Most troubling to those responsible for the efficiency and morale of our space-going pioneers are the suicides of *active residents* of the Censorinus base."

Young Eisenhower turns to the man sitting to his right in

the NBC newsroom. "This is James L. Bodine, official NASA spokesman for Moon-related programs."

A close-up of Bodine, smiling sedately. "Good morning, David."

EISENHOWER: "Good morning, Jim. Could you tell us, please, the identity of the latest moonbase suicide?"

BODINE: "We're now in the process of notifying that person's family. So I don't want to disclose that information yet. I'm sure you understand our need for discretion."

EISENHOWER: "Of course. How, then, did this latest tragedy occur and what does NASA plan to do to minimize the chances for a sixth suicide at Von Braunville?"

BODINE: "Please recollect that dying on the Moon is easy; it's staying alive up there that's hard. As in all our previous cases, David, the would-be suicide left a dormitory dome without enough protection against the lunar near-vacuum. That was deliberate, we believe. It was also fatal. As for what NASA plans to do—"

EISENHOWER: "How do you know that the victim wasn't —forgive me, Jim—murdered?"

BODINE: "We don't send murderers to the Moon."

EISENHOWER: "Ideally, NASA doesn't send suicides either, but this is apparently the fifth in not quite six years. Why couldn't this one, or one of the four others, be a murder?"

BODINE (somewhat testily): "Because it simply isn't."

Gus squints at Bodine's off-center mouth and flinty eyes. "How do you know? What makes you so sure?" He remembers Kirsten. He remembers the disappearances of those long-haired hippie singers in the early 1970s, not to mention the ambiguous fates of Jane Fonda, the brothers Berrigan, and the editors of the *New York Times*, the *Chicago Daily News*, and the *Washington Post*. Cronkite is reported to be in exile somewhere in the Caribbean, and Tad Kennedy has been ruined by Chappaquidick—was it a setup?—and strong drink.

BODINE (continuing): "Our people at Van Braunville confirm that the suicide was a suicide. They're very upset. They found this person lying next to a moondozer about thirty yards from the airlock of the dormitory dome. The deceased had walked that far before dying of asphyxiation."

EISENHOWER: "Oxygen, oxygen, everywhere, but not a molecule to breathe?"

BODINE: "Yes, I suppose it *is* ironic."

EISENHOWER: "But now you'll take steps to counteract the mood swings and depressions of moonbase personnel?"

BODINE: "*Most* of our people don't suffer these violent bouts of depression, David. We have athletic facilities, TV broadcasts, films, excellent food, a wonderful microfiche library, and almost anything else that anyone could want. We believe—"

EISENHOWER: "Opportunities for sex?"

BODINE (*taken aback*): "David, you know as well as I do that nine tenths of our moonbase personnel are male and that the women on hand there are monogamous wives and mothers. A question like that is pretty close to juvenile mischief making."

EISENHOWER: "Then what do you believe is at the root of this spate of suicides, Jim?"

BODINE: "It isn't a 'spate.' We've been in space only a very short time, historically speaking, and on the Moon for only the past seven-eight years. We know more about rocket propellants and orbital velocities than we do about the human brain. It shouldn't come as a complete surprise that the psychological stresses of living in near-weightlessness for long periods, on another world, still elude our full understanding."

EISENHOWER: "Will we rotate our moonbase personnel more often to offset our ignorance?"

BODINE: "More frequent rotation of personnel is of course a possibility, but our latest suicide wasn't actually a long-termer, and maybe we'll simply try to monitor the psychological state of each astronaut, technician, and scientist more closely. We may also try beautifying Von Braunville with plants and allowing each worker at the station to have a personal pet of some kind. These strategies have proved helpful with prison populations, David, and although our people aren't prisoners, of course, they do live under extremely tight and confining conditions."

EISENHOWER: "That's fascinating, Jim, and I wish we had time to pursue it further. However, it's time for a commercial break—after which I'll be back to tell you how

Canadian law-enforcement officials"—full close-up on young Eisenhower—"believe that dogs as sniffers-out of illegal drugs in airports and prisons may have had their day. Our neighbors to the north think that gerbils—tiny, ratlike rodents that can be trained to detect one illicit odor each—may become an even more valuable weapon against runners, dealers, and users than Fido has been. Don't go away."

Gus smiles. He's sorry about the new suicide at the moonbase, but the fact that NASA might rocket pets into space to comfort the guys up there, along with Eisenhower's little teaser about gerbils, tickles him. But he'd better get something to eat and go on out to West Georgia Commons to see about his animals. Almost reluctantly, then, he clicks off *The Today Show* and shuffles into his bedroom to dress.

After eating a couple of sausage biscuits at Hardy's, Augustus climbed back into his little Honda Civic. He still had some time to kill before the Pet Emporium opened at ten, and although he needed to go in at least an hour early, to check on his "critters," to arrive now would be to make it a painfully long day. He decided to cruise for a while. Traffic was bad, people going to work and so forth, but Gus liked the bustle of downtown, particularly around the main square, with its fountains and its gallant-looking statue of Lafayette.

He circled the square twice, headed south past Charlie Joseph's (makers of the best chili dog in the world), and eventually wound up cruising down Hines Street past the Chattahoochee Valley Art, Film, and Photography Salon.

Glancing to his right, he saw a good-looking woman—she had on heels, a tailored business suit, and a wide-brimmed hat like those sometimes worn by the models on the covers of Vera's *Vogues*—exit onto the porch of the salon; she locked the glass doors behind her and came down the steps into the tiny walled courtyard. Here, only her hat visible, she pivoted and strode around the salon toward the parking lot.

Behind Gus, an impatient nine-to-fiver was leaning on the horn, trying to blast him through the traffic light before it changed again. At last, Gus got the Honda rolling, but his main thoughts were that he had just seen Grace Rinehart, the foremost patron of the Art, Film, and Photography Salon, and that the famous actress and the mysterious woman who had bought two Brezhnev bears from Cal yesterday morning were the Very Same Person.

Gus felt like a fool. He should have guessed. However, Grace Rinehart hadn't wanted anyone to know her real identity. And so she had entered incognito and paid in cash.

What gives? Gus asked himself, already feeling an acid stomach coming on. Am I in trouble? Is Pickford in dutch? She was spying on us. She didn't need to buy Brezhnev bears from me. Her husband's the guy who first imported the critters from Mother Russia. Now he breeds them over by Woodbury. I get my own "bears" from Berthelot wholesalers. For Miss Rinehart to buy them from me is like a sheik flying over here to buy a can of oil at K-Mart. Except, of course, the lady had an ulterior motive. What, though?

Gus eventually got his Honda onto the four-lane out to the mall and cruised along it thinking about Miss Rinehart. She must have spent the night at the salon. Because of her many contributions to the facility and her leadership in having the building renovated, the salon committee had given her a suite of rooms on the second story. It was rumored that she spent more evenings in the building than she did at the Berthelot estate, for her husband was often in Washington. Anyway, Hiram and Miss Grace couldn't, and didn't, always cohabit nowadays, and some folks found their private lives grist for catty speculation.

For example, it was widely rumored that Miss Rinehart sometimes invited old Hollywood cronies out to LaGrange— leading men from the 1960s and early 1970s—and ushered them into the salon in the dead of night for "reunions." A Rinehart-and-Whoever Film Festival. In the upstairs screening room, she and her guest would watch one of her old films, and then one of his, and then maybe a film featuring both of them, and so on, alternating starring vehicles until they wearied of their celluloid ego orgy and retired to her hidden suite to costar in a more conventional festival of indulgence.

Gus found these rumors as titillating as anyone, but he didn't trust them very far. Miss Rinehart was an asset to the community, a woman who had once helped turn the tide of negativism threatening to wash out the American effort in Vietnam. Moreover, her Liberty Americulturation Centers had made prosperous, productive citizens of thousands of talented Vietnamese, many of whom would eventually go back to their homeland—still as American citizens—to convince their old-style compatriots that the New Vietnam should apply for American statehood. As the fifty-first state, their country would cunningly formalize its special relationship with the United States: full partnership in tomorrow's preeminent politicoeconomic system.

Manifest Destiny with a trans-Pacific dimension.

Well, Gus reflected, that Miss Rinehart is a mighty smart lady for figuring all that out, but her being smart only makes me that much more afraid of her.

Augustus Kemmings parked his car behind West Georgia Commons, unlocked the rear door of the pet shop, and went inside to reassure his babies of something he himself no longer believed, namely, that everything was going to be A-OK.

10

In the recreational lounge of one of the dome-capped caverns of Von Braunville at Censorinus, three of the moondozer operators at the O_2 plant were watching a tape of the premier show of the 1981–1982 season of *Star Trek*, the fifteenth straight year that Captain Kirk, Mr. Spock, and the multinational and multispecies crew of the starship *Enterprise* had carried out their five-year mission "to boldly go where no man has ever gone before"—at least on network television.

Air Force Major Gordon Vear, selenologist and ferry-shuttle pilot, stood in the rear of the lounge watching the tired 'dozer jockies watching their huge video screen. Spock, who for the past three seasons had been wearing a Vulcan earclip on his right ear, told Kirk that unless their new engineer, an eight-foot-tall Alpha Crucian by the name of Traz, coaxed more power from their engines, their refitted starship would probably stall in its unprecedented attempt to traverse the outer layers of the gas giant into which a Klingon amphibian craft had already plunged.

"What utter rot," Vear murmured. When I was nineteen, I used to think ol' Spock was truly hot stuff. The episodes— once in a while—had *some*thing to do with real philosophical issues or social concerns. For the past twelve years, though, it's all been space opera, melodrama, and half-assed Hollywood mysticism. Getting to the Moon ruined *Star Trek*. I mean, *ruined* it. Getting to the Moon and the goddamn Board of Media Censorship.

Making his way to the door, Vear collided with Dan Franciscus, a ferry-shuttle copilot and selenonaut.

"Where you off to?" Franciscus asked.

"Out for some fresh vacuum, Daniel. I can't take much more of this hokey argle-bargle." He nodded at the screen.

"Come on, Gordo, it's a gas. You just gotta sit back and let it knock you into warp-speed mindlessness. Then everything's A-OK, you're cruising hyperspace." The lieutenant looked more closely at the major. "'Fresh vacuum'? You gonna suit up?"

Vear smiled. "Thought I would, Daniel. Don't intend to take an unsupported hike the way Nyby did."

"Did you know I was on the up-flight to the transfer ship that hauled that poor bastard back to Kennedy Port?" NASA had concealed word of the week-old suicide until just a few hours ago.

"I'd heard, Daniel. You and Colonel Hoffman."

"Did you also know that Von Braunville's got a slump-pit cavern whose only purpose is to warehouse coffins? Fifty of 'em in there, one for every manjack and jillfem assigned here. Forty-nine, now. NASA's lifted the Boy Scout motto: 'Be Prepared.' But if we're bombed by a meteorite, who the hell's gonna peel himself out of the plagioclase to put everybody else in their boxes?"

"No idea, Daniel. No idea." Vear wanted only to escape. One of the 'dozer jockies kept casting irritated looks at Franciscus. He'd seen this *Trek* a dozen times; still, he was anticipating the moment when the *Enterprise* split the surface of the gas giant and began plowing through its murk in pursuit of the renegade Klingons who had murdered Chief Engineer Traz's brood-sibling.

Heedless of the annoyed man, Franciscus said, "And it's no damn fun finagling a coffin from one airlock to another in lunar orbit, either. I don't *ever* want to do that again. Spooky."

"I've done it, too, Daniel."

"Yeah, that's right, you have. You pulled a tour here in '78, didn't you?"

"Could you guys hold it down?" the 'dozer jockey asked. Vear could tell that although he was trying to be polite, he would have liked to punch the lieutenant's lights out.

Franciscus ignored him. "You're not supposed to suit up

after a work period, Gordo. Commander Logan frowns on ECA"—ECA was a jocular selenonaut acronym for Extra-Curricular Activity—"that 'one, needlessly depletes our oxygen reserves; two, puts expensive NASA equipment at risk; and three, endangers the lives or health of anybody—one's self included—working at Von Braunville.' Besides, Gordo, you can get to your dormitory unit through a tunnel."

"Have you ever tried to see the stars in a tunnel, Daniel?"

"Can't say that—"

"If you have, you're probably blessed with X-ray vision. I'm not so blessed. If Logan or anybody else wants me, tell 'em I'll be in when I'm in. Catch you later."

Franciscus, detecting the major's impatience, said, "Yes, sir," and shut up. Vear went around the narrow hall to a suiting room, pulled on his vacuum gear, affixed the portable life-support system (PLSS) that would sustain him outside, and single-handedly worked the air lock releasing him to the surface. In the old days, these procedures would have required at least two sets of hands, but now, thanks to advances in both suit design and moonbase architecture, a guy could accomplish them—fairly easily—solo.

Of course, as Vear exited, an alarm sounded throughout the dome, and a computer in the headquarters hemisphere halfway around the bleached lunacrete of the O_2 plant also noted his departure. Vear knew about, and approved of, this precaution. He was a small amber light on a safety technician's console and would continue to gleam there until his mortal body came back inside.

Unearthly, thinks Gordon Vear, taking in Von Braunville from the floor of the Censorinus crater. Despite its name, the base looks less like a city than it does a construction site in a great monochrome desert. During the fourteen-day sunlit period, moondozers operate round the clock, gouging shovelsful of anorthosite out of the crater's floor to feed the oxygen plant. One 'dozer is working now, moving like a spindly balloon-tired stegosaurus so that the plant can process about five tons of lunar dirt every twenty-four hours, turning it into O_2 not only as a component of the breathable air both here and in the earth-orbiting station known as Kennedy

Port, but also as a fuel for the three different types of ships required for Earth-Moon voyages.

Of course it's unearthly, you dummikins, Vear rebukes himself. Where do you think you are anyway? Las Vegas?

Inside his helmet, the major laughs. Because Nixon's Travel Restrictions Act puts such a cramp in casino business, the military services allow their personnel to use acquired leave to visit Las Vegas, Atlantic City, and the Miami Strip. In fact, you can fly to one of those places, space available, for *nada*, and in '79, after returning from his first lunar tour, Vear made an eager pilgrimage to Vegas. The fact is, some neon lights and a few one-stop wedding chapels would make Von Braunville look an awful lot like that down-on-its-luck Nevada city.

So our moonbase isn't *that* unearthly, he thinks, smiling. Not if you compare it to the most desolate terrestrial outposts you know. It's just hellfire hot or damnation cold, and so implacably deadly either way that it's little wonder Logan doesn't want us to go out alone. On the other hand, how else would I ever find any solitude on this slaggy lump of basalt, KREEP norite, and jumbled breccias if I *didn't* go out alone?

Raised a Catholic in Louisville, Kentucky, Vear also sometimes finds himself comparing Von Braunville to Gethsemani, the monastery near Bardstown, Kentucky, where the Trappist writer and monk Thomas Merton spent most of his adult life.

Make up your mind, Gordon. Is your moonbase a gambling casino or a monastery? Well, a little of both. Depends on your point of view. Just being up here's a gamble, of course, but the monastic aspect of our life comes through in the fact that we're crammed together in a finite amount of life-supporting space and have to adjust to one another's omnipresent bodies—and to one another's annoying quirks—to keep from going nuts and committing actionable mayhem. Isolated as we are, 240,000 miles from Earth, we almost never—paradoxically—get any privacy. And rejuvenating privacy is what most of us need.

Vear, seeking privacy, climbs a rugged natural pathway on the eastern flank of the crater. Von Braunville nestles below. The slope, mercifully, is not severe, and slowly he gains height on the base and blessed distance on its regs and recriminations. He has air for four hours; his suit's cooling system will keep his blood—praise God and NASA—from boiling; and despite the sweat gathering on his brow, under his arms, and behind his knees, Vear is enjoying this . . . well, couldn't he legitimately call it a "star trek"?

The stars shine scattershot, fiercer and more numerous than he ever experienced them in Kentucky, and although officially he is off duty, he can also, in his role as selenologist, look down at the rocks—powdery, glassy, crystalline— through which he treks and later justify his outing as "research."

Privacy, Vear reflects, is what Nyby needed, even if Logan and some of the NASA boys believe that it was our isolation —a mistaken sense of cosmic estrangement—that goaded him to kill himself. To hell with that, Vear thinks grimly. What pushed Nyby over was the fact that there was almost always somebody in his face, telling him what duty to do, and how to tackle it, and when to get it done by. It was Nyby's sense of enforced association, with no real intimacy, and his awareness that true control of his life lay elsewhere that walked him down the plank to suicide. Maybe somebody should have talked to him—by way of *confessing* him, I mean—but as it was, everybody was always talking *at* poor Roland, commanding, coercing, constricting.

A twinge of guilt afflicts Vear, and he halts in a spot with a fine view of both Von Braunville and the eastern crater rim, beyond which—if you grab yourself a flyer and ride it a good hundred and fifty miles—lies the near shore of the Sea of Fertility. I wish I were there now, the major thinks. More privacy, more solitude, and more room to mull my guilt over Nyby, a specialist in materials science who dropped out of our lives—precipitated himself out, I guess you could say—by taking a short walk.

Vear's guilt arises from a memory of a conversation with Nyby two weeks before he took this walk. The major saw him at chow one day and, noticing his depression, approached him afterward to ask if he were all right.

"I feel like people are sitting on me, sir."

The "sir" was obligatory, not mere politeness. Although part of the official scientific contingent, Nyby was also a commissioned naval officer and a selenonaut. Commander

Logan had insisted—not unreasonably—that he, like others, pull double duty.

"What do you mean, sitting on you?"

At the door to the chow hall, they had to whisper to maintain the confidentiality of their exchange.

"I'm covered over," the kid said. "I can't breathe."

"You need to get away. I know the feeling."

"I *can't* get away. I barely have time to eat and sleep. And when I'm awake and working, I'm at somebody else's beck and call. Everything I do, Major Vear, is other-willed."

"How long've you been up here now?"

"Four months. Nearly five."

"Well, that means seven more to go. That's a long time for a young person, Roland, but you can stick it out."

"You're assuming that going home will take care of my problem. But it's just more of the same, Major. In some ways, considering the way things used to be, it's even worse."

"I'm not following you."

"Forgive me, sir, but I'm probably lucky that you're not. All I can say is that up here there's a built-in, ecological rationale for tyranny. Pardon me, I mean *authoritarianism.*"

"And back home . . . ?"

"Excuse me. I'm two minutes late for my shift." Nyby brushed past Vear into the corridor.

"Damn your shift. I'll answer for your tardiness. Let's sit down and hash this business out."

Nyby hesitated. "Do you really want to take this on, sir? I mean, *really.*"

And what did you say? Vear admonishes himself. Nothing. You hesitated, and Nyby, bright boy that he was, picked up on it.

"That's what I thought. I don't blame you, either. Thanks for being concerned, but I've got resources of my own, Major." And he broke off their talk and reported for his shift.

Although Vear bumped into Nyby on several occasions over the next two weeks, neither alluded to their brief colloquy in the chow hall. And then, of course, time in which to allude to it ran out. Completely.

Please, dear God, Vear prays, forgive me. And Roland, wherever you are—you forgive me, too, okay? I don't think you believed in anything but your work, and in your ability to use the lunar vacuum and its low gravity to create strangely unique crystals, but if you committed mortal sins either by not believing or by renouncing the gift of life, both you and God must forgive the one whose hesitancy may have greased your slide to . . . well, to hell.

This thought, suit or no suit, PLSS or no PLSS, scalds Vear to the marrow. PLSS, God, PLSS, Roland, he prays: forgive.

After a time, a kind of uneasy calm settles on the major. He studies the stars. He bathes in cold, blue Earthlight. He looks out into Censorinus at the solar dishes planted to the northwest of Von Braunville like a huge garden of mirrors on stilts. Suggesting a collaboration between Lewis Carroll and H. G. Wells, they provide power for the domes and the power that enables the O_2 factory to convert plagioclase—$CaA1_2Si_2O_8$—into usable oxygen.

Up here, though, Vear is exhilaratingly alone. "I *vahnt* to be alone!" he shouts, deafening himself. Alone to expiate my guilt. Alone to commune with God. He wishes that he could have given Nyby some of this solitude, some of this privacy. Maybe that would have helped the kid. If, of course, the kid had had a faith that made his solitary moments something other than deadfalls for loneliness, snares for his sense of futility.

Because you can carry being alone and unknown too far. And the same goes for the desire for privacy.

What was it that Thomas Merton had said on this point? Another acute observation. Vear finally recalls it: "And to be unknown to God is altogether too much privacy." Exactly. You want solitude, a chance to reflect, but you don't want your retreat from others to deprive you of the company of God. That's not privacy, that's the ultimate loneliness, absolute desolation. And, unfortunately, it may have been exactly what Nyby achieved in the enmiring press and hubbub of Von Braunville. If not long before.

Everything went off the rails in 1968, Vear concludes. Oh, yeah, we won the war in Vietnam, and we're colonizing the Moon well ahead of anybody's expectations, given the budget cuts that NASA was about to absorb between 1969 and 1971, when that friggin' mess in 'Nam nearly forced us to shut down Saturn V production and my brother almost lost his job in the

Michoud Plant in New Orleans—but what have we gained but an ice-cream rasher of international prestige and steady employment for a few thousand people building rocket stages and guidance and control units?

Star Trek started going downhill in '68, it stank on ice in '69, and it's been an embarrassment to humanity ever since. Our Constitution's been shredded, our civil liberties have been stomped on, and we've got a president who dresses up the White House guards like Ruritanian dragoons. You can get by okay, I guess, if you're working for the government, especially the services, or if you're a business person with the proper contacts, or if you're a celebrity who's made a right-minded mint or whom King Richard has invited to a command performance. Otherwise, you'd better grub and kiss ass, or else hide away in the country and stay deep in the weeds praying that the No-Knocks never find you.

Praying. That's what I came out here to do, Vear thinks, not to rile myself up reflecting on Nyby's fatal weltschmerz and the way I've avoided common hardships by going to the Air Force Academy and taking flight to the Moon. Still, '68 was the year that it all went off the rails, and that was the year that Thomas Merton died, too. In December. After the national elections. He accidentally electrocuted himself with a fan after taking a shower in a cottage near Bangkok; he'd been touring the Far East discussing monasticism and meditation with the Dalai Lama and other Buddhists.

Vear has always considered Merton's death—for so searching and holy a man—ludicrous, a vaudeville jape unworthy of God. But here above Von Braunville, he begins to regard it as a mercy. Maybe the Holy Spirit had been whirling in the blades of that defective fan, breathing grace upon Merton even as the fan—*a fan, for Christ's sake!*—shocked him to the roots of his being. How a mercy? How a gift of grace?

Well, Merton had fought the good fight—for justice, for peace, for the greater glory of God—and his death, at the painfully early age of fifty-three, spared him the necessity of witnessing either Nixon's gutting of the Bill of Rights or the American people's lamblike complicity in their own slaughter. Vear remembers that in Merton's *Asian Journal*, circulated posthumously in *samizdat* copies among many

Catholics, the man expressed satisfaction that Kentucky had not voted for George Wallace in the '68 election but tremendous disappointment that Nixon had beaten Herbert Humphrey.

"Our new president is depressing," he declared in his journal. "What can one expect of him?"

Well, thinks Vear, I'm glad you didn't have to live through the early years of his administration to find out. If an electric fan hadn't killed you, *that* would have, and you deserved the mercy of your slapstick electrocution in Thailand. And what a breathtaking mercy—literally—it was. Breath*giving*, too.

Vear shakes his head, no easy thing to do in the TV-like box of his helmet. You've got to stop worrying about these matters, Gordon, and commune with your God. That's what you came out here to do.

So the major climbs farther up the "path" on the jumbled slope of the crater rim and finds a refrigerator-sized boulder, capsized, on which to lower his butt and rest. Seated on it, he says a psalm from memory and later the Lord's Prayer: "Our Father, Who art in Heaven, hallowed be . . ."

He mumbles on, eventually concluding, ". . . the glory forever. Amen." He feels a little calmer, but not much. And so he swings into prayers for his family, his city, his state, his nation, the planet, the entire cosmos. Even though wonders surround him, his eyes close, and he goes into a kind of trance in the chapel of his suit and the cathedral of Censorinus.

"Give me some sign of Your presence," Air Force Major Gordon Vear pleads. "Some small sign that You hear me. . . ."

Opening his eyes, he detected movement above him on the eastern rim of the crater. The movement startled him. His stomach dropped and his scalp tingled. You weren't supposed to see movement on the Moon—not unless it derived from human activity at Von Braunville, the random impact of meteorites, or maybe the effects of some rare, residual volcanism.

In this case, meteorites and volcanism had nothing to do with it, and, squinting, Vear saw through his grimy faceplate that a human figure was staring down on him—indeed, on the entire base—from the rampart of Censorinus. The figure seemed to be either a child or a dwarf; a *black* child or dwarf. It was framed by rugged fractures of lunar rock, wedged between them on the rampart like a medieval soldier in the notch of a castle wall. The most startling thing about the figure, even more startling than its size or its race, was that it had no protection against the lunar vacuum. No suit. No PLSS. In fact, it was wearing—if Vear's eyes were not deceiving him—blue jeans and a white dress shirt.

11

"Why would she come here to buy Brezhnev bears?" Cal asked Mr. Kemmings. "It makes no sense."

"I know that. I was asking myself the same thing on the drive out from town."

Cal, as good as his word, had reached the pet shop only a few minutes after his boss and for the past half hour had been cleaning out the shit from the puppy and kitten pens or else replacing the spattered newsprint in half a dozen rattan bird cages. Mr. K. was upset. He had arrived upset, having spotted Grace Rinehart at the arts salon and recognized her instantly as yesterday's customer in cape, sunglasses, and duded-up riding apparel. Something was going on . . . but what?

To Cal, the fact that he had sold the famous film actress and Americulturator a pair of naked guinea pigs seemed the least of his troubles. Today, at least. Yesterday, the mystery of the woman's identity had bugged him bunches, especially when she'd asked him if he'd ever been in hot water with the law, but today he couldn't let himself worry too much about the Secretary of Agriculture's wife. Maybe she'd been checking out the Brezhnev bears to see how those on sale in pet shops measured up against the ones that her bigshot hubby Hiram bred—whether they seemed healthier, less healthy, or somehow subtly different from the Berthelot cavies. Maybe she had wanted to inject a little jet-set cash into the local economy, even with a nonessential purchase. Cal refused to speculate. After all, he had a more urgent concern: Yesterday he and Lia had been visited by a dead man who could not remember that he was, or had been, a controversial American writer.

Mr. K. finally picked up on Cal's mood. "How you doin' today?" he asked. "You better?"

"Yes, sir. The shock's worn off."

"Did you hear about the latest suicide at Von Braunville?"

"On the car radio driving up, yes, sir, I did."

"Sad," Mr. Kemmings said. "Sad."

"Yes, sir. Death's nearly always sad." No truer words were ever spoken, Cal thought. Unless you were suffering like crazy or long past your prime, death fell on you with all the welcomeness of a bout of genital herpes.

"On *The Today Show*, this NASA fella said that maybe they'll send pets up there to help the moon folk fight depression. Pets and plants."

"Umm," Cal said, using a cloth soaked in boric acid to wipe the matter out of an Airedale puppy's eye.

"Wouldn't I love to have a piece of that concession?" the old man admitted. "Wonder if they'll take bids."

"I doubt it. Buddy-buddy favoritism will come into play. If they did, though, you could probably undercut the competition with a thousand-dollar parakeet or a million-buck black snake. NASA's about like the Pentagon when it comes to getting took."

"Careful there, Pickford. Careful."

Mr. K. put a finger to his lips to stress the need for caution, but he was smiling, and Cal smiled back. Then Mr. K. left to wait on a customer, leaving Cal to finish wiping gunk from the eyes of yet another Happy Puppy.

Last night, returning to Pine Mountain from the nursing home, Lia had said, "Listen, Cal, I lost the fish pin you gave me. It fell off my chair in the chapel onto the floor, and even though I got down on my hands and knees, I couldn't find it."

"I never gave you that pin."

"You did. You just don't remember. It stood in for a ring at our wedding in the Garden of the Gods."

"Lia, we were married in Arvill Rudd's house."

"Kai—Philip K. Dick—the man who came to see me this morning—he told me not to lose that pin. He called it, jokingly, I think, a linchpin."

"It was on your blazer when you got home from work tonight, Lia. I don't think you took it to the nursing home with you at all. You can relax."

"I didn't think I had, either. But it was in my pocket when I got Phoebe down to the chapel, and looking at it, I saw you and me as we *should've* been at our wedding. Then, damn it, I lost it."

All the way home, Viking prowling the backseat like a creature from Norse mythology, Lia had worried about the fish pin that Cal could not even remember giving her. Finally, in their apartment, she had rummaged her jewelry boxes, double-checking, and in only a moment her fingers had tweezered out the pin that she thought she had lost in the nursing home.

"You must not've had it with you there."

"But I did, Cal. I swear to you, I really did."

"Maybe you had two of them all along."

"Until this morning, I didn't know I had even *one*."

Putting up the bottle of boric acid and ignoring the yaps of a terrier who didn't want him to leave, Cal recalled that this whole fish-pin mystery had irritated him. Lia had suffered a delusional spell triggered by the trauma of taking on a resurrected dead man as a client. On the other hand, if you could believe *that*, why not the additional improbability that a pin lost in Warm Springs could pop up an hour later in a jewelry box in Pine Mountain?

Because empirically received physical laws didn't all start falling to pieces at once. At least a *few* things had to go on nonsensically making sense.

"I think Kai put it back for me," Lia had said. "He must have wanted to give me another chance."

Your mother dips snuff, Cal had wanted to reply, but right now, this morning, he began to weigh the possibility that Lia's bizarre theory was correct, and finally he saw it not only as a cogent but also as an inevitable explanation.

Kai—P. K. Dick—wanted them to know that in all the unforeseen trials ahead, he was on their side. They could count on him—or, that is, his lingering aura—to support and uphold their fight for justice in a reality—*this* reality—

through which evil had already spread like a many-fingered oil slick.

That's right, thought Cal sardonically, Lia and I are agents for truth, justice, and righteousness, and our secret ally is a coffee-drinking, snuff-dipping ghost who can't always keep from fading off into Nowheresville when he drops in to see us.

What was it that Dick, ineptly superimposed on Emily Bonner's crippled body, had said last night in the nursing home? "You know better than I do why I've picked you out." But I don't, I really don't. I'm a displaced Sangre de Cristo ranch hand, taking care of house pets when I ought to be seeing about livestock—calves that bawl, colts that balk, and bulls that'll butt down fences.

That, Phil, is the reality *I'm* homesick for. . . .

At noon, while Mr. Kemmings drove downtown for a chili dog at Charlie Joseph's, Le Boi Loan came into the Pet Emporium. Cal was surprised to see him. In the eight weeks that Cal had been at the mall, he had never encountered the Vietnamese outside the confines of Gangway Books. Lone Boy took his duties there seriously, and, his Americulturation aside, he apparently didn't much enjoy window shopping or browsing through other stores.

Cal had bought a Chick-Fil-A sandwich and returned with it to the pet shop. When Lone Boy tentatively entered, Cal was seated on an empty puppy cage in the back having lunch. In the forward half of the shop, the Vietnamese eyed the enormous green parrot on its perch near the cash register, squinted askance at the snakes, and openly admired the energetic hamsters and gerbils.

Like a little kid in somebody else's house, Cal decided. All it would take to make him leap ten feet straight up was the word *boo*. So Cal rattled the ice in his cup to let Lone Boy know that he was not alone in the shop.

"Howdy, Calvin," Lone Boy said. "What's going down?"

Cal lifted his sandwich and then his paper cup. "Only lunch, Lone Boy. What can I do for you?"

"Yesterday you were all bent out of shape by that Dick fella dying. Just thought I'd see how you were getting along."

Another surprise. Cal was touched by Lone Boy's embarrassed concern. He would've never figured the Vietnamese for the type; ordinarily, Lone Boy affected a tough-guy exterior that Cal, early on, had pegged—perhaps unfairly—as proof of a basic shallowness of purpose and character. Today, though, the tough guy had left Gangway Books to come inquire about his frame of mind.

"I'm okay, Lone Boy. I'm doing okay."

Lone Boy looked nervously around the shop. "I put your Pouch House order in, Calvin. Don't sweat it. Soon as those books hit my counter, I'll run 'em down here to you."

"You don't have to do that. I can—"

"Hey, I *want* to, okay? I can see what it means to you."

"Stupid sentimentality, Lone Boy. I associate that guy's books with Colorado, old friends, a whole different world."

Abruptly, Lone Boy appeared to lose interest in the matter. He wrinkled his nose in distaste. "How can you choke down your lunch in here, Calvin? I mean, you know . . . the *stink*."

Cal laughed. "Think this is bad? You ought to hang around a feedlot for beef cattle in ninety-plus-degree temperatures."

"I'd gag. I have to have it, you know, *clean*—before I can enjoy whatever Tuyet's fixed me for eating."

What could you say to that? Cal could think of only banalities and so kept his mouth shut. This was a strange visit. Now that he had fulfilled his sympathy-dispensing role, Lone Boy seemed to be at loose ends, and Cal had no idea how to help him. They had very little in common, Loan's employment in a bookstore and Cal's love of reading notwithstanding, and unless Lone Boy decided to buy some guppies or a Brezhnev bear or something, they were probably doomed to a long session of smiling and nodding.

But Lone Boy said, "You live in Pine Mountain, don't you?"

Cal admitted that he did.

"And how does somebody looking for your house find it?"

Cal gave Lone Boy directions, the straightforward ones that he gave everyone who wanted to find his place: You came down Highway 27 from LaGrange, turned right at Pine

Mountain's first traffic light, and stopped at the red-brick duplex on the corner of Chipley Street and King Avenue. Easy.

"Why do you ask?"

Lone Boy hesitated before saying, "When the weather improves, we should meet—y'all, the Bonner-Pickfords, and us, the Loans—for a burger cookout. For relaxing. For friendship's sake."

That's nice, Cal thought. You've invited yourself to my house for dinner. We don't even have one of those pot-bellied metal grills that you push around on lopsided rubber tires.

Suddenly, Lone Boy crimsoned. "That was rude as hell, wasn't it? Forgive me, I didn't mean to impose my whole everlovin' family on you and your woman. All I meant was—"

"No sweat, Lone Boy. Maybe we could get together in Roosevelt State Park one weekend. They've got plenty of grills."

"No, no. I should've invited you and the missus to *our* place first. Fuckin' bad manners." He shook his head. "That's what I *meant* to do. But I didn't get much sleep last night. Sometimes working two jobs strings me out and makes me stupid."

"Really. It's okay."

Still embarrassed, Lone Boy rocked on his heels. "You'll have to come to our place one of these days."

"That'd be nice." In fact, maybe it wouldn't be bad at all. Cal had seen Lone Boy's little girls in Gangway Books with their mother one afternoon, and he couldn't imagine encountering a more appealing, a more handsome, family.

But their conversation had reached another impasse. Lone Boy peered about self-consciously, scratching a fingernail against the glass of an aquarium. He *looked* ready to go, but apparently had no idea how to manage a graceful exit.

Finally, he said, "Did you know that Grace Rinehart was once in a movie version of *The Broken Bubble of Thisbe Holt*?"

"Yeah, I guess I did. Vaguely."

"Only a few people got to see it. Rinehart had it yanked from circulation and bought up all the prints."

"I think I'd heard that, too."

"Well, I'm one of the few people who's seen it, and Rinehart stunk up her part. I mean she was lousy."

What was the point of this story? And where had Lone Boy seen a film unavailable since the early 1960s. It occurred to Cal that Lone Boy was lying. Not about the badness of Rinehart's acting in *Thisbe Holt*, but about having seen the movie. But why bother to lie about such a thing? Was Loan trying to forge a bond between them, letting Cal know that although giants might walk the halls of West Georgia Commons, they did so on feet of clay? Or did he even know that the actress had visited the Pet Emporium yesterday?

"Everyone has off days," Cal said noncommittally.

"Lucky for Rinehart she can buy up the pudding proof of hers."

"I guess so."

"See you later," Lone Boy blurted. "Come down to Gangway when you can and put in another weird-ass order."

"How about a video cassette of *Thisbe Holt*?"

"Don't you wish? Don't you wish?" Lone Boy backpedaled away from Cal and exited onto the main concourse of the mall.

Later that afternoon, Cal was going past the glass cage housing My Main Squeeze, the boa constrictor, when the air seemed to redden and the muscles in his arms and legs to lose their elasticity. He felt, suddenly, as sluggish as a snake must after gulping down a rasher of nine white rats. He halted, reaching out to the glass to steady himself and noting that the strange redness of the shop's atmosphere had moved by osmosis into the corridors beyond. All the shoppers in West Georgia Commons, including the patrons of the pet store, had stopped moving; they stood in dreamlike frozen postures wherever the shimmering redness had captured them.

Cal himself could only barely move, and surveying the bizarre scene, he found that the mall reminded him of a vast classical ruin filled with black-cherry Jell-O. Every person in the tableau was a morsel in a tinted aspic of stasis.

"My God," Cal said. He could hear these words, but everything else—nearly everything else—was silence.

What wasn't silence was a bumping on the glass behind his hand; looking, he saw that My Main Squeeze had lifted the forward coils of its body and was spiraling toward the screen-covered lid of the cage. If the boa kept rising, it would push the lid back and spill out into the shop.

"Stay where you are, Squeeze. Ain't nothing out here for you. You couldn't possibly like black-cherry Jell-O."

"It's me." The boa halted. "Have you already forgotten?"

"Mr. Dick?"

The boa's blunt-nosed head, beady eyes, and flickering tongue hypnotized Cal, freezing him as the redness had frozen everyone else. Except that, if he really tried, he *could* move; it was only his astonishment transfixing him.

"I guess. Whatever my name is, I talked to your wife yesterday morning and to you last night, and I'm back for a few minutes."

With difficulty, Cal indicated the grotesque red-black gelatin quivering all about them. "How did you do that?"

"*I* didn't do it, Pickford. I'm benefitting, momentarily, from the phenomenon, but its true author is the demiurge whose messenger I am. I see that now."

"Demiurge?"

"The subordinate deity responsible for this reality. It can do whatever it wants to here. We're only its puppets, no matter how self-sufficient we may think ourselves."

"Not very," Cal admitted.

"Yeah, well, that's right. Yesterday morning, I came back from the dead in a resurrection body. Last night, as a plasma quivering around the material form of your wife's mother. But today, alas, only as a goddamn herpetological ventriloquist. This must've been the way Satan felt in the Garden of Eden. Anyway, it's a reverse progression, Cal, a devolution, and I sure as hell don't know if I'll be back again. Certainly, I don't know what shape you'll find me in next time. I admit it. The voice that's using me—that's letting me talk through this snake—it's fickle. It's struggling to impose order on events just the way that you and I do in our own daily lives. Ineptly."

"Whoa. You're confusing the hell out of me."

"Listen, the important thing for you to remember, Pickford, is that there're other realities and some of them are better than this one. Some lots better. Some only a little. Some frighteningly worse. When I'm disembodied, I can float among them, searching for the best of all existing worlds to plop down on this one. Call it stereographic imposition, if you want to give it a name."

"I don't want to give it anything, Mr. Dick. I just want out of this humongous weird you're laying on Lia and me."

"Float like a butterfly, sting like a . . . well, I don't have any sting in this state. Death doesn't, either. I'm going to need help to make anything at all happen. I can float from reality to reality, looking, testing, but my ability to effect a stereographic imposition—*that's* severely limited. You see, the demiurge doesn't want to invest me with too much power, fearing I'll take on greater importance in this reality than its true author. So I'm probably going to drop out of sight for a while—not my doing, Pickford, but the demiurge's. Granted, it permitted me to return from the dead, but it's also a jealous sucker, and its jealousy has resulted in my devolution—in three neat steps—from man to mist to talking boa. It set entropy loose on me, and now I'm depending on you—you and your pretty wife—to keep entropy from devouring us all for good. You guys have got to engineer the redemptive shift."

Was this how the serpent in the Garden of Eden had talked to Eve? Surely not. If Mr. Dick was tempting Cal, and he seemed to be trying to, the precise nature of the temptation was impossible to characterize.

"You're talking in generalities," Cal said. "You want Lia and me to, uh, 'engineer the redemptive shift.' *How*, for God's sake?"

"By taking risks," the snake said, bumping the glass. "By not permitting yourself to get too cozy."

"Cozy?"

"Look, opportunities will soon start appearing. Your first response to most of these will probably be distaste. A reluctance to follow through. It's easier to rehash a routine—to get out of bed at the same hour, eat the same kind of cereal, and totter off to work just like you've been doing for the past ten years."

"I've only been working here since Christmas."

"Coziness sets in—that's all I'm saying. And it's the archenemy of evolution, of healthy change. Look for opportunities to defy it. From whatever unlikely quarter they may come."

"All right. I will."

"Prove it."

Cal was startled by the peremptory demand. "How do I do that?"

"By letting me out of this cage."

Cal hesitated. The snake appeared to be speaking, of course, but the truth—the ostensible truth—was that Philip K. Dick's disembodied spirit was using the boa as a mouthpiece, to give both a location and an undeniable dramatic burden to his remarks. Why, then, would Dick ask him to let Squeeze out of its cage? It would not be Dick who benefitted from the release, and the boa might find its sudden freedom more a trial than a boon.

"Come on, Pickford. Take a risk. Do it."

So Cal struggled against the cumbersome redness to undo the hasp and lift the cage's lid. Immediately, all his strength left him. A statue, he stood with one arm supporting the lid as Squeeze flowed up the glass, through the gap, and directly onto Cal's body; then the boa rippled over his shoulder, around his back, and under his armpit. Cal was aware of the snake's darting tongue, the ease with which it could have crushed him.

"Flying colors," the P. K. Dick voice said. "You pass with flying colors."

Whereupon the boa constrictor unwrapped Cal as effortlessly as it had just wrapped him, coiled back into its glass prison, and slumped neatly to the gravel on its bottom. Cal closed the lid and found that the paralyzing redness had miraculously separated out into nearly all the hues of the visible spectrum.

The Crimson Interlude, as Cal had already begun to think of it, had abruptly concluded.

The people in the mall were moving again, and Mr. K. came back to Cal to tell him to stop worrying about the boa escaping. Squeeze was perfectly content in the cage, and Cal could quit messing with its lock and go back to work.

"Yes, sir," Cal said bemusedly. "I'll do that."

12

"Hey!" Vear shouted, even though the dwarflike figure among the lunar rocks could not possibly hear him. "What the hell are you doing up there?"

He staggered backward, perilously near the edge of his natural ramp, to get a better view of the unsuited person above him. The dwarf—a black man with bandy legs, a barrel chest, and a face that reminded Vear of a Klingon alien's from *Star Trek*—leapt dreamily aside, disappearing behind the rocks. By rights, the man should have been dead, a victim of vacuum or blood-boiling heat. Knowing this, Vear had to question what he had just seen. Maybe he hadn't seen the dwarf at all. Maybe this solo excursion, along with the fatigue that a guy could develop even in lunar gravity, was causing him to hallucinate, to see *the thing which is not*.

But you asked God for a sign, Vear reminded himself. What if that bowlegged black homunculus was God's reply? No human being can live out here, of course; and if it's miracles that demonstrate God's existence—His readiness to intercede in human affairs—well, you've just witnessed one wingding of a miracle.

The major considered walking up the jagged slope to verify what he had seen, but, a hundred feet or more above him, debris clogged his way. Besides, it was much farther to the crater rim—although weirdly slumped or eroded at this point in its arc—than it looked, and Vear had neither the stamina nor the oxygen for a round-trip visit to the high ground from which the dwarf had vanished. And if the dwarf were an illusion, what would he accomplish making such a trip? For that matter, if the dwarf were a sign from God, dangled before him and then teasingly withdrawn, what would he gain? Only, it seemed, his own undoing.

Breathing hard, Vear told himself that he had better sit back down. Rest your weary bones, brother. See if you can't get your dizziness to depart. Recklessly, he performed a couple of kangaroo hops to the boulder on which he had been perched before the coming of the homunculus. Then, gingerly, he lowered himself to a smooth upper facet of the rock and sat there catching his breath and blankly cogitating. Be careful what you pray for, his daddy had always warned him. You just might get it.

Don't think, don't fret, don't pray, Vear thought. Just rest. Empty your mind and rest. Rest is what you need before you try to go back down to Von Braunville. Rest is what you need before you tackle, again, the tedium and the trials of living in the pockets of fifty people—well, forty-eight—who resent your bad habits and personality tics at least as much as you resent theirs. And so Vear closed his eyes and stopped cogitating. He descended into himself for a spiritual renewal akin to, but different from, praying. He let his mind empty, and he kept on going down.

Back in his own dormitory unit, after shedding his suit in the chamber next to the airlock, Vear hugs the corridor wall, moving along it to the cubicle he shares with Peter Dahlquist, a computer specialist whose primary task is troubleshooting problems at the moonbase. Dahlquist is also one of Vear's crosses, a tinkerer who has turned their room into a workshop for off-duty projects and a warehouse for all the spare parts, gizmos, and doodads that he has accumulated cadging from any supply officer or ferry-shuttle pilot willing to hear him out.

Indeed, as Vear circles in on their room, he looks up to see a Leonardo da Vinci-esque contraption—a bird of balsa, clear plastic, wire, rubber bands, and, astonishingly, gray and white feathers—flapping dreamily toward him through the narrow corridor. He has to lift his arm to keep the toy bird from striking him in the face, and the bird pirouettes harmlessly to the floor, whispering.

"Sorry," says Dahlquist, appearing from around the curve

of the corridor. "How do you like my mock mockingbird?"

"It's prettier than your mock turtle, I guess. But the turtle wasn't a threat to put your eye out."

"You've got a visitor."

"A visitor?"

"In our room. Make sure your gig-line's straight and buff up your brass. Figuratively speaking, I mean."

"Who is it? Logan?"

Dahlquist picks up his toy bird. Older than Vear but blond and boyish-looking, he says, "It wouldn't be hard to make one of these for everybody at Von Braunville, Gordon. Some of the NASA bigwigs want to send us pets, but these'd do as well, don't you think?"

"Dolly—"

"Less costly than boosting up a bunch of cocker spaniels from the Cape. No upkeep. No anxiety about keeping them healthy."

"Who the hell's here to see me, Dolly?"

Dahlquist strokes one wing of his mock mockingbird and examines its balsa belly to see if the crash snapped a rubber band. "I'm not to tell you. I'd knock before going in, though." He pats Vear on the shoulder as he ambles on by.

Vear gazes bemusedly after Dahlquist, both wanting and not wanting to tell him about the strange apparition he saw above him on the rim of Censorinus. Don't, he warns himself. They'll say you're insane and ship you home. Great. Going home could be just the ticket. If only it weren't catch-22 time. You'd be crazy to want to stay on the Moon, they'll say, so if you don't, you must be sane, and we can't send you home unless you're crazy. . . .

Worriedly, Vear proceeds down the corridor to the room—a room like a triangular pie wedge—that he shares with Dahlquist. Here, hesitantly, he lifts his knuckles and knocks.

"Who is it?"

My Lord, Vear thinks. What a bellow. But he gives his name and rank. "This happens to be my room," he adds.

"Come in. But hurry up and iris the door behind you."

Shaken, the major obeys the basso profundo's command. Inside, Vear finds two men in three-piece suits, one of them—the older—seated in a cleared space on the edge of

Dahlquist's messy bunk, and the other—the owner of the sea-deep voice—standing next to his employer with one hand in the pit of his opposite armpit. The major also notices that this gorilla—an exceptionally neat and fragrant-smelling primate—is wearing, with his gray civilian suit, a jaunty green beret. This chapeau paradoxically identifies him as both a veteran of the Vietnam War and a Secret Service man. The personage sitting on the bunk with his legs crossed, after all, is none other than the President of the United States.

"Mr. President," Vear says, even in his surprise snapping to attention and saluting.

"Okay, okay, Major. It's good to see spit and polish out here, miles and miles from the world that nourished us all, but it's only us three fellas now and let's not stand on ceremony." He gives Vear a sweet, black Irish grin. "Which is one reason, incidentally in that connection, that I sat down."

Vear, after dropping his arm, can only gape. What have I done, he wonders, for the President of the United States to come all the way from Washington, D.C., to Von Braunville, Censorinus, the Moon, to confront me in my own cramped living quarters? Am I about to be court-martialed? Now the President is waving his hand with spastic authority.

"You can leave us by ourselves, Ingham," Mr. Nixon tells his beret-wearing bodyguard. "I'm in no danger from this patriotic Air Force officer, and our chat will go better if the major doesn't feel menaced by someone bigger and stronger than he."

"Yes, sir," Ingham agrees, reluctantly exiting.

"A great guy," the President tells Vear, nodding at the irising door. "A two-time winner of the Medal of Honor, once for heroism at Quang Tri and once, as you must know, for kneecapping that coward Hinckley when the bum tried to bushwhack us in front of the D.C. Hilton. Ingham could've plowed the nut under, but the compassion he learned in Vietnam—the empathy for the suffering of others—well, I for one know that those hard-won virtues stayed his hand even in a moment of crisis."

"Hinckley went on trial just recently, didn't he, sir?"

"Between you and me, Major, the bastard's practically sitting in the chair."

Vear continues to stand, unsure how to comport himself in this discussion.

Nixon waves him to the chair—ominous word—at Dolly's desk and workstand: a kipple of duct tape, batteries, potentiometers, even melted Crayolas. "Be at ease, Major. Never mind that a guy as famous and powerful as the fourth-term President of the United States has dropped in on you. Even my office gets messy sometimes, usually before the maids get to it. Every man needs a place he can unwind—San Clemente, Key Biscayne."

But what are you doing at Von Braunville? Vear thinks, raking a seat for himself at his roommate's workstand. Why are you here? The major's every vital sign—breathing, pulse —tells him that he is terrified.

"I'm sure you'll be as glad as I am to know that the cause of my would-be assassin's delirium—Flossy Jodelle, that cheeky piece of tail on *Right This Way, Mister Dailey*—uh, well, our Secretary of Broadcast and Print Media, Mr. Reagan, longtime anchor on the *CBS Evening News*—Ron has recently assured me that Miss Jodelle's contract isn't being renewed next season. This will prevent her from planting evil seeds in the minds of other overweight young men who might one day recover their sense of direction.

"Ron did just what the situation demanded. I'd be a piss-poor American if I didn't appreciate—which I do—his efforts to keep our young men upright. It's possible, of course, that this bum was already irredeemable, but we've gotta do all we can to save those who still haven't betrayed both their manhood and their country. Miss Jodelle's expulsion from an otherwise wholesome TV series is an important step in that direction."

"Yes, sir," Vear says, numbed by this flow of information and rhetoric. He almost wishes that Ingham, the agent in the beret, would return to absorb a little of the President's jibber-jabber.

The two men sit in the pie-shaped room, at the heart of Major Vear's dormitory cavern. The fact that they have almost nothing in common but their nationality and their language establishes a gulf greater than the six feet actually separating them. We're maybe 240,000 miles apart, Vear thinks. Metaphorically, I'm sitting on a Moon rock, while you, sir, are sunbathing in Key Biscayne.

"But you're probably wondering why I've come— unannounced, as it were—all these miles to talk to you."

"I'm wondering when you arrived, Mr. President, and why you've singled me out for the honor of this meeting."

"It's well you should wonder, Major. I've visited every great nation and many of the far less consequential ones on our wonderful planet, but this is my very first trip—indeed, the very first trip of any world leader—to the bleak but profitable surface of the Moon, and I think that this feat—as unsung as I've arranged for it to be—must surely rank as the most remarkable, since the dawn of spaceflight, ever achieved by a major world leader.

"My friend Billy Graham, our new Secretary of Nondenominational Godliness, once chided me for going overboard in my description of the triumph of Apollo 11, but even Billy—were he sitting with us now—would surely agree that *this* lunar visit is 'extraordinary.' After all, I was sixty-nine this past January, two years younger than Mr. Reagan, and it takes a lot of courage for a man my age to undertake such a journey. But I'm not going to exploit any of this to puff myself up. For which reason—a very sound reason—we're going to rap in strictest confidence. And why I want you, Major, to preserve the confidentiality of our meeting."

"Of course." Vear looks at his hands, not at the heavy-jowled, familiar face of the President. "Sir, from my knowledge of the launch schedule at Canaveral and of the frequency of t-ship flights from Kennedy Port to Moon orbit, you must've come in on the same transfer ship that picked up Nyby's body. If that's true, it means you've been here several days, undercover or incognito."

"That's exactly right. They knew who we were in the t-ship, of course, but before boarding the ferry shuttle, my bodyguard and I disguised ourselves with latex makeup patriotically provided by a cabinet official's wife. You know her as Grace Rinehart, but make no mistake: She's a loyal helpmeet to Secretary Berthelot."

"Have you been with Commander Logan since arriving, then?"

"No. I was sick a couple of days and had to get accustomed—as any semielderly person would—to the goddamn giddiness that even younger lunar travelers may experience. But for everything taken, something's given, and vice versa—a credo I try to live by. You see, my convalescence gave Ingham time to hang out my pinstripes and to iron this lovely shirt by Gant.''

Otherwise, thinks Vear, you'd be sitting here in your skivvies.

"However, let me make it abundantly clear, Major, that I'm not here simply to chitchat. There's a method in my madness, just as there was when I told our brave B-52 boys to unload on the dikes in North 'Nam and flood half that country. Believe me, we wouldn't be on the Moon today if I hadn't—in my inspired 'madness'—ordered those strikes.''

"Mr. President—''

"I stayed out of sight because I was ill, but also because I wasn't about to let the Russians here at Von Braunville—according to intelligence reports, we've got four—deduce the purpose of my visit. Whether ill or not ill, I can ill-afford to play—call it, if you like, Russian roulette—with our national security.''

"Sir, you could go to their dorm and *count* the Soviets who are here. Their names are Gubarev, Nemov, Shikin, and Romanenko.''

"Of course they are. I didn't for a moment think their names were Smith, Jones, Davis, and Anderson.''

Make your long story short, Vear silently pleads. Tell me why I'm having to endure this pitiless presidential prating.

"You know, Major Vear, that while more than a hundred and fifty flags fly at the United Nations, the one that flies the highest is the double standard. We may cooperate with the Soviets in certain areas, but they and their puppets still vote against us in the General Assembly and goad every tinhorn despot who's 'unaligned'—and some of our fair-weather allies—to do the same fucking thing, and I'm not going to go down in somebody's backbiting revisionist history as a jerk who mollycoddled the commies.''

"No, sir. I'm sure you're not.''

"It's good to hear you say so. Well, this is what I've come to report: NASA is on the brink of outfitting an expedition to Mars, for the purpose of space industrialization, with landings scheduled not on the Red Planet itself but instead on each of its two moons, Demon and Fabian.''

"Deimos and Phobos, sir." (Quemoy and Matsu—Vear thinks—he might've remembered.)

"Whatever. We're going to crack apart those two little black suckers for their carbon. It's a long haul, but the tremendous advantage of the trip—make no mistake about my commitment to fuel conservation—is simply that the energy expenditure is *less* than what we use on our Earth-Moon/Moon-Earth runs! At least, if you don't count the oxygen taken up for breathing purposes on our ferry shuttles and then pumped into the t-ships for the voyage to Kennedy Port. So I say let's not count the oxygen."

"That's fine with me, Mr. President."

Nixon, for the first time, stands up. Making a fist, he tells Vear, "Let me say forthrightly that we're going to cut the fucking Russians out of this one, Major. We have no wish to reprise our Apollo-Soyuz Test Project hanky-panky or our joint Eagle-Bear Heavy Lift Vehicle Launches. So the Rooskies will find—'feel the heat,' to be hip about it—it's their bad behavior worldwide that's put them in hot water with Dick. No carbon from the Martian moons for those guys. And I for one intend to kick Comrades Smith, Jones, Davis, and Anderson clear the hell out of Von Braunville."

"Sir, they're scientists—"

"And good ones, too, I don't doubt. But they're also commies, who got propaganda before pabulum, and if one bad apple can spoil a whole barrel—which it can (Ezra Taft Benson used to say that all the time back when Ike was in office)—well, those four guys can surely infect the otherwise robust population at this great lunar installation. That's why I didn't want them to know I was here—you don't tell the bugs when you're calling the exterminator—and that's why I intend to pack them all off on the next t-ship to, uh, Venalgrad."

"I don't think that's going to be a popular—"

"If I cared more for personal popularity, Major Vear, than for a reputation as a no-nonsense ass-kicker, I'd've never been elected to four straight terms as President of the United States."

Don't open your mouth again, Vear cautions himself. This guy will eat you alive and spit you out like a Macintosh pip somewhere south of the Sea of Fertility.

"Major—may I call you Gordon? You're entirely welcome to call me Mr. President. Great. Well, Gordon, the reason I've invaded your room like this is to ask you to show both your gumption and your national spirit commanding, as it were, our historic Mining the Moons of Mars Mission, which I've personally dubbed, in all our top-secret memos, the 4-M Agenda."

Vear's stomach flip-flops. This is the barb that he has been waiting to feel, the hook that the President has set with a glib but painful yank. Vear fears that soon he will overload and go thrashing about Von Braunville in uncontrollable spasms of protest and self-pity.

"Sir, this is my second tour at Censorinus. The Mars flight, round-trip, will have to take—well, what?—*at least* two years, especially if NASA's going to use a minimum-energy trajectory, and I'm not sure I can handle a fourth full year away from home. You can't know how much I'd like to see Kentucky again."

"As much as I'd like to pay a secret visit to my childhood home in Fullerton, California, I suppose. But you'll be able to do that before the 4-M launch. Accept this assignment, Gordon, and you'll be taking the t-ship back to Earth with Ingham and me. You're a bachelor, right? Well, a man without a family is just the sort to lead this expedition. If disaster—God forbid—should strike, you won't regret your passing quite so much as a family man."

Vear finds that he is hyperventilating and struggling to keep the President from noticing. Help me, God. Give me words to say to this august bonehead.

"Sir, I'd hoped to finish out my second tour and then to resign my commission. For a long time now, it's been in the back of my mind to become a religious in a holy order."

"A religious?"

"A monk. Like St. Francis of Assisi. Like Thomas Merton. A religious, sir."

"But it's my understanding—feel free to contradict me, but I often consult on such issues with Secretary Graham—that you'd be in a monastery—monkeyhouses, I affectionately called them when I was a Quaker—much longer than you'd ever be in an Interplanetary Vehicle System, or IVS, carrying you to Mars. How can you compare the two or more years of the 4-M Agenda to the *lifetime* that your Catholic zealots will unquestionably demand of you?"

"But I don't compare them, sir! Traveling in a spaceship for however long isn't anything like taking vows!"

King Richard holds up his hand and waves it consolingly. "Hey now, calm yourself, Gordon. Take it easy, son."

Vear grabs a solenoid from Dahlquist's desk and brandishes it at the President. "Take it easy yourself, dad! Roland Nyby did himself in because of you! Because your fucking administration has every one of us in a merciless squeeze!"

"Every society has its weaklings, Gordon. Its crybabies, its losers, its bleeding hearts. You can't expect the President of the United States to take personal responsibility for the shortcomings of the fuckups."

Mr. Nixon is ballsier than Vear has supposed. He is standing firm, wearily eyeing the major. Well, naturally, Vear thinks, you don't become the most powerful man in the West—hell, on the entire planet—by bowing to unsupported threats and empty gestures. Let him know that you intend to turn his ski-slope nose into a bloody little flap and then go over there and do it.

Thus encouraging himself, Vear advances. Mr. Nixon glances at the room's irising portal and coolly nods his bodyguard in.

Ingham pounces on Vear, slapping the solenoid from his hand and shoving him backward over Dolly's workstand. Silicon chips, vacuum tubes, strands of copper wire, pliers, potentiometers, capacitors, computer boards, and sundry other bits of hard and soft clamjamfry go flying. Vear falls backward into it, while Ingham comes down on him with his linebacker's face either grinning or grimacing and his forearm falling on Vear's Adam's apple and pressing down harder and harder as if to utterly crush it.

For Ingham, this is the Hinckley business all over again, and he is enjoying another chance to empathize with the sufferings of others (an ability he learned in Vietnam) not by refusing to hurt Vear but by declining to kill him outright.

"Gaaaah!" the major protests. But Ingham continues throttling him; and after seeing the President's indifferent face from the corner of one bulging eye, Vear disappears into the dark. Into the midnight, he hopes, or at least temporary reprieve.

"Here's the auxiliary air. See if you can rouse the idiot."

"Gordon! My God, Gordon, get to your feet!"

Vear opened his eyes. Two men in spacesuits—their NASA name strips identified them as Franciscus and Stanfield —hovered over him on the ledge above Von Braunville. A lovely slice of planet Earth floated overhead, filling the rugged bowl of the crater with cobalt shadows and an ice-blue luminosity.

"He told me he was going out for a little 'fresh vacuum.' He said he didn't intend to pull a Nyby."

"Yeah, well, maybe the fucker—I beg your pardon, Major—lied to you."

Stanfield was trying to hook up an auxiliary air supply, and Franciscus was slapping him on the helmet with his enormous white gloves. Vear blinked, struggled to rise. Stanfield held him down and continued carrying out the PLSS attachment procedure.

The two men's voices, when they spoke, bumbled around in the box behind Vear's faceplate like a pair of angry bees. Relaxing, he let his colleagues do what they had to do to recall him to . . . well, to what? Reality, he supposed. The mind-numbing reality of life on the Moon. The eerily beautiful reality of the satellite's monochrome surfaces and changing purple shadows.

Alternately cursing and joking, they walked him down the crater ledge and into the headquarters hemisphere, where, as nearly fully recovered as he was going to get today, Vear listened to Commander Logan call him a nincompoop and a threat to moonbase morale and a thoughtless spendthrift of resources necessary for the survival of every person—not just Gordon Vear, but every person!—assigned to their facility. The characterization nincompoop offended Vear more than any of the others; and as soon as Logan had spoken it, he let all the other crap blow past him like day-old newspapers on a windy city street.

When you had just approached the High Mucky-Muck of the United States with an intent to kill, listening to a nonentity like Logan rave on was an insufferable anticlimax.

Later, Vear had a long session with Dr. Erica Zola, a

cognitive psychotherapist, who tried hard to determine if he had gone outside to commune with God, as he insisted, or to do a Roland Nyby, which, greatly peeved, he heatedly denied. He told Dr. Zola that he had seen a black dwarf in blue jeans on the near rim of Censorinus and that Richard Nixon had come to his and Dolly's room to ask him to head up NASA's Mining the Moons of Mars Mission. He understood that the Nixon episode was the consequence of "lunar rapture," if you wanted a term for it, because he had let himself get fatigued and had never even come inside. But the appearance of the dwarf, well, that episode may have actually occurred. After all, he had seen the homunculus early in his outing, wondering even then if he were hallucinating but discounting the possibility because he had seen the crippled figure etched so distinctly above him.

"You realize that it had to be an illusion, too," Dr. Zola told the major. "Nobody—giant or dwarf, peon or president —can survive in their street clothes on the surface of the Moon."

"That's the popular wisdom."

A small woman with large eyes and worrisomely discolored teeth, Dr. Zola laughed. She had a big laugh for so small a woman. It got Vear laughing, too, and he liked laughing along with her even though their laughter inevitably seemed to sabotage the credibility of the *nanophany*, as she facetiously called it, explaining that she had based her word on *theophany*—"a visible manifestation of a deity"—but that *nanophany* meant "the visible manifestation of an impossible dwarf." Which set them both a-giggling again, and the session wound down into a mild joke fest and some comforting small talk.

"Okay," Vear finally asked her, "what're you going to tell the boss?"

"I can't divulge the gist of your latest psychological profile, Major. You know that."

"Come on, ma'am. We're friends, aren't we?"

"You're not a hopeless neurotic, if that helps you. You've had a bad experience. You're still mourning Nyby. You've got a lot of unexorcised guilt over your handling of that matter. I'm not going to recommend that you be sent home, though."

"I'll give you my next paycheck."

And they laughed again, because Vear had no desire to return to Earth until his full tour was up, no matter what he had told the President during his oxygen-starved dream on the crater ledge. He was a NASA man, by way of the U.S. Air Force, and not a Carthusian or a Cistercian monk, and he took pride in doing his duty, even if a son of a bitch like Commander Logan or King Richard was trying to dictate to him the questionable elements constituting that duty. He had a lot of anger to exorcise, as well as guilt, but he was sane, damn it! Sane, sane, sane!

Still later, back in his pie wedge, confined to quarters until Commander Logan had studied Dr. Zola's latest profile of him, Vear found—to his relief—that the jumble atop his roommate's desk was the same jumble that he remembered from earlier. A scuffle with a Secret Service man had not imparted new chaos to the hodgepodge.

The major sat down on his bunk, precisely where the President had perched during their dream colloquy. My subconscious viciously maligned the man, he thought. But a person in power has to be able to stand the heat. With power comes responsibility, and abuses of this responsibility deserve our contempt more than do the venial sins of the powerless. Thank God my fantasy—at least until I met with Dr. Zola— was a private one. They can't court-martial a guy for *dreaming* he's punched the boss in the nose, can they?

Dahlquist came in. He told Vear that he looked pretty good for somebody who'd nearly hallucinated himself into heaven.

I must've mumbled deliriously, thought Vear, about that goddamn homunculus—maybe even King Richard's "visit"— on my way downslope with Franciscus and Stanfield. Now those two turkeys are running around Von Braunville telling my loony fantasies to everyone with the time to listen and the gall to try to figure out what caused them. Half the base thinks I'm suffering a metabolic imbalance. The other half thinks that, like Nyby, I blew a gasket because of isolation and overwork. They believe that, like Nyby, I tried to check into the Hotel Thanatos. Forever.

"I wasn't trying to kill myself!" Vear shouted.

"I know you weren't," Dahlquist said. "You'd never give me the satisfaction of inheriting the other half of this room."

"Dolly, you've got three quarters of it already!"

Dahlquist shrugged and raked a place to sit down on the chair next to his workstand. A moment later, he was assembling a toy bird like the one he'd thrown at Vear . . . when? But he *hadn't*. That was simply a part of your dream, Gordon. Nevertheless, your roommate's putting a mock mockingbird together, and that wasn't a project he'd started before your great outdoor adventure—not, at least, that you can recall. Up until yesterday, he'd been building globelike stereo speakers to hang in the dining room for piped-in Earl Klugh and Spyrogyra concerts.

A shiver fishtailed down Vear's spine; its coldness seized him like the chill of Censorinus itself.

That sleep period, dozing, the major saw a small black figure, his body powerful but pain-racked, doing cartwheels and dancing jigs on the crater floor. The dwarf's face was businesslike rather than joyful. Whenever Vear approached him, he dematerialized, only to crop up an instant later on another stretch of moonbed or an outcropping of black feldspar high above the flats. Vantages from which he would also soon disappear . . .

The next "morning," Vear awakened to find Dahlquist sitting at their room's microfiche reader, alternately reading and worrying a pencil across a yellow legal pad.

"What gives?"

Dahlquist turned about, knocking a coil of wire to the floor. "I found out yesterday—during your dream quest for the solace of extinction—that a writer I used to like a lot died earlier this year. The library here's got only one of his books on microfiche, *The Man Whose Teeth Were All Exactly Alike*, and I was just giving it a quick perusal for old times' sake."

"Philip K. Dick," Vear said.

"You know him?"

"My brother Frank bought me a copy of *Valis* before the Board of Media Censorship seized its second printing. I couldn't bring it up here, of course, but I read it."

"*Valis* was his last book, Gordon. Cranky, impenetrable stuff. Atypical. He went off the rails mentally a few years after Kennedy was shot and got nothing else into print—if you overlook *Valis*—after a semidisaster called *Nicholas and*

the Higs. This one here"—he tapped the microfiche reader—
"well, it's Dick pretty much at the height of his powers. He
was a favorite of mine when I was a teenager. William
Golding, J. D. Slazenger, and Philip K. Dick, young Peter
Dahlquist's personal Big Three."

"I can't believe you were reading anything other than
physics texts and math books, Dolly."

"Believe it. I was ahead of my time, Gordon. Or behind
it, maybe. A dyed-in-the-tapestry Renaissance man."

Vear was oddly touched by his roommate's nostalgic
recollection of a writer who had been important to him as a
high-school kid. He wondered aloud if Dolly were taking
notes from the microfiche card of *The Man Whose Teeth Were
All Exactly Alike*.

"No, no," Dahlquist hurried to reply. "Nothing like
that."

"What, then?"

"Well, I didn't sleep too well last night—I kept thinking
that Dick had died awfully young: fifty-three."

The same age that Thomas Merton died, Vear thought.

"What I *wanted* to think about was making a flock of toy
birds—in my spare time—so that everyone at Von Braunville
could have one, but what I kept thinking about instead was
Philip K. Dick and the unfairness of the way his life turned
out. The unfairness of his early death."

"Yeah?" Vear prompted.

"So I thought I'd write something that expressed those
things, or *tried* to express them. I labored as if to give birth to
Pikes Peak, Gordon, and what I squeezed out instead was a
couple of silly lines of poetry. And that's what I finally got up
and wrote down on my pad."

"Let's hear them."

"You'll either laugh or get mad. When you're not being a
mean bastard, Gordon, you're being the quintessential Catholic."

"I won't laugh. I won't get mad."

They volleyed the matter for a while, Vear feeling that it
was crucial that Dolly read him the lines he had composed,
and at last the major's pie-wedge partner surrendered and
read them: "'Philip K. Dick is dead, alas. / Let's all queue up
and kick God's ass.'"

13

La ia depresses the key on her intercom unit: "Shawanda, is he here yet?"

"No, ma'am. Nobody's here. Nobody but me, anyway."

"Let me know as soon as he arrives."

"If he do, ma'am, would it be all right if I cut over to the Victorian Tea Room and buy me a breakfast roll?"

"What for? You've had breakfast, and it's still a couple of hours till lunch."

"I don't want to watch that spooky white man do his ghost-away again. Had me 'bout nine bad dreams on it since it happen, and I ain't lookin' to set up another week's worth."

Lia sighs. "I pay you to stay in the office, Shawanda."

"Yes, ma'am."

"Our luck, he won't be back, anyway. It's just that, you know, the way things're going, it'd be nice to have *someone*— even a dead amnesiac in a resurrection body—come staggering in."

"'Specially, he got that fat wallet in his hip pocket."

"Just let me know if he shows up."

"Maybe he'll jus' up and appear in there beside you 'thout even usin' the door."

"God, I hope not."

But, imagining Kai opting for that kind of melodramatic advent, Lia laughs. Then she releases the talk key and leans back in her chair to wait for the day to begin. So far this morning, she's simply been reviewing old cases and fiddling with the notion of making a grant application.

Kai, Lia figures, won't be back. Since last week's session, he has appeared—if *appeared* is the word—twice more, but only to Cal, first as a talkative nimbus around her mother in the nursing home and then as the voice of My Main Squeeze in the pet shop.

Speaking through the snake, Kai had hinted that he was taking a ghostly holiday and that Cal and Lia could best help him by waging war on entropy. However the hell you did that.

I wage war on entropy, Lia thinks, by counseling people and by receiving payment for my services. I can't do either, though, if I don't have any clients.

She wants Kai to come back up the stairs and into her office. She will settle even for his smug materialization in her lounger. So long as he comes, she won't try to stipulate the manner of his arrival. Beggars can't be choosers, and sometimes she thinks her practice in Warm Springs will reduce her to beggary.

In the six days since Kai's last appearance, the world has returned to normal. Locally, *normal* means that Lia is averaging little better than two clients and a referral a day.

In the world at large (Lia skims the various sections of this morning's *Atlanta Constitution*), *normal* means that Argentina and Great Britain are about to go to war over the ownership of the Falkland Islands: a Gilbert-and-Sullivan donnybrook here at the dawn of the moonbase era. Amazing.

Elsewhere, martial law has entered its fourth month in Poland. Afghani opponents of the Soviet puppets in Kabul continue to snipe at their oppressors. In Iran, the resourceful son of the late Reza Pahlavi has crushed a new coup attempt by Islamic fundamentalists. Meanwhile, in Washington, D.C., Joel Hinckley, Jr., is pleading "not guilty by reason of insanity" to a federal charge of trying to assassinate President Nixon in 1981.

"Joel," Lia murmurs, "you're doomed."

Four other people have tried to kill the President since 1975: Squeaky Fromme; an ineptly Americulturated North Vietnamese by the name of Mai That; Sarah Jane Moore; and a member of the Beach Boys angered by the four-concert-a-year limit placed on rock groups by an arbitrary postwar extension of the Pop Performance Licensing Act of 1971. All these would-be assassins paid for their effrontery by sitting down in electric chairs, and Lia has little doubt that Joel Hinckley, Jr. (who allegedly shot at King Richard to impress the female lead of a popular TV series about congressional pages called *Right This Way, Mister Dailey*) is also going to fry.

If only the government would let me work with failed assassins, Lia tells herself, I could make a half-decent living.

As for Cal, he has been intently rereading his Dickiana. Since talking with Squeeze, he has averaged a novel a night, beginning with *The Doctor in High Dudgeon*, going on to *Do Androids Dream of Electric Veeps?*, *Flow My Tears, the Policeman Said*, and *No-Knock Nocturne*, and concluding with *They Scan Us Darkly, Don't They?* and *The Dream Impeachment of Harper Mocton*.

This last novel has spoken to Cal with especial force, and last night, as they lay in bed with Viking sprawled on a nearby rug, he kept reading sections of it to her aloud, repeatedly interrupting her already fitful attention to a piece in the *Journal of Clinical Psychology* on the symptomatology of paranoia.

At one point, Cal said, "Listen, Dick's set up an alternative history in which an evil president by the name of Harper Mocton—another Nixon figure—works his will on the American people by an institutionalized form of mind control. Every household has either a TV or a microcomputer with a video display terminal and—"

"Wait a minute. That's a freedom *we* don't have. TV, yes, but in the early '70's, Congress made it unlawful for individuals to own computers without an exemption to the Computer Licensing Act."

"I know that, Lia. What I'm trying to—"

"You almost have to be a defense contractor or an executive in a big steel firm to win an exemption. I couldn't get a computer in Colorado, and I'm not going to get one here in Dixie, either. The licensing procedures are unfair. You have to do volume business to qualify. Your work has to 'increase American prestige' or 'redound to the benefit of national security.' Blah blah blah.''

"Look, I know all that," Cal replied impatiently. "Nixon had Congress place a ban on microcomputers—home computers, Dick calls them in *The Dream Impeachment*—because he was afraid they'd give private citizens, particularly those with a high-tech background, easy access to top-secret info. He was scared. Back then, he didn't want us to have microcomputers because of the war; now he doesn't want us to have 'em for fear the resulting info explosion will light up all the filthy little rats' nests he and his cohorts have pieced together during their thirteen years in power."

Lia tapped the photocopied manuscript in Cal's hands. "Isn't Dick's evil Harper Mocton afraid of the same sorts of thing?"

"Nope. In this book, Mocton uses people's TV sets and computer screens to overpower them with propaganda. He controls every arm of broadcasting—"

"Bingo."

"—and he's always using the networks and the national computer link to tell everyone how lucky they are that he's their *jefe*, a method of mind control that Mocton's perfected."

"So he has no trouble getting reelected every four years?"

"He has no trouble getting reelected *every day*, Lia. There's a computer referendum on his administration every evening during the news. All the people watching key into their consoles a Yes or a No. The results are instantly toted by the Great National Computer in the Mocton White House on Maui. Ninety percent of the people vote Yes. The ones who vote No are visited by thugs similar to our No-Knocks. The dissidents are either reeducated or declared crazy, and Mocton's reign goes on and on."

"It can't go on forever. The book's title is a giveaway."

"No, it doesn't. What happens is, a computer genius—a kind of Middle American Einstein working in secret in Van Luna, Kansas, a guy by the name of Eric Gipp—taps into the Great National Computer and programs it to include with each broadcast from the Oval Office a subliminal message. This message is flashed at the viewer over and over again at speeds too great for the human eye to fix. It says, MOCTON IS A

LIAR. DREAM HIM TO JUSTICE TONIGHT. Almost everyone in the country subconsciously registers it and tries to obey its cryptic suggestion."

"So your computer-genius hero is brainwashing everybody, too?"

"Well, there's *some* moral ambiguity here, Lia, but Dick shows that people obey Gipp's hidden message because they subconsciously recognize its truth. They want to regain control of their lives by obeying a command that holds out that promise."

"Tricky stuff, Cal. These folks are going to regain control of their lives by adopting somebody else's view of reality?"

Cal's forehead wrinkled in irritation. "Look, you can either adopt a false view of reality or one that's more or less in tune with things as they actually are."

"How are things, actually?" She gave him a perky smile.

"Hey, don't be cute. Aren't you in a line that weighs people's mental health by how well or poorly their perceptions of the world conform to some objective standard of reality? Well, in this book, Mocton's presentation of the world and his exalted place in it is a lie, and Gipp's subliminal computer message is an antidote. If the population's been turned into a bunch of zombies, you first have to plan an attack that'll reverse things and dezombify 'em. You fight fire with fire."

" 'Dezombify'?"

"Damn it, Lia!"

"Okay, okay. Calm down. What happens next?"

"Listen, I'll read you a passage." And he let the photocopy fall open on his lap and read to her aloud.

Two hundred million Americans, children and adults alike, began to dream Harper Mocton to justice. Some of these Americans dreamt that the President met a physical comeuppance exactly suited to a wrong that he had either committed or commanded. If he had maimed someone, he was himself maimed. If he had killed someone or ordered a murder, he was himself murdered. Whatever physical harm Mocton was known to have caused, he himself suffered.

Some Americans dreamt that Harper Mocton was caged in slime and stink in a federal prison. Others dreamt him staked out on an ant hill in the middle of the Great Plains, his flesh peeling from his brow like ancient red wallpaper. A few dreamt Mocton was chained to a man-sized rock in the asteroid belt, and still others imagined that cosmic justice had funneled him into a black hole beyond Pluto's orbit and that the awesome gravitational forces of this hole would fling the evil man into a dimension of pain and darkness unknown to any other living creature.

"That's some pretty sadistic dreamers old Harper's got angry at him there," Lia said.

"Hang on. That's not all."

"There's more? Dick fetches Mocton back from oblivion at the bottom of a black hole?"

"He hasn't really been zapped to the bottom of a black hole, Lia. That's only what some folks *dream* happens to him after they start obeying Eric Gipp's computer message."

"Oh. Go on."

But most Americans dreamt that no bodily punishment could ever humble this latter-day scourge as well as strong reminders that they were finally taking off their blinders and seeing him for what he was. A manipulator, not a magician, an opportunist not a benefactor. They knew that he would regard his own murder, or any truly colorful punishment, as one more addition to the legend of Harper Mocton. And they knew that he would not be able to stand any punishment that *undercut* this grandiose legend. And so many of those heeding Gipp's summons to dream Mocton to justice dreamt situations in which he publicly humiliated himself.

Eventually, by sheer weight of numbers, these dreams began to come true. Mocton could not resist them. He would go on television to speak, and the first words out of his mouth would be a confession of wrongdoing: "In my maiden race for office, I accused my opponent of child molestation. I actually paid kids to step forward and vilify him." Or: "You may be the suckers who elected me, but I've always thought you a contemptible crowd of pricks, cunts, faggots, and feebs, altogether undeserving of the leadership I'm busting my ass to provide."

"Jesus," Lia said. "I can't imagine an elected official talking like that."

"Of course you can't," Cal said. "Which is why it's funny."

"*Funny?* You think it's funny? A president admitting that he falsely accused someone? A president calling us dirty names?"

"Sure. And so do you. It's just that's it's funny in a really dreadful way you're afraid might be true."

"Cal, you're—"

"Listen, Lia darlin'. Listen."

Mocton could not believe that he was saying such things aloud. First, because they showed him to be such a monster; second, because they were either true on their face or painfully true to his hidden feelings. He could avoid these damaging revelations, he found, only if he refused to speak over the airways or in public; and soon, to prevent self-incrimination, he made the sad decision to confine himself to the White House.

Meanwhile, Gipp continued to afflict the TV and video-display screens of the nation with the subliminal legend, MOCTON IS A LIAR. DREAM HIM TO JUSTICE. And everyone oppressed by Mocton continued to dream his downfall. Hundreds of millions of dreams left an impress on reality, and Mocton could feel them warping his reign toward its end, knocking entire days, weeks, and months off the otherwise fixed span of his presidency.

Finally, Mocton resolved to make a last attempt to confront the nation and save his reputation. Terrified that he would betray himself again, he studied his notes, tested his voice, and found that he felt pretty good. Maybe I'm going to beat this thing,

he thought. As soon as the TV camera's red light
came on, however, he opened his mouth and vented
a meaningless barrage of cartoonish duck sounds:
"Quack, quack, quack, quack, quack."

Here, Cal stopped reading. He said that the novel went on
to show how Gipp and a coalition of dreamers make Mocton
answer for his crimes at a Senate trial. This trial "actually"
takes place only in the minds of the participants. Although a
good dream for those upholding justice, it is a nightmare for
Harper Mocton.

At the end, Eric Gipp, acting prosecutor at the dream
trial, points a finger at Mocton, "Your punishment is this:
Bereft of your office, you go forth to harvest the contempt of
your victims. That's all, but because your victims are almost
beyond number, it may be more than enough."

After the dream impeachment, Mocton loses his first
computer referendum. Pretty soon, he's wandering the conti-
nental mainland, carrying a begging bowl. Many people take
pity on him and give him something, but every contribution
so greatly chastens him that by the final paragraph of Dick's
novel, he is only a ghost drifting across the landscape, his
substance utterly depleted by the charity of people whom he
expected to spit upon and revile him.

"Ah," said Lia. "An allegory."

"All Dick's unpublished novels are allegories. But this
one mirrors our situation so closely that it's almost a kind of
lens through which to look at our own time and decide what
to do."

"Right. We *dream* Richard Nixon out of office."

"Lia, read your goddamn article. It's not a patch on what
I'm reading, but maybe it'll keep you from talking crap."

"Stop patronizing me. Nobody *dreams* a bad president's
demise."

"Look, dreaming in *Harper Mocton* is symbolic of joint
action—cooperative action. Don't be such an all-fired literal-
ist."

"But, Cal, our situation and Dick's *don't* mirror each
other. Nixon's popular. Most Americans don't want to boot—
to dream him—out of office. *You* may, but you're an atypical
case."

And so they argued the extent to which President Nixon

could count on grass-roots support. Lia held that he rivaled Franklin Roosevelt at the height of his popularity, while Cal contended that five assassination attempts in eight years proved that a reservoir of ill feeling lay at the bottom of the national mood. Lia replied that assassins were not reliable gauges of popular opinion—they were slaves to private psychoses, just as Cal had become a slave to his pathological hatred of the President. This analysis prompted Cal to turn away from her and finish *Harper Mocton* without reading any further passages aloud.

Lia, in self-defense, focused her attention on the article in the *Journal of Clinical Psychology*.

"Dr. Bonner," Shawanda's voice said, "you've got a visitor."

"Kai?"

"No, ma'am. It's—"

But the door to the office opened, and Grace Rinehart—Lia recognized her at once—strolled in from the waiting area and began an unabashed assessment of the little room's décor. Lia's first thought was that it couldn't possibly measure up to Miss Rinehart's patrician standards; anxious, she rose to greet her visitor. Cal had said that this woman might drop in, and today Lia was finding that her husband was an uncannily accurate prophet.

"Very nice," Grace Rinehart said, "Plants always cheer a room, and the way you've arranged those old black-and-white photographs of your family—it is your family, isn't it?—well, that's a homey touch that ought to calm even the jumpiest client."

"Thank you," Lia said. "Won't you sit down?" She indicated the lounger.

"Oh, no. Not there. I'd rather have a straight-backed chair, please. That's for contortionists."

Shawanda brought in the requested chair, and Miss Rinehart sat down. She was wearing a navy-blue dress with white polka dots, a bright red scarf, navy pumps, and a white jacket with navy piping on the hem, pockets, and sleeves. Her hat—selected, Lia thought, by the wardrobe mistress of a movie company specializing in bravura remakes of World War II *films noirs*—was a pillbox number with the hint of a black veil depending from the front. The veil scarcely touched Miss Rinehart's forehead, but its shadow laid a spider's web on her brow. Shawanda gave Lia a looky-what-we've-got-us-here expression and then retreated dutifully to the outer office.

"You know who I am?"

"Yes, ma'am, I believe I do."

"Please don't call me ma'am. I prefer Grace, or Miss Grace, or something equally informal."

"All right." But what you really want, Lia thought, is a title that helps you think of yourself as ever-youthful, ever desirable, and ever happy. Informality has little to do with it. But never mind. It must be hard having to compete with celluloid images of the person that you once were but clearly are no longer. . . .

"Are you and your secretary discreet enough—mature enough—to keep my dealings with you to yourselves?"

"Certainly." Just give us that chance, Lia prayed.

"Would you *object* to taking me on as a client?"

"Of course not." But if you could hear my heart pounding, Lia thought, would you think me strong enough to do the job?

Lia and the actress stared at each other appraisingly, and the psychologist began to wonder why Grace Rinehart, whom patriotic wits liked to apostrophize as the Liberty Belle, would show up in Warm Springs looking for help from a no-name practitioner when she could easily afford the services of any high-powered shrink in the world, from a Viennese Freudian to a Manhattan pharmacotherapist. That she had materialized in Lia's office was a small miracle, not one quite so inexplicable and alarming as Kai's appearance a week earlier, yet still one extraordinary enough to provoke disbelief and suspicion. Lia rose from her place behind her desk and began to pace the hardwood floor at a small distance from her would-be client. Her would-be *celebrity* client.

"Miss Rinehart, what do you want me to try to do for you and why have you chosen me to try to do it?"

"For God's sake, didn't I ask you to call me by my first name? If you can't meet that little request, Dr. Bonner, maybe you're—"

"Call me Lia."

"—maybe you're—" The actress stopped. It dawned on

her what had just happened. She laughed. "I was going to say that if you couldn't even get my name right, maybe you're not the one I need to help me at all."

"Maybe not." Lia resumed pacing. "But, Grace, I still don't understand *what* you want me to do. Or why you want me to do it."

"Why do people ever go to head doctors? To have their heads screwed back on straight, I suppose. And why you? Well, I met your husband not too long ago, and you're relatively near, and I'm tired of spilling my guts to bearded men in turtleneck sweaters. They're far more interested in my bank-book and the unholy myth of my on-screen/off-screen Sex Life—capital *S*, capital *L*—than in my self-doubts and my recurring depressions. So I thought that maybe, just maybe, a woman from a similar background would find it easier to cut through all the Tinsel Town tinsel and empathize with me in a way that the shrinks in turtlenecks never quite manage. Which is why I'm here. Please take me on without trumpeting the news all up and down the front and back sides of Pine Mountain."

"Ensuring confidentiality is a rule of my profession."

"Of course it is, Lia. Of course it is."

"But I'll be interested in every aspect of your life—personal, financial, political, professional—that may be contributing to the problems tormenting you. Nothing can be out of bounds in our talks if I'm to help you confront and exorcise these torments. Is that agreed, Miss Ri—Grace?"

Of course. However, I have some stipulations of my own."

Lia halted. She clasped her hands behind her back and stared at the actress with an apprehensiveness bordering on dismay. What stipulations? And would it damage her professional credibility to yield to them? I've lost Kai as a client, Lia thought, and though I'm not that crazy about taking on someone as high-strung, spoiled, and unpredictable as Grace Rinehart may prove to be, neither do I want to kick away a chance to treat her. I *need* this client.

"All right," Lia said warily. "What stipulations?"

Leaning assertively forward, Grace said, "I want to meet with you somewhere other than this office."

"Where?" Lia blurted, surprised.

Grace waved away her question. "Second, I insist that you set aside for me—I'll pay for the privilege—one whole day out of each week. On that day, you'll be not only my personal psychotherapist but also my companion. You'll go where I go, interviewing me as we travel together."

Lia could feel her blood rising. "Friends make lousy shrinks, Grace, and trying to conduct an interview while driving around the countryside would be a lot like trying to compose a sonnet while playing roller derby."

"I didn't say 'friend,' I said 'companion,' and—"

"Does the distinction matter?"

"—and there's no place as conducive to confession as the front seat of an expensive car cruising along on a lovely spring day."

"The front seat of a car?"

"Or a secluded spot on Berthelot Acres. Or a private room at the Fort Benning LAC. Or maybe even my suite at the Art, Film, and Photography Salon in LaGrange."

"But why?" Lia protested. "Psychologists don't ordinarily make house calls. For the simple reason that—"

"They want to *control* the shrink-shrunk relationship."

"Not true. We just want our clients to make real progress at as many sessions as possible. That's why we don't meet them in casinos full of one-armed bandits."

"Baloney, Lia. All you need's a little privacy and quiet. You don't need an isolation booth with your nameplate on the door."

"Is this an isolation booth?" Lia gestured at her office. "A medieval torture chamber?"

"Those are my conditions. That we meet in quiet places other than this office. And that you set aside one full day each week for my session. Even if it lasts no longer than an hour."

Lia felt hassled and violated. That another woman was mapping out this ego trip, and demanding that she get aboard, bugged her even more than the "conditions." You just didn't let a client dictate to you. It was also galling that Grace Rinehart, thinking a woman might empathize more than a "turtleneck," had no misgivings about pushing a fellow female around to access this empathy. There was something predatory about her mind. A life of celebrity and privilege undoubtedly accounted for it.

"Well?" the actress said.

"Let's make Wednesday your day," Lia replied, hating herself for surrendering but anticipating not only the money that she would earn but also the insights into the minds of the rich and powerful that she would surely acquire. Besides, ever since her first week in Warm Springs, Wednesday had been her slowest day.

Shawanda is astonished when Lia dons her coat and goes clumping down the stairs with Grace Rinehart—but scarcely more astonished than Lia herself. An hour before noon and she is leaving on a wild-hair jaunt with the wife of the Secretary of Agriculture, a woman as well known today for turning Ho Chi Minh fans into raving capitalists as for bringing a new image of Southern womanhood—self-reliant, smart, and foxy—to the silver screen.

Of course, Grace hasn't made a new film in three years, and the widespread perception of her as an ideologue, a zealous defender of conservative ideals, has begun to dilute her reputation as a film actress. Even during her Hollywood heyday—the decisive years of the Vietnamese conflict—many people in the industry respected her political connections more than her acting ability, and most agree that she ruined Jane Fonda's career even before the latter's vocal support of Ho's gang culminated in her disappearance. Grace also did much to send Paul Newman back to Broadway, where he toiled in relative obscurity until landing the part of the boozy ex-astronaut in *Terms of Endearment* and finally winning an Academy Award.

In any case, Grace made her influence felt during the 1970s, as much as a patriot as a thespian, and Lia wonders if she regrets having mixed the two. Her wedding in 1978 to Hiram Berthelot, a Georgian whose grandfather had made a fortune in textiles, has gradually—inevitably—untied her from the film industry, and Lia feels sure that the severing of this identity-giving knot has at last begun to unravel her new client.

"Where to?" Lia asks. They are seated next to each other in the front of Miss Rinehart's Cadillac, cruising at Ye Old Double Nickel (Cal's derisive nicklename for the speed limit) and moving out of town on a narrow two-lane. Woodbury—

Berthelot Acres—has to be their destination, Lia decides, but she still finds it easy to get lost amid the pine-fretted hills that rise up and fall away from the tiny communities abutting one another on the southern edge of the Piedmont shield.

"Relax and enjoy the ride," the actress says, her eyes hidden by mirrored lenses that go jarringly with her outfit.

The Fleetwood whisks them through the greening countryside—past fields full of clover or rusted autos, railroad embankments thick with new kudzu, and a portable signboard on which someone has spelled out this tripartite message: DEER PROCESSING / FATBACK / JESUS SAVES.

At last they reach the turnoff—a long gravel drive through upward-sloping meadows of moist spring grass—to the latter-day fiefdom called Berthelot Acres. Here, Grace Rinehart lives with her husband (when the secretary can get away from Washington), and here they try to lead normal lives despite their status as Hotshot Politico and Famous Activist Actress. However, two burly Secret Service men guard the entrance to the place. And so large is the estate that if it were set down in Europe, somewhere near Monaco or Luxembourg, it would qualify for UN membership.

It seems to Lia that they glide forever up the entrance drive, on either side of which graze imposing specimens of reddish cattle. These animals have the elegance and coloring of well-groomed Irish setters. Grace informs Lia that they are Santa Gertrudis cattle, first developed on the King Ranch in Texas by a complicated series of crosses between shorthorn and Brahman stock, and that here on Berthelot Acres Hiram has more than a thousand head. Lia marvels at the clean wooden breeding pens that grid the rolling meadow to her right and also at the number of healthy red beasts nibbling at the stretches of lawn between the rectangular pens.

"Cal would love this," she tells Grace.

"Your husband may be working in a pet store, but he's still got calluses on his palms and an unmistakable cowboy squint."

"You were disguised. You bought a couple of Brezhnev bears."

"Mmmm."

"Why would you do that? You said to keep you company, but you hardly need to *buy* Brezhnev bears, and—"

"Hardly."

"—and you scared Cal to death. He didn't know who you were then, but he was afraid you were checking him out, spying."

"Does your husband have something to hide?"

This question chills Lia. *What have I got myself into, riding around with this Nixon administration zealot? Am I betraying Cal by being here? No, no. He himself told me that Kai wanted us to take risks, to reach out to opportunities that might at first strike us as, well, repugnant.*

"I'm sure he's got no more to hide than most of us," Grace says before Lia can manage a reply. "Those guinea pigs were gifts for a friend of mine's children, but I fibbed—told a white lie—to keep from, ah, blowing my cover." She chuckles at this expression. "I can't go out as myself without attracting notice, Lia, and I weary of the attention. Sometimes I resort to melodramatic subterfuges. I'm terribly sorry if I gave your husband a bad moment."

"*Several* bad moments."

"He's not secretly pining for Herbert Humphrey or Jimmy Carter, is he? I'll think less of him if he is."

"It's not illegal to feel a fondness for the loyal opposition."

"A fondness is fine. Seditious rancor is something else."

That ended the conversation. The Cadillac crested a hillock of grass and day lilies capped by a stand of oaks, and Lia caught her first glimpse of the Berthelot mansion, an antebellum house with a portico, fluted white columns, and at least six towering red-brick chimneys. A gargantuan solarium, all glass and hanging plants and wrought-iron furniture and sculpture-surmounted fountains, grew out of the Berthelot mansion on the north, and a small army of peacocks marched the nearby parade fields like a scattershot drill team with no instructor to coordinate its strutting.

Grace introduced Lia to the Secret Service men, veterans of the Vietnam War, who had trailed them up to the house in a vehicle like an armored golf cart, and, once inside, to a black housekeeper who set table places for them in the solarium and served them lemonade and deliciously oniony chicken-salad sandwiches with pickle slices and potato chips.

Over this meal, Grace began to talk. She said that she had come to Lia because she felt that she was beginning to disappear from life, leaving behind maybe fifteen half-decent films and the nationwide chain of Liberty Americulturation Centers that had won her the Freedom Medal. These things were her gifts to posterity, but she herself was going transparent, and this terrified her. It was probably a fear of aging that lay behind her visions of turning into mist or wind, but knowing this did not banish the fear, and she wondered how she could make herself real again.

Lia realized that they were sessioning, that this was the part of their day for which Grace Rinehart had expressly hired her; she set down her chicken-salad sandwich, took out a notepad, and began to scribble notes. A tape recorder would have been a real help, but Lia wasn't going to interrupt the flow of her client's recital to ask for one.

The business about disappearing—fading out—gave Lia an abrupt shock of recogniton. Grace Rinehart was afraid of succumbing to a spiritual state that mirrored—metaphorically—the physical fadeout to which Kai, or Philip K. Dick, had recently succumbed. She was afraid of disappearing. Coincidence? Or synchronicity? Also (and this was almost as disturbing to Lia as the analogy between Grace and Kai), the end of Dick's novel *The Dream Impeachment of Harper Mocton* featured the symbolic dematerialization of its title character. What was going on? Could nothing hold these unhappy people to the planet?

"Coffee?" Grace Rinehart asked.

"Coffee doesn't work, either," Lia said.

"I beg your pardon."

"No, thank you. That's all I meant. I can't drink it unless it's decaffeinated, anyway."

"I'm sure we've got some decaffeinated somewhere."

"No, it's all right. I'm fine." Jeena, the housekeeper-cook, came by to refill her glass of lemonade.

Even before Jeena had left the solarium, Grace was confessing that Hiram, her third husband, probably had no idea how rootless and uncertain she was feeling these days. Her first two husbands had been actors, callow guys with swashbuckling profiles and raging libidos—damned if she hadn't made the same mistake twice—both of whom had begun cheating because their own careers had devolved into dramatic donkeywork: a sidekick in a dumb TV cop show, a shill for aspirin. *Her* career, meanwhile, was rocketing skyward like a Heavy Lift Launch Vehicle. Old Tweedledum and Tweedledee—it was hard to recall which had been the cop and which the pitchman—had been able to handle the bruising of their male egos only by screwing every leggy starlet who came their way. And so these "marriages"—ha!—had fizzled out in divorce.

Hiram, however, was as dependable/faithful as sunrise/sunset. If he had a failing, it was work. Therefore his ignorance of her—Well, what to call it? Her "midlife crisis"? That was popular terminology nowadays, wasn't it? Anyway, Hiram stayed busy talking with wheat farmers, dairy ranchers, farm-equipment manufacturers, agribusiness lobbyists, and so on. He was constantly plugging away for grain shipments to Africa and the Soviet Union, lower interest rates on farm loans, and the end of every federal price ceiling on beef, mutton, and pork.

Lia listened to this synopsis of Hiram Berthelot's career with real sympathy, in part because even Cal liked him. Indeed, Cal and Arvill Rudd thought Berthelot the gutsiest member of Nixon's third- and fourth-term cabinets. Who else, they argued, had had the brass to tell King Richard that the price ceiling he'd fixed for beef in 1973 was a monstrous disaster for the cattle industry and only a temporary boon for the American consumer? But that's exactly what Berthelot had done, and there was some evidence that Nixon had heeded his words.

Grace was still talking, and Lia's hand was tiring. Politics, Grace allowed, was an even nastier trade than show business. It bugged her how often some yellow-dog Democrat in the House or the Senate accused Hiram of a conflict of interests. They didn't like him raising cattle, they disapproved of his owning a large block of prime pasture in Meriwether County, they objected to the fact that he'd arranged the first shipment of Brezhnev bears from the Soviet Union and now raised the critters—along with a thousand head of Santa Gertrudis cattle—on Berthelot Acres. They had no right to object. Hiram had signed all his income from these enterprises over to the Liberty Foundation, a nonprofit patriotic organization, and the Senate had long ago ruled that he was not technically in violation of any of the conflict-of-interest statutes pertaining to cabinet members.

Why are you telling me all this? Lia wondered. She had stopped taking notes. You're my client, not your husband, and although I need to have as much background as I can to help you, a lot of this seems overdetailed and extraneous.

Outside the solarium, the branches of two elm trees had filled with goldfinches. The birds clung precariously to these branches, pecking away at seeds or buds. Lia, sipping her tea, watched them teetering like circus aerialists on the cascading limbs.

"I think it would help," Grace said, "if I saw more of Hiram."

"Why don't you go to Washington to live, then?"

"I hate that city. It's bitchier than Los Angeles."

This remark, insofar as Lia could judge, concluded their first formal session. Grace beckoned to Jeena, who entered the solarium and cleared away their dishes. Then the actress got up and led Lia outdoors, through a gauntlet of potted ferns and down the back side of the hill on which the mansion perched to a long whitewashed barn with three cupolas and three antique weather vanes.

One of the Secret Service agents, a big guy named Twitchell, joined them about halfway down the hill and accompanied them to the barn. Which, Lia decided, was actually a converted chickenhouse. When they stepped through the west-end door, she could smell—not the sickening odor of barnyard fowls, but a delicate gaminess betraying the presence of . . . guinea pigs.

"Three or four of them don't smell bad at all," Twitchell said, "but when you get just beaucoup bunches of 'em in the same joint at one time, well, forget it. Nude or no, their tiny bods can perfume a place as fast as a—" Twitchell blushed, and Lia understood that he had almost framed a scatological figure of speech.

"I know what you mean," she said.

As far as the eye could see in the converted chickenhouse —with its green indoor/outdoor carpeting, overhead warm-air blowers and fluorescents, and metal food and water trays—Berthelot's half-nude cavies cavorted. Amused, Lia looked at all the pink varmints, with only their manes to make them "cuddlesome," and wondered again why the American people had taken them to their hearts. These guinea pigs were more popular than war orphans or March of Dime poster kids, and Lia knew that Hiram—good guy or no—was making money hand over fist peddling the little buggers to pet stores and other breeders. Besides, the Liberty Foundation was Grace's baby, and if it were getting all of Hiram's profits from beef and cavy raising, well, she and Hubby Dear were probably raking a pretty sum off the top of these contributions.

"Would you like one?" Grace asked. "If you would, it's yours. Just pick it out."

"I don't think it would get along too well with our husky. And I really don't want to take my pay in barter items."

The actress stressed that she had not intended barter as her way of paying her bills. Then she jolted Lia by saying, "You're not doing all that well yet, are you? In your practice?"

Twitchell was leaning over one of the low wire fences, trying to pet a pale-maned pig that kept scooting to and fro among its chittering buddies to avoid his hand.

"They don't like to be touched on their heinies," Grace shouted at Twitchell. "Rub its nose. That, they like."

Lia was thinking, Is she trying to humiliate me? I've come out here to session with her. Now she's insinuating—correctly —that my practice isn't much of a practice. The unspoken implication is that I'm a charity case. She even wants me to accept a Brezhnev bear. Maybe this is how Cal felt when Mr. Kemmings tried to foist a pair of the little stinkers off on him. . . .

"You aren't, are you?" Grace insisted.

"Things are starting to turn around," Lia said through clenched teeth. "It just takes awhile."

Grace Rinehart studied Lia in a way that made her feel that she had a bra strap showing. Then she said, "Come on, young lady. You and I are going to Columbus."

"Columbus?"

"Well, Fort Benning."

"Fort Benning?"

"Specifically, the Liberty Americulturation Center."

"But I need to get back to—"

"You've given me the entire day, remember?"

"Shawanda rides home with me. She won't know what—"

"We'll telephone her. Does she drive?"

"Yes, but—"

"Well, she can drive your car home. On our way back from Fort Benning this evening, I'll drop you off at your house, and she can pick you up in the morning."

"But—"

"What's the matter? Did you bring your car keys with you?"

"Yes, but there's a duplicate set at the office. Only—"

"That's wonderful. Don't second-guess me. It's decided."

And it was. Lia found herself using the Berthelot telephone in a large white room off the solarium.

Soon afterward, she was sitting beside Grace Rinehart in her Cadillac as it slid down the winding gravel drive. Behind them in the portico—Lia glanced back to see this—Twitchell was holding a Brezhnev bear to his lapel. After waving them good-bye, he began to pat the cavy on the back as if trying to burp it. Meanwhile, the other agent, Scarletti, followed them to the gate in the armored golf cart, eating the Cadillac's dust all the way.

As soon as they were on the highway, Grace popped a tape into her player. It was José Feliciano wailing a hip rendition of "The Star-Spangled Banner."

14

Grace Rinehart and her passenger reached the outskirts of Fort Benning, the sprawling army installation south of Columbus, by two that afternoon. Grace drove her Cadillac down the four-lane onto the post, turned below the army hospital, and went on past the mall housing the commissary and the PX to a vast enclave where all the World War II era buildings had a forbidding official aspect. A war college of some sort, the officers' club, the enlisted men's dining hall, the quartermaster's barracks, the motor pool.

Lia felt that she had entered a foreign country. Even when she saw a Burger King amid all these austere structures, she regarded it as she would have a McDonald's in the center of Mexico City—as an anomaly that in no essential way undid the estranging exoticism of the place. She was an outsider here, a tourist, possibly even a captive being paraded before an indifferent and already victorious enemy. As a spit-and-polish platoon came trotting along the road to the chirpy hut-hutting of a red-haired DI in a wide-brimmed hat, she had to fight the urge to duck from view. Even after realizing that her window glass was tinted against Tom Peepery, she could not relax and enjoy the sightseeing.

"What's the matter?" Grace asked her.

"I don't know. I guess that army posts make me nervous."

"They ought to *calm* you. My God, this is a bastion of American strength and resolution."

Of course it was. On the other hand, the sound of helicopters swinging low over the parade fields—*thwup-*

thwup-thwup-thwup-thwup!—and of soldiers jogging to quick-time rhymes called out by career disciplinarians was painfully daunting. It recalled to Lia the war years: the divisive 1960s, the repressive early 1970s, the insane euphoria of victory when the bombing of North Vietnam's irrigation dikes and the push into Hanoi by a joint force of ARVN regulars and U.S. Marines had broken the backs of the Reds and brought the long agony of the Indochinese conflict to a surprisingly decisive end. Grace Rinehart's hero, Richard Nixon, had achieved this triumph, primarily by refusing to mute American power and by ordering Harry Kissinger to portray him at the Paris peace talks (ah, the irony of that epithet) as a Hitlerian madman who would do anything to obtain his goals. This cynical characterization had not been a lie.

Briefly, the hard-won triumph had been sweet. Soon, though, it had acquired a bitter taste—the apotheosis of the President, the institutionalization of repression, the crazy glorification of all things military. So how, given this dismaying history, could Lia ever feel at ease on an army post?

The Cadillac—some good distance from the Burger King—turned onto a street in an area where only a few barracks-like buildings dotted the brown meadows of the post. Lia soon caught sight of a painted sign near one of these structures: LIBERTY AMERICULTURATION CENTER, GREATER SOUTHEAST, FORT BENNING FRANCHISE.

From the outside, the center looked closed. It had no windows, only outsized clapboard shingles—all of them dingy—resting on a concrete foundation at least three feet high. Grace parked her car on a diagonal near the hanging wooden sign, and she and Lia climbed a series of steps to the porch giving access to the entrance bay of the center. In this bay, everything was vast and shadowy, but Lia, squinting, could see corridors leading off it at weird and distant angles and rooms giving on these halls in the brightnesses beyond. Eventually, she also began to hear voices, most of which echoed scratchily across the gloom.

Grace said, "We first set up these centers for the Vietnamese, our enemies as well as our allies. The South Vietnamese really only needed pep talks and fine tuning, but the redeemable commies—Northerners that we thought might be able to influence the diehard Reds back home—they needed out-and-out conversion and hypnagogic reinforcement. As you can probably guess, the two or three years right after the war were our busiest times in the centers. Lately, I'm afraid, it's been a little slow."

If what I'm seeing right now is any indication, Lia thought, it's more like D-E-A-D than S-L-O-W.

"We're going to stay at it, though," Grace confided. "We still have a number of Vietnamese to Americulturate, of course, but in recent months we've begun to diversify. Now we deprogram Muslim extremists for the new Shah, Castroite revolutionaries from Central and South America, and captured Marxists from Africa. Naturally, working with hostiles is harder than dealing with those predisposed to love us, but the rewards are greater. Unfortunately, it's also difficult to capture and transport the hostiles back here so that we can do something with them."

"Who's here now?"

"A few Vietnamese, a few wild-eyed Islamic terrorists, several Sandinista guerrillas from Nicaragua. But mostly, even yet, it's the Vietnamese—for which I'm grateful."

"Does it depress you that the main work of your centers seems to be winding down?"

"Sure. A little. First the film career. Now this. Wouldn't you be depressed?"

Lia said nothing. As her eyes adjusted, she realized that the bay was a kitchen and dining area. Ovens, stoves, stainless-steel tubs, and big wooden butcher blocks bulked in the dimness. Dozens of fold-up tables insulated the wall next to the street.

"Pollard!" Grace shouted. "Pollard, you've got company!" The echo of this shout ping-ponged around the room in a way that made Lia cringe.

A small, neat man in civilian clothes appeared in the mouth of one of the far corridors and then came tap-tapping across the open bay to greet them. Grace introduced him as Ralph C. Pollard, the director of this center; he shook Lia's hand with a single limp pump. He had a silky mustache, a pair of wire-rimmed glasses, and five or six strands of snow-white hair sweeping over one ear in a coiffure otherwise dark and youthful. He could have been anywhere from twenty-five to forty; nothing in his demeanor enabled Lia to make a more precise estimate.

"What's going on today, Pollard?"

"As always, that depends on which room you're in, Grace," he said. Apparently, she called the director by his surname even though he was obliged to use her Christian name. "If you'll just come with me, ladies, I'll give you a tour."

Lia was glad to get out of the bleak entrance bay. Was it any less oppressive when lights were gleaming, pots boiling, and people sitting at the tables for their meals? Naturally. It had to be. Maybe if she and Grace had arrived at noon, her first impression of the center would not have been so negative. Well, Pollard was going to try to reverse that impression, and Lia told herself that she must do her damnedest to help him. Negativism was a killer; it was certainly Cal's least winsome personality trait.

The LAC director led them to the first door in the hallway from which he had come. Looking into the room, Lia noticed that it was decorated to resemble the interior of a subway car; it had false windows, with rectangular advertisements slotted into metal frames directly above them, and fake-leather seats that rested flush against the sides of the car. Floor-to-ceiling support poles lent an air of authenticity to this unorthodox décor, as did the spray-paint graffiti—most of it inauthentically bland—rippling over the walls and many of the ads. Tobacco firms, banks, soft-drink companies, and auto manufacturers had all bought ad space, but big concealing smears of crimson, blue, or ebony made it seem unlikely that these various concerns were getting their messages across.

Ten or twelve people—they *looked* Vietnamese—slumped or stood in the make-believe subway car, taking turns sharing recent good or bad experiences with their fellow passengers. Lia could not follow their talk very well—not because they were speaking Vietnamese but because speaker units at each end of the car were flooding it with clickety-clackety subway-train noises. Moreover, everybody seemed to be swaying in their stationary conveyance as if it were actually hurtling them through the catacombs under New York City.

"This is a leaderless group-therapy session," Pollard told Lia, *sotto voce*. "Everyone participates on an equal footing."

"I don't know," Lia said. "I think the ones sitting down might have an advantage."

Pollard gave her a wan, tolerant smile. "Right. Because this is supposed to be a subway car. Good, good." Absent-mindedly, he wiggled the knot of his tie. "I meant, of course, that each person has an equal chance to contribute, to bring up problems they've had handling American manners and mores. Or they can tell the others an inspiring success story. In this part of the LAC program, members of our support groups meet once a week for six months."

"Why do you distract them with the subway-car getup?"

"It's not meant as a distraction," Grace said. "It's a means—an additional one—to acculturate them to our socie-ty. Two birds with one stone. Besides, they don't always have the same backdrop against which to share their stories. We change the sets from week to week."

Pollard said, "Last week, it was a small-town barbershop. It's also been the lobby of a movie theater, the waiting room of a Midas muffler shop, and the first-class section of a 747 jumbo jet flying from Los Angeles to Hawaii."

"Not to mention a hospital ward, the interior of a mobile home, and a diner right out of an old Edward Hopper painting."

Isn't that a lot of trouble to go to? Lia thought. And doesn't it cost bundles of money to refit this overgrown confessional every week? Aloud, she said nothing. I've stumbled into a Mad Tea Party in Grace Rinehart's batty Wonderland, she told herself, biting her tongue to remain silent.

"We have the members of the support group design and construct the sets themselves," Pollard said. "It's yet another way to make sure they're exposing themselves to edifying Americana. We grade them on their choices and then on how well they render the sets they actually do."

"And where do these poor people get the money to do them?"

"They're not 'poor people,' Lia," Grace rebuked her. "Neither in a material nor in a spiritual sense. Some of them are already quite well off, having begun businesses or service organizations of their own. Most of them have a real creative flair, which shows to good advantage in their set-making. Sometimes—to answer your question—they use their own money; however, the Liberty Foundation always pays for most of what they need."

When the clickety-clackety clickety-clackety of the subway tape briefly subsided, Lia heard one of the men declare, ". . . and so I have overcome my natural aversion to tossing beer or soda cans from the windows of moving vehicles." Every member of the man's support group, whether sitting or clinging to a pole, applauded him for his accomplishment. All, Lia noted, but one young man who appeared to be suffering from a private distress.

"Let's move on," Pollard said.

They did. Lia saw a room in which a small group of people were watching a kinescoped episode of *I Love Lucy*. Pollard told her that the students had already seen or would later see episodes of *Amos and Arnie*, *Highway Patrol*, *The Honeymooners*, *Dragnet*, *Leave it to Bunny*, *Ozzie and Harriet*, *Father Knows Best*, and *The Andy Griffith Show*. Todd Turner, the owner of Channel 17 in Atlanta, a cable network whose programming consisted primarily of old movies, old television series, and sporting events, had helped LAC/GSE acquire many of these episodes, and so Grace considered him a special friend of the Liberty Foundation. Lia noticed that two of those undergoing Americulturation in this room were tactlessly "resting their eyes."

Gesturing the two women onward, Pollard indicated the next door along the corridor. Here, Lia found herself gazing in at a smartly dressed young woman who appeared to be lecturing her charges on responsible consumerism. From the table before her, she lifted two cans of sliced cling peaches in heavy syrup, one a name brand, one a generic product; then she showed her students a designer box of Kleenex tissues and a modest box of nonproprietary tissues. After these demonstrations, she stressed that upwardly mobile Americans— Benjamin Franklin's admonition "A penny saved is a penny earned" notwithstanding—would opt for the status-imparting and economy-boosting name-brand goods rather than the less attractive and less expensive generic products. Thrift without taste was un-American, but a pretty prodigality was patriotic.

"I regularly buy generic items," Lia whispered. "If we want to make ends meet, we have to."

"Well, you were born here," Grace whispered back. "You can get away with a little tactical scrimping."

"But not these people," Pollard said. "Foreign-born citizens who buy generic goods are in danger of making

themselves feel like generic Americans, rootless and nonde-
script. It's psychologically important for them to identify with
name-brand products. That's why, at graduation, we give
them Adidas T-shirts and Papermate pens and tote bags from
Macy's."

The director nodded at the next door down the corridor.
"Come on, then, ladies."

I hope you're including yourself in that category, Lia
thought, not because she believed Ralph C. Pollard gay or
even off-puttingly effeminate but because there was something quintessentially bitchy about his manner. He was, she
concluded, a patronizing creep, and this tour was depressing
her, wearing her down, in a way that even an uneventful work
day in Warm Springs could not do.

The next chamber they came to was a small auditorium. It
had a low stage at one end, the backdrop to which was an
immense—yea, an almost sardonically big—American flag.
Previously, they had stood outside each therapy or lecture
room, but this time Grace walked boldly in. As soon as the
fifteen or twenty Vietnamese sitting in their theater chairs
saw, and recognized, her, they came to their feet, enthusiasti-
cally applauding. Lia knew immediately that this display of
respect and affection was both spontaneous and real; the men
in the room were truly glad to see her. Even the young man
on stage, whose presentation Grace had interrupted, was
applauding. He wore a beige helmet liner and slapped a
swagger stick repeatedly against his palm to show his delight
at the unexpected advent of the Medal of Freedom winner.

"Let me apologize for breaking in on you," Grace said,
urging quiet with her hands. "We don't mean to put you
behind schedule. It's only that I wanted Dr. Bonner here"—
she indicated Lia—"to see how well you all're doing and what
great talents many of you possess. Please, now, go on with
what you were doing."

That said, Grace led Lia and the director along the wall to
the rear of the auditorium, where they found standing room
and crossed their arms and waited for the man in the helmet
liner to resume his presentation. Which, unabashedly, he did.

It took Lia only a moment to comprehend that he was
re-creating the prologue to the film *Patton*, George C. Scott's
eloquent address to the troops. And he was re-creating it

well, if not altogether expertly, striding this way and that, enunciating each syllable as though it had been engraved on a gold tablet, and using his swagger stick—it and the helmet were his only props—to punctuate Patton's jingoistic but somehow moving harangue. Everyone in the little auditorium paid strict heed, and when he was finished, there was clapping for him as loud and heartfelt as that which had greeted Grace's arrival.

"Very good, Pham Kha Son," the actress told him, and the young man, taking off his helmet liner and facing everyone in his Calvin Klyne jeans and his Arrow shirt, shyly acknowledged her praise. He seemed embarrassed as well as gratified by it.

Pollard, leaning across Lia, whispered, "He's just had his name legally changed to Frederick Cason, Grace. That's what he'd like you to call him."

"Very good, Mr. Cason," Grace said aloud. "With your speaking ability, I think you should run for office."

The man's smile broadened, and he came down from the stage to pass the helmet liner and the swagger stick to the next performer. This was a fellow even younger than "Frederick Cason," undoubtedly a teenager, who bowed accepting his props and then tripped almost daintily up the steps to the stage. Soon, he, too, was reprising the George C. Scott speech—in a voice exotically inflected and disconcertingly high-pitched. Still, he seemed to know what he was doing, and if he were less compelling than Mr. Cason, Lia knew that it was his physical appearance and his boyish voice rather than his lack of acting talent that made him so.

As he was swaggering and haranguing, Grace said, "This is not only Americulturation, Lia, it's a kind of assertiveness training. We bring only the men into this track, and we make them deliver the prologue from *Patton* because it's a real flag-waver that requires whoever's doing it to drop that self-effacing Asian gentlemanliness that undercuts their ability to compete in the West."

"Amen," said Ralph C. Pollard.

A Mad Tea Party, Lia thought. Everything I've seen here is an invitation to high tea with the March hare and the dormouse. But before she could think further on the insanity of this and other LAC activities, Grace eased past her, beckoning her to follow, and they left the auditorium, turned into another corridor, and walked along it—a long way—to a different sort of room.

Here, they stood outside the door, which, uncharacteristically, was both shut and locked. Lia gazed into the room through a pane of glass fortified with wire in a mesh of interlocking diamonds. On six simple beds lay six comatose people, all of them, if skin color and physiognomy meant anything, Middle Easterners, probably Arabs. Two of those lying zonked on their monastic racks were young women. Electrodes or sensors of some kind were taped to these persons' pulse points—at their arms, throats, and temples—and each of them wore a set of padded earphones. Lia could tell that even though they all had their eyes closed, beneath their lids their eyeballs were desperately jitterbugging. Expressions common to seizure victims came and went on their youthful faces. A man in a wrinkled white smock moved among the beds, monitoring both his patients and the tape machine into whose hypnagogic propaganda they were collectively plugged.

"You don't have to tell me," Lia said. "I can guess."

"The drugs have no bad side effects," Grace assured her. "They simply heighten our subjects' receptiveness to the tapes." Turning to Pollard, she asked, "What are they listening to today?"

"These are newcomers, Grace. Palestinians. They're getting an introductory lesson in Arabic about the sanctity of each person and the need to love our neighbors as ourselves. Etcetera. It's not *that* foreign to them. We'll be moving on to democratic ideals and the practical satisfactions of capitalism as soon as we've got them fully indoctrinated in the basics. Teaching them the satisfactions of American popular culture, well, that'll have to wait until we're sure they're not going to backslide into fanaticism."

How do you define *fanaticism*? Lia wondered. I could come up with a definition that would include you, Grace, and all the other LAC wizards trying to make the world safe for Nabisco, the Chrysler Corporation, and the CIA.

Abruptly, an anguished cry echoed down the long corridor toward them. Behind this cry came the sound of running feet, a commotion completely unexpected in the solitude and gloom of the center. Lia looked back the way they had come to see one of the young men from the subway room careen around the corner, bounce off the wall, and stumble midway down the long hall toward them. He looked wild-eyed and distraught. As soon as he saw them—specifically, Pollard and Miss Grace—he halted, bending at the waist as if hugely winded and then straightening again to raise one lean arm into the air and to shout, "I am not a goddamn American, you vultures! I am not from Indianapolis! I am Vietnamese! If I must suffer such indignity in this place, then—*pfui!*—I spit on it!" He spat on the linoleum, and Lia was shocked to see that the ejected strand of saliva shone a baleful crimson in the half-light of the corridor.

"My God," she murmured.

And then the young man's pursuers—fellow students and center employees—appeared in the mouth of the turnoff, sliding into view like Keystone Kops, and would have advanced and captured him, Lia supposed, if Grace had not held up her hand and shaken her head to indicate that they should leave him be.

"Vo Quang Lat," she said, "aren't you only a couple of months away from receiving your certificate?"

"Fuck my certificate!" he shouted. "Fuck it!"

A buzzer began to sound, an amplified burr that made the whole labyrinthine building quake. The noise—the continuous cycling of the alarm—seemed to go on forever. Vo Quang Lat began to stalk them again, his bloody-looking mouth shaping reproaches, curses, accusations, scoldings, all his recriminations rendered inaudible by that damned blatting.

"Stay where you are, Lat!" Pollard cried. "You're going to get yourself in deep trouble!"

But Lat kept coming.

Lia thought, What's he going to do? Throw himself on Pollard? Try to strangle Grace? Is he lumping me with them simply because I'm standing here beside them? And who gave him that vicious punch in the mouth? His teeth must be rattling in his head.

Now Lia could hear what the imperfectly indoctrinated Lat was spieling: ". . . I'm sick of these games! All I want is to go home. Is that too much to ask? And is it too much to ask that you stop trying to turn my country into Disneyland and all our people into Mouseketeers?" The Vietnamese spat again, another distressing dollop of crimson.

As the alarm continued to sound, Lat's pursuers began to surge forward again. Grace thrust out her hand to stop his advance, but even when the LAC worker in the white smock came out of the locked room, Lat, shaking his fist and cursing, kept coming. Lia stepped back, but Grace told him calmly that he would regret this behavior, he would especially regret forfeiting his certificate on the brink of full Americulturation.

Lat wasn't listening. One hand plunged into the pocket of his pleated slacks and emerged with . . .

Lia couldn't see, and she had no chance to weigh Lat's action because two military policemen—MPs—appeared in the corridor at her back, knocking aside a pair of heavy swinging doors and jumping to opposite sides of the hall to protect themselves if the madman they were trying to apprehend was armed. Each MP was carrying a pistol, and when they saw the crowd behind Vo Quang Lat, one MP, speaking loudly, urged its members to retreat as quickly as they could. Lia knew that these army cops feared that if they had to shoot, a stray bullet might hit a bystander.

"Drop it!" the other MP shouted.

Pollard got down on all fours. Grace, Lia, and the man in the white smock hurried to press themselves against the wall.

Lat, confused, watched his pursuers retreat into the auditorium corridor, then pivoted back around to unriddle Pollard's bizarre behavior. When he took his hand from his pocket, both MPs—knees bent, legs apart—fired a pair of shots. The noise was deafening. Afterward, Lia understood that either she or Grace had screamed. Probably me, she thought. Probably me.

Meanwhile, Vo Quang Lat clutched first his arm, then his belly, and gracelessly collapsed.

A liquid redness poured from his mouth, a deep scarlet that had already dyed his lips and discolored his teeth. The hand taken from his pocket scattered beads—a broken rosary?—onto the scuffed linoleum of the corridor.

They've killed him, Lia numbly marveled. They've just up and killed the poor fella.

As one MP knelt beside Lat, Grace, cucumber cool, took Lia by the elbow and led her to the shooting victim. The other

MP helped Pollard up, and soon all six of them, including the man in the lab coat, had gathered about the fallen Vietnamese. Lia, to her chagrin, was crying.

"He's not dead," Grace said. "The MPs attached to LAC never use real bullets. They're equipped with high-compression tranqs. The impact knocked Lat down, but the drugs are only now beginning to act. Except that Miller there"—she nodded at the kneeling MP—"pulled out one of the darts. To keep from sending our friend to cloud-cuckoo-land for longer than he needs to be there."

"But the blood—"

Miller picked a bead off the floor, stood up, and placed it in Lia's hand. "That's a betel nut," he said. "And all this filthy red crap you see on the dude's mouth and shirt, well, it's only the juice from the betel nuts he was chewing."

"We thought maybe he had a pocketknife or something," the other MP said. "That's why we hurried to tranq him."

Grace said, "Vietnamese peasants chew betel nuts to deaden their senses to the poverty of their lives. Not Lat, though. He put in a supply so that he could spit defiance—literally—at our center's work." She wheeled on the LAC's director. "Didn't anyone see this coming, Pollard?"

"Lat seemed to be doing fine, Grace. If anything, he seemed ahead of schedule. This was, uh, wholly unexpected."

"Shit," Grace said. "Shit to the seventy-seventh power."

The MP named Miller, Lia noticed, was scrutinizing her jacket. "I like your pin," he said in a low, confidential tone. "And I just want you to know that I'm a Christian, too."

On the drive back up Highway 27 to Pine Mountain, Grace assured Lia that she had seen the Fort Benning LAC on a very unusual day. In the nearly twelve years that it had been operating, you could count recidivist lapses like Vo Quang Lat's on the fingers of two—possibly three—hands. Of course, this estimate didn't include hard-core terrorists or guerrillas, who were virtually a different breed from an ally as grateful as the South Vietnamese or even from foes as beaten and woebegone as the Red army of the North and their National Liberation Front—that is, Vietcong—comrades.

"What's going to happen to Lat, anyway?"

"Why?" Grace asked.

"I was just wondering. I mean, will he be punished? Put in a cell somewhere or . . .?"

"Executed?"

"Surely not. I mean, for suffering a kind of breakdown while undergoing the Americulturation process?"

"Of course not. Absolutely not. We'll counsel with him and then start over again."

The Cadillac cruised smoothly through the dapples of light and shade overlapping Highway 27 from the pine trees standing sentinel to the east. On Lia's left, that early evening sun was raying red spokes through the ragged trees, plunging earthward near Lannett or Opelika, and Lia felt that she had been away from Pine Mountain for years, not merely a single afternoon.

"How would you like to go to work for us at the Fort Benning LAC?"

Lia fought to keep from barking her astonishment. Right. Me, a product of the precrackdown antiwar effort, shrinking Oriental egos for King Richard. Just my agreeing to session with you has probably put my marriage in jeopardy. Going to work at one of your centers would spell D-I-V-O-R-C-E for sure. I can imagine what Cal is going to say about my afternoon already. But hire on with you? Ye gods, it doesn't bear thinking about. . . .

"I take it that's a no?"

"I've got my own practice, Grace."

"And I've seen how staggeringly well you're doing with it, too, haven't I?"

About as staggeringly well as you seem to be doing nowadays at your LAC, Lia thought. But she said nothing.

"You could counsel with difficult cases. Lat, for instance."

"I'm not trained to Americulturate, Grace. It's wholly beyond my expertise."

"That's not so. Our first session convinces me that you can do just about any kind of psychotherapy you put your mind to."

"Not this."

"Why not give us one day a week?"

"I've already committed myself to giving you one day a week. I can't give up another."

"What if it were the same day?"

A terrific uneasiness stole over Lia. "Please don't make that a condition of taking therapy with me, Grace. You'd be backing me into a corner." Of course, Lia reflected, it may be that you enjoy backing people into corners.

The Fleetwood's tires hummed on the asphalt. The sun's rays slanted into the car like blood-slathered knives.

"Let me tell you something," Grace said. "A confidence. Not one having to do with my feelings of aimlessness and ennui, but a confidence involving Hiram and my relationship with him."

Spare me, Lia prayed. For now, anyway, spare me.

"The President has pledged not to run again, to retire to San Clemente and write his memoirs. Well, it's entirely possible that he'll endorse my husband for the '84 Republican nomination. If you climb aboard now, Lia, you'll be a virtual shoo-in as the First Lady's psychotherapist. Being First Lady will probably get me out of my doldrums for good, and being my personal shrink, that'll make your whole career. You'll never have to grub for clients or status again. The world will beat a path to your couch."

"Lounger."

"Whatever. I want you to think about this, Lia, and I want you to discuss it with—" She stuck.

"Cal?"

"Of course. With Cal. The President believes that after the thrashing he gave Jimmy in '76, Georgia deserves another candidate, and Hiram—even if his only elected post was as a representative to the state legislature—is just the fella to succeed him. I'm going to help Hiram, and I want you to help me."

"I'm not a politician, Grace. I'm not a campaign worker. I do cognitive psychotherapy."

Grace turned her head slightly and gave Lia a look of such smug contradiction that Lia was both angered and intimidated. I don't like what's happening here, she thought. This woman is trying to substitute her various private greeds for my own will. What scares me is that she may be able—somehow—to pull it off.

They crested the mountain, purred past Callaway Gardens, and coasted into the sunset-flooded town, where the actress left Lia at her doorstep, dismissing her with a nod and driving back uptown to Highway 27.

Lia noticed, with both relief and gratitude, that Cal's beat-up '68 Dart was already parked on the edge of the yard. Her own hubby was safe at home. Nyah nyah nyah, she thought at the Cadillac's retreating taillights. That's one thing I've got on you, lady: my sweet, stable, satisfying marriage. And she entered their apartment to give Cal a kiss and to ask him how his day had gone.

15

Aping John Wayne's walk, Twitchell, minus his beret, ambled through West Georgia Commons mall. In Gangway Books, he spoke briefly with the young woman at the register, then strolled on up the concourse to a video-game arcade called the Barrel of Fun. He entered this noisy place through a paneled opening that looked like the mouth of a big wooden barrel lying on its side.

Where are you, my gooky gook gook? Twitchell sang in his head. Come to Daddy, do.

It was dark in the game room. Purple and amber lights from the video screens fractured the shadows, but the kids standing at the consoles—truants? dropouts?—were mere cutouts, not recognizable people. Twitchell had to make two circuits around the room to find Le Boi Loan.

Lone Boy was standing in a nervous stoop at a game called Phun Ky Cong. Twitchell, the father of two teenage boys, smiled; he had played this baby himself. It was a big favorite of the kids. Or, at least, it had been a year or two ago. You used your joystick to move a figure called Grady Grunt through the Tunnels of Cu Chi in pursuit of a Viet Minh guerrilla named Phun Ky Cong. Whenever you got Grady close enough, you pressed your button and blasted away at Cong's narrow ass with a flamethrower.

It wasn't all that easy. Cong was always trying to maneuver Grady into a pitfall lined with bamboo stakes or directly beneath a tunnel opening through which Cong and his VC buddies could drop a skull-cracking rock. If that weren't enough, Twitchell recalled, you had to fry *five* Phun Ky Congs before Grady could advance to the next video stage, an even more labyrinthine and treacherous level of the Cu Chi tunnels.

Twitchell stood at Loan's shoulder, watching. From the upright boxes all around them burped peculiar noises: *Pop-pop-pop! Blippa-blip-blippa! Ka-pow-pow-pow!* As always, the sound effects made Twitchell nervous, and as soon as Lone Boy had positioned Grady in a good place to barbecue Cong, he put his hand on the little guy's shoulder.

"How's it goin', sharpshooter?"

Lone Boy's hands came off the box's controls. He whirled, his eyes showing a lot of white. "Hey, you shithead, I'm on my fuckin' lunch hour!"

Twitchell said, "I'm sure you are, Loan." Such defensiveness, such empty bravado. The poor gook's scared to death.

On Lone Boy's screen, the Cong figure, unhampered, dug a tunnel under Grady Grunt, causing Grady to plummet into a net that closed around him like a string bag around an onion. A peppy little dirge played. The game was over. Lone Boy had lost.

Lone Boy glanced at the Phun Ky Cong console. "Fuck it all to hell! You cost me my goddamn quarter!"

"I'm trying to save you something worth a helluva lot more than that. The respect of a very fine lady."

"You're gonna give me another quarter, dork."

"Hey, man, a Green Beret gives no quarter." Twitchell strong-armed the feisty Lone Boy to a corner of the Barrel of Fun where two forlorn pinball machines stood. No one was playing them; no one was going to play them. "Does the word *reindoctrination* ring any bells with you, my friend?"

It sure as hell did. The little guy's face altered. Now he knows where I'm coming from, gloated Twitchell.

"Who are you?" Lone Boy asked, trying to regain his composure. He pushed the Secret Service man's hand off his arm.

"You already know what you need to know. I think we can skip my name."

"I *don't* know what I need to know. Like, for instance, what do you want?"

"When're we gonna see some results?"

"I know where he lives. I took some time and found out where he lives."

"The lady I've mentioned—even *she* knows where he lives. So that's nothing. What else have you got?"

"Two-three days ago, I took this order of books to him, a whole bunch of Philip K. Dick's stuff. He was glad to get it."

Christ, thought Twitchell. "Big fuckin' deal, Loan. When're you gonna move? That's our question."

"Listen, I work days. I work evenings. Sometimes, I got to sleep, don't I? And see my family?"

"You agreed to a set of conditions."

"I can't go in there while they're in there, can I? It only leaves me days, and I work days."

"Take one off. Phone in sick."

"And they've got a dog. A big mother. They keep him chained out front while they're away."

"Go in through the back."

"This dog, man, it'll hear me. It'll bark. It'll eat me up if it gets off its chain."

With that, Twitchell again grabbed Lone Boy's arm. He pulled the Americulturated Vietnamese to his side and walked him through the mall to the parking lot behind it. The little guy kept jerking his elbow, but Twitchell refused to let him go and pretty soon they were standing over the trunk of a late-model Dodge. A jalopy laid rubber at the other end of the mall; a high-flying jet braided its contrails through a tenuous macramé of spring clouds.

"Use this." Twitchell handed Lone Boy a military pistol and a flat rectangular case.

"Shoot him? I won't shoot him. First, I'd take your goddamn program all over again."

"Look in the case."

Lone Boy looked. His expression betrayed his puzzlement.

"Use those instead of conventional ammo. They'll knock him out for a while. That satisfy your goody-two-shoes conscience?"

"How many?"

"Just one. The extras are if you miss. Precautionaries, I s'pose you could call 'em."

Lone Boy was staring at the pistol, hefting it. Twitchell gave him an empty shoe box from the trunk and told him to put the pistol and the tranqs away.

"Tell you something else you need to know. This Cal Pickford you're supposed to be tailin'—his wife's mother kicked off last night. The funeral's tomorrow at two. There's gonna be some sort of get-together afterward at Brown Thrasher Barony, the farm that Dr. Bonner's brother works on. The whole clan's probably gonna be out there. At least until dark."

"You expect me to do it in the *day*time?"

"You got an excuse for every other time." He did, too. And, Twitchell noted with pleasure, this simple remark had sobered him. Loan was staring into the shoe box with pursed lips and a furrowed brow. Weighing the merits of the suggestion.

"Okay," he said presently. "Okay." He walked back toward the rear entrance to the mall, clutching the shoe box under his arm like something salvaged from the wreckage of a tornado.

Twitchell lifted his imaginary flamethrower and squeezed off an imaginary burst at Le Boi Loan's narrow ass. Gotcha, he silently exulted, gotcha gotcha gotcha, my gooky gook gook you.

16

The worst has to be over, Cal thought as he escorted Lia from her mother's grave to the silver limousine. They would ride with Jeff and Suzi Bonner and the Bonners' children, Martin and Carina, from the cemetery to Brown Thrasher Barony. Everyone who had ever cared about—who had ever had even a nodding acquaintance—with Miss Emily would drive out to the farm, too, bringing platters of chicken and ham, bowls of cooked vegetables, pitchers of tea, pie tins of various desserts—enough stuff to keep the British and the Argentine warriors in the Falklands going for weeks.

It would be an ordeal, this postfuneral reception, but not as much of one as the two days they'd spent in the Meriwether Memorial Hospital after Miss Emily's devastating heart attack in the Eleanor Roosevelt Nursing Home. At the hospital, they'd known almost from the beginning that they were simply waiting for her to die. And certainly the reception would be less of an ordeal than their trip to the mortuary in LaGrange to view the body. There, Lia had cried so much—cool psychotherapist or no—that it looked as if each eye had taken the impact of a hard-hit tennis ball.

In fact, she *still* looked that way, and Cal kept pulling her to him in the backseat, squeezing her shoulder, tracing the enflamed circles under her eyes with a solicitous finger—until, tiring of this attention, she grabbed his wrist and gently settled his hand into his own lap.

The worst *has* to be over, Cal reflected. Miss Emily's in the ground, the eulogies have all been spoken, and folks are gathering around Jeff and Suzi, Martin and Carina. And Lia and me. Even me, Cal Pickford, the outsider son-in-law whom Miss Emily sometimes seemed to regard—unfairly—as the Angel of Death.

Suzi and the boy Martin were in the backseat of the limousine with Lia and Cal. Jeff and the girl Carina were up front with the callow young driver from the funeral home.

The Bonner kids, eleven and nine, respectively, were downcast imps today, grieving as deeply as any adult—but with more hurt and less understanding—and saying nothing at all.

Good kids, Cal decided. Really admirable, first-class little persons. He had never noticed their dignity before. They had always seemed to him standard-issure children, adequately tousled and freckle-ridden, neither marvels of brilliance nor monsters of brattiness. But now their grief was bringing them into focus for him, distinguishing them in startling ways. They had lost someone who mattered, and Cal could empathize.

As for Suzi, well, she was a decent person, too. Oddly solemn even on happy occasions; aware, maybe, that Martin and Carina were growing up in a different world. Nowadays you didn't make waves. If you danced, you danced to the music of the ski-nosed piper. The solemnity that her kids were displaying today would stand them in good stead later. They wouldn't have much to laugh about if things kept going as they were, and Suzi—even from a position of moderate privilege—knew it.

Cal looked at the back of Jeff's head. His sister's brother. A guy who didn't deserve a wife and kids as neat as these. Not that he was a jerk—only that he had surrendered to the status quo. He managed a horse farm for an indulgent absentee landlord, a man named—truly now—Denzil Wiedenhoedt, who'd made his money back in the 1950s selling and installing wall-to-wall carpet.

Jeff had it too good under Wiedenhoedt: The injustices worked by this administration on folks less well-connected meant nothing to him. Jeff was ignorant of these injustices; he *strove* to remain ignorant of them. Which was one reason that he disliked Cal and wished that Lia had married a local boy.

Maybe you're not being fair, Cal cautioned himself. After

all, there's a black stablehand—Kenneth "Horsy" Stout—at the farm, and Jeff keeps *him* on the payroll.

And when you first got here and were struggling to find work, Lia asked Jeff to hire you—not as a replacement for Stout, but as a supervisor or an extra hand, roles that Jeff was already filling himself. So possibly, Mr. Pickford, *you* resent *Jeff*.

Cal began to fret. Did he resent not only his brother-in-law but the black stablehand? Certainly, if not for Stout, Cal might have had a job on the horse farm from the beginning. . . .

Suzi broke into his worry: "I'm surprised that Grace Rinehart and Secretary Berthelot came, Lia. You must really be impressing her. For her to put in an appearance, I mean."

That's what it was, Cal thought. An appearance. The woman is super at making appearances. Her *life* is an appearance.

Aloud he said, "Just what we needed at Miss Emily's funeral, a couple of bigwigs and some gun-toting Secret Service geeks."

"She really looks great, doesn't she?" the limousine's driver said. He was wearing a dark suit and, despite the balmy weather, a pair of calfskin gloves.

"I'd rather have security at a funeral than not," Jeff said, without turning around. "What's the matter, Cal. Did they make you nervous?"

"It was a show, Jeff. Neither of those people knew your mama, and neither of them really gives a"—the kids in the car dictated Cal's word choice—"a fig that she's died. It's all politics."

Lia said, "I'm not crazy about the way Grace goes about doing some things, but she's not an unfeeling person. Her coming to the funeral today was a show, all right—a show of concern."

"It was sweet she came," Suzi agreed.

"And what about Hubby Hiram?" Cal asked, annoyed.

"He came because he was home from D.C. and Grace wanted him to come. That's just the way good husbands behave. He could've been a no-show easily enough. I imagine he's got plenty to do, what with his cattle, and his Brezhnev bears, and all the hassles over price supports and so on."

"But the agents in their green berets," Jeff said, still facing front, "they make poor ol' Calvin antsy. Something must be eating Calvin. Probably his conscience."

Fuck you, Cal thought. But he said, "I don't like the Gestapo, Jeff, and I don't care what color their hats are."

"Gestapo?" the driver said. "You mean Germans?"

"Secret Service men aren't No-Knocks," Jeff replied. "They're not even all that secret. They wear their berets to show us that they're completely on the up-and-up."

"To intimidate us, you mean."

"Cal, you're a true paranoid."

"I'd like to wear a beret some day," Martin said.

"You'd look silly in it," Carina told him, a disembodied voice from the front seat.

Suzi kept Marty from replying, and the driver, looking into his rearview mirror, said, "They've got the next three cars after this one, folks. If one of you all's antsy about 'em bein' along, well, you're gonna have 'em at the party to be antsy about, too. Hope there's plenty of food."

Cal glanced over his shoulder. The next car in the procession was Grace Rinehart's cordovan-colored Cadillac. Today, though, it carried a pair of beret-wearing agents. Miss Rinehart and Hiram Berthelot were in the backseat of the trailing auto. Behind that one, visible when the mortuary limousine turned onto a county road, was a third armor-plated luxury car. Dozens of other cars of all shapes, sizes, and makes trailed after.

This isn't a funeral procession, Cal thought. It's a goddamn convoy.

"I invited Grace to come," Lia said. "I phoned her yesterday and said she was welcome. Secretary Berthelot, too. Was that all right?" Lia looked past Cal to Suzi for a yea or a nay.

"Sure, it was," Suzi said. "Our house is your house, Lia. You know that. Invite anybody you like."

Tiglath-pileser the Third, Cal thought. Attila the Hun. Adolf the Hitler. Anybody at all.

Brown Thrasher Barony nestled about six miles northwest of Pine Mountain. It comprised sixty acres of land, a dozen high-strung thoroughbreds, possibly twenty quarter horses, and a stable vastly larger than the Bonners' house.

Although no tightwad, Denzil Wiedenhoedt felt that most of the money spent at the Barony should go toward maintaining its fences and grounds and toward feeding and caring for the horses. However, upon learning of Miss Emily's death, he had wired the Bonners a thousand dollars to have a huge canopy erected in front of their house (an ill-disguised doublewide trailer) and church tables moved on to the lawn to accommodate all the people, himself included, attending the postfuneral reception. He had also provided for portable toilets, valet parking, and a jukebox draped in ebony bunting.

This jukebox was playing the sort of pious music that caused Cal's teeth to ache. From the roots up.

Under the high, fringed canopy, Lia was being consoled by ten different people at once; the Secretary of Agriculture was talking with Wiedenhoedt; and Miss Grace was standing at one of the tables politely declining autograph requests and spooning out field peas, candied yams, and greens (turnip, mustard, or collard) to whoever walked past her with a designer paper plate. Probably thinks she's Jesus washing the feet of the disciples, Cal decided.

Two Secret Service men hovered near the Liberty Belle, while four other agents guarded Berthelot and Wiedenhoedt, peering at the crowd like yard bulls casing a hobo jungle for troublemakers.

It seemed to Cal that everyone in Pine Mountain, plus a hundred other souls, had showed up. Mr. Kemmings was there, and Cal took him a plate at a table near the doublewide and talked with him for several minutes. Then he saw Shawanda Bledsoe with some of her friends and family members and waved them up to the serving tables so that, later, they could brag that Grace Rinehart—yes, *the* Grace Rinehart—had actually slopped them some sweet 'taters and greens at a white folks' funeral whoop-de-doop.

Cal tried to signal Lia a couple of times, but it was no use—she was beset by comforters. Finally, he abandoned the front lawn and hiked down the neat dirt road from the Bonners' house to the stables. Pearl bushes and flowering quince danced their colors at him. Meanwhile, the music from Denzil Wiedenhoedt's idiot jukebox, along with the folksy hubbub from the tables, began to fade, and he could hear faint whinnyings from the barn. The acrid, provocative smells of horseflesh also swirled out to greet him.

The stable's huge doors—big enough to admit a couple of trucks—stood open, revealing facing rows of gray-painted stalls, maybe twenty on each side, and a floor of poured concrete so well scoured that it gleamed like ivory. The door at the far end of the barn looked as far away as Italy, but skylights in the steepled ceiling shed sunshine across the entire distance, pillars of crisscrossing butterscotch. Dust motes and pieces of either hay or straw swam in these beams, reminding Cal of unknown life-forms in a colossal but waterless aquarium.

He walked down the row of stalls, listening to the hollow tap of his Sunday oxfords and looking at the nervous thoroughbreds. My God, he thought, they're beautiful. Each horse had its name on the stall: Golightly, Divine Intervention, Radioactive, Ubiquity, and so on.

Beyond the far doors, more horses were grazing; therefore, some of the stalls were empty, and Cal paused at an empty unit to study its design. He noticed immediately that Horsy Stout had built a ledge around this stall at the same height as the concrete water trough—so that he could stand on this platform to wipe down and curry his charges.

Me and Horsy Stout, Cal thought. Two men in the same general line. Him with his horses, me with my Brezhnev bears.

Aloud, Cal said, "I need a hit."

He searched for a place. The aisle between the stalls wasn't it. Thoroughbreds were sensitive. Smoke annoyed them, and they'd whicker and rear if you lit up around them. If you upset them too much, they'd bang around in their stalls—almost willfully—until they'd gashed a flank or splintered a hoof, as if conscious of the fact that doing themselves damage was the best way to make you rue your behavior. We're expensive suckers, their attitude said, and if you don't treat us right, we'll go into your goddamn pockets to punish you.

At last, Cal came to the saddle room. It had racing saddles resting on sawhorses or stacked on a plywood table. And because Wiedenhoedt had quarter horses for both farm work and recreational riding, three fanny-burnished Western saddles hung from one wall. An assortment of bridles, blinders, and bits depended from wooden pegs next to them.

The saddle room also had clothing lockers, a television set, a couple of easy chairs, and a refrigerator full of soft drinks and beer. Even better, a shower for weary riders was wedged behind the half wall supporting the lockers.

Privacy.

Cal eased through the little room and into the shower stall. No one had used it recently—its avocado-colored tiles were dry. And so he had no compunction about slumping into its corner in his good suit and rummaging his pockets for reefer makings.

From an inside jacket pocket, he took his Pouch House paperback of *The Broken Bubble of Thisbe Holt*—from the set that Le Boi Loan had hand-delivered to him in the Pet Emporium the day before Miss Emily's heart attack. With a fresh imprimatur from the Board of Media Censorship, this was the only mainstream Dick title that Cal had not read yet. Because of the hospital vigils and the dither of funeral preparations, he had had no chance to crack this copy until now. He felt a bit guilty about reading while the reception was going on, but nobody was really missing him, and he didn't plan to be gone that long, anyway.

Cal toked once or twice on his cigarette before turning to page one, chapter one.

Instantly, he had a vision of Miss Emily lying in state in an odd dimension beyond time. This vision, he knew, had nothing to do with the marijuana. It was a mental image conjured not by *Cannabis sativa* but by grief, his own and Lia's.

There, at the shower stall's open door, Miss Emily floated up before him, levitating on a cloud or a shroud (a shroud or a cloud, Cal thought in silly singsong), her thin face waxen and her hands beside her like plaster-of-Paris claws.

"Once alive but now dead." The most profound banality, or the most banal profundity, that any human being could utter.

A mystery.

The paperback of *Thisbe Holt* slipped from Cal's grasp. He kept his eyes on Miss Emily, but took several quick drags—violating every code of reefer etiquette known to him—to sustain this image of his dead mother-in-law.

Not possible.

Almost at once she began to mutate, her features melting as if hot lights had struck them, then re-forming as if unseen hands were shaping them from underneath. A shocking rearrangement of cheek bones, brow, nose, chin, eye sockets, mouth. Lia's mother's face, gone. From its waxen slag, a second female face emerged, this one belonging to Cal's own dead mother, Dora Jane Pickford.

Cal couldn't move. He felt the reefer burning his fingers, but did not drop it. This face was his mother's, all right. As she had looked in '71. As he *imagined* she had looked in her casket—even though he had never seen her in it.

Before he could speak to her, Dora Jane's face began to alter. This time he had an idea what to expect, but even when the features slumped, pooched upward again, and came together to reproduce the face of Royce Pickford, his father, Cal was startled in spite of himself. Taken aback.

Miss Emily's death, he knew, had triggered this vision, but knowing that did nothing to make the sight of his long-dead parents less heartbreaking. Just as his sympathy for his wife's loss did nothing to make his sympathy for himself any less trenchant.

Finally, Cal dropped his cigarette and, sucking the blisters that had popped up on his hand, scooted forward to touch Royce Pickford's floating corpse. Immediately, his father dissolved and Cal was squatting on the edge of the shower stall—about to topple headlong into the saddle room. About to bellow like a steer going under the sledgehammer.

King Richard's first-term vice president has come into Denver a day before the Victory Rally. The city has scheduled a parade down Colfax Avenue, and "Speero the Heero" —as the kids in Boulder enjoy referring to him—is going to be its ringmaster.

Cal has driven up from Arvill Rudd's ranch in Gardner to see the show. At five or six different roadblocks, he has assured the state police that he is a gung-ho patriot, not a depraved hippie, and he has pulled off this improbable stunt by stuffing his Indian braid under his Stetson, saying yessir and nosir twenty-thousand times, and repeatedly demonstrating that the carrier in his pickup contains tiny American flags—not Molotov cocktails.

On Colfax, Cal positions himself near a group of soldiers from Fort Carson. Business people, well-dressed mothers with preschool children, college students in coats and ties, and a wide variety of other onlookers—none of them, tellingly, counterculture bohemians—line the same sidewalk. Cal is astonished that the makeup of the crowd is so different from what it would have been only two years ago, when nearly every longhair, Jesus freak, and raving peacenik in the land would have converged on Denver to tell Speero the Heero where to stick it and why.

But the mood in the nation has undergone a radical—ha! call it rather a remarkable *conservative*—shift, and King Richard and the Congress that he has blandished and bullied have made it harder and harder for the antiwar party to obtain a forum. In fact, Senators Morse and Fulbright have changed sides, citing the intransigence of the North Vietnamese government and the atrocities committed by its troops against thousands of South Vietnamese civilians during the Tet Offensive of 1968.

Cal himself knows some kids, erstwhile flower children, who have recently accepted the argument that the conflict in Indochina is *not* a civil war (as the peace movement's abashed leaders still shakily contend), but a clear-cut case of naked aggression. The aggressors are Uncle Ho's crimson legions; the transgressed against are the valiant citizens of the democratic South. Converts to this view—King Richard's bluntly articulated view—often sound to Cal like born-again Christians. They are fervent in their faith, and they can talk of nothing else.

The soldiers next to Cal on Colfax burst into applause. One of them shouts, "There he is!" The sounds of two different marching bands—one from a local high school, one from Fort Carson—collide, reminding Cal of a sardonic symphony by Charles Ives.

The Vice President is on the lead float (which resembles an aircraft carrier), standing at its prow inside a plastic cylinder meant to protect him from unfriendly missiles. He is speaking, and his amplified words echo through the long canyon of Colfax like the pronouncements of an apoplectic judge.

". . . the blithering bumpkins who tell you that up is down

and down up!" he cries, scowling. "Well, now we no longer even begin to believe them. Their day has died, and ours has dawned. So look around. If you see one of these grim, grousing gushers of guileful gratuitousness, gouge him in the groin!"

What the hell does *that* mean? Cal wonders. Nobody here seems to care. It sounds as if Speero the Heero has just kicked ass, though, and the color of his language—magniloquent mauve—seems to've tickled everybody's funny bone.

But soon enough the Vice President has passed by, and although several of the soldiers chase after his float, waving their caps, Cal has come to Denver for another reason. Victory rallies like this one have been taking place for about three months now, in strategic cities across the country, usually with a high-ranking administration official as grand marshal. New York, Cal remembers, got Kissinger. Boston, Melvin Laird. Chicago, William Rogers. And so on.

But Cal has no interest in bigshots—only in blood-relation little people.

A year ago, Royce and Dora Pickford, who ran a weekly newspaper out of Snowy Falls, Colorado, not to mention a few head of cattle, were arrested for taking an anti-administration stance and sending copies of the seditious *Huerfano Warrior* through the U.S. mails to every major political figure in Washington. But *arrested* is the wrong word: Cal's parents simply disappeared. Only after weeks of persistent and dangerous inquiry was he able to find out that his father was in the state prison in Canyon City and his mother in a "safe house"—*safe house* was the government's own obfuscating term for it—at Ent Air Force Base in Colorado Springs.

His father, a tough but honorable man, in a facility designed for murderers, rapists, and their violent ilk. His mother, the most gentle and gregarious of women, forcibly cloistered away from her family and friends.

These were, and are, outrages. True outrages. But no one will allow Cal to visit either parent. Once, when he drove up to Ent to look for his mother's "safe house," base security caught him and escorted him to the city limits, warning that further unauthorized encroachments would lead to his own arrest.

By working through several nervous elected officials from his own county and congressional district, Cal was at last able to get his parents' addresses. He now exchanges monthly letters with his mother in locations that keep shifting (although her address stays the same) and with his father in Canyon City, but he feels certain that any news about Royce sent to his mother, or any news about Dora sent to his father, gets obliterated with black ink or excised with razor blades before the Board of Citizen Censorship forwards his communications. It probably doesn't matter much, though, for his parents' letters to him are always either carefully inked-out or intricately windowed, and there really isn't that much news for him to pass on. Still . . .

So Cal has come to the Victory Parade. He watches a troop of buckskin-clad cowboys ride past on their skittish horses, followed by a band of sad-looking Utes on foot. Two of the Utes are doing random dance steps that appear to have no connection with anything else going on.

A rumor that Cal has heard—and that he wishes both to believe and *not* to believe—says that at least one float in every Victory Parade is given over to the display of dissidents. The crowd gets to boo and catcall them, a tension-releasing opportunity that has been inaugurated and vigorously championed by two of King Richard's most influential aides. This idea—so the Rumor has it—came to these men while watching films of American POW's being paraded through the streets of Hanoi by their North Vietnamese captors and abjectly enduring the abuse of the crowds. The first thought of Nixon's aides was to do that very same thing with captured North Vietnamese soldiers, but the expense of transport and the fact that such action violates the Geneva Conventions—a potential public-relations disaster in the world at large—led these men to consider substituting home-grown dissidents for enemy foreigners. And that is what has happened. Or so saith the Rumor.

Ticker tape, or a convincing facsimile, drifts dreamily through the urban canyon. A piece of it lands on Cal's shoulder.

Behind the Indians, a battalion of men in yellow hard hats comes surging up the avenue laughing and flashing victory signs. This is the two-fingered V beloved of King Richard and recently reclaimed from the dissidents, who were using it as a peace sign, but it still amazes Cal to see it lifted in support of the war.

The noisy hard hats are *not*—Cal belatedly sees—a formal part of the parade but some patriotic enthusiasts who are fanning out on both sides of Colfax and giving miniature American flags to anyone not already waving or wearing one.

"Here, mack," a huge hard hat says to Cal. "Show the colors."

"That's okay. I've got a couple in my pocket."

"What in crap they doin' in your pocket?"

"At least I haven't got it sewn on the seat of my pants." Cal hopes that this remark sounds like brotherly banter.

"Yeah. Good thing. We'd have to yank your pants off and boot you in the place where you'd been sitting on it." A hearty laugh. And more laughter from two other well-muscled men—one in a white T-shirt, one in an open-collared work shirt—who join their friend on the sidewalk beside Cal.

"At first, I thought you guys were marching," Cal says, afraid that they will spot the braid stuffed up under his hat.

"We are," says the man in the T-shirt, gesturing with his lunch sack. "Marching for God and country."

"Even when we're standing still," the third hard hat adds.

They've got me corralled, Cal thinks. And look: There're more guys just like them across the street, standing in two- or three-man groups around the other spectators. Their yellow construction helmets pick them out.

"Is there a float of dissidents today?" he says, not merely to make conversation but to obtain an answer to the question that has been nagging him all morning.

"Yeah. It's coming. And this is probably the best stretch of Colfax to catch it on, too."

" 'Catch it'?"

The hard hat with the flags peers into Cal's face. "See it, I mean. It's good and wide here. What'd you think I meant?"

Cal murmurs an inaudible reply, and the man turns aside.

To loud applause, a contingent of Green Berets strides past. A pair of fighter aircraft roars by overhead. And then, a block down the avenue, a hostile grumble begins to swell, a many-voiced jeer that ripples down the sidewalks and back and forth across Colfax, growing louder and nastier the nearer it draws.

Beyond the turrets of two state-of-the-art tanks, Cal sees the red cab of a tractor truck and the open semitrailer on which this Victory Rally's object-lesson dissidents have been made to ride. The semitrailer has clear plastic sides but no roof, and as it approaches the portion of the avenue that Cal is sharing with the hard hats, several of these men's cohorts start running into the street and pelting the plastic walls of the trailer with rocks or eggs or rotten produce.

The rocks bounce back—dangerously—but the eggs and vegetables and fruits splatter and stick, turning the trailer's clear shields into ugly abstract-expressionist murals. And behind the murals, in loose-fitting prison garb, are the dissidents themselves, maybe thirty in all, some flinching away from the impact of the missiles, some huddled together on the bed of the trailer, pretending in vain that they are elsewhere.

"Christ," Cal blurts.

"Here," says the second hard hat, drawing a good-sized rock out of his paper sack. "Lob this mother up and over."

"Yeah," says the third man, himself taking a rock. "That way, you'll have a decent chance of bloodying one of 'em's head."

Cal drops the rock and runs into the street. The semitrailer is grinding past. Desperately, he paces it, peering through the smears of egg yolk and pulped tomato at the prisoners enduring this shameful test.

Unconstitutional, he thinks. Unconstitutional! By God, this is fuckin' unconstitutional!

But it's happening, and as he jogs beside the truck, he takes a rotten cantaloupe half in the shoulder. An egg grazes his Stetson, knocking it from his head and releasing his Indian pigtail. Now, nearly all the hard hats and many of the other spectators are doing what the guy in the T-shirt advised, namely, tossing their missiles up and over the shields and watching them plummet on the prisoners like V-2s dropping on London during the blitz.

This, in fact, is a blitz in microcosm, and the jeering of the hard hats echoes among Denver's buildings like so many raw shrapnel bursts. Cal hears, too, the sounds of rocks rebounding from metal, plastic, and even fragile human bone.

It's Cal's father who sees him first—who, hanging to a strap near the tractor cab, reaches up and taps the back of his head to pantomine the fact that Cal has lost his hat and that his Indian braid is exposed. His mother, her temple already bloodied, appears from under Royce's arm. Seeing her son, she warns him off, shaking her head and making shooing motions with her palms. Cal continues trotting beside the semitrailer, shouting, *"Mom, Dad! Mom, Dad!"* and distractedly fending off the moldy oranges and the chunks of asphalt hurled against either it or him.

Eventually, though, Cal stumbles and falls, tripping over some debris in the street, and by the time he has regained his feet and caught up with the trailer, the barrage from the spectators—led by the gleeful hard hats—has become a lethal rain, and Royce and Dora Jane Pickford have thrown themselves down on the bed of the vehicle to cover the bodies of people younger than they.

It's hard to see through the smeared murals on the shields, but another block and a half up the avenue, Cal notices that his dad's prostrate body is reacting to each new missile blow not like a man experiencing pain but like a puppet spasming in reply to a touch or a nudge. As for his mother, he can no longer even find her in the pile of bodies shifting on the trailer bed.

"Mom, Dad! Mom, Dad!"

Someone hits him across the back with a board—possibly a canoe paddle—and he goes down facefirst on the July concrete, twisting over and up to avoid being pinioned there. Nevertheless, a hard hat—a bullish fellow about Cal's own age—briefly straddles and rides him, meanwhile working his pocketknife to cut off the braid that has identified Cal as a troublemaker.

It is only after Cal has frantically fled this hard hat that he realizes what a favor—given the mood of the city—the guy has done him. Without the pigtail, he looks respectable enough, and he can go anywhere he wants, a cowboy on the town.

There is nowhere in this town to go. Dry-eyed but

occasionally dabbing at his face with a handkerchief, Cal locates his pickup. Then he drives back down I-25 toward Walsenburg and Gardner. Doing so, he feels the hurt seep up from the cuts and bruises inflicted on him in the city; he senses, too, the beginning of the long hurt that his parents' violent deaths will exact from him. Probably for the rest of his days.

Cal opened his eyes to discover that his visions of Miss Emily, Dora Jane, and finally Royce were fled phantoms. He was alone in the saddle room, down on all fours in its shower stall. His eyes were like scoured china cups, empty and dry. His mouth was lined with flannel.

Finally, he thought. Finally, you've got it out. Lia's mama's death did it for you, cowboy. Now all you need to do is cry.

Cry.

You cried for Philip K. Dick, didn't you? A man you never even knew. A dude you knew only through his weird but wonderful books. And if for him, then why not for your own ever-lovin' parents? Why not for them, Calvin?

Painfully, Cal got to his feet and picked up the roach lying on the tiles. As he stripped it, he funneled the unburnt grass into his jacket pocket and sucked his blistered hand. It wouldn't do to leave any evidence of his sad little party in Brother Jeff's horse barn. Brother Jeff would probably report him to the Georgia Bureau of Investigation.

The Gee Bee Eye.

Cry, he instructed himself. Cry, Cal, cry. For the first time since watching them die, you've abreacted the experience of losing your parents. It hurts, damn it. It hurts like hell. But you've done it, and that's good.

You're not home yet, of course. Not yet. This was a lonesome abreaction, without benefit of guide or counselor, but at least you've taken the first step Lia's been after you to take. You've summoned the long-suppressed. You've gone from a state of amnesia to one of anamnesis. What Kai called the loss of amnesia.

Cal considered his situation. He was confused. *Abreaction* was one of Lia's psychological terms. It meant the remembrance and the cathartic discharge of pent-up emotional material. Usually, you achieved both recollection and discharge with the aid of a trained therapist. Getting to *anamnesis*—Kai's word—put you only halfway there. Cal had just got there by himself, but he could not go any further alone. Not just now, anyway. Discharging the pain of his recollection—going from simple anamnesis to curative abreaction—was going to require help. Without help, Cal understood, he would never be able to cry for his parents.

"Cry, damn you! Cry!"

Nothing happened.

Frustrated, Cal struck the tiles of the stall. Then he grabbed the shower head and twisted it so that it was directed down at him like a gun muzzle. The heels of his hands fumbled at the hot- and cold-water cocks, finally rotating them and bringing down a deluge so prickly and icelike that he yelped.

But Cal stayed under the spray, and soon his hair was plastered to his skull, his nose dripping like a spigot, his best suit soaked from lapels to cuffs, and his copy of *The Broken Bubble of Thisbe Holt* beginning, like something dead, to bloat. His socks squished inside his oxfords, while all around him fell the tears—the cold, unremitting, redemptive tears—that he ached to cry himself.

17

Lone Boy's Datsun whistled down 27. He and Tuyet had often taken their girls to the beach at Callaway Gardens, south of Pine Mountain, so the drive was not unfamiliar. Today, though, miles from Pine Mountain, he hooked a right on a pothole-riven county road and swung past Brown Thrasher Barony.

Jeepers! he thought. The place is jumpin'. Looks like Sale Day at Bill Heard Chevrolet in Columbus.

Seeing the tall canopy on the lawn and all the cars parked in the meadow west of the Bonners' doublewide eased Loan's worry. The stooge hadn't lied to him. There *was* a postfuneral party going on here, and Cal and his wife had to be among those celebrating—uh, commemorating—her mother's kicking, so to speak, the bucket. So their apartment in town would be empty, unguarded.

Certain that no one who knew him had seen him, Loan whistled away from the Barony—and toward Pine Mountain —not on 27 but on Butt's Mill Road. To avoid the traffic uptown, he turned near the rundown community tennis courts and angled through a neighborhood of clapboard and modest brick houses. He came upon the Bonner-Pickfords' duplex on Chipley Street from the east rather than the west. And saw their Siberian husky, nose on forepaws, chained in the front yard under a redbud tree.

Empty, yeah.

Unguarded, no such luck.

Loan turned left on King Avenue and parked the Datsun behind the old Swish plant across from the duplex. He was wearing a black jacket and a yellow hard hat. If anyone saw him, he hoped that he would be mistaken for a telephone repairman or a county surveyor, someone just official-enough-seeming to deflect suspicion. He had the military pistol, loaded with tranqs, under his jacket, and if anyone got too nosy or belligerent, well, he supposed that he could send them to dreamland. A prospect that failed to work like Speedy Alka-Seltzer to settle his stomach.

Hands in pockets, he strolled south on King, casting a glance at the big silver-black dog as he crossed Chipley and noticing with faint alarm that it was watching him. Stupid, Loan thought. You should've parked at a restaurant or something and then approached the duplex from behind, never allowing that monster bowwow to catch sight or smell of you. Too late now, asshole.

Azaleas were blooming along King. Dogwoods, too. Several of the houses had flowerbeds around their porches, flaming pink and orange and purple. Thank God, though, no flaming people peering at the flaming flowers. An empty street. Lone Boy used its emptiness to stomp matter-of-factly around the landlords' side of the duplex and then on up to the Bonner-Pickfords' kitchen door.

Viking, as they called their big-mother husky, was out of sight and quite gratifyingly silent. The only good bowwow, thought Lone Boy, is a quiet bowwow.

He took a pocket calculator out of one pocket and held it up to the door as if doing something official. Then he studied the lock, mulling how to get in without a commotion. He put the calculator away and felt in his pocket for a length of clipped coat hanger that he had brought from LaGrange. He maneuvered this wire, pointed end first, into the lock opening.

Don't let them have a dead bolt, he prayed. Please, Holy Jesus, no dead bolt.

The probing coat hanger bent, and Loan, cursing, had to struggle to pull it out again. Worriedly, he surveyed the backyard and the alley between the duplex and the clapboard house next door. No one was watching, but he could hear traffic grinding through town, only two blocks away. He probed at the lock some more, sweat trickling down his flanks, a mustache of moistness shining above his lip.

Then, bitterly, he tossed the wire away. A decent LAC

would've given us breaking-and-entering training, he thought. Watching old Hitchcock movies on TV just didn't get it.

A heating-and-cooling unit rested near one of the apartment's rear windows. Lone Boy climbed on top of the unit, jimmied loose the window's lightweight screen, and dropped this screen into the grass. The window itself was unlocked, and Loan, not believing his luck, forced it open by banging the heels of his hands against the top sash. Rattling and creaking, the window rose, and Loan could see into the Bonner-Pickfords' bedroom. Leaning across the gap between the duplex and the cooling unit, he peered at his victims' belongings. Startlingly, they reminded him of the kinds of junk that he and Tuyet owned: cheap pine dressers, a bookcase of planks and cinder blocks, a swag lamp. Etcetera.

Rob your buddy, Lone Boy mockingly encouraged himself. Go in there and steal from your friend at the mall.

Another part of him said, altogether sincerely, Just go home, Le Boi Loan. Give up this dirty mission.

But if you don't do it, asshole, you'll have to get "refreshed" by the people at Miss Grace's fuckin' LAC.

Yeah, well, so what?

What do you mean, so what?

Will that be any worse than this? Than playing thief to save your fuckin' self some time and embarrassment?

And it seemed to Lone Boy, suspended like a bridge between the duplex and the cooling unit, that, in this impromptu argument, his better half was mounting the stronger case. He should shut this window, climb down, and go home to Tuyet and the girls. Whatever vindictive punishment the Liberty Belle decided to mete out, well, he must accept it as his due. At least he wouldn't have to deceive his conscience every night to get a little sleep. . . .

Then he heard the Growl. Off to his right, padding around the east wing of the L-shaped duplex, came the imperious Viking. Loan had to look under his arm to see the husky, but the Growl gave him to know that unless he took action, he would soon be dog meat. He could jump down and run, but felt sure that Viking would overtake him before he reached the street. He would die of blood loss, his jugular spurting like a Roman candle. Meanwhile, straddling Loan, the dog would be disgustedly gagging down the flesh and veins torn from his throat.

Not a good choice, Lone Boy decided.

As Viking continued to advance, stalking rather than charging, Loan realized that the dog had slipped free of the collar to which Cal usually attached his chain. Vike had probably shaken it while Loan was banging at the window. In any event, the animal's growl got deeper and more savage-sounding with each menacing step toward the cooling unit.

Loan closed his eyes. What would Daredevil do in a situation like this? Daredevil, Matthew Murdock's superhero alter ego, was blind, of course, but Vike's growl would have alerted him to danger long ago. Maybe, in fact, as the husky tried to pull free of his collar, Daredevil—with his heightened senses and reflexes—would have detected the telltale jangling of dog tags, or even the beating of the animal's heart, and sauntered around the duplex to befriend the husky and to recinch and tighten his collar.

Thinking, Listen, asshole, you ain't no fuckin' Matt Murdock and you ain't got no supper powers, Loan opened his eyes and saw that Viking was about to leap. He'll knock your ass right into the grass, and you'll die with his fangs dripping venom into your eyes. So do something at least halfway smart, Lone Boy, and . . . MOVE!

The only way to go was through the window. Lone Boy propelled himself into the bedroom, losing his hard hat as he struck the rug. He scrambled up, tugging at the pistol under his coat. Viking had already achieved the top of the cooling unit—Loan could hear his claws scritch-scratch-scritching on the metal—and a mere second or two later came exploding jaws-agape through the window.

"Holy Jesus!" Loan cried, stumbling backward, careening into the hall. Maybe six feet away, a hollow-paneled door stood ajar. Loan jumped for it, insinuating himself between its edge and the doorjamb. As he did, he grabbed the inside knob and slammed the door shut after him.

A narrow bathroom contained him. He pushed a button locking the door. Viking crashed against this panel—an upright sheet of stained elm—and kept on shouldering it. Loan freed his pistol, pointed it, backed away, and climbed into the bathtub. He drew the shower curtain to and waited, glad for both a hiding place and a little breathing room—if the dog actually managed to splinter the door.

At least, Loan thought, he's not barking. He's a growler. But I hope to God the neighbors don't hear him. I'm a No-Knock now, a No-Knock without credentials. If they catch me, they'll say I'm a fuckin' breaker and enterer, a bad-guy Phun Ky Cong. Which'll be the end of my Horatio Alger hopes. O my beloved Tuyet, what the screamin' fuck am I doing here?

With his pistol protruding from the shower curtain, Lone Boy waited. Viking had stopped ramming the door. In fact, he had stopped growling. Now he was whimpering, yapping like a chihuahua, and intermittently pacing the corridor.

A lull, of sorts.

It lulled Loan, who, soon enough, let his pistol barrel drop and sat down on a triangular seat built into the shower stall. A brief rest, he thought. A brief rest and then I'll get up and do something about that furry mother.

KRESSH!

Loan scrambled up again, his pistol leveled on the door. The dog had resumed battering its hollow panel.

On the second collision—KRAK!—the button locking the door popped up. On the next impact—CHOK!—the bolt pulled clear of its harbor. On the third—KLUDD!—the door banged open, admitting the husky, who came flying at Loan in a flurry of snapping teeth and redly pinwheeling eyes. The door, flapping back, hit Viking in the flank. Although he yelped, the blow did not slow his attack.

Frantically, Lone Boy squeezed off a shot. A tranquilizer dart struck Viking in the throat; the percussion of hammerfall grumbled like August thunder. Deafened, Lone Boy fired again and again, at least five times, panicked by the tearing pressure of the husky's teeth on his arm. As the descending weight of the animal bore him backward into the shower spigots, he tried to resist but at last gave up and slid down the tiles like a murder victim in a grade-B movie. A moment later, he was amazed to find that he had cracked neither a vertebra nor his vulnerable pumpkin head.

Hey, asshole, *you're* okay, but you've filled this beautiful dog with No-Knock knockout drops.

Lone Boy crawled out from under. Gracefully, he eeled

his way over the tub's edge and then leaned back in to look at Viking's body. But the husky's eyes were already filmed, like those of a reptile. The dog resembled an elegant fur coat unceremoniously dumped in the Bonner-Pickfords' bathtub.

You've got to move your skinny little tail, Loan told himself. If anybody heard all that boom-boom-booming, you're doomed.

And if you're doomed, you might as well make an effort to do what Miss Grace sent you to do. Right? Yeah, right. So see if you can find Mr. Pickford's incriminating pile of Philip K. Dick *samizdat* manuscripts and haul them back to Her Majesty as hurry up as ever you goddamn can.

Arm throbbing, eyes not altogether focused, Lone Boy stumbled about the duplex apartment, rummaging it for the Dickiana that Miss Grace wanted. He looked in bookcases, behind the sofa, in dresser drawers, in closets, under beds, in kitchen cabinets, and finally in the olive-green trunk where Cal actually kept them. He laid the embroidered cushion on top of this trunk aside, lifted the lid, and gazed down—with a kind of addled awe—at the spiral binders that were Cal's prize possessions.

You've come this far, he thought. So finish up right and take 'em all—they're your passports to freedom and prosperity.

Loan got a grocery sack from the kitchen, a double-duty bag, and filled it with the binders. Nine in all. Crazy stuff. *Now Wait for Last Year. Do Androids Dream of Ambitious Veeps?* Stuff like that. Gonzo-weird crap that only a pinko or maybe a dude on horse would keep around.

That was the sad thing about home-grown U.S. citizens. A lot of them didn't know what they had.

The grocery bag with nine spiral binders in it was heavy. Loan supported it at his middle, knees bent, and let himself out the front door, just as if he lived in the duplex. Then he staggered across Chipley Street to the old Swish plant and around it to where his car was parked. Although it was still afternoon, and painfully bright, no one paid him any heed. Maybe they were all still out at that fake wake at the Barony. If so, Miss Grace's stooge had given him a fine, fine tip.

Goddamn, Lone Boy thought, driving home to LaGrange. Free at last. Great God Almighty, I'm free at last. . . .

18

When the rains stopped, Cal looked down. Beside him, shaking water from his muscular forearms, stood Kenneth "Horsy" Stout, Jeff Bonner's stablehand. He had just turned off the shower spigots, and he was squinting up at Cal from his concave, ebony face with a look hinting that Cal had just blown a billion cerebral neurons.

"S'pose to get nekkid 'fore you hop in here," he said. "Do it *that* way, you mess up your duds."

"Hello, Horsy," Cal said. "I was trying to cry."

"Your wife gonna cry when she sees what you done to your suit."

"She'll cry when she sees everybody else seeing what I've done to my suit."

"Reckon so. So whyn't you come on out here and change, Mister Cal? 'S mostly all ridin' garb, but it ain't soaked through like the duds you're wearin' now."

What have I got to lose? Cal thought. He followed the crippled dwarf, a black man in his early fifties, into the saddle room and sat down in his drenched suit in front of a locker that Horsy had just opened.

While Cal was removing his garments, the stablehand brought him a large, fluffy towel, a clean pair of boxer shorts, an undershirt, and some black socks. In the locker, Cal found riding britches, a silk shirt with puffed sleeves (Douglas Fairbanks or Errol Flynn might have worn it in a 1930s swashbuckler), riding boots, and a polo-player's cap.

"I wear this crap, I'm going to look like a friggin' dude."

"Gonna look like Eve's bare-ass Big Daddy if you don't."

So Cal dried himself and grudgingly pulled on the equestrian gear. Everything was a near fit, even the boots. While he was tugging them on, Horsy brought him a beer from the refrigerator and sat down on the end of the bench with a can of his own.

Cal quit tugging at his boot long enough to take an eye-burning swallow. A malty cold roared down his throat, washing away some of his shame at being dressed like an Ivy League Tory.

"Thanks."

"Sorry 'bout Miss Emily, Mr. Cal."

"Did you know her?"

"When I was little—'course I *always* been little—she was one soul who didn't treat me like no freak. So I'm sorry 'bout her. 'Cep' for the horses, I'da been at her funeral."

"Are you always out here, then?"

"Near 'bout. Sometimes I gotta be other places, 'course, but I hafta have somebody take me there."

"Mister Jeff? Miss Suzi?"

"If they ain't too busy. If they is, well, then, somebody else—'cause I *do* like to travel, Mr. Cal."

This was news to him. Cal supposed that Horsy confined himself to Brown Thrasher Barony not merely because his duties so dictated, but also because he felt uneasy under the prying eyes of strangers. (Of course, he had once seen Horsy sitting in a tree on Highway 27, but that had been an hallucination, and he sure as hell wasn't going to mention *that*.) Actually, though, Cal knew only a few basic things about Horsy, most of which he had gleaned from the Bonners or his own haphazard observations.

Horsy had his living quarters in the stable—not in the saddle room but in one of the haylofts over the thoroughbreds' stalls. A bed, an army footlocker, a chifforobe, a reading lamp, not much else. But he liked the privacy of this arrangement, and Suzi said that she had often seen him gamboling about the stable, swinging from rafter to rafter, climbing barricades, even tightrope-walking the tops of stalls. He inhabited the place, in short, much in the way that the hunchback Quasimodo had inhabited the cathedral of Notre Dame. His dwarfism had crippled him, causing intermittent flashes of agony in his legs, hips, and chest, but he had the upper body strength of an ape (no racial slur intended—it was a surprising compensatory fact of his unique build), and he refused to let his pain, even when severe, restrict his activity.

As for his background, it was all local. A woman not herself a dwarf, Elizabeth Stout, had raised Kenny without any help from his father, who could have been any of four or five different men. And Kenny survived because of his mama and the fanatic protectiveness of an older brother, Eldred, who fought bullies and catcallers at the first snide or abusive syllable.

After World War II, Eldred had laid out some of his hard-earned cash to buy Kenny a shaggy, sway-backed pony, which the Stouts had kept tethered to a chinaberry tree in the backyard. Kenny had fed it hay and broken it to the bridle.

Now, apparently, Horsy had no surviving family in the States. In 1965, in Selma, Alabama, Eldred had suffered a ruptured spleen during a direct-action voters' registration campaign organized by Dr. Martin Luther King. A year later, in an Atlanta hospital, he'd died from complications. As for Horsy's other brothers and sisters—and his septuagenarian mama—they'd put their names, uncoerced, in a federal hopper for the Return to Your Roots Program begun by the Nixon Administration after the defeat of the North Vietnamese. Three years ago (about the time Jeff was taking over the Barony for Denzil Wiedenhoedt), their numbers had come up, and they'd all gone off together on an ocean liner bound for Nigeria. Sick to death of fightin' King Richard and his followers' bullshit, they said. Horsy had stayed at home because he liked his job and had no heavy political gripes to level at anyone. And because he was doubtful that very many horses lived in Nigeria, anyway.

"Where do you like to travel to?" Cal asked him. "Besides into Pine Mountain."

"Oh, all over."

"Inside Georgia, you must mean. The Travel Act makes it hard for folks like us to go anywhere else."

Horsy finished off his Budweiser and crushed the aluminum can in his fist. "Mister Cal, I go anywhere I've a mind to."

Sure you do, Cal thought. Anywhere you've a mind to,

even the topmost branches of a pine on Highway 27. "Well, like where?"

"Like Selma, Alabama. Like Washington, D.C. Like Santa Ana, California. Like ol' Von Braunville on the Moon."

Cal laughed, shaking his head. Horsy had a better sense of humor than he would have expected.

"Jus' got back from the ol' Moon a week or so ago, Mr. Cal. Nice 'n' dry. Nice 'n' quiet. I always like it."

"You always like it?" Cal said, bewildered.

"Yes, sir. Even though it warn't only me that was there this last time but a brand-new pilot angel from the Holy Ghost. A new pilot angel that took me over during one of my spells."

What the hell, thought Cal. What is this crap? Horsy just got back from Von Braunville, which he'd visited with a "pilot angel"? Does that make sense, or has the Black Dwarf of Br'er Jeff's Barony flipped his ever-lovin' wig?

But Cal also experienced a sensation of macabre *déja vu*—what a psychotherapist might call paramnesia, the re-membering of events that are only now taking place.

"Spells, Horsy? What do you mean, spells?"

"It's been happenin' to me ever since I was a young'un, Mister Cal. My pony—I called him Phineas, after a uncle of mine—well, Phineas one time cut loose with me on his back and run me up under a clothes line in this white lady's backyard, knockin' me on my tailbone and bustin' my head. So now and again, ever since, I take spells that jus' decommission me for a hour or so. While I'm down, decommissioned-like, I travel."

"You travel?"

"Yes, sir. But only if a pilot—a angel, you see—comes in to fly me off to wheresoever we're goin'. Las' week, well, it was the Censorinus base. I had me a fine time."

"Nice and quiet. Nice and dry," said Cal dazedly.

"Yes, sir. Relaxin', like. Even if this new pilot that took me did make me jump and tumble some."

Spells. Cal recalled Suzi's speaking of Horsy's problems in this regard. Occasionally, it seemed, he would black out and lie comatose anywhere from thirty to ninety minutes, and then awaken again, not groggy and defeated but alert and (to all appearances) refreshed. He refused to see a doctor for this condition, saying—insisting, in fact—that he'd gone as a boy: Elizabeth had taken him, and later Eldred had too, and all the doctors could tell them was that he'd suffered a strange but not life-threatening injury to the right side of his brain.

Not life-threatening, Suzi said, *if* Horsy blacked out while he was lying in bed or sitting in a chair, but potentially fatal if he was stricken while doing acrobatics in the rafters. Oddly, though, these blackouts always occurred when he was somewhere relatively safe, in bed or at table, and he had survived them so long without hurting himself that even Jeff, the worrywart of the Bonner clan, had conceded that he was unlikely to kill himself or anyone else succumbing to one of his spells. Still, it was always in the backs of their minds that Horsy would probably die from an unforeseen side effect of these spells, if not from the physical complications of his dwarfism, and they had all had to work like crazy pretending that Horsy Stout was—as he himself claimed to be—"as healthy as a horse," "as stout as a stud."

"So if anyone ask you to," the dwarf was saying, "you go."

"Asks me to what? Go where?"

"Why, to the Moon, of course. If anybody ask you to go there, you gotta do it. Very edyucashun'l."

"I think maybe I'd better get back to Lia, Horsy." Cal rose, gathered up his wet clothes, put them on hangers, and, at Horsy's suggestion, hung them in the shower stall to dry. He picked up the bloated copy of *The Broken Bubble of Thisbe Holt* and, reluctantly, dropped it into a wastebasket.

Then he and the dwarf exited the saddle room and strode side by side—Cal walking casually, Horsy half trotting—toward the immense open doors through which the eastern pastures were visible.

Before they reached the doors, Grace Rinehart, Hiram Berthelot, and Denzil Wiedenhoedt appeared in this sunlit opening and came on into the barn, squinting to adjust to its butterscotch-tinted gloom. Two Secret Service men remained outside, ostentatiously on guard.

"Horsy," Wiedenhoedt cried, "Secretary Berthelot wants to view the thoroughbreds! Let's give him a tour!"

"'Scuse me, Mr. Cal. Duty done jus' called." He hobbled off toward the two men, who had separated from Miss Grace to stroll past Divine Intervention, Ubiquity, Valerian, and the other nine thoroughbreds whose stalls made a ritzy train through the tunnel of the stable.

Hiram Berthelot waved at Cal, to acknowledge his existence, but Wiedenhoedt was too busy showing off his horses to waste his time on pleasantries.

Now, though, Miss Grace was stalking Cal. She met him in the center of the cathedralesque barn.

"We have a proposition for you, Mr. Pickford," she said.

" 'We'?"

"Hiram and I. Lia still hasn't formally agreed to do LAC work for me, or to cast her lot with Hi when we make our presidential bid in '84, but she's coming 'round. She sees that I'm not such an overbearing soul, not such an ogre."

"Did you come to Miss Emily's funeral to convince her of that?"

Grace drew back as if Cal had flicked her in the nose with his forefinger. "You're not still upset because I bought my Brezhnev bears from you under false—false but harmless— pretenses? Or are you?"

"If you're rich, white, right, and over twenty-one, you can buy Brezhnev bears under just about any pretenses you want. I guess you qualify."

Now her squint was appraising rather than pupil-adjusting. "I really don't like your tone, Mr. Pickford."

"What if it were higher?" Cal essayed a falsetto: "Would you be more favorably disposed? After all, us high-toned folks gots to stick together."

"Up yours, *Prick*ford." She started to turn and leave, but Cal grabbed her elbow and turned her about. He had flown headlong into a hurricane, talking to her as he had, but now he would behave, and maybe even redeem their meeting by showing her that even a has-been hippie could change his stripes . . . from American-flag campiness to designer *haute couture*.

"Wait. I'm sorry. What proposition?"

"Is there someplace else we could talk, Mr. Pickford? I feel like I'm in an empty church."

Escorting her by the elbow, he led her to the saddle room,

but, outside its door, she said, "My God, it smells like a combination leather shop and locker room in there. Are you trying to establish your credentials as a full-fledged male?"

"Not that I know of. I was only trying to find a semiprivate place to talk."

"Not here. Even outside would be better."

So he led her down the northern side of the stable, where the quarter horses had their stalls, thinking that they could sit on a bench in the shade of one of the building's eaves. Meanwhile, Hiram and Denzil, the Katzenjammer Kids, were playing Radioactive a surprise visit—about a mile across the vault of the stable—and the horse was snorting and stamping as if not all that glad to see them. Cal could sympathize.

Grace stopped at an empty stall, pushed its door inward, and said, "This'll do. This is fine."

The saddle room won't do, Cal thought, but a horse stall is okay? All right. Suit yourself. He entered behind the actress, thinking of her as an actress, and they sat down on one of the plank ledges that Horsy had built to get himself closer to his work. Two bales of hay were broken and raked out in the corner, but otherwise the stall was immaculate, almost as if Horsy had disinfected every square centimeter.

"Bouquet of Lysol," Grace said.

"Yeah. You wouldn't want to play any leather games in here. Or change your gym shorts, either."

"Would you stop sparring with me? For just a few minutes?"

"All right. What proposition?"

"Hiram wants you to come to work at Berthelot Acres."

Although Cal had resolved not to be tempted by anything that this woman said or did, his heart began to rev. Good-bye to the Happy Puppy Pet Emporium. Hello honest-to-God cattle ranch. If you can't work for Arvill Rudd, then why not for the sockdolager Secretary of Agriculture? But Cal mastered his excitement. "Why?"

"Because you're a cowboy. Or were. And we've got cows."

"Santa Gertrudis cattle."

"That's right. Big-beamed reddish-brown creatures."

"Lia tells me they're beautiful."

"Beauty's in the eye of the beholder. I prefer horses." She

made a gesture that took in the whole of Brown Thrasher Barony.

"I hear you also have Brezhnev bears."

"But you wouldn't be responsible for them. Unless you wanted to be. They're doing fine as is, I think."

"Your cattle aren't doing fine?"

"They're all right. But Hiram feels they'd do even better if we had someone knowledgeable to watchdog and care for them."

This is like a dream come true, Cal thought. Woodbury isn't that much farther from Pine Mountain than the pet shop is, and you'd love the work, you really would. In fact, seeing as how Lia already has her office in Warm Springs, it might be smart for us to move over there. . . .

The actress was studying him, trying to ascertain the content and flow of his thoughts.

In hopes of throwing her off, Cal said, "I've got a really good boss right now. It'd be hard to stop working for him."

So Grace told him what he would earn if he signed on as foreman at Berthelot Acres. She added that Lia and he would be allowed to rent a house, in either Woodbury or Warm Springs, for what they were now paying for their duplex apartment. Other benefits would accrue when they began supporting Hiram's bid for the presidency.

"King Richard's never going to abdicate."

"He's announced that he is. I believe him. Sixteen years at the helm is enough to wear down any man, no matter how great. And I hate that sophomoric epithet 'King Richard.' The people elected him four times, by bigger majorities every time, and he *deserves* to retire to all the honors befitting a man of his accomplishments."

"Amen. Hallelujah."

"Your mama's water must've been a bath of cynicism. You're blind and mean-spirited."

"I see a few things. I love some others."

"If you love yourself, or your wife, accept Hi's offer. You won't get another as good if you live to be ninety."

"What if Hiram—Secretary Berthelot—gets cut off at the pass at the Republican National Convention?"

"What do you mean?"

"I mean, it's hard for me to see him as President Nixon's

successor. If he can't get the nomination, there go your dreams of First Ladydom, Miss Grace."

"But you'd still be Hiram's foreman, and Lia would still be my therapist."

"Wait a minute, now." Cal sought the actress's eyes. "If the President does decide *not* to run, wouldn't he endorse Westmoreland rather than your husband? Westmoreland's been the veep since '76. He's popular, and he's far better known than your husband. So why wouldn't Westmoreland be the nominee?"

Grace smiled. "He's a former general."

"Right. You remember President Eisenhower, don't you? He got his start in the military, I hear."

"And that's why Dick, when Carter came along, got the baseball commissionership for Agnew and pep-talked Westmoreland into running with him. Turnabout, he felt, was fair play, and since *he'd* served as vice president under a man who'd once been a general and a war hero, Dick thought it fitting that a man who was a general and a war hero serve under *him* as vice president."

Dick, Cal thought. Dick, Dick, Dick. The name had different resonances for him than it had for Grace Rinehart.

"And that's one reason," she went on, "Dick isn't going to want to back Westmoreland's candidacy in '84. He remembers Eisenhower's warnings about the 'military-industrial complex,' and he wants a civilian—a real civilian—to follow him."

"So says the man who turned the Pentagon loose on Indochina?" Cal was incredulous. "You're kidding."

"I'm *not* kidding. You see him as a hateful stereotype that has nothing to do with the person he really is."

"I guess that's possible. He never invited me over for a drink so I could get to know him better."

"More sarcasm. But the fact remains: He wants a civilian to succeed him, and the civilian he has his eye on is Hiram."

"He has his eye on lots of civilians, Miss Grace. Sometimes he plucks them out of his eye and puts them on a list."

"Look, Dick's decided that Hi's his man, and what Dick decides, well, that's what happens."

"Yeah, but the best laid plans of lice and ladies . . ."

Where do we go from here? he wondered. She thinks Hi's

going to be our next president, and I don't. She thinks Westmoreland's in line to be dumped, and I don't. She thinks Dick's the cat's meow, and I don't. *Her* Dick, that is. *My* Dick—aka Philip K., aka Lia's Kai—is dead, or mooning about somewhere between death and resurrection.

"Do you want the job we're offering or not?"

Cal shut his eyes. In rapid sequence, he saw floating before him the dead Miss Emily, the dead Dora Jane Pickford, and the dead Royce Pickford. When he opened his eyes again, the temptation to say yes had fled utterly. But he had a twinge—a brief internal tugging—hinting that his self-righteousness was stupid and that he was passing up a perfect chance to get back at those who had robbed him of both his youthful idealism and his parents.

"Well?"

"No, ma'am, I don't think so."

Grace Rinehart was beautiful, stunning even with sweat on her forehead and her hair mussed. Now, though, minute crow's-feet tracked the corners of her eyes and her irises enlarged.

"Pardon me," Cal said. "No, *miss*, I don't think so."

Grace's bugeyes returned to normal. "Yes, it's an affectation, wanting to be called 'miss' when I'm over"—humorously, she mumbled an unintelligible age—"and on my third marriage. Lia tells me as much. I say it's only showbiz, but she insists that it derives—this affectation—from my fear of growing old."

Cal had no idea what to say to this speech.

"Don't you fear that? Growing old? Nearing death?"

"What I fear," Cal said, "is stagnating. Getting old may not have all that much to do with it."

"And you don't think you're stagnating working in, uh, the Happy Puppy Pet Emporium?"

"Maybe." (Cal feared that very thing. My job bores me silly, he silently admitted.)

"Then why won't you hire on? Why won't you all get aboard our presidential express while it's still working up steam?"

"Probably because I'm a Democrat."

After staring at him blankly for a moment, Grace Rinehart began to laugh. Her laughter had no malice or mockery in it, only joy in the absurdity of Cal's professed political allegiance.

"I'm sorry," she said. "It's just that I can't imagine who you intend to place your Democratic faith in. Kennedy wiped himself out at Chappaquiddick, Humphrey's dead, Mondale might as well be, and Jimmy—dear Jimmy—that smilin' peanut farmer undid even the Solid South for your pathetic crew. You all practically had to pay that dumpy man Asner—a television actor, for pity's sake—to run last time, and the President just blew him away. I don't know what else you could've expected, Mr. Pickford. Or who, so far as that goes, you think you're going to sacrifice next time."

Cal gave her a wan grin. "Maybe Mr. Spock. He's about due a shore leave from the *Enterprise*."

This wasn't half so funny as admitting that he was a Democrat. Grace pursed her lips—sympathetically, he thought—and brushed a tangle of hair out of her eyes. Another impasse, another awkward silence. Cal wanted to get up and leave, their talk seemed to be over—but Grace herself made no move to rise. Damn. What could he say to blunt his refusal of her job offer and to ease his anxiety? What conciliatory word?

"Time hasn't done you in," he essayed. "You're still a looker, Miss Grace."

"In the evening. Under light like this." She looked up at the slant-set skylight. Then, with no other preamble, she slowly undid the top two buttons of her dress.

Cal stood up. "Listen . . ."

She stopped. "You were hoping . . . well, not hoping, exactly, but wondering if perhaps I'd do something like this."

"No. No, I wasn't."

"Wondering what it would be like to screw a film star. To be able to tell yourself, lying in bed next to the faithful Lia, that you'd done so."

"Miss Grace, that's not—"

"It hadn't crossed your mind? Not at all? Not even the way a spiderweb might brush your forehead?"

"Jesus," Cal said. "Jesus."

"Perhaps we *should've* talked in the saddle room. At least the stink there would've proved to me which gender you belong to."

"Listen, you're not seriously proposing that we get down in the hay together, are you? On the same afternoon that my wife's mother was buried? With kaboodles of other people doing tangos around us on the very premises where you'd like us to get intimate? Is that your latest proposition?"

"I seldom make much noise. What about you?"

"My father told me never to put myself in a place where I had to fuck anybody with my pants on. I'm not about to take them off, borrowed or no, in a setup as spacy as this one. *Mrs.* Berthelot."

She smiled, a sorrowful rather than a sardonic smile. "You'll regret walking away—*and* your jackass nobility— later."

"I don't think so."

"No?"

"No. Have you ever balled anybody in the hay? Try it with Hiram. It'll make your cute little fanny itch for a week."

With that, Cal exited the stall; he walked all the way across the stable's concrete floor, past the beret-wearing agents at its entrance, and back down the lane of flowering quince and azaleas toward the canopy under which Lia sat. Approaching, he could hear Denzil Wiedenhoedt's jukebox blaring "That Old Rugged Cross."

After showing his boss's boss and Secretary Berthelot around the stable, Horsy went back to the saddle room. He fixed himself a corned-beef sandwich and laid hands on another beer. An easy day, once you got past poor Miss Emily's funeral.

While toddling around the saddle room sipping and eating, Horsy glanced into the wastebasket. There sprawled the water-logged book that Cal had discarded, *The Broken Bubble of Thisbe Holt.* Horsy fished it out. It looked semi-interesting, but it was all swole up with shower water, as fat as a June-bug grub. It would have to dry out for him to read it, and, once it had dried, it'd still be plump and hard to thumb.

Later, he carried it to his rafter room above the thorough-breds and put it on his bedside table. Later yet, sitting in his barrel chair, he began perusing the sodden book. As he did, one of his spells ambushed him, and he was lifted through the stable's ceiling like Elijah going up by a whirlwind into heaven. . . .

19

"My God!" Lia cried. "My God!"

Cal hurried into the bathroom after her. His hand moved to her nape; his fingers began to knead the tautness there.

"The No-Knocks," he said. "The stinkin', goddamn No-Knocks."

"What did they do to him, Cal? What did they do?" But she knew already. Vike's absence from his spot under the redbud tree had been their first clue that something was, in Cal's words, "bad wrong."

And then the front door, unlocked and ajar. Dirt stains on the living-room carpet. Followed by their discovery of Viking lying in the bathtub like a mound of ragged wolf pelts.

Cal knelt beside the tub to check the husky out. Lia stared down with her hands gripping her face as if to let go would be to allow it to fly away. The funeral, the ordeal at the Barony, and now this. Numbing capstone to a day that, until now, had not been as bad as she had expected. Driving home from the Barony with Cal dressed—inexplicably—like a polo-playing pirate had lightened her mood, as had the thought of collapsing on the sofa with her shoes off and a stiff drink in hand.

"Tranquilizer darts," Cal said. "See 'em." He lifted the dead weight of Viking's head and struggled to turn it toward Lia. "One or two would've probably only knocked him out—he was big enough to handle a fair-sized dose—but whoever did this, riddled him with the goddamn things. I count five. No, six." He eased the great head down again and carefully began plucking darts.

"Vo Quang Lat," Lia said.

Cal glanced up at her in puzzlement.

"The Vietnamese they tranq'd the day that Grace drove me down to Fort Benning."

"Well, your conniving bitch was behind this, too."

"No. This was a break-in. Just a break-in. Why would Grace want to kill our dog?"

Even as she said this, though, Lia knew that Cal was right, that the woman with whom she was now profitably counseling one day a week had ordered this hit. Why, though? Why kill poor Vike, her four-legged sweetheart? Well, because he had posed an obstacle to the No-Knock looking for incriminating evidence against either Cal or her. As this awareness dawned, so did an expression of disgust on Cal's face. He came out of his crouch and pushed brusquely past her into the hall.

"Your *samizdat* manuscripts!" she cried. "Your Dick novels!"

"You think you have to tell me? You think I don't know?" A moment later, from the library, he shouted, "They're gone! Damn it all to hell, *they're gone!*"

Lia went to the door. Cal was on his knees beside the trunk, shuffling through the remaining kipple, mostly letters, notebooks from college, some innocent *samizdat* manuscripts that no one but Cal could possibly care about. The most precious remaining items were of course the letters from his parents. He held a batch of them in his hands, like stocks that a down-trending market has rendered nonnegotiable. He looked both comic and pathetic. Why hadn't he just burned his dangerous Dick material before their move from Colorado? Hadn't she asked him a dozen dozen times?

"Have you ever mentioned my Dick collection to her, Lia? Did you ever once let it slip that I had this stuff?"

"Cal—"

"*Did you?*"

"Yeah, sure, that's all we ever talk about! How may I get my hippie hubby in deeper dutch with King Richard's Court? 'Outlawed P. K. Dick novels? Yes, Miss Rinehart. A whole trunk of them. When would it be convenient for someone to break in to get them? I hope it won't be too much trouble for your hired thug to murder our dog while he's picking them up. Oh, really. That's wonderful.'" Lia, gritting her teeth, began to cry.

"I'm sorry," Cal said.

He came to her and embraced her. As he held her, they heard their landlady, Mrs. McVane, yoo-hooing from the front door.

The woman came on into the apartment. Her husband was in the hospital in Columbus with a troubling numbness in his arms, but she herself had just come home from the reception at the Barony.

"Lia, darlin', what's happened? What *else* has happened?"

"A break-in," Cal said. "A goddamn break-in."

Calmly, Lia disengaged from Cal's comforting arms and hooked her elbow through Mrs. McVane's so that she could escort the woman back to the front door, assuring her landlady with every step that they would be fine, they just needed a little time to straighten things up and grieve for poor Vike.

Mrs. McVane expostulated with Lia, begging to be allowed to help, volunteering to call up two of Roger's friends to assist Cal in carrying the husky outside and burying him. Poor Lia's second burial of the day. Such a pity, such a pity.

It took about ten minutes to maneuver the woman back into her own half of the duplex. She was sincere in her desire to help, and Lia appreciated her concern. But the last thing either she or Cal needed now was another well-meaning deluge of compassion. They had stood in a rain of solicitude ever since Miss Emily's death, and Lia would melt—dissolve and runnel away—if she had to endure its merciless mercies for even five more minutes. Aloneness was what she required. Cal, too, probably. Tomorrow, of course, or the day after, further consequences of the No-Knocks' break-in would reveal themselves, and their lives would change again. . . .

Lia reentered the apartment and closed the door. Mama dead, Vike gone, Cal's Dickiana stolen. Disaster on disaster.

Where was Cal now? Lia found him in their own bedroom, sitting cross-legged on the floor with the window open behind him and the screen missing. In his lap rested a bright yellow hard hat such as those worn by men working construction. Cal had his hands on this hat as if it were a fortune-teller's crystal.

His face, meanwhile, was twisted with emotion. Tears beaded at the corners of his eyes and made snaky red paths down his cheeks. Lia was surprised to see him responding so vehemently to Viking's killing. He was usually more reticent, more reserved. Even Miss Emily's death had not prompted him to cry. In that event, he had been her comforter, not her fellow mourner. Maybe, of course, this was his response to a culminating series of shocks.

"What is it, honey?" Lia asked. She knelt before Cal, put her hands on his collarbones, and kissed his forehead.

"I'm abreacting," he told her, his voice as thick and frayed as unraveling hemp. "Finally, Lia, I'm abreacting." He lifted the yellow hat as if it would explain this strange remark.

It clarified nothing for Lia, not yet anyway, but there was so much muted hope in the gesture that she said, "Good. That's very good, Cal. . . ."

Later that evening, Le Boi Loan was on duty in the Save-Our-Way convenience store on Highway 27 out of LaGrange. Pleading illness, he had missed his shift at Gangway Books to do his No-Knock dirty work for Grace Rinehart, and now he really did feel ill. A knot kept shifting in his belly; his brow burned as if smeared with Ben-Gay; his hands were as cold as the ice in a Sno-Kone machine.

Perhaps he should have gone on home to Tuyet and the twins. Of course, then he would have had to lie to them to explain his early departure from the mall. Better to report for work at Save-Our-Way and make some money than to shirk his second job and to deceive his wife. But, dear God, he could still hear the echoes of his pistol shots and see Cal Pickford's beautiful Siberian husky muzzle-down in the bathtub.

Shit, but his gut hurt! If only there were a new *Daredevil* to take from the whirl-rack and read. But there wasn't. The June issue wasn't out yet, and recently he'd heard rumors from a pair of comic-book fans who frequented the store that Frank Miller, the only artist-writer to make *Daredevil* come alive for them, was about to jump from Marvel to Stupendo, and that he might even leap from comic art to the design of campaign posters and the development of animated TV spots for whoever became the Republican presidential candidate in 1984. That was still a good ways off, but it showed that Miller had his eyes set on the future.

Maybe you should take up drawing again, Lone Boy told himself. You were pretty good for a while.

And so he brought a pad of paper out from under the counter and with a red Bic pen drew a caricature of King Richard throwing out the first ball at the opening game of the Washington Senators' new season. But the ball was a hand grenade, and the player trying to catch it was the Senate's minority whip, who always tried to block passage of any bill favored by the President.

Maybe you could start a comic, mused Lone Boy, devoted to the adventures of, say, "Masterman Milrose."

Angrily, Loan wadded up his drawing and dropped it in an empty box behind the counter. A dumb-ass idea. All the good superheroes have already been invented, and if the President were going to have a series devoted to *his* heroics, he'd get Frank Miller to do it and not some fuckin' upstart Americulturated Vietnamese with no track record. A really dumb dumb-ass idea, asshole.

Loan's head ached, his stomach sloshed sea-sickeningly, and his tongue felt like a woollybooger. He found some aspirins in a tin next to the cash register, used his thumb to push them into a cup of lemon sherbet from the dairy bar, and ate them with a plastic spoon from the picnic-supplies department.

He still felt lousy when a car roared up and parked in front of the shop. The dork who'd given him the pistol and the tranquilizer darts climbed out and came rolling into Save-Our-Way as if he owned the place. He nodded, paraded up and down every aisle, and halted at the magazine and paperback rack near the checkout counter.

Here, the stooge lipsynched *National Enquirer* headlines and ogled the bazoomas of the gals on the covers of such books as *Tart, Tender Torment,* or *Tender, Torrid Tart.* Literary junk food that sold in depressing quantities even out at Gangway Books.

The only other person in the store, a tek-school student

who'd been playing a video game, lost his last quarter and left.

"'Dju get 'em?" the stooge asked, still casually spinning the whirl-stand of paperbacks.

Lone Boy continued eating lemon sherbet.

"I asked you if you got 'em, gook."

"And gook to your goddamn racial insults. Stick 'em where the *E. coli* roam, numbnuts." Figure that out, Lone Boy thought, grim in his certainty that the stooge would try to strong-arm him.

Instead, the burly man said, "Forgive me, Mr. Loan," and came to the counter with three paperbacks, none a bodice-ripper. Loan saw that they were self-help titles, the topmost being *Eliminating the Negative: Individual Affirmative Action for the Underconfident*.

"They're for my wife's brother," the stooge explained, not in the least embarrassed. "He's on a self-improvement kick."

"Okay, good. They've all been big sellers lately. But you've missed one that *you* might like, too."

"Yeah? What's that?"

"*Twenty Days to More Discreet and Satisfying Nose Picking*. I think there's a copy behind *Flame's Flaccid Fury*."

Miss Grace's emissary simply stared at him—contemptuously, it seemed to Loan. Then he said that he had come for some books that weren't on sale at either Save-Our-Way or West Georgia Commons and that if Lone Boy didn't have them, that'd be too bad, not only for him but for his family, too: Lone's refresher course at the Fort Benning LAC might turn out to be more time-consuming than anybody had expected.

"They're in the trunk of my car," Lone Boy said. His stomach dropped again. The sherbet in it, the aspirins that he'd eaten, roiled in him. This was his final chance to keep the *samizdat* manuscripts out of Grace Rinehart's clutches, and he could tell already that he had blown it, that he was giving in to the worst qualities in his makeup: ambition, greed, disloyalty.

Lone Boy led his visitor outside to his Datsun. The transfer of the stolen Dick novels—in a brown grocery sack—took less than thirty seconds. The Secret Service man set them on the floor of the backseat of his automobile. Then, from the inside pocket of his sports coat, he pulled out a flimsy pamphlet, which he thrust emphatically at Loan.

"Here. A token of Miss Grace's appreciation." He went around the nose of his car, climbed in, and drove away.

Lone Boy stood on the raised sidewalk outside the Save-Our-Way store, under the magnesium glare of its fluorescents, watching the evening traffic go by. He knew without looking at the pamphlet that the agent had given him—at Grace Rinehart's bidding and with her full complicity and connivance—an advance copy of the June issue of *Daredevil*.

It wasn't thirty pieces of silver, Lone Boy supposed. But it would do, it would do. . . .

"Do you know when I realized I was getting old?" Mr. Kemmings asked Cal the next morning at the Pet Emporium. My Main Squeeze was stretching out lazily for a long postprandial nap.

"No, sir," Cal said, his mind not really on either Mr. K.'s words or Squeeze's lassitude.

"It must've been Lia's mother's funeral that made me remember this, Pickford. I've been to too many funerals, and each one makes me think of all the others. Anyway, I believe I first knew I was getting old when Keith, our son, was about fourteen.

"We didn't have central heating. We used—I still use—space heaters. Dearborns burn either natural gas or propane, depending on where you live. When you turn a space heater on, it takes the chill off the air, but it also sucks all the moisture out of it. Folks who stay indoors a lot end up with parched mucous membranes and sore throats."

Cal was absentmindedly listening to this spiel as he restocked the shelves with flea collars and fish food.

"What we used to do—to keep some humidity around us—was put a little pan of water on the ledge in front of the flames. Worked, too. Only thing was, in really cold weather, when the flames were ripplin' high, turnin' the grate stones orange, well, the water in your pan would evaporate pretty damn fast. You had to keep toting in a teakettle to refill it. Got to be a pain."

"Reckon it did," Cal said, thinking, What's the point, Mr. K.? What are you trying to tell me?

"So once I thought of getting Keith to do it. I was watching TV and didn't want to get up, and I must've thought a tractable teenage kid would do as well as a footman. But Keith was watching, too, and didn't want to do it, either. Not only did you have to fetch the kettle from the kitchen and fill the pan, you had to take the joker back. *Two* trips, and the hallway between was cold.

"Keith grumbled and moaned when I asked him, but soon enough went off to do it. When he came back from the kitchen, though, he wasn't toting the kettle. He had a load of ice cubes in his hands, and just as I was about to shout, 'Hey, boy, what the hell're you doing?' he dropped those cubes— clunketa-clunketa—into the heater pan and came over next to me to watch the TV again.

"I was on the verge of scolding him when I thought, What for? That took some ingenuity. I'd've never thought of it. But Keith thought of it right off, a way to get water to the space heater without making two trips. And only a fresh mind—I told myself—could've come up with it. Me, I was pushing senility, and all I could do was marvel at Keith's cleverness." Mr. K. chuckled in memory and appreciation.

But, Cal reflected, the kid's been dead for seventeen years; he didn't even last until his twentieth birthday. History's a goddamn devourer of children. A ravenous eater of the brave, the trusting, and the uninitiated.

"You and Lia doing okay today?" Mr. Kemmings suddenly asked.

"Yes, sir. We're fine." Cal had already decided not to burden his boss with an account of the break-in or of Vike's unjust fate, and, with difficulty, he stayed mum even under the man's solicitous questioning. Over the past several weeks, he knew Mr. K. had come to regard him as a surrogate child, and Cal had a genuine filial respect for Mr. Kemmings, too.

Around eleven, the telephone rang, and Mr. K. said, "Yeah, he's here. Just a minute. I'll have him pick up." He made a shooing gesture, urging Cal into the combination office and stockroom at the rear of the Pet Emporium.

Cal went. He lifted the handset and pushed a lighted button.

His caller said, "I'm renewing our offer. Hire on as

foreman at Berthelot Acres, and I'll forget yesterday's stupid rebuff. For that matter, *both* stupid rebuffs."

Here it comes, Cal thought. Here it comes.

"Hello?"

"I'm here," Cal said.

"And things have changed, haven't they? Your illegal *samizdat* collection is in my hands. Damningly, it includes a letter to you from the author. Possession of such material is a violation of the emended Bill of Rights. A federal offense punishable by from three to fifteen years in prison, depending on the extent and nature of the illicit holdings themselves."

"Philip K. Dick is a respected American writer."

"You're sparring with me again, Mr. Pickford. That reputation is based on his pre-Nixonian output. Unfortunately, the books you own—or owned—were written later, in a seditious and hostile spirit, when the author was failing emotionally and disintegrating intellectually. They couldn't find publishers, and no one pretends that they have any literary merit."

"*I* pretend that they do. Only it's not a pretense. They lack status with the keepers of the status quo because they're defiantly antiestablishment. Angry, not soothing. Compassionate, not cool. Crude, not refined. Whacked-out, not rational."

"That's a very pretty speech, Mr. Pickford. Did you steal it from *A Dictionary of Synonyms and Antonyms*?"

Cal shut up. He hadn't, but it must have sounded like it. And pretty speeches, whether original or pilfered, whether heartfelt or hypocritical, made no difference, anyway. Grace Rinehart had him where she wanted him, and that—damn the bitch to hell!—was in her and Hiram's clutches.

"Still there, Mr. Pickford?"

"Yeah, I'm still here. When do I start?"

"As soon as possible. Give notice today." She rang off.

"Why in fuck did you have to kill our dog?" Cal asked the empty receiver. Then he hung up and slumped against the wall. His whole body was trembling.

After a while, Mr. Kemmings came back to see about him. "You all right, Cal."

"Mr. Kemmings, I'm afraid I've found another job."

The old man—two decades older than he'd been when his late son taught him about toting ice cubes—looked briefly stunned. Then he recovered and nodded.

"I knew I was going to lose you. You're on your way up. Don't worry, though. You'll leave with my blessing. I'm just grateful I had you as long as I did."

Grace Rinehart's Cadillac rested in the gravel horseshoe of an overlook in Roosevelt State Park; its two occupants were gazing out over the tree-studded checkerboard of Pine Mountain Valley. This was the first time that Lia had seen the actress since Miss Emily's funeral. Knowing that Grace had ordered both Vike's murder and the theft of Cal's Dickiana, Lia hated herself for having taken this ride. A woman of courage would've told Miss Grace where to stick it. She certainly wouldn't be sitting in her car listening to her unload the psychic freight of her girlhood.

"You're not taking notes," Miss Grace said. "During our first session, you took notes."

Lia gave her client a malevolent look. Today, she thought, I'm the one who's fading out. I'm vanishing from the lofty branch of my self-esteem like a Cheshire Cat. Why? Because I don't have the pluck to resist your bullying tyranny.

"I want you to take notes."

Lia dug into her purse and extracted a tiny tape recorder. "May I use this instead?"

"That'll be fine. Just so long as you have a record." Miss Grace scrutinized Lia appraisingly. "You really don't want to be here, do you?"

"Frankly, no."

"Then tell me to drive you back to Warm Springs."

Stop it, Lia wanted to shout. Stop tormenting me.

"Because I'll do that. And you'll merely forfeit the honor of my company and the bounty of my fee. Of course, Cal's quit his job at the pet shop, and if you won't be my therapist, I doubt that Hiram's going to want to keep your hubby on as foreman. Then you'd *both* be out of work, wouldn't you?"

"Blackmail," Lia muttered.

Miss Grace hit the car's horn with both fists; the resultant outcry echoed bleatingly over the valley. "It's blackmail, all right, but not because I enjoy exercising power, Lia. It's just that I want you and Cal working for us, it's very important to me that you understand our point of view."

Get out of this car, Lia urged herself. Get out and walk down the road past the Civilian Conservation Corps swimming pool and on into Pine Mountain. Maybe you can hitch a ride before you've worn the soles off your wedgies. But she remained where she was, a dead lump in the actress's hearselike limousine.

"What happened to your dog was an accident."

Lia's pulse quickened, and the words that came out of her mouth had so much bitter energy that she and Miss Grace were stunned by them: "You can talk about anything else you feel like, *but don't, for God's sake, talk about Viking!*"

The other woman looked at her with an odd commingling of awe and amusement. Then she toed off her shoes, pulled her legs up under her on the plush front seat, and gestured a command: Turn on the tape recorder. Emptily, Lia obeyed.

"When I was little, the most important man in my life was my daddy. He was career Air Force, and, now that I think about it, he was built a little like Hiram, taller by a couple of inches but as solid as a fireplug.

"I was born in Valdosta, Georgia. Daddy was stationed at Moody Air Force Base, near there, training all these handsome young guys to be fighter pilots. When I was two, he violated regulations and took me up in a trainer for a ride. Nobody knew but him, my mama, and me, and I can still remember sitting on Daddy's lap watching the nose of that stubby silver plane go angling up into the sky's terrific blueness and then lickety-split back down at the flat red fields shimmering with heat on every side of Valdosta.

"My father loved me to death. He must've been a little crazy, too, because on some later illicit flights—we did this half a dozen times before I turned five—he let me take the joystick and fling our airplane up and down like one of his shavetail trainees. Me, a mere baby, squeezing the joystick and rocketing us around the south Georgia skies just as if I knew what I was doing. Of course, Daddy was there to take over if I screwed up—if I got us climbing so fast that we stalled out or if I bucked us into the beginnings of a death spiral. That was damn good to know, Lia. I never felt insecure piloting one of Daddy's trainers. Never."

What a story, Lia thought. The Freudian implications of your infant joyrides are as plain as blood on a wedding gown. In spite of herself, Lia found that her self-involved client was involving her, too. Recapturing her attention. Neutralizing the anger that had nearly led her to get out of the car.

"What's the point of this reminiscence?" Lia asked. "I mean, what do *you* think the point of it is?"

"I don't know. It was the last time in my life that I remember feeling truly secure. And it happened in circumstances that most little kids—boys and girls alike—would probably find frightening, don't you think?"

"Probably."

"Daddy was a rock, though. He believed that the United States of America was the City of God on Earth. He volunteered to fly in Korea because he figured the Red Chinese would swamp that peninsula and take Japan and all of Indochina if we didn't stop them there. He flew F-84s for sixteen months of our so-called police action. Later, he left Mama and me for some top-secret training at Edwards Air Force Base in California, and it wasn't until he died in a U-2 overflight of the Soviet Union that we found out what Daddy'd been doing. This was in 1961, at the very beginning of Jack Kennedy's administration, not long after the release of *The Broken Bubble of Thisbe Holt*, and it never made the news. Kennedy and Khrushchev were meeting in Vienna in June, and neither that Russian pig nor our fair-haired Massachusetts Democrat wanted another U-2 incident to shoot down their talk the way the Francis Gary Powers fuckup had sabotaged Ike's last scheduled summit with Khrushchev.

"It was a mockery. Daddy overflew Russia to combat communism, but our playboy president and their plowboy premier both pretended that he hadn't even been there. Why? So that JFK and Nikita could look like big shots for the home folks. Which was when I realized that this Kennedy jerk—the guy who'd recently withheld air cover from the Bay of Pigs freedom fighters—was no more trustworthy than the fat man who'd had my daddy shot down. Then and there I started looking for a conservative alternative to Kennedy. I found him in Barry Goldwater."

Oh, yeah, thought Lia, I remember him. He was the patriot who stood up at the Republican National Convention in '64 and declared, "Extremism in the defense of liberty is no vice." Johnson swamped him, but Goldwater's unsuccessful campaign that year paved the way for Nixon's comeback in '68, and the Democrats haven't been able to mount a convincing challenge since.

"So everything you've done since then politically," Lia said, "you've done in memory of your father? Is that it?"

"Of course. There's no doubt about it. And if he could see how my work—my Hollywood activism, my Americulturation programs, my consistent support of Dick's domestic and foreign policies—has contributed to the current health of our nation, well, Lia, I know, really know, that he'd be proud of me. The way he was proud of me for flying that training aircraft—taking its joystick and putting it through its paces— when I was a little girl of four. Shit, yes, he'd be proud. If only he could see. . . ." The actress's voice faded into a breathy sibilance.

Meanwhile, a great melancholy descended on Lia. Grace Rinehart was a megalomaniacal superpatriot with an Electra complex. Her daddy had given her phallic control of an Air Force trainer during her toddlerhood. Later, when she was building a screen career that would have secured his everlasting admiration, he had perished over the Soviet heartland during the administration of a man she could only regard as an opportunistic rake in his private life and a self-seeking traitor in the public performance of his presidential duties. These disparate episodes had shaped the woman's psyche in ways that would probably resist a decade of conscientious therapy, and Lia could not imagine sessioning with her another week or two, much less ten years.

I'll never make this fanatical bitch like herself, she thought bitterly. Even if I make some small headway, I'll do so only at the expense of my own peace of mind. I'm a woman diminished, and how a diminished woman can heal a woman who secretly believes herself unworthy of her dead daddy's love is a mystery I'll never wholly fathom. . . .

20

Vear felt someone shaking him. Rolling over, he saw Dolly, his pie-wedge partner, mouthing something urgent.

". . . a visitor," Dolly's lips finally gave voice. "We've got a visitor, Gordon."

But I've already talked to the President, Vear thought, trying to shove Peter Dahlquist's hand aside. I almost killed him with one of your finagled solenoids. But his bodyguard strangled me, I woke up, and none of it had really happened. . . .

Dear Lord, am I about to have another of those episodes? Vear asked himself.

Panicked, he swung his feet to the floor, almost booting Dolly in the groin, and found to his relief that he was in his room, the quarters to which Commander Logan had ordered him confined (except for shuttle-pilot missions and trips to the mess hall) days upon days ago. It was an even greater relief to see that their visitor was not King Richard but Von Braunville's resident psychotherapist, Dr. Erica Zola.

A woman? In his and Dolly's pie wedge? Wasn't that against base regs?

"Forgive me," she said, "for imposing on you like this. I know how much you value privacy. But an impossible thing has happened, and my orders are to take you and Peter with me to a place where we can safely commune."

"Safely commune?"

"The words of the one who sent me, quoted verbatim."

"Commander Logan ordered you to take my roomie and me someplace where we can . . . 'safely commune'?"

"She isn't talking about Commander Logan," Dolly said.

What the hell's going on? Vear wondered. His commander wanted him to stay in his dormitory dome under a kind of self-monitored house arrest, but Dolly and this woman were urging him to follow them to a tryst with a mysterious order-giver who apparently *wasn't* the base commander.

"You're not talking about the President, are you?" Vear asked.

"Gordon, I've had my own nanophany."

"Nanophany?" Dolly asked Erica.

"Dwarf sighting," she said. "*Impossible* dwarf sighting."

Jumpsuited and barefoot, Vear grabbed her by the shoulders and looked down into her pleasant but vaguely lupine face. "You mean you saw the same dwarf I did? That proves I'm not out of my gourd, doesn't it?"

"I don't know what it proves. Maybe that I'm out of mine."

"You *talked* to him?"

"He's waiting for us, Gordon. All three of us."

Dolly said, "But *I* never saw a dwarf cavorting outdoors without a suit. What the hell does he want with me?"

"Perhaps he'll tell you, Peter. Come on."

"Wait a minute," Vear said. He was growing suspicious. This was a practical joke. Franciscus and Stanfield had recruited Erica to help make him look like an idiot in front of everybody serving at Von Braunville. She would lead him—and the slyly dissembling Dolly—to an "empty" sanctuary in the next dome, and when they got there and let themselves in, Franciscus and all the others would jump out dressed like the Seven Dwarfs. They'd have signs around their necks identifying them as Grumpy, Doc, Bashful, Dopey, etc. One of them might even be wearing blackface and a sign proclaiming himself (hi ho; ha ha) Darky.

"What's wrong?" Erica asked.

"I'm disappointed in you, that's all." Angrily, Vear outlined his suspicions. He paced and fumed. It wasn't surprising that the personnel at the moonbase should fall prey to boredom, but trying to alleviate it by making cruel sport of someone who'd suffered an upsetting hallucination on a crater ledge, well, that was behavior worthy of cretinous fifth graders, not of professionals who took pride in their professionalism.

"What if this had something to do with Roland Nyby?" the woman countered. "Would you still regard it as a barbarous ruse?"

Vear stopped pacing, stopped fuming. No, he thought. If this has anything at all to do with Nyby, you'd never turn it into an excuse to ridicule me. Or anyone else. You'd do just what you're doing now, namely, come to our room and summon us forth. And if I were anything but a horse's patootie, I'd pull on my dome slippers and follow you.

"Lead on, McDuff," Vear said.

And so Erica Zola led Major Gordon Vear and the civilian NASA official Peter Dahlquist, computer troubleshooter, out of C dome, through a little-used connecting tunnel, and into a slump-pit cavern. This cavern, vitrifoamed and lunacreted, served the base as a warehouse for auxiliary supplies and as a motor pool for its 'dozers and exploration vehicles.

Several of the sealed bays in this cavern were airless. Erica had to pause at two or three airlock doors to determine the oxygen levels beyond them before proceeding. Even Vear, a ferry-shuttle pilot, felt like a trespasser here, and he was glad that the amber lights on the tracking console over in HQ dome worked only for base personnel who ventured outdoors.

Dolly had brought one of his mock mockingbirds. Each time they had to stop, he would wind its rubber band and let the artificial bird go flapping about in the tight corridors of the warehouse cum motor pool. This clumsy flapping annoyed Vear, who tolerated it only because it did not bother Erica and because Dolly was plainly fighting to overcome several serial bouts of nerves.

At last, well below the floor of the Censorinus crater, Erica escorted them into a chamber—its atmosphere of 27% oxygen and 73% nitrogen was oddly musty—stacked with boxes of commercial snacks, cans of soft drinks, and crates full of jars of cocktail cherries, boysenberry jam, and Spanish olives. These were food items that several American firms had paid NASA to ship to Kennedy Port and then on to Von

Braunville for promotional purposes. Most of these goods were less than sterling; they warranted warehouse space only because Commander Logan—so the rumor went—had promised a Soviet cosmonaut with whom he had become friendly that the cosmonaut could take a few crates home and sell their contents on Moscow's black market, where almost *any* American-manufactured item was regarded as a prestigious acquisition.

"Here?" Vear asked, glancing around.

"This way," Erica replied. She led them to a sorting stand and told them to fetch three metal stools that workers in this chamber used to reach goods on the upper shelves. Vear wondered where the dwarf was. No one had jumped out at him with a Dopey or a Sneezy sign. Too bad. Such a "surprise" would have been more uplifting than stumbling into this eerie gloom and silence.

"I guess we have to wait," the psychotherapist said.

"But where did you first see him?" Vear asked.

"In my room, Gordon. Just a few minutes before I came to get you and Dolly. He said it was lucky you guys were rooming together because I wouldn't have to disturb anybody else fetching you down here to this rendezvous."

"Okay. And then what happened?"

"He disappeared. He faded out and was gone."

Dolly passed the time by launching his mock mockingbird at the soda-pop cases at Vear's back. Vear finally retaliated by batting the damn thing from the air as it flapped past him on its seventh languorous flight. But why the hell am I so jumpy? the major asked himself. We're anxious, that's all. Like a couple of monks taking their tonsures from a man with pruning shears . . .

Someone appears at the head of the sorting stand. Vear tries unsuccessfully to wrap an identity around this figure. He feels an oscillating uncertainty, warmth giving way to fear, fear giving way to warmth. Are the others similarly affected? Dolly and Erica are staring raptly at the spot where the homunculus slips in and out of focus.

A hologram, thinks Vear. Franciscus and Stanfield have set up a goddamn holo-projector in here.

But the figure slowly acquires resolution, being—just as

Erica has indicated—a Negroid dwarf. He wears blue jeans and a white shirt. The shirt billows almost imperceptibly at the sleeves and shoulders, like wings in a faint breeze.

Before Vear can think of a greeting that does not sound flip or nincompoopish, the dwarf turns to the modular storage unit behind him and takes down a package of soda crackers. Then, again at the sorting stand, he shakes out three crackers, mumbles a prayer or an incantation, and nonchalantly shies the crackers across the table. Vear catches his sedately floating cracker as if it were a small square Frisbee. As both Erica and Dolly catch theirs.

"Take, eat," says the dwarf. (His accent is a kind of basic Californian.)

The three people at the sorting stand eat.

Then the dwarf pulls down three cans of grape soda, pongs their special spouts, and slides them across the table to his guests. Vear briefly wonders why he, Erica, and Dolly—moonbase personnel of long standing—should now regard themselves as this apparition's "guests," but guests, like it or not, is what they are.

"Take, drink," says the apparition.

Vear drinks. So do Erica and Dolly. The only one who neither eats nor drinks is the dwarf, who now seems familiar to the major, not simply because he saw him on the crater rim a few days ago, but because both Dolly and Erica appear to recognize him, too.

"Elijah!" declares the psychotherapist.

"Jesus H. Christ!" says the computer specialist.

"Thomas Merton?" suggests Vear, tentatively.

The dwarf chuckles modestly. "Elijah. Christ. Merton. What can I say? You guys aren't even close. I may've been taken over by Elijah once upon a time, Dr. Zola, but when his spirit abandoned me—back in '76—well, I tried to kill myself. As for Christ, you might get a point or two, Mr. Dahlquist, but only if you're broad-minded. What did you mean that H to stand for?"

Dolly looks confused. "Nothing. It was a profane H, part of an oath. Like when somebody says, 'Jesus X. Christ!'"

"Well, X is the symbol for *chi*, the first letter of Christ if you're writing in Greek. I was sort of hoping, you know, that your H stood for, uh, 'Horsy.' But in English, not in Greek."

Vear feels the hair on his nape dancing, like tiny, filamentous snakes swaying to an unheard flute. Nothing of what the dwarf has just said makes any sense. All Vear understands is that even in misidentifying the apparition, Erica and Dolly have named a *part* of his identity. They've come closer to defining him than either they know or the homunculus is yet willing to concede.

"As for Merton," the dwarf continues, "well, that's flattering, I guess. Seriously flattering. But so what if we both died when we were fifty-three? Coincidence. Stupid coincidence. All Merton and I have in common is our unshakable faith that the Transcendent exists and that It'll talk to you if ever It decides you're worth the effort. And that's about it. That and a quest to understand whatever the fuck we're being handed when the Transcendent finally deigns to speak."

"You told me you'd identify yourself," Erica says. "So why do you have us playing this silly guessing game?"

"*You* guys started zapping out names. Not my fault. But if you still want to play, here's a hint: *Confessions of a Crap Artist.*"

"Philip K. Dick?" Dolly hazards.

"Good, Mr. Dahlquist. The *K* stands for *Kai*." Kai hops onto the table and sits cross-legged. Glorified but hazy, he shimmers there. "Go ahead. Eat. Drink. We may be here awhile."

"We can't *afford* to be here 'awhile,' " Erica protests. "We've got duties to perform, appointments to keep."

"I meant subjectively," Kai says. "Outside this chamber, no time at all is passing. It's stalled. Von Braunville's enchanted, like Sleeping Beauty's castle. If you stuck your head into one of your colleague's rooms, you'd see a red fog hanging over everything and your colleague suspended in that fog like a grape in a bowl of black-cherry Jell-O."

I'm hallucinating again, Vear thinks. Or I'm dreaming. Erica and Dolly aren't really here, and I'm playing out this "nanophany" in a remote corner of my dreaming mind. When I wake up, I'll still be confined to quarters for my trek outside the domes. Nyby will still be dead. Erica won't remember anything about this, and Dolly will have started making mock mockingbirds by the dozens. To boost morale. Which, by now, may be unboostable.

"True, true," Kai, alias Philip K. Dick, tells Vear. "This is a dream, an hallucination. On the other hand, isn't life a dream? And this dream, right now, is more real for you than anything else happening around you. If you decide *I'm* an irreality, well, *you'll* get cancelled, too. Goes with the territory, Major."

This speech frightens Vear. It has the ring of authenticity, as if this dwarf, Dick's current hypostasis, knows exactly whereof he speaks. So play along, the major advises himself. Pretend that this is really happening so that a failure to pretend doesn't wipe you totally out of existence forever.

"If you're Philip K. Dick," Vear says, trying to disguise the quaver in his voice, "why do you look like . . . *that*?"

"Because I'm dead, Gordon, and my own glorified body has only recently ascended to the Holy One. But my consciousness—my soul, you know—hangs on here because the demiurge of this creation (a decidedly lowercase creation) has charged me with rectifying the nightmare that made Nyby and the others up here commit suicide. I mean, up here you can watch how bad everything's going down there, and your despair's enlarged by your perspective on the whole mess. And by the bleakness of your surroundings."

"But a dwarf?" Dolly says. "A black dwarf?"

"Well, the dwarf himself is still alive. I'm just piloting his body. From what I can guess about him, inhabiting him as I do, the angelic hierarchy and some other intermediate souls have also made occasional use of him. He permits it, this Kenneth 'Horsy' Stout, because essentially he's a good man. Also, he likes to travel. He regards benevolent possession—by angels, by in-betweener gofers like me—as a sort of reward for bearing with the handicap of his dwarfism. For overcoming it."

"And is that Stout's actual physical body?" Vear asks. (If any aspect of this situation deserves the designation "actual.")

"It's an incorruptible, virtually indestructible version of his physical body. Glorified before it's time, you know, but subject again to all the slings and arrows that flesh is heir to—at least, that is, when I return it to the consciousness, or soul, dormant in its physical husk. Which lies in a stable outside Pine Mountain."

"Wait a minute," Dolly says. "If you don't take this person's body or soul, what exactly *are* you taking?"

"Not taking. Borrowing. What I'm borrowing is a *potential*, the spiritual body that Stout will become when he himself dies and is raised incorruptible from death."

That's like taking a loaner from next year's new-car models, Vear thinks. Can't be done.

Kai says, "When I borrowed his posthumous potential this time, Horsy was reading a book of mine, and my novel triggered anamnesis in me. Suddenly, I lost my forgetfulness, and remembered my name, and recalled that I'd been to Von Braunville once before. Just to case the joint."

"Why would you want to 'case the joint'?" Vear asks. "What at Von Braunville is of any interest to a ghost?"

"I'm not a ghost, I'm an apparition-at-one-remove. I cased Von Braunville because the core of religion is service to the needy, and you guys up here and all the people on Earth are definitely in need. I wanted you to resolve the problem yourselves, but now I don't think you can, and so I've come to help. And I've come here because I've got good intelligence —divine, or at least demiurgic, intelligence—that this is where you three guys, and maybe a couple of others, can best engineer the redemptive shift."

Dolly says, "What do you mean, 'redemptive shift'?"

"Getting rid of this oppressive historical reality and calling up a freer, more humane reality. Lately, I've been able to visit—or my soul has—an attractive alternative to this time line, and that's the one you guys need to shift over to. You can do it from Censorinus by taking a forthcoming opportunity—one you'll probably never get again—to abreact history."

Vear has not been able to follow Kai's argument very well, but he can see that Erica Zola looks preternaturally alert. Her eyes, normally quite big, now seem as large as gongs.

"'Abreact'?" she says. "You're putting a psychological term in a strange context. Could you be a little clearer, Mr. Dick?"

"Please call me Kai. Okay. Look at this. In your profession, doctor, *abreact* means to express and discharge a heavy emotional burden—unconscious shit—by talking it out in a session with a therapist. Someone like you. But let's broaden *abreaction* to give it an historical application."

"But how? The term's specific to my field."

"How else but by analogy, Dr. Zola? Just suppose that beneath this historical reality lies an unconscious dimension of suppressed events—an entire suppressed history, in fact—that we can bring up and make manifest by . . . well, by *abreacting* them. We'd change history. We'd free these trapped occurrences, permitting them to supplant the warped events making up our own nightmarish time line, and the latter would submerge and sink out of sight, out of mind. Which would effect the redemptive shift—yeah, I know, I'm mixing metaphors—that I've been talking about."

"It's a neat analogy, abreacting a suppressed time line," Dolly says, "but—"

"But what, Mr. Dahlquist?"

"You're assuming that history, like consciousness, has layers. Or, if not layers, unseen collateral cousins. I don't assume that it has either, and if I did, Mr. Dick, I'd wonder how you propose to get the suppressed layers, or the invisible collateral cousins, up into the sunshine."

"I don't think you're hearing me. I'm not *assuming* anything. I've gone over to this other time line. I've walked around in it, I've examined my own place there, and I've taken note—O my little ones—of the big discrepancies between that time line's events and this one's."

Vear's mouth is cottony. He takes a swig of grape pop and asks Kai to fling him a few more crackers. Kai closes the lid on the box and shuffleboards it to him. Vear grabs a handful of crackers and passes the box to Dolly, who liberates a share for himself before proffering it to Erica. Meanwhile, warm grape drink fizzes on the major's tongue with all the pizzazz of a day-old glass of Alka-Seltzer. Why, he wonders, does Kai call us 'O my little ones' when he's so small himself?

Dolly says, "What *are* the major discrepancies, Mr. Dick?"

"I can't enumerate them. It would take too long. Things are better there. Better, that is, *by comparison*. The upsetting thing to me is that although the two time lines run nearly parallel until 1968, one of the big differences *before* '68 is that over here I'm an important American writer but over there I'm a purveyor of genre trash. That's their critical consensus, anyway. That I wrote crap—mindless sci-fi about parallel times, paranoia, androids, aliens, and God. Shit like that."

"Books like *Valis*?" Dolly asks.

"Yeah. Of course, I wrote speculative stuff like that even in your time line, but it's all unpublished. What hurts is that, over there, it's the *only* part of my work, by and large, that's seen print and the literary establishment—the *New York Times* and that bunch—dismisses it as pop-culture trivia. In their view, I belong to the trash stratum and my work is eminently dismissable.

"I do have a cult following over there, but *A Time for George Stavros*, *Pilgrim on the Hill*, *The Broken Bubble of Thisbe Holt*—no one in that time line even thought 'em worth publishing. My cult is a fuckin' category cult, sci-fi fans who think Phil Dick has a pipeline to the Deity. I mean, I guess I should be glad to have a cult, but it's awful knowing that my early realist novels didn't rate publication over there. And I've got a group named for me—the PKD Appreciation Society—full of kids who believe *They Scan Us Darkly, Don't They?* is better than *Nicholas and the Higs*."

Erica takes a sip of grape pop. "But that's the time line you want us to shift over to? A time line in which you're regarded as the trash slinger that the Nixon administration, over here, has been trying to label you for years."

"Hey, listen, don't think I like it. I *don't* like it, having a part of my canon fall between the cracks and disappear. But if that's the price to be paid to abreact a freer time line, fine. I mean, it's a small sacrifice, and who am I in the big picture? The genuinely big picture. Just a writer. That's all."

Erica sets her soda can down, eases herself off her stool, and walks toward the dwarf with her hands on her hips, pondering what Kai has just told them. Kai, watching her, raises his hands in a gesture signifying, That's close enough, don't come too near, I'm not ready for contact. Erica respects his prohibition but lingers at the edge of his spooky aura, and Vear finds himself admiring the psychotherapist for her courage.

"Isn't there any other downside to this shift?" she demands.

For everything taken, something's given, Vear thinks, recalling his imaginary talk with President Nixon. And vice versa. And it's the vice versa that scares us. What must the world at large—not just Philip K. Dick—give up to abreact this freer, more humane time line? An important question.

Kai says, "I'm not supposed to talk about the differences that occur *after* '68, Dr. Zola. I'm only permitted to say that for the most part, it's a better world than this one."

"Who's doing this permitting and not-permitting?" she demands.

"I think that goes without saying, don't you?"

"Then maybe this cult of yours—in the suppressed time stream—is correct in thinking that you have a pipeline to the Deity."

"Yeah, I guess I do. But I'm a spirit now, and I wasn't then. And, technically, this discussion is taking place wholly *outside* time. Don't use it as a measuring stick for my activities when I was mortal, either in this time stream or another."

Vear steels himself to speak. "You've given us the personal downside of the alternative history you want us summon, but you *have* to tell us if there's a major political price to pay. You can't expect us to conspire to 'abreact' your submerged time line—however the hell we'd do that—while we're ignorant of the global consequences. Your readiness to sacrifice your literary reputation to make things 'better' doesn't prove you've taken every important issue into consideration."

Dolly says, "Tell us *some*thing about this other reality."

From his Buddha posture, the dwarf sighs. "Okay, two things. Are they good, bad, or both at once? It'll be up to you guys to decide. I'm here to rescue the United States—not necessarily the world—from the situation that it's got itself into. I really see no alternative. But because I'm enlisting you to help me, I guess you deserve *some*thing in the way of information."

"Give, then," says Erica, audibly impatient.

"Okay. First, the United States loses the Vietnam War. Or we put our South Vietnamese allies into a position that automatically loses it for them. Same difference."

"That's no small thing," Vear says. "That would drastically alter the balance of power in Indochina. And I can't imagine that it'd be for the better, Mr. Dick."

Dolly says, "And the second thing?"

"Because of the prolongation of the war and our retreat before the North Vietnamese, the space program gets put on hold. In the 1982 of my submerged time line, the U.S. doesn't have a moonbase. Von Braunville doesn't exist. In fact, it probably *won't* exist any time before the turn of the century."

Vear listens as both Dolly and Erica tell the dwarf that these seem incredibly dubious examples of how abreacting the suppressed time line is going to improve the world. He must be joking. Is King Richard's reign—one authorized and acquiesced in by the vast majority of Americans—so terrible that they should risk permitting a communist victory in Vietnam and the complete dismantling of the American space program?

Kai, still in the lotus position, explains that they object to the proposed abreaction because they fear that these two startling changes may ramify into unknown historical horrors. Well, they're taking a short-range view of the matter. Besides, Kai's suppressed time line features the full restoration of constitutional democracy in the United States, the example of which has long-term benefits that override the not inconsiderable disadvantages of the defeat in Vietnam and the slowdown—*not* the complete dismantling—of American efforts in space.

The submerged reality, though far from perfect, is *better* than this one. Nyby would not have died there, neither would the other NASA people who committed suicide at Censorinus. These deaths are insignificant statistically, given the population of the United States, but have great symbolic import and a telling correlation to the increase in suicides nationwide. Moreover, the fact that King Richard's reign has unaccountably flourished has given immeasurable aid and comfort, globally, to totalitarians of both the right and the left. The execrable Return to Your Roots Program is blatantly racist in intent and execution. And, according to an outlawed watchdog organization, the number of administration "enemies" who simply "disappear" has nearly doubled every year since the defeat of the North Vietnamese in 1974. The fact that the media are under administration control has either disguised or excused these abuses of power, and most Americans prudently look the other way.

"But why come to us?" Dolly asks. "Us of all people?"

Recites the dwarf, gazing at the chamber's ceiling, "'Philip K. Dick is dead, alas. / Let's all queue up to kick God's ass.'"

Dolly's elegy, Vear thinks. Kai overheard Dolly's little

elegy and from it deduced his potential sympathy for the abreaction of a "more humane" time line.

"And Major Vear? He's on my side because he hates our drift to totalitarianism and admires the late Trappist monk Thomas Merton. He's been waiting—he didn't know it, but he has—for a chance like this to come along."

"And me?" asks Erica Zola.

"You're a former classmate of a young woman named Lia Pickford, née Bonner. You briefly met her husband while attending school in Colorado Springs, and the three of you partied together one evening with a bottle of wine and some top-grade pot and a contraband Jefferson Airplane album playing in the background. You resonated in time to the music. You got off on a P. K. Dick reading that Cal Pickford subjected you to. And you found yourself agreeing—while high on liebfraumilch and stoned on Colombian Gold—with everything negative that he and I had to say about You-Know-Who. Of course, then you returned to your studies and forgot the whole evening, but maybe my manifestation has triggered anamnesis and you know what I'm saying again. Possible?"

Erica appears stunned. You hit it on the head, Vear thinks. She's trying to digest what you've told her.

"I remember," she admits. "You're right."

"But you sublimated your love of justice to a personal quest to become one of the first five women to serve at Von Braunville. And you succeeded. Congratulations."

"Thank you," Erica says, dubiously.

And then no one speaks for a time. Vear can tell that as weird as this audience with the dwarf is, all three of them—not one of whom has ever been much of a rebel—relish the opportunity to help the Kai manifestation topple the tyrant whose government has given them their jobs. They long to effect the mysterious abreaction that will erase a U.S. victory in Indochina. That will cause the domes of Von Braunville in the crater called Censorinus to vanish from the lunar landscape as if no one ever built them.

Which, if the abreaction succeeds, no one will have. . . .

Dolly says, "Okay, we're game, Mr. Dick. But *how* do we do what you want us to do, and *when* do we do it?"

"Watch and wait," says the dwarf, relentlessly fading.

* * *

As soon as the apparition was gone, Vear walked to the end of the sorting stand. He put his palm on the spot where Kai's bottom had rested. It was warmer than nearby areas of the tabletop. Was it possible to hallucinate a "haint" that was . . . *real*? He had just done so. In the company of a respected psychotherapist and a computer scientist famous for his spaced-out rationality.

"Did this happen?" he asked them.

Neither replied. With them, however, he saw that the box of crackers from which they had eaten and the cans of grape soda from which they had drunk were no longer on the table. Nor could they find an open crate that might have held the cracker box or a break in the row of soda cans to show that Kai had removed three for his bewildered guests. All that proved to them that the dwarf had been there was, yes, the warm spot on the sorting stand.

"And our memories that this really happened," Vear said. "You *do* remember this experience the same way I do, don't you?"

The three of them compared. Their individual memories of the past forty minutes matched. What had happened had happened. Or else they had shared a common hallucination.

Erica led them out of the various bays of the warehouse cavern and into the tunnel to the men's dormitory dome. As they walked, they noticed that the air had a pinkish tinge, as if a cloud of red smoke were in the final stages of dissipating. The domes' filter system was working to suck up the anamolous smoke—from what? from where?—and to vent it out onto the lunar night.

Or was it?

Seeing two of their NASA colleagues frozen in midstride, Vear recalled that Kai had said that, objectively speaking, no time at all would pass while they talked to him.

Back in their own room, Dolly confirmed this claim. They had returned to their dormitory hardly a minute after leaving it. So none of them would show up late this "morning" for an assignment. Like the air in the domes, they were completely in the clear. All they had to worry about was the puzzling import of their outrageous collective memory. . . .

21

Lone Boy entered the Happy Puppy Pet Emporium. Mr. Kemmings, the manager, was alone in the shop.

Cal had been gone two weeks now, and Lone Boy feared that the authorities had sent him to a federal prison—possibly even the decrepit, overcrowded one in Atlanta still housing Cuban prisoners of war from the successful invasion of that island in 1975. Its communist dictator Fidel Castro had been hanged on live television at an undisclosed site in the States, but many of the soldiers still loyal to his dishonored cause remained incarcerated in the Atlanta pen.

Nixon justified the cost of keeping them there by using them as exchange bait in any international situation in which American citizens were taken hostage, a policy that had proved a brilliant and popular political coup. Loan himself admired it immensely, but the thought that Cal Pickford might be sitting in a cell next to an embittered, die-hard Castroite amplified his feelings of guilt. He had betrayed Pickford to avoid the inconvenience of a LAC refresher course. He had sold him out for a *Daredevil* comic book.

"What can I do for you, Lone Boy?" said Mr. Kemmings.

"I want to buy a pet."

"For your girls, I'd imagine. A parakeet? A Brezhnev bear?"

"My girls already have Brezhnev bears. One each." Gifts, Loan resentfully told himself, from that ruthless American patriot Grace Rinehart. Bitch of all bitches.

"Oh, really? Where did you get them?"

Uh-oh. Mr. K's feelings are hurt you didn't buy your pigs from him. Hurriedly, Lone Boy said, "They were given to us by a family friend. Hey, would I buy one of those skinned Ruski mutants from anybody but you?"

Mr. K's face uncrinkled from its disappointment, crinkled again from pleasure. "Well, if they've already got 'bears,' what else do you think they'd like?"

"Not for the girls, sir. For me."

"Oh. A dog? Dogs're man's best friends. Of course, parrots can be good company, too, and they live a long time."

Lone Boy made no answer. He walked deeper into the shop. He halted only when he had reached the smeared glass cage holding the boa constrictor that Cal and his boss had always jocularly called My Main Squeeze. The snake, snoozing in a dun-colored stack of its own coils, seemed to have increased in girth since Lone Boy's last visit. Looking at it, he shuddered . . . but knew that it was the perfect gift to terrify and humiliate the woman who'd forced him to do a great evil to avoid a little personal pain.

"This."

Mr. Kemmings was startled. "Squeeze? You don't really want Squeeze. Nobody wants Squeeze. He's expensive."

"That's all right. I've been saving."

"So's his food, Lone Boy. You have to feed him mice."

"That's okay, too. I don't go ga-ga over mice."

"It'll be a pretty big shock for the twins, Loan. Sort of like making them watch Squeeze eat their Brezhnev bears."

"I'm not going to take it home. I'm buying the boa for someone greatly in sympathy with reptilian ways."

Mr. K. nodded, but Loan could tell that he did not really want to sell. His reluctance would have dissuaded him from writing a check for My Main Squeeze except that Lone Boy could still see the Bonner-Pickford's husky dead in their bathtub. Further, insomnia plagued his nights, and he could no longer sit down to eat without suffering a surge of nausea that had limited his recent fare to white rice, apples, and tea. Grace Rinehart had to pay.

"Have you made any plans to get Squeeze to your friend?" Mr. K. asked. "Do you have your car?"

"It'll be a hassle—but I'll manage, I'll manage."

* * *

Cal cradled the gelding's forefoot between his legs, working at it with a hoof pick. A pair of quarter horses that Hiram Berthelot had bought from Brown Thrasher Barony were already well pedicured (Horsy Stout had taken care of them), but the feet of Berthelot's four middle-aged quarter horses needed work. Over the winter their hooves had grown extra horn, or split, or both. And once the tardy spring roundup began, these horses would be at a risky disadvantage if Cal failed to trim, file, and pick.

"Doin' fine, now," he soothed the gelding. "Just hold steady."

It was backbreaking work. Cal had been at it for nearly eleven hours. The saddle of muscles near his lower spine creaked like old leather, and a numbing ache blanketed him dorsally from shoulders to hips. Somehow, though, it felt good. G-O-O-D.

Can't say I'm crazy about the way I got this job, Cal thought, but the job itself is the job I was born for.

Right now, his foremost anxiety was that Lia might already be expecting him home. Also troubling was his nagging awareness that she still bitterly resented Grace Rinehart for causing Vike's death and for blackmailing both of them with the Damoclean sword of those stolen manuscripts. Lia viewed his employment on Berthelot Acres as slavery, while he regarded it as salvation, a private Return to Your Roots program that had given him back his real identity. Or, at least, *part* of it. Nowadays, you couldn't hope for much more.

The horse trap and stable on Berthelot Acres lay about half a mile from the mansion itself. Cal was glad to be at this remove. That he spent most of his work time alone did not bother him. In fact, Berthelot—four days after Miss Emily's funeral, two days after the phone call to the pet shop—had told Cal to do all that was necessary to get ready for a roundup by mid-May. Cal had not seen the man since. Preparing for a roundup—even in Georgia—was a straightforward, if fatiguing and time-consuming, operation, and Cal had been doing it alone to keep from having to hire extra hands until it was time to gather the cattle.

A portable radio on the floor near his stool played a song by Hank Williams, Jr. Next, an upbeat ditty by Berle Haggard (like Miss Grace, a recipient of the Medal of Freedom).

Country-western stuff dominated the airwaves nowadays, and although Cal could get one soft-rock FM station from Atlanta —at least in good weather—the saccharine pap passing for rock 'n' roll on that station made him want to puke. Better a patriotic twang from a guy in a Stetson than a sappy lovesong from another Barry Manilow clone.

And then the seven o'clock news. It began with an account of British casualties and successes in the Falklands Islands since the arrival of its naval task force. Cal listened with less than half his attention, dumbfounded that this strange little war was really taking place.

A pox on their little war, he thought. Finish cleaning up this horse's foot and get your broken-back body home to Lia.

"How's it going, Cal?"

Cal dropped the pick and toppled off his stool.

His new boss, Hiram Berthelot, had entered the prefab stable. The man reached down, clicked off the radio, and lifted Cal off the hay-strewn floor. He seemed to be alone. No Secret Service man had come into the corrugated building with him, and neither—much to Cal's relief—had Miss Grace.

"Fine," Cal said brightly. "Okay."

The Secretary of Agriculture was stocky, four or five inches shorter than Cal—an impressive figure despite his lack of height. His expression was one of bulldog pertinacity and playfulness, and his body suggested power, an amiable, lived-in power that did not have to demonstrate itself to prove that it was there.

Largely because of Arvill Rudd's approval, Cal had liked this man—at least in the abstract—almost from the beginning of his career in Washington. Berthelot had tweaked the President about imposing a price ceiling on beef in '73, during the tenure of his predecessor, and he had managed to keep his nose clean—so far as the media would let you know, anyway —in the six years of his own secretaryship. Now, in fact, King Richard was apparently secretly grooming Berthelot to follow him as president.

"You're here awfully late. I'm glad you are, I wanted to talk to you. But your missus might be worrying."

"It's possible she'll be late, too. Her practice has picked up considerably since I came to work over here."

"Grace thinks the world of her, I know that much."

Yeah, yeah, thought Cal. Grace thinks the world of

whomever she can most easily manipulate. Not excluding yours truly. The object of a seduction attempt on the Wiedenhoedt horse farm.

And, Cal told himself, the secretary was as untrustworthy as his famous wife. You couldn't trust *anyone* in this administration, and if Berthelot sometimes seemed an okay sort—wielding amiable as opposed to vengeful power—well, that was only in comparison to the other current members of King Richard's court.

And so Cal found himself growing increasingly suspicious of his new boss's visit and immediate motives.

Hoping to conclude their conversation quickly, he told the man what he had to do before they could begin their late roundup of Santa Gertrudis calves. One more horse to pedicure. The repair of a compressible branding chute. A bulk purchase of Cutter 3-way vaccine. The sharpening of every dehorning tube in the equipment shack. And, after all that, the hiring of a decent roundup crew. Which here in Meriwether County, Cal thought, will be like flushing all-star ice-hockey players from the African bush. . . .

"Wait a minute," Berthelot said. "Hold it."

"It sounds like a lot, sir. But we should be hard at work by the end of the week—if I can find five semiexperienced guys."

"We'll mechanize as much of the work as we can. On the other hand, you're going to *miss* this spring's roundup."

"I beg your pardon." He felt his stomach tighten. Miss this spring's roundup? Wasn't that one of the reasons he'd been hired? To oversee the branding, vaccinating, castrating, and dehorning of the secretary's precious calves? Had he changed his mind? Had he or Grace decided to indict Cal for possessing *The Doctor in High Dudgeon*, *No-Knock Nocturne*, and all the other anti-Nixon novels that some anonymous No-Knock had stolen from his trunk?

The secretary said, "Don't worry. I'm not firing you. You'll be back for the fall roundup."

"Back? Back from what? I don't get it, sir."

"The President and I want you to undertake a special mission. How would you like to visit Von Braunville?"

"The Moon?"

"Unless they've moved it, that's where Von Braunville is."

"But why?"

"Since '78, we've sent civilians from six different professions up there. A teacher. A journalist. A theologian. An athlete. A poet. The mayor of New York. How would you like to be the first . . . well, the first *cowboy* to set foot on the lunar surface."

"Not very much, sir." But immediately he recalled the phantom Phil Dick's admonition to try risk taking and Horsy Stout's advice to visit the Moon if ever he got the chance. In the wake of these memories, a disorienting dizziness assailed Cal. He grabbed the top of a stall to steady himself.

"Look, it's an honor."

"But why a cowboy? And why me?"

"Actually, your mission will be to oversee the shipment of six cavies—Brezhnev bears—to our personnel in the Censorinus crater. Three males, three females, two of which will already be pregnant. Once you're up there, Cal, you'll show our people how to take care of their new pets. You'll return on the very next t-ship sent out from Kennedy Port, and your entire stay—traveling time included—won't be much more than three weeks."

"Cowboys aren't cavy keepers, Mr. Secretary."

"Yes, I know. But shipping heifers to the Moon is out of the question. Consider the Brezhnev bears shippable stand-ins."

Pets to improve the morale of moonbase personnel, Cal thought. And me, blackmailed again, their tin-can-riding Hopalong Castaway, rootin' tutelary drover of a miniherd of guinea pigs.

"There's a man over in Alabama I can get to boss this roundup, Cal. He's done it before. Once you're back, you're back for good, and you won't be sidetracked again."

"Didn't the other civilians have to take some training in Texas before NASA'd let them go up?"

"The training time got shorter with each candidate. They'll do you in a week. But you leave day after tomorrow. Forget your work here. Start thinking lunar adventure."

"I'll go on one condition." Foolish bravado, thought Cal, but it's worth a shot.

"You're in no position to lay down conditions, I'm afraid."

"Nevertheless."

"Okay. For my curiosity's sake, if for no other, what is it?"

"That the Brezhnev bears that we take up are purchased by NASA from the Happy Puppy Pet Emporium."

Berthelot boomed with laughter, bending over to accommodate his biggest guffaws. Then, sputtering, he said, "Done."

"Done?"

"Sure. I don't give a damn whose Brezhnev bears get sent. You think the Happy Puppy's got a couple of pregnant females?"

"Probably."

"Because every person up there should have one. Eventually, at least. And why ship fifty when they're such prolific breeders?"

No, that would be stupid, Cal thought. But what if moonbase personnel don't *want* them? Cal smothered this question because the President, the Secretary of Agriculture, and NASA's Texas-based bigwigs had clearly already decided exactly what Von Braunville's inhabitants required to stay happy and productive.

"Your loyalty to Mr. Kemmings is admirable, Cal. I hope it's a trait you transfer to your current boss as well."

When Cal did not reply, the secretary said, "We'll have NASA requisition all six cavies from the Pet Emporium. Mr. Kemmings can expect payment by Friday—as soon as his 'bears' have a clean bill of health from a USDA cavy inspector. I'll send one of our men to West Georgia Commons tomorrow to check them out."

"Doesn't NASA have to take bids on the animals?"

"What the hell do you want?" Hiram Berthelot flashed. "Your old boss to sell us these cavies? Or NASA to go through the legal procurement channels that your 'condition' —since you've decided to pull strings—nullifies? Please tell me."

My God, thought Cal, I've riled him. Of course I have. I ask for an exemption from the rules, which he grants, and then I hint that he's not playing fair.

Abashedly, Cal said, "I'd like NASA to buy them from Mr. K."

"Done. I said so, didn't I? Now shut up about it."

Immediately, though, the secretary was smiling again. He had worn blue jeans, a denim jacket, and a pair of work boots to the corrugated-metal building, and he helped Cal put up the horses for the night. He moved with contagious energy around the machine-shed stable, filling six big coffee tins with rolled oats and murmuring nonsense to the horses as he slotted the cans into place in their stalls. Then, in the drifting twilight, he walked with Cal to the rust-pocked Dart under an elm not far from the shed.

"Your dinner's gonna be cold. Better scram."

"Yes, sir."

But, to Cal's surprise, Berthelot climbed into the front seat and sat there with his hands on his thighs.

"You want a ride up to your house, sir?"

"No, Cal. I want you to go to your trunk, open it, and fetch me the spiral binder lying on top of your spare."

The muscles in Cal's lower back seized and spasmed. A chill clutched his chest. How had the bastard known? How had he found out? Like a zombie, Cal did as Berthelot had just asked. Then he reached the binder through the window to his boss and squeezed in behind the steering wheel.

"Ah, yes. *The Dream Impeachment of Harper Mocton.* By the late Philip K. Dick."

"How did you know I still had it?"

"Because you had all the other illicit Dick titles. Why would you neglect to acquire this one?"

Cal was desolate. Venus was rising in the April sky, above a stand of pines, but the sight of it failed to alleviate either his bitterness or his sense of loss. The thief had missed this binder only because Cal had been carrying it around in the trunk of his car. And, with his other manuscripts stolen and Viking dead as a result of the break-in, he'd taken heart from this small victory. All else might be gone, but he still had his copy of the novel in which Dick had envisioned a bloodless popular uprising against presidential arrogance. And accidentally retaining *The Dream Impeachment of Harper Mocton*, out of all the titles in his trunk, seemed to Cal a sign of . . . well, of divine favor.

Now, though, he was about to lose both his *samizdat* manuscript and the small triumph of his uninterrupted owner-ship of it.

Berthelot handed the binder back to Cal. "I don't want

this. Just wanted to see if my hunch was correct. Before coming into the shed, I peeked under these seats." He slammed the front seat with the heel of his hand. "Nothing. And since the trunk was locked, I had to bully you into opening it to prove to myself that you still had the binder. The No-Knock would've found it if it'd been in your apartment, and he didn't."

"I could've put it in a safety-deposit box. I could've hid it in a hollow tree somewhere."

"Could've. But didn't. I was right."

Cal held the binder on his lap, waiting for the other shoe to drop. The Berthelots already had plenty of blackmail material on the Bonner-Pickfords. Why had the secretary bothered to scare him to death making him bring forth this manuscript? Simply to impress him with his ratiocinative abilities?

"What'd you think of the book?" Berthelot said, nodding at it.

"Vile, seditious garbage. Trash in every possible sense of the term. Sci-fi schlock unworthy of publication."

Berthelot smiled. "No. What do you *really* think of it?"

Why? Cal wondered. Are you going to tape my response?

"It's weird," he said aloud, "but it has real literary merit. Besides, I like what happens to Harper Mocton in it. I wish—" Go ahead, Cal. Hand this smiling, two-legged piranha your liver. "I wish we could do the same to our own royal quack."

"Ah."

Venus twinkled above the nearby hills like the white-hot head of an invisible candle. An odor of horse manure and machine oil lilted through the Dart on the twilight breeze.

"I think you should know that along with the guinea pigs, Cal, you'll be accompanied to Censorinus by President Nixon."

In a second-story chamber of the Berthelot mansion, mirrors and video screens abut one another on the walls. They give the chamber windows on every occupant's soul, eyes on the outer world, and a fractured looking-glass review of Grace Rinehart's cinematic past. Each of these glass rectangles is a shard in a silent kaleidoscope of images. None of the mirrors now has a human face in it, but all the video screens stutter with dramatis personae, some of whom are twenty years dead, some of whom are broadcasting live, all of whom are as silent as mimes.

"Hiram, I don't get it. I worked like a nigger to maneuver Cal Pickford into your employ."

"*Our* employ, Grace. He's still in it."

"But you're sending him to the Moon! You and Dick are sending the ranch foreman you've been searching for for three years to Von Braunville! Why?"

Berthelot, dressed in silk pajamas and an embroidered bathrobe, lowers himself to the edge of their circular bed. Grace sits in a fortified position at its center. A striped bolster chair supports her back; from chair arm to chair arm, ramparts of fringed pillows make a semicircle in front of her. With the master remote in her left hand, she is obssessively changing channels, rewinding movie scenes, pausing the action here, speeding it there, turning every phosphor-dot window in the room into a pointillist turmoil of light and color.

"I've told you, Grace—to tend to the 'bears.'"

"But I promised him he wouldn't have to do that."

"He understands that it's an honor. That he won't have to do it again. It's okay. Please stop worrying."

"Lia won't like him being away for so long, and she'll hate me even more than she does now. At our last session—I told her how you and I met—she kept taking pencils from her purse and snapping them in two. She must've broken a dozen. We were sitting in a booth in a restaurant in Manchester, and with every snap, another head would turn. I was disguised again, of course, but that stupid snapping made my position pretty goddamn insecure."

"You can buy a therapist, Grace, but not somebody else's love or good opinion."

Caustically, Berthelot's wife says, "Benjamin Franklin? Oscar Wilde? From whom do you steal your epigrams?"

"I make them up myself. Banal though it may be, it's true."

"Listen, Hi, it'll be different when you're president. She'll be glad to see me coming then. So will everybody else."

"I'm not going to be president."

Grace stops pushing buttons on the master remote. The video screens windowing the ceiling and the magnolia-print wallpaper grow conspicuously less agitated. "Say that again."

"I'm not going to be president."

Grace sets the remote down and stares hard at her husband. "Of course you are. You've got Dick's backing. You'll turn aside all your Republican challengers, including General Willie, and in the November election you'll swamp whichever mealymouthed nonentity the donkey-brain Democrats send out naked against you. Don't *ever* tell me you're not going to be president."

"But that's what I'm telling you, baby."

"Who, then? Who?"

"I don't know. Maybe no one. Certainly not me."

Grace rises from her fortress of pillows like a cobra from a snake charmer's basket. "Why the fuck not?"

Berthelot reaches out and touches his wife's hair. "Look, I *could* be president, baby. But I'd hold the job in name only. It's becoming clearer all the time that President Nixon has no plans to give up power—only the visible trappings of his office. He's settled on me as his titular successor only because he thinks I'm a wimp who'll be easily manipulatable once I've been sworn in."

"But you're *not* a wimp!"

"I'm grateful for your testimony to the contrary."

"How do you know these things?"

"One of the President's aides had lunch with me a week or so ago. He told me to beware of the endorsement. 'It's the kiss of death,' he said."

"Which aide?"

"I can't tell you, baby. Of all the White House ass lickers, though, he's the one with the cleanest tongue. He's got a line to all the reliable scuttlebutt, and he talked to me straight."

"Ass lickers? They're not ass lickers, they're—"

"Hush a minute and listen. This guy told me that the President has decided to endorse me to ensure my victory. The last person he wants to succeed him is Westmoreland. Willie's got a mind of his own, and he's been champing at the bit these past six years to shed the veepship and run for the Oval Office. I'm to deflect Willie's ambitions. Then, once I'm in, dear old Dick's gonna shove his fist up my butt and dance me around like a hand puppet."

"That's pure poppycock, Hi. In the first place, if Dick's so in love with power, why doesn't he just run again? He'd take sixty percent of the vote. In the second place, you'd never let him get away with that kind of manipulation."

"Going for a fifth term might sully his reputation. FDR still catches hell in some quarters for making it to a *fourth*."

"But Roosevelt ran for a fourth in the middle of a world war. You don't just bail out of a situation like that."

"Okay. And Nixon's war? It's over. Running again, in more or less settled times, may make him look greedy for the very thing that he *is* greedy for—self-aggrandizing power. Sure, he'd like to go down as the only fifth-term president in history, but not in a way that suggests that that was his only reason for running."

"But it wouldn't be. I'm sure it wouldn't be."

Berthelot says nothing. On a pool-table-sized screen directly overhead, his wife—fifteen years younger—drops a bra strap for a blond actor later killed in a terrorist bombing in London.

"Anyway, Hiram, once sworn in, you could shake Dick— not that you'd have to, not at all—and do whatever you pleased, letting your conscience guide. You'd be the president, not him, and the Constitution would hold you up. What could he do?"

"What we did to Pickford. Blackmail me."

"Dick wouldn't do that. Besides, how could he blackmail you? You're a straight arrow. The only true one I've ever met."

"My source told me that the President has become increasingly self-willed and ruthless since the O_2 plant at Censorinus came on line. Privately, that is. On public occasions, he's still pretty much the old 'New Nixon,' but when alone with his intimates he's more of an autocrat than he was when he was prosecuting the war.

"I take the aide's assessment on faith. I've been to plenty of cabinet meetings, and I've long had the feeling that the President approves of me. Still, I'm hardly an intimate. Is it so hard to believe that for hidden reasons of his own he's cultivating a new ruthlessness, from which he may need to be saved?"

"You're saying he's ill? You're saying that this illness might lead him to try to blackmail you?"

"I am, Grace. Yes, I am."

"But blackmail you with what? How?"

Berthelot turns his eyes away from the pale woman in her fort of pillows. On a screen near a low white enamel bureau, his wife—seven years younger—leads a band of crewcut volunteers along a tangled Cambodian trail. When any of its weary members stumbles or hangs back, she impatiently semaphores.

"With you," he says, returning his gaze to her. "My informant tells me that your beloved Dick—now a very sick man—would try to manipulate me by threatening to ruin your reputation. There are films, he says. Not Hollywood productions, mind you, but footage surreptitiously shot in and around the Art, Film, and Photography Salon. And the President would release these films to his friends in the media if I proved an intractable doer of my own will rather than his."

Grace stares at her husband, her eyes like burnt pennies in a fuse box. "What are you going to do?"

Stretching one arm toward his wife, Berthelot leans across the bed. When she pushes his reaching fingers aside, he dog-walks over the mattress until he is just outside her fort of fringed pillows. Then he rises on his knees and tries to kiss her on the lips. She shows him the profile of her jaw. Glancingly, his mouth mumbles at the rigid line of bone she has presented him.

"Gimme a li'l sugar. Jus' a li'l sugar, baby."

"I asked you what you're going to do."

"A li'l sugar'd make us both happy. But you're not going to give it to me, are you?"

"This isn't the time."

"It's the place, Grace. And with jus' a li'l effort, baby, you could make it the time, too."

"Stop it, Hiram." She turns her head, gives him a perfunctory kiss, and quickly draws back.

"That wasn't much. It was almost nothing. But it's got my mojo runnin', baby. It's got my mojo justa jukin' along at ninety plus."

"I hate it when you talk like you think a horny redneck would. I really hate it, Hiram."

Berthelot takes the woman's face in his hands and bestows

kiss after kiss upon it. Slow, delicate, tender kisses. "You love me, don't you?" he asks her. "You really love me?"

Grudgingly, Grace says that she does.

"Would you stop loving me if I didn't become president? Would you shed me and find some eager young stud to fill in for me?"

Grace does not reply.

"I wouldn't be able to stand that," Berthelot tells her. "You know my secret. You know you've got the only li'l ignition switch that could ever crank my mojo."

"Hiram—"

"The ten years before I met you, I was as dead as a junked four cylinder. Nobody could rev me up. Then you, baby."

"All you're talking's lubrication. Crude, crass sex."

"All I'm talkin's love," Berthelot whispers. "You really think I could go the way I do with you—go 'n' keep a-goin'—if it wasn't love that stoked me to it?"

"If you truly love me, you'll back away."

"Baby," he rebukes her.

"I mean it. I mean what I'm asking."

He stares at her for a moment, touches her hair, and then, more awkwardly than not, rolls to the edge of their bed, eleven billion light-years from her fastness of pillows.

"What are you going to do if . . ." Grace runs down.

"If the President tries to blackmail us?"

In her fort of fringed bolsters, she imperceptibly nods.

Standing up, the Secretary of Agriculture surveys the chamber. The empty mirrors and the teeming video screens. He loves this woman. Deeply loves her. Her every image—no matter the medium, the production, or the year—deserves the whole of his attention. So, of course, does she. Looking at her again, he puts his hands in his bathrobe pockets. He wants to reassure and hearten her, the vulnerable woman inside the famous one.

"What am I going to do?" he asks rhetorically. "Baby mine, O my little baby, I'm going to cure the President."

"The Moon?" Lia cried. "What do you mean, the Moon?"

"Just listen. Just be quiet a few minutes and listen to what I have to say. . . ."

22

Berthelot arranged an exemption to the Travel Restrictions Act so that Lia could fly to Houston with Cal for his week of training and then to the Cape for the takeoff. To Lia's surprise, NASA treated Cal and her like celebrities. It was as if she were a stand-in Grace Rinehart, a personal emissary of the famous wife of the powerful man who, according to the latest Capitol Hill gossip, was King Richard's handpicked heir and successor.

A friendly, fortyish astronaut was Lia's liaison officer. He took her to see portions of Cal's weightlessness-training program; he showed her films of the beautifully choreographed construction of Kennedy Port and of the historic Bicentennial groundbreaking at Von Braunville. And, in his company, Lia toured a vehicle-assembly building and attended private briefings on rocket propellants, orbital mechanics, and lunar geography.

Later, she was fitted for her own space suit and given a spin on a long-armed machine that put bone-flattening centrifugal pressure on her entire body. The "vomit comet" scared her only a bit more than did the bucking mechanical bull in a local dancehall that Cal made her ride on their single evening away from training. Cowboys, she decided, had a built-in awareness of the unsettling hazards of zero g, and she was glad that it was her pigtailed hubby (NASA had let him keep his Indian braid) going into space instead of her. On the other hand, she wasn't all that happy that *he* was going.

One night, at the suburban home where NASA had quartered her, Lia had a long talk with the wife of her astronaut liaison. This woman told Lia that not everyone who went up came back down. Since 1977, two Heavy Lift Launch Vehicles (reputedly unmanned) boosted from the main pad at Canaveral had suffered annihilating explosions before reaching Earth orbit. Further, the government had relocated the families of the killed crew members before they could spread word of these disasters to others in the Texas-based community of astronauts. You knew that they had died, though. Why else would the members of the same HLLV mission receive simultaneous transfers that scattered their families willy-nilly across the country before the men themselves had even returned to Houston?

But the space program was more important than individual lives, the astronaut's wife murmured. So no news got out, and NASA kept launching tin cans on huge, unpredictable Roman candles. Finally, the woman realized that she was upsetting her guest and hurried to add that two explosions in six years really wasn't all that many. Besides, for two years, they had been flinging the shuttle aloft on an immense fly-back booster that obviated the need for expendable external tanks and colossal solid-fuel rockets. In fact, NASA's safety record was a sterling one when you compared it to the number of auto accidents every year . . . prior, at least, to the passage of the Internal Travel Restrictions Act.

In Florida, on the morning of the takeoff, Lia joined Cal in a battleship-gray antechamber near the booster flight line. She put her hands on the chest of his jumpsuit and fiddled with the tiny pull on one of its zippers. But why are they sending you? she wondered. Why you rather than some other equally or even better qualified cavy keeper?

"Don't worry, Lia. God's not going to let anything happen to six innocent Brezhnev bears."

"Not to mention the President of the United States."

Cal put a finger to his lips. "Shhhh."

Berthelot had said that Nixon would be going to Censorinus on this same mission, up from the Cape on the HLLV shuttle *Clemency* and from Kennedy Port to lunar orbit aboard the newly commissioned transfer ship *Checkers*—but King Richard had attended none of Cal's training sessions, and Lia did not believe that he had traveled to Houston to prepare. This morning, however, David Eisenhower had announced on *Today* that his father-in-law really did intend to be the world's first head of state to visit the Moon, and both Cal and Lia had a sense that something grand and furtive was happening just out of their view. Still, they had seen nothing to confirm their suspicions, and no one was talking.

"The whole country's just learned that the President is turning astronaut. Why do *I* have to be quiet?"

"He may be near enough to hear you," Cal said.

"Impossible. My flesh isn't crawling. Besides, you're right—God's more likely to preserve you guys for those two pregnant pigs' sakes than for the bastard who had Viking knocked off."

"Shhhh."

"God may also approve of the fact you all've got an Episcopal bishop going along."

This was true, and it was one of the many odd aspects of a very odd mission. Bishop Joshua Marlin of the Georgia diocese of the Protestant Episcopal Church, Hiram Berthelot's personal friend and confessor, had trained with Cal in Houston, subjecting himself to calisthenics, jogging, and the dizzying torments of the "octopus arm"—as he and Cal had dubbed that machine—in order to prepare for the flight. And, for a ruddy fifty-year-old man of substantial girth and dubious eyesight, Marlin had acquitted himself remarkably well. Lia, along with Cal, had had lunch with the bishop on three occasions, and she was comforted by the knowledge that he would be sitting in the crew chair next to her husband's on the *Clemency* and later on the *Checkers*.

Cal said, "Bishop Marlin has blessed this flight and everyone on it—Colonel Hudner, Major Levack, me, even that Secret Service guy who made only every third training session in Houston. Marlin jokes with us, too. Calls this the 4-P Expedition."

Lia waited for Cal to explain.

"Pets, Plants, Priest, and President. Up we go to propitiate the demons of despair."

"And what else? You're holding out on me." For Lia knew that preflight anxiety did not fully account for Cal's reticence.

"I don't know. Nothing I can talk about."

"This is happening because of Kai, isn't it? Because he

wants to obliterate this reality with a better one." As soon as Lia had said these words, voicing for the first time what both of them had intuitively known since departing Georgia for NASA headquarters, a low-grade but persistent terror settled in her heart. She clutched Cal to her and held him. But the terror throbbed on and on.

"It's going to work," he whispered.

"So you say. But, afterward, will either of us have any idea what we've done? And if whatever it is you're going to do *doesn't* work, this may be the last time we'll ever hold each other."

"Hush."

"*Damn* that haint! And his amnesia, and his stereographia, and all his troublemaking unpublished sci-fi!"

"Shhhh!"

Lia pulled back from Cal. "And you, too, so far as that goes, for being the 'lens' that focused him on Warm Springs!"

"It would've happened even without me, Lia. Somehow or other, it would've happened without me."

His fatalism, his certainty, enraged her. She wanted to ball up her fist and strike his chest again and again—so that he could experience maybe a *tenth* of the terror-bred pain that was racking her even as she tried to bid him a respectable good-bye. But good-bye for how long? It was possible that Philip K. Dick, Bishop Marlin, Cal, and their undisclosed confederates at Von Braunville would so violently rend the fabric of this historical continuum that no one wrapped in it now would ever wear it again as anything other than a shroud.

And Cal was trying to shush her!

"If you loved me," she said, "you wouldn't rush off in pursuit of this megalomaniac dream."

"If you loved me, you'd know there's nothing megalomaniac about it. I'm scared shitless, Lia. But what do you want me to do? Go out there and tell Colonel Hudner, 'Hey, man, gotta get on home and fix our sump pump. Catch you next trip'?"

"What's going to happen, Cal? When will we next see each other? And where? Or will we at all?"

"God knows, Lia. God or the demiurge."

Okay, she reflected. It's inevitable. He's trained for this trip, and he's going, and I'd be the worst sort of obstructionist female if I derailed the whole thing by making him stay. A bitch of a wife. A monkeywench in the reality-reshaping conspiracy of Kai, Cal, and their presumptuous lowercase demiurge. Which is why another bishop's going instead, and why I've got to stop badgering Cal and give him my own feeble blessing. . . .

Lia stepped back and, with trembling fingers, undid the pin on her blouse. Then she dropped the tiny intaglio fish into a pocket on Cal's NASA jumpsuit.

"Keep this with you," she said. "Always."

They kissed, a kiss longer and deeper than any she could recall since their courtship. After which he strode away from her like a hero in a western movie. Only a fleeting glance over his shoulder cracked the veneer of his stoicism, redeeming him as the flesh-and-blood creature she had married.

As she climbs the steps of the Chattahoochee Valley Art, Film, and Photography Salon, Grace Rinehart imagines that the cameras are rolling. A night scene. A mystery woman going to an assignation with a mystery man.

In the absence of her work-absorbed husband, what other option does she have? She could stay in the Berthelot mansion awaiting Hiram's next visit, but the intervals between these visits seem to grow longer, and with only filmed images of herself for company (her own face and figure endlessly multiplied on the screens around her), the nights protract and demoralize.

So I'm going to meet my lover, she tells herself an hour after midnight, unlocking the iron-barred door and stepping inside.

The reflection of the red traffic light at Hines and Railroad Streets glares in the foyer window; it spills its winking stain on the white stone floor. Grace stands in the dark, imagining that the director has cut to an interior shot taken from great altitude; her foreshortened body gives the scene an impressionistic air of claustrophobic menace. Anyone viewing the scene in a theater would intuit, entirely from the camera angle, that a probing pair of eyes has sighted Grace and from henceforth will track her remorselessly through the salon.

Turn on the lights! every anonymous viewer wants to cry. Don't be an idiot! Turn on the lights!

But she is thinking, My lover's already here, and he's kept the galleries dark to heighten the glamor of our tryst. Our director concurs. The darkness will incite his two principals to a storm of photogenic passion that light would render . . . well, commonplace, if not downright tawdry and repellent. So let me go to my lover in the dark, and let our high-speed color cameras follow me to him as if I were in danger instead of heat. . . .

Whom has she enticed here from among her sexiest former leading men? James Garner? Cliff Judson? William Shatner? Or maybe it's one of the younger bloods. Keith Carradine? Fordham Hayes? Geoff Bridges? She can't remember whom she telephoned long-distance, or whether that person was serious about accepting her invitation or only facetiously flirty, but as she stolls from the foyer into the gallery of Popular Americana, she senses that her lover awaits her aloft. If he refuses to disclose his presence, he does so not only to sharpen their appetites for each other but also to increase the dramatic tension of this footage. Like her, the man is a pro, and a pro is ever ready to sacrifice even immediate carnal fulfillment for a stunning cinematic coup. So she grins as she strolls, but, each time the camera intercepts her face-on, hides her grin behind a pout of bemused expectancy.

The signature Grace Rinehart pout.

"Luciano!" she calls. (Luciano seems a good fictional name for whoever awaits her.) "Luciano, are you here?"

The question echoes up and down among the galleries.

Continuing to stroll, she circles the pedestal on which sits a bronze icon of Checkers—the Nixons' dog during the presidency of Dwight D. Eisenhower and the namesake of the t-ship taking Dick, Cal, and Bishop Marlin to the Moon. Grace lets her fingers caress the bronze furrows on Checkers's muzzle (no wonder the Nixons loved this dog) and then wanders on to the next statue, a sensuous marble effigy of MariLou Monroe, that bastard JFK's secret playmate. The camera cuts from this moon-white Monroe to shadowy living woman and back again. A slow-motion do-si-do of cinema goddesses.

"Luciano!"

The name reverberates, its ultimate *O* spiraling up the helical stairway to the photography gallery, the screening room, and the concealed bedroom to which Grace often retires when Hiram is away. That must be where her mysterious paramour has concealed himself, too. With a crane-mounted camera dollying back to accommodate her advance, she mounts the stairs.

Nobody in the photography gallery. Nobody in the uphol-stered seats of the screening room. Nobody in her hidden bedroom.

Luciano, it seems, wants to make her search. Filmically, this strategy has a certain Hitchcockian charm, but Grace has begun to resent the stuck-up sonuvabitch's dedication to elusiveness. She marches from one end of the second floor to the other with a clumsy swagger betraying her mood.

"Damn it, Luciano! Get your butt out here!"

No answer. Did he miss his flight? Did he lose the key that she sent him? Has he been detained by a death in the family, a movie shooting, a personal-appearance commitment? Well, he should have called to tell her. But of course nearly every actor in Hollywood, whether sixteen or sixty, is a self-absorbed adolescent. Their dismaying similarity to her first two conniving husbands is clear. Shouldn't she know better by now? Yes, sir. She definitely ought to know better.

"Keep shooting," Grace commands. "I know I lost it there for a minute, but I'm getting it back. Really, I am."

She goes to the screening room's projection booth, rum-mages in its film library, and finds an unmarked canister that she stuck behind the others two or three years ago. Luciano hasn't shown, but at least she can show herself. And show herself to fresh, if not brilliant, advantage by sprocketing into the projector a film made while she was still a mere girl. Filming an actress in the process of showing one of her own films is too self-referential an approach to be very entertain-ing, but let the director in her head keep 'em rolling, anyway. She's always been her own best audience, and *The Broken Bubble of Thisbe Holt* is probably worth at least one more viewing before she dies. She was horrendous in it—it was a truly bad film—but she probably never *looked* better in any of her starring or co-starring roles. Which is the reason she has saved this solitary print of the film after buying up and cold-bloodedly destroying nearly every other copy.

Soon, she sits slumped in a center-aisle seat in the screening room while the second movie she ever made burns silently—she has turned down its soundtrack—on the high white rectangle opposite. Two-dimensional images prance and preen on this surface. Today's face is lit by the tattered radiance pouring down from the wistful visage of her nineteen-year-old self. And Grace is certain that yet another camera is filming the interaction between her and the immature goddess glowing in celluloid apotheosis.

This certainty persuades her that a climax of some sort must be nearing, that she cannot be sprawled here eyeing her daughter—no, not her daughter: a younger clone of her continuous self—solely to gratify a craven desire to sidestep the aging process. Something is about to happen . . . not up on the screen but in the theater of the absurd of her very life.

"Luciano!" she calls again. "Luciano, I'm giving you one more goddamn chance!"

"Here, I am," Luciano declares, and in the phallic guise of an eight-foot-long boa constrictor he rises from the floor between her stretched-out legs and holds his blunt reptilian head only inches from her own. Luciano's tongue flicks out, a split filament full of annihilating electricity, and the brushing touch of its two cold prongs deadens Grace's lips and stops her heart.

"My God!" she reflexively exclaims.

Goggle-eyed, she recoils from Luciano's kiss, grimly clutching the arms of her seat. She fails in mid-recoil, consciousness going out of her with her last line of dialogue. Luciano balances on his nether body, staring sidelong into her eyes like a rapist robbed of some ambiguous satisfaction.

Meanwhile, this creature sees in the glassed-over hemispheres of Grace Rinehart's eyes the twinned image of an immortal goddess, all of whose childish laughter erupts from her like gunfire in a perfect vacuum.

Two days out from the modularized space station Kennedy Port, the transfer ship *Checkers* was dog-paddling—coasting—away from Earth toward the Moon. To Cal's eye, the t-ship resembled a huge dunce cap sitting atop two immense fuel tanks, the smaller tank containing O_2 (oxygen) and the larger H_2 (hydrogen). In fact, the hydrogen-holding bottom tank was as large as the entire upper portion of the *Checkers*, and Cal had the chagrined sense that even Flash Gordon or Buck Rogers would have considered their vehicle a technological albatross.

The President was actually aboard. However, he spent

most of his time in a passenger area just above the crew deck in which Cal floated with Bishop Marlin and the two NASA crew members, the pilot Colonel Hudner and copilot Major Levack. Nixon had for company the whip-thin Secret Service man, Griegs, who had trained off and on with Cal and the bishop in Houston, and another Secret Service agent, Robinson, who played cameraman whenever the President wished to make a TV broadcast to his expectant Earthbound audience. Each broadcast was "historic," and during each one Nixon repeated that he had chosen to visit the base at Censorinus for three very good and sufficient reasons:

"First off, my fellow Americans—indeed, my fellow Earthlings—I go to Von Braunville to lift the hearts of the brave men and women who have sacrificed so much to serve us on our barren lunar outpost. Like Dear Abby, I care.

"Second, I go to Von Braunville to leave my mark on history. What other leader has dared so much in the face of such odds?

"And, third, I go to Von Braunville to speak to its forty-plus pioneers—and, incidentally in that regard, to all of you sitting by your TV sets—a message that will expand the dimensions of the American space program and eventually bring home to you even richer blessings than it has to date. God bless you, every one."

In one telecast from the *Checkers*, the President brought Joshua Marlin on camera, introducing him as the "distinguished spiritual leader of Georgia's God-fearing Episcopalians." He announced that taking the bishop to the Moon—an idea first suggested by Secretary Berthelot—was another new strategy to bolster the morale of Von Braunvillians. And the selfless Bishop Marlin—bless his heart—had agreed to serve as their chaplain for three months.

Watching this broadcast with Colonel Hudner and Major Levack, Cal saw the bishop smile myopically, clasp his hands, and make a crowd-acknowledging gesture more typical of a prizefighter than a clergyman. But Nixon did not permit him to speak, and a moment later Marlin came swimming back down to the crew deck to tell Cal that the President wanted him to get *his* fanny up to the passenger deck now doubling as a broadcast booth. He also wanted Cal to bring with him one or two of the Brezhnev bears.

"You're kidding," Cal said.

"No, Calvin, I'm not. The President sees this as a fine 'video opportunity.' A chance to show off his personal warmth. To score a few points *with* tottery Leonid Ilyich in Moscow. And *against* him in the Vigorous Leader Sweepstakes."

Bishop Marlin explained that Brezhnev was reputedly miffed that his American counterpart had opted to one-up him like this. So the President hoped to cool him down by showing the Soviet cavies in a broadcast. At the same time, he was not unaware that magnanimously spotlighting the pigs would underscore the fact that *he* was taking them to the Moon and Leonid *wasn't*. From these facts, the world could draw its own conclusions about the health of the American and Soviet space programs and the countries' two leaders.

Cal pushed off to get the Brezhnev bears. Jesus, he thought, what an idea. The cavies had been a nuisance from the beginning; the possibility that they would tremendously cheer the selenonauts struck him as remote. Housed in two plastic boxes on the crew deck—so that Cal could tend to them—the pigs squeaked continually, noises so similar to computer beeps that Hudner often thought that either Houston or Kennedy Port was trying to signal him.

Worse, the "bears" had little understanding of zero-g hygiene, and Cal spent a lot of time vacuuming drifting pellets out of their boxes and trying to repair the improvised filter that was supposed to keep their pee from separating out into free-floating droplets that jaundiced the crew deck's atmosphere. Because of the guinea pigs, things were always about to go blooey—equipment failing, tempers pulled thin—and Cal was more than ready for the *Checkers* to rendezvous with the ferry shuttle that would set them all down on the Moon. A surface where "up" and "down" were not arbitrary terms and you could exercise your God-given right to take a piss without a lot of clunky zero-g paraphernalia.

"Come on," Cal coaxed, reaching into one of the double-walled plastic boxes. "You guys've got a presidential summons."

The cavies, who had learned to hang themselves by their manes on the strips of Velcro lining the rear walls of their boxes, were not impressed. Cal had to grip their naked bellies and pull; the result was a ripping sound like that obtained yanking a Band-Aid off an unhealed wound. Fortunately, having chosen two plump males to meet the President, he had to do this only twice, but these two squealed histrionically, thrashed their little legs, and tried to bite him. The overlooked male and the three females, hanging like Lilliputian sides of pork on their own Velcro strips, squealed and kicked in sympathy.

And it doesn't help much, thought Cal bitterly, knowing that everyone else sees this as the Calvin Pickford Comedy Minute. For the colonel, the major, and the bishop were amusedly following his efforts and trying hard not to snigger.

At last, he had the cavies free. He let them go, and in the open space of the cabin they struggled, treading air for purchase and finding none. God, they were ugly, obscene in their nudity and in their futile wriggling. Cal's first inclination was to cram them into socks to restore a degree of decorum to the cabin.

But that, Cal knew, was a prudish urge. He spurned it, opting to shepherd the cavies toward the ladder by shooting jets of air at them from a squeeze bottle. And so they rose, a binary of helpless rodents, pig-paddling about each other, energetically squeaking.

Cal hand-over-handed his own way to the upper deck, emerging into this jungle of ferns, caladiums, hydrangeas, and miniature evergreens to find himself facing Robinson's camera and Griegs's perpetual scowl. Nixon, too, was eyeing the helical waltz of the guinea pigs and the jack-in-the-box arrival of their keeper.

Boosted by the squeeze bottle, the "bears" kept going; Cal had to grab each of them by a foot to prevent them from colliding with the floor of the cargo bay capping the passenger decks. He also feared the possibility of their getting lost in the foliage of the various plants bracketed to the pegboard walls.

"All right," said the President. "Let's shoot, boys. Billions of people are waiting to see this."

Whereupon Griegs towed one of the guineas to the President by a hind leg and Robinson began televising its summit with the Leader of the Free World. Soon, the other pig joined their deliberations, and finally even Cal got to enter the picture. The two men and the two bare cavies circled one another in a parody of friendliness, the nauseous implications of which put Cal in danger of barfing in front of half the world's population, not excluding his wife.

But, by dint of will, he kept his gorge down, and the President told the multitudes that Cal Pickford, the first working cowhand in space, had foregone the pleasures of post-hole digging and bovine midwifery to escort Brezhnev's babies to the Moon and that for this sacrifice he deserved three cheers from every English- (and maybe Spanish-) speaking person watching this broadcast.

And, to his chagrin, Cal smiled to consider that millions of Americans were even now rising before their TV sets to bellow, in unison, "Hip hip hooray for Cal Pickford!"

A biological accident interrupted this reverie. The plumper of the two cavies discharged a swarm of pellets, which floated around the two men like wayward planetoids. Cal had to take the nozzle off his squeeze bottle and chase them down. Nixon stayed calmly affable through this impromptu business —human, almost—as if tickled by the spectacle of an erstwhile cowhand collecting BBs of cavy dung in a container meant for Co' Cola.

But after the broadcast, the President—it was hard to deride him as "King Richard" when you were floating alongside him in a fragile tin can one hundred thousand miles from Earth—rebuked Cal for wearing an Indian braid.

"That goddamn hippie hair string," he said, "has no place on a mission like ours. The *Checkers* was built for tradition-respecting souls, and if you don't cut that doo-whanger off before we go into lunar orbit, pigs or no pigs, I'm going to send your calloused butt back to Kennedy Port with Hudner and Levack."

"None of our NASA colleagues objected, sir."

"Then they're not the sticklers for clean-cutness they should be, and I'm ashamed of the sorry peckers."

"Yes, sir."

After which the President withdrew into himself, veiling his worry-cratered eyes behind a look of such aloof malignity that Cal was frightened. What had happened to the semi-human Richard Nixon of five minutes ago? It seemed that he had metamorphosed into a real-world hypostasis of Philip K. Dick's fictional Harper Mocton. Even Robinson and Griegs, former Green Berets and veterans of the Indochina triumph, wanted nothing to do with him now. Although both men remained on the upper deck, they strove to get as far from their employer as possible. Meanwhile, the President swam to his passenger chair, strapped himself in, and sat there like an effigy in a department-store window.

"How'd it go?" Bishop Marlin asked when Cal had returned to the crew deck. "Aside from the pellet spill, I mean."

He and the pilots, all dressed in T-shirts and flight pants, had been watching on monitors attached to a pegboard wall. Hudner and Levack were upside down to each other, watching TVs similarly oriented and fiddling with broken pieces of t-ship hardware.

As for Bishop Marlin, he was blowing balls of water through a straw, four of which—lovely fragile spheres—wheeled about him in an accidental orrery a good deal more elegant than the one that had just attended Cal and the President.

"He wants me to cut my braid," Cal said. "The look on his face would've popped every one of your bubbles."

"I know," Joshua Marlin said. "I know."

Major Levack cut Cal's braid, and the remainder of their trip—another day and a half of relentless coasting—made Cal think of a voyage from life to death, across a Styx of ebony vacuum. Nixon had taken the role of Charon, and everyone else aboard was a soul on the way to . . . well, what? Oblivion, probably. Even those rascally damn Brezhnev bears. Against all expectation, Cal found himself mourning the varmints as earnestly as he mourned his lost braid, and his dreams were all nightmares.

Sometimes, though, Bishop Marlin would read from Revelation, and the words he read were these: " 'And night shall be no more; they need no light of lamp or sun, for the Lord God will be their light, and they shall reign for ever and ever. . . .' "

"The snake didn't kill her," Langland, the police captain, told Hiram Berthelot. "That's an old wives' tale, the notion that a boa constrictor will squeeze a human being to death."

"Yes?"

"It was fright that did it, we think. It's cold in the salon, and the snake, sensing the warmth of your wife's presence, went to her instinctively. She was watching a movie, though, and didn't notice until it was practically in her face."

"Which caused her heart to stop?"

"Yes, Mr. Secretary. That's what we think. The boa coiled up in her lap and stayed there even after her body had begun to cool. It didn't constrict her, though. There are no signs of contusions, hematomata, or broken bones."

"Where did the goddamned snake come from?"

Langland flipped his notepad out. "West Georgia Commons. The Happy Puppy Pet Emporium. The manager, Augustus Kemmings, sold it to an Americulturated Vietnamese by the name of Le Boi Loan, alias Lone Boy, a bookstore and Save-Our-Way clerk."

"Then *he* killed my wife."

"It's highly likely that he established a set of circumstances that *led* to your wife's death, yes, sir."

"He introduced the boa into the salon. That was premeditated, and it qualifies as murder."

"With something like this, Mr. Secretary, you're not likely to get him on murder one. Manslaughter, maybe."

"Manslaughter be damned. This was premeditated. *Pregoddamn-meditated*. And that's murder."

"If a boa constrictor were a lethal weapon. But the DA's gonna have a hard time making that argument stick, especially since these snakes don't ordinarily crush and eat human beings. Besides, we're fairly sure the autopsy will indicate heart attack, and a halfway decent defense attorney is gonna try like hell to suggest it may've been a response to the movie instead of the snake. We have no proof that the boa didn't climb into her lap until *after* she'd died—only a reasonable conjecture."

"Is this sleazeball Lone Boy in custody?"

"No, sir."

"Why the hell not?"

"We sent a car out to his house. He wasn't there. His wife didn't know where he was, either. We've got an APB out, though, and his Datsun shouldn't be that hard to find."

"I appreciate your calling me, Langland, but I don't want news of this spilling to anyone. Understand?"

"Yes, sir. And I'm sorry, Mr. Secretary. Really."

Berthelot made no reply. He went out to the street and climbed into the limousine that his bodyguard cum chauffeur, Jared Twitchell, was driving. The secretary sat beside him in the front. Briefly, they spoke. The street lamp coated the limousine with a waxy glow, and nearby elms shook their night-entangled canopies.

"The Barrel of Fun?"

"Yes, sir."

"Surely, the police would've checked there already."

"It's a funny place. Game consoles. Booths to climb in. Lots of black-light posters and dimness."

"Yes?"

"It's possible they missed him."

The Lincoln made the trip from midtown LaGrange to the suburban mall in less than eight minutes. Then the Secretary of Agriculture and his bodyguard strolled through its central concourse and up to the huge capsized "barrel" allowing them entrance to the video-game arcade. They went inside.

Hundreds of outré noises assailed Berthelot. Computer blips. The chuckles of intragalactic weaponry. The whirr of electrified cormorant wings. The furnace roars of Technicolor dragons. The annihilating pileups of animated racing cars. With these noises came weird hues and a disorienting ambience of fractured lambency. Berthelot staggered through the arcade, and it seemed to him that he had entered another continuum.

Maybe you have, he thought. Maybe the new continuum's already here. If so, all the old laws have been abrogated. The only laws you need to obey are those that impinge on your conscience, Hiram, and those that don't, well, they must be obsolete. He read the names of the games. Asteroids. Fragger. Centipede. Drac-Man. Phun Ky Cong. Defender. Bigg-Bugg. And others that escaped him, their designations scrolling around the canopies of the booths into which their players ducked and disappeared.

The place was full of kids. And a few shadowy toughs who could have been anywhere from eighteen to thirty-eight. They shot Hiram Berthelot and his bodyguard bleak, socket-eyed glances that turned their faces into either jokes or insults. Twitchell, undeterred, went patrolling through and past them as if they were substanceless spirits, wraiths in impalpable leather. After two circuits of the arcade's token-dispensing kiosk, he found Le Boi Loan huddled in a booth purporting to be the cabin of a transdimensional voyager. He grabbed the Americulturated Vietnamese by the lapels of his jacket and shouted his boss's name.

Berthelot took over for Twitchell, who didn't want him to. He leaned into the booth to study the foreign features of the man who had murdered his wife. Le Boi Loan cringed away. His face—his helpless cringing—infuriated Berthelot, who moved his hands from the lapels of the chickenshit's jacket to his scrawny throat.

This is the way I squeeze my foe, he thought. Squeeze my foe, squeeze my foe. So early in the evening.

His fingers felt Adam's apple, lymph nodes, and vertebrae, and tried to bring them all together into a lump no larger than his clasped hands. *My* Main Squeeze is just as effective as your Main Squeeze, he thought, all the while squeezing.

Lone Boy began to kick. Twitchell, standing at Berthelot's shoulder, muttered something about the inadvisability of wreaking vengeance on Grace's murderer in so public a place. Already, the secretary was attracting attention.

"Let me do it," Twitchell said. "It's what I'm paid for."

But Berthelot braced his feet and shrugged the bodyguard aside, bearing down even harder on the thrashing Loan. He, too, was aware that some of the game players in the Barrel of Fun were trying to determine the exact nature of this struggle, but he interposed his back—no inconsequential barrier—and did what he had to do. The horror of life without Grace Rinehart, film actress, patriot, and soulmate, sustained him in this effort, and when Le Boi Loan had finally ceased thrashing, he opened his fingers and saw that deep creases disfigured his victim's neck.

"It's all right," he consoled the dead man. "We shall not all sleep, but we shall all be changed."

"What?" Twitchell said. "What're you telling him?"

"Nothing," Hiram Berthelot replied, backing out of the cockpit of the transdimensional voyager. "Only that he was a mean little bastard and I hope he rots in hell."

* * *

Matt Murdock, alias Daredevil, cannot believe it. His superpowers have left him, and his archenemy, Kingpin, has choked the very breath from his body.

But why? What has he done to deserve this? Surely, putting a snake in the screening room at the salon—scaring the Kingpin's mistress a little—doesn't warrant so violent a response. Can't the tight-assed guy take a joke?

I'm dying, Murdock thinks, amazed: I was blind, and now I'm dying. Kingpin, lord of the criminal underworld, has defeated me in one-on-one combat.

And in his last window of consciousness—the final panel of an adventure gone bad—Murdock glimpses the faces of a bereaved woman and two distraught little girls. The faces, he notes, are Oriental and hence bewilderingly foreign. . . .

Grif Langland, the police captain, could not believe what Hiram Berthelot had just told him. How could he? The Secret Service man assigned to the Secretary of Agriculture kept contradicting his boss, saying that it was he, Jared Twitchell, who had killed Le Boi Loan and not the insistent Berthelot.

"Twitchell, will you shut up and let me confess?"

"No, sir. I'm not going to let you take the rap for something I did. Besides, I'm *authorized* to do that sort of thing."

"Nobody's authorized to commit murder, Twitchell. At any rate, no one *should* be." He looked at Langland. "I took it upon myself to break the law, and now I'm turning myself in."

"Listen to Agent Twitchell," Langland said, as uncomfortable as he could ever remember being. He didn't want to arrest the most famous Georgian in national politics since Jimmy Carter. Everybody from Atlanta to Waycross would clamor for his scalp, and, with King Richard's help, they just might get it.

"I committed murder, Captain Langland."

"'Justifiable homicide,' call it. You had your reasons."

"*He* didn't do it," Twitchell said. "*I* did."

"It wasn't premeditated," Berthelot said. "Pure impulse. I loved my wife. You'll never know how much. But impulse killing's still killing, and not even a member of the President's cabinet is above the law. Arrest me. I demand to be arrested."

Think, Langland told himself. Think. "Sir," he said, "there's no reason at all for any of this to get out."

"Damn it! You think I want a cover-up? No Berthelot has ever ducked responsibility for his acts, and this administration doesn't countenance cover-ups!"

Langland was glad to hear Twitchell say, "Listen to me, sir. Taking the rap for this . . . this accident . . . wouldn't be in the national interest."

"That's horseshit," Berthelot retorted.

"President Nixon's out of the country—off the goddamn planet, in fact—and letting this fuckin' news out while he's away would be . . . *un*patriotic. You'd afflict the administration with a terrible scandal just when it least needs it."

"He's right, Mr. Secretary," Langland put in, grateful that a hulk like Twitchell could mount convincing reasons for . . . well, for covering up a murder by a cabinet member. In spite of himself, Berthelot appeared to be mulling the Secret Service man's appeal to his patriotism. "You can't drop this kind of bombshell while the President's on an historic trip to the Moon."

The secretary slumped dejectedly into a coaster chair. He shut his eyes, rubbed his temples, and grimaced.

"You should ask President Nixon's advice," Langland said.

"Right," said Twitchell. "But you'd distract the hell out of him if you asked him while he's commuting to Von Braunville."

"I've killed a man!"

Said Twitchell evenly, "I've killed lots of men."

"Just forget about this matter until the President comes home," Langland said. "Then see him. Meanwhile, my department'll take care of any embarrassing loose ends."

Berthelot groaned. But, Langland saw, they'd knocked the props out from under him. He was an honorable man, but he was also a patriot, and his patriotism required that he seek King Richard's approval of his confession before going public with it.

Thank God, thought Langland. Thank God for small mercies.

23

L ia sat in her office waiting for Grace Rinehart to show. It was Wednesday, and, with Cal finally at Von Braunville, she began to anticipate—almost with pleasure—the itinerary that her least predictable client would seek to implement today. A luncheon at In Clover in LaGrange? A drive through Roosevelt State Part? Another visit to the LAC at Fort Benning?

Bemused and impatient, Lia struck her intercom button. "Isn't she here yet, Shawanda?"

"No, ma'am," replied Shawanda Bledsoe's voice.

"She's forty minutes late. If she doesn't get here soon, you and I might as well go home. Nobody else is scheduled."

"You want me to call out at her place?"

"Why don't you? I'd like to know what's going on."

Lia fiddled with her notes. Then the intercom unit buzzed, and Shawanda said, "I got this man, Dr. Bonner. Said Miss Rinehart's 'unavailable to the telephone.' "

"Is she going to make it today? Did he tell you that?"

"The man he didn't say. Said she's going to be 'out of pocket'—whatever the fool *that* mean—indefinitely."

"Oh, great."

"Told me your fee's going to come, anyhow. That's good."

"Yeah, I guess it is." But Lia craved a distraction from both mundane paperwork and Cal's out-of-this-world mission as much as she did an income guarantee. With Grace Rinehart's patronage and Cal's job at Berthelot Acres, they were better off financially than they had been even in their best year in Colorado. Unfortunately, a theft, a murder, and a blackmail effort—all directly traceable to Miss Grace and her husband—continued to rankle, and Lia often felt that she was eating humble pie—hell, *subservient stew*—every time that she sessioned with the actress.

Shawanda buzzed her. "Got you a call, ma'am. You want to pick up on line two for Missus Phoebe Flack?"

Phoebe Flack? Her mother's roommate at the Eleanor Roosevelt Nursing Home? What in the world did she want?

"Hello," Lia said.

Phoebe Flack's querulous voice said, "Doctor Lia, it's me, your mama's friend." She gave her name and reminded Lia of all that she had done for Miss Emily during her stay in the home. Doubtfully, she wondered aloud if maybe the "busy doctor" could drop by for a few minutes to see her.

"These *are* business hours, Phoebe. I'm working." Or would be, thought Lia, if my queenly client would ever get here.

"Whenever you can, then," whined the woman.

"But what's this about, Phoebe?" Possibly, of course, the poor old gal was just lonely. But Lia didn't want to think about this possibility because guilt—wholly appropriate guilt—would require her to take action to ease Phoebe's loneliness.

"I've got something for you. Didn't think I should put it in the mail. It's too valuable to mail."

What could Phoebe Flack have for her? Lia wondered. Especially if it were valuable. Probably a photograph, or a diary, or a stray family memento. Otherwise, her call made no sense. Despite having been roommates, Phoebe and her mama had never been close; they were "friends" only if that word meant "glorified acquaintances."

Instantly, Lia resolved to visit Phoebe. "I'll be right over," she said. Let Grace Rinehart, if ever she left off being "out of pocket," sit in the waiting room cooling *her* heels.

And so Lia hung up and walked from her office on Main Street to the nursing home. Phoebe Flack was parked in her wheelchair in the lobby, predatorily near the plate-glass doors. Lia kissed her on the cheek and pushed her down one of the Lysol-scented corridors to her own room, which she now shared with a woman whose skin seemed to have been made from lacquered tissue paper. The two women did not acknowledge each other, nor was Lia able to wrest a greeting from the Origami Dowager in the next bed.

"What is it, Phoebe? What did you want me to come get?"

"Just this, Doctor Lia." Phoebe reached into the pocket of her robe and withdrew a circular tin that Lia did not recognize. Once in her own hands, however, the object disclosed itself as a yellow can of Dean Swift's snuff. Lia got the top off, sniffed the brown grains, struggled to keep from sneezing.

"*Phshhuuuw*," she said. "Why are you giving me this, Phoebe?"

"It was in the very back of your mama's dresser drawer, Doctor Lia, and I figured you'd want it."

"It wasn't my mother's, Phoebe. Even if it had been, there'd hardly've been any need to give it to me." Lia placed the tin on a bedside table. "Keep it, dispose of it, I honestly don't care what you do with it." Is this what the flaky Phoebe Flack had made her take off work to come see about?

"And something else," Phoebe said. She rotated her wrist and opened the cage of her fingers. Now Lia saw the gold intaglio profile of a fish on a beautiful lapel pin. The sight made her heart catch. A moment later, as if she had just completed a long run, it began to pound.

"Where'd you get that?"

"A maid cleaning the chapel found it. She turned it in at the nurses' station. They said whoever described this lost piece of jewelry could have it back. I claimed it, kept it. But when your mama died, I started feelin' guilty. So it's yours again, Doctor Lia. Can you forgive me for doin' what I did?"

Stunned, Lia said, "Certainly. Of course."

She walked dazedly back to her office in the April sun. Once, Cal had said, "Maybe you had two of them all along." And she had replied, "Until this morning, I didn't know I had even *one*."

Well, she definitely had two now. Of course, the second was in Cal's possession on the Moon, but the first pin—the one she'd lost—she was clutching hard enough to burn a fish brand into her palm as indelible as those that Cal burned into the flanks of cattle.

Kai, punning, had called the pin a linchpin, and had warned her about losing it, but now Lia was fretting the upsetting enigma of there being *two* linchpins—was that possible? was it likely?—and trying to find an answer to the puzzle.

Back at the office, Shawanda told her that Miss Grace still had not arrived but that Suzi Bonner had called to invite her to dinner on Saturday evening.

"Formal? Informal? What?"

"I guess it's more dress-down than dress-up, ma'am. Miss Suzi said you all was set to do some horseback riding before dinner."

"All right. Thanks."

Lia went into her office and sat down at her desk. She put the fish pin on her blotter and stared at it. It was real. It glinted in the sunlight coming through the slatted blinds, and its imprint was there in her hand like a seraphic seal of approval. Why, then, did she feel so woozy and confused?

The assembly center/dining hall in B dome is festooned with plants, giving it the fake serenity of a sauna in a forward battle zone. The incongruity of crimson-touched caladium leaves and mint-green ferns in a shell of rock and aluminum may account for some of Gordon Vear's nervousness. On the other hand, a day after the ferry shuttle *Daisy Duck*'s landing on the lunacrete pad near the solar array, the President is going to address Von Braunville's citizens, and Vear has an uneasy feeling about the likely gist of his remarks.

Nearly everyone at the base is crowding into the dining hall; only essential communications personnel and the 'dozer jockeys who must keep digging plagioclase feldspar for the O_2 plant will be absent. Coming in with Dahlquist, Vear sees the "cowboy" Pickford sitting in a chair near the podium and beside him the Episcopalian sky pilot Joshua Marlin.

Sighting the bishop calms the major. Marlin isn't a Catholic, of course, but he's closer to it than Easson, the Baptist physicist and chaplain, who is on his way home to Earth aboard the *Checkers*. And, when the crunch comes, Marlin is going to help them abreact history and set this topsy-turvy time line to rights. How, Vear doesn't yet know, but it will happen because of a ghostly dwarf; the determination of Erica Zola; Dahlquist and Vear's bewildered complicity; and the aid of the newcomers sitting up front awaiting the entrance of the President. Primarily the bishop.

"I want to sit in the back," Vear tells Dahlquist.

Dolly whispers, "Relax. This'll be a *pro forma* glad-to-be-here speech that every politician makes on the campaign trail."

"He isn't campaigning."

"Dream on. He's always campaigning."

Vear elbows his roommate toward a chair in the rear, and the hall keeps filling. Ubiquitous murmuring. A palpable current of excitement in the refiltered air.

And all this for a *pro forma* glad-to-be-here speech? No, sir. Not likely. The President has come to the Moon to wow them, and Vear remembers the fugue that he experienced on the interior crater ledge.

He remembers, too, the docking maneuver in lunar orbit, when the t-ship *Checkers* and the shuttle *Daisy Duck* met to exchange cargoes and passengers. The hookup lasted forever. Why? Because you just couldn't refuel the t-ship and push its many goodies through the docking ports into the shuttle in a mere fifteen minutes. And they hadn't. It took nearly an hour, Vear recalls. And during those grueling sixty minutes, only the President and the Secret Service man Griegs declined to help with the work. Indeed, Nixon paddled past Vear into *Daisy Duck*'s air lock soon after instrument readings showed that it had a breathable mix of oxygen and nitrogen.

As in his lunar hallucination, the major came to attention and saluted the President. But Nixon kept on floating. Eerily, the look on his face perfectly matched the one that he had worn nodding Ingham into Vear's pie wedge during that hallucination. But Ingham existed nowhere *except* in the major's fugue—Robinson and Griegs were the names of the men on *this* trip, a trip indisputably real—and, there in the cramped air lock of the t-ship, Vear knew that he was once again about to lose it.

Speak to the man, he encouraged himself. You can't allow the President of the United States to go by unacknowledged.

And so he barked, "Good to see you again, sir. We trust you all had a good crossing."

Griegs, wedging himself into the lock next to the major, said, "Yeah, it was fine."

Nixon finned himself around and studied Vear for a minute. "What do you mean, 'again'? We've never met, have we, Major?"

"No, sir. I should've said 'in person.' I've seen you on TV so often it just *seemed* like 'again.'"

The President's expression hardened; his jowls quavered as if he were contemplating a reply. Instead, he favored, or chastised, Vear with a scowl of such crude intensity that the major could feel his own face crimsoning. Then Griegs shoved Vear out of the way, and the President and his bodyguard strapped themselves into seats in the shuttle.

After which, not a little shaken, Vear oversaw the exchange of all the other passengers and the transfer of the cargo aboard the *Checkers* to *Daisy Duck*'s underslung craw. Guinea pigs. Plants. Cowboy. And a Protestant Episcopal bishop.

And surely, Vear thinks as the PA system begins to pipe in "Hail to the Chief," Bishop Marlin is going to make a helluva lot more difference to us than Brezhnev bears, imported greenery, or that anxious-looking Pickford fellow.

In fact, Pickford looks as nervous as Vear feels, and it's hard not to sympathize with him. In the few words that the major and the guinea-pig keeper—Lord, what a job!—exchanged on the flight down, Pickford seemed an okay guy. When *Daisy Duck* swooped across the Mare Crisium mascon (an ancient meteorite whose deeply buried bulk accelerated the shuttle, shaking it with gravitational effects that Vear is still learning to conquer), Pickford truly enjoyed the extra speed. He shouted, "Ride 'em, Major!" while everyone else, Marlin included, was as quiet as a Cistercian.

Up front, people are beginning to stand. Vear sees the bishop, Pickford, Franciscus, Gubarev, Nemov, and many others rippling to their feet; soon everyone in the hall is upright. Commander Logan enters from the galley. The President emerges a step or two behind him with his Secret Service bodyguards, both of whom, today, are wearing their green berets and expensive civilian suits. Nixon raises his arms over his head, showing the V for victory sign and smiling tightly. Griegs and Robinson bookend the podium, each of them near a hanging fern basket.

"Hail to the Chief" stops playing, everybody sits, Commander Logan introduces the President, and up he steps to speak. Vear leans forward, curious to know if Nixon's words will in any way echo the words spoken to him during his lunar rapture.

Nixon begins to talk. He says many of the things he said in his broadcasts from the *Checkers*. (Strangely, this speech is not being televised home—even though it *is* going out by radio to all base personnel not in the hall.) He has come to lift the dejected, to see Von Braunville firsthand, and to deliver a message of great importance to everyone working for NASA.

"And what about the Russians?" Vear asks Dolly, whispering. Gubarev, Romanenko, Nemov, and Shikin are on the Moon courtesy of NASA, but they are Soviet scientists and military men.

Dahlquist shrugs.

Shortly, the President is comfortably into his speech, and Vear notes that after every big topic heading, Nixon is saying, "I am a Von Braunvillian." A flourish lifted from John F. Kennedy's "*Ich bin Berliner*" address of the early 1960s. Nearly everyone on hand, sensing a refrain opportunity, joins Nixon in asserting, "I am a Von Braunvillian!" Applause accompanies these boasts, and now even the Russians are lending their voices to the chorus. Vear has to struggle to keep from joining it himself; eventually, though, he begins to wonder *why* he feels obliged to resist.

The President pauses. All along, his gestures have had that spastic quality—almost a robotic mechanicalness—typical of his speech-making behavior. As he stands wordless before his fellow Von Braunvillians, his eyes go glassy and his jowls perceptibly inflate, as if something in the hall has annoyed him. Vear feels the hair on his nape rising and his palms turning cold.

"My fellow Von Braunvillians," the President says, "within the next six months the United States will launch a manned expedition to Mars. Four people here among you have been selected for this extraordinary mission. Their surnames—I list them alphabetically rather than by rank—are Berry, Franciscus, Hoffman, and Vear."

Stunned silence. Then the selected men's colleagues, rising as one, burst into applause. Vear feels his skull ballooning like a bellows, and nothing about the moment seems real. He is suffering another hallucination. Or is he? Dolly's hand on his shoulder has substance, doesn't it? The hurrahing of his comrades is palpable, isn't it?

But do any of them care that he doesn't want to go to Mars? Do any of them know that this unlikely scene parodies the President's distressing revelation to him during his lunar fugue?

Of course not. How could they?

The din dies. Chairs scrape as everyone sits.

"Usually, of course, we consult with our astronauts to see how they feel about a dangerous mission, but in this case we chose our fellas on the basis of service records, psychological profiles, and peer ratings. These guys came out on top. Make no mistake: We'd never send anybody unequal to the task, and Messieurs Berry, Franciscus, Hoffman, and Vear are more than equal to it. If they *haven't* got the gumption to go, just let 'em say so, without the least prejudice to their careers, and we'll slap in some gung-ho alternates to take up the slack."

Romanenko, a Soviet cosmonaut and materials scientist, gets to his feet. "Mr. President, my countrymen and I applaud this great endeavor, too. We pledge our support. And if you must try to find these 'gung-ho' alternates, please overlook us not."

Approving murmurs. The cosmonaut nods to acknowledge them and then sits again.

Nixon glares at Romanenko. At last, he says, "The only place you and your countrymen are going, Major, is home."

Warily, Romanenko rises again. "But why, Mr. President?"

"We can maintain a token Soviet presence here at Von Braunville better with Brezhnev bears than with live commies. Six cavies for four cosmonauts. I for one see that as a pretty fair trade."

Stung, Romanenko lowers himself into his chair. Even

Vear, in the midst of his personal shock, sits aghast at this unanticipated presidential rudeness, and no one in the entire hall speaks. Like Romanenko, like Vear, no one has any idea what to say or what good mere speech can possibly do. Playing superpower politics with men you have to work beside every day is impossible, and the major is embarrassed on the President's behalf. So, it seems, is *nearly* every other American in the hall.

Finally, Shikin, the youngest of the four Soviets, stands and says, "Mr. President, that is an insulting—"

Nixon cocks his head and autocratically raises the palm of one hand. "Spare me. Communism is something a country—likewise Von Braunville—is infected with, not something it chooses. So let me make it perfectly clear that I'm taking action against a latent plague. You guys always say that what's yours is yours and what's ours is negotiable. Well, I'm not going to give you a single piece of this Mars mission. The Red Planet will never be the Red Planet in any sense that the Kremlin approves. And if that means the end of détente, good riddance."

Greatly daring, Shikin advances toward the podium. The agents flanking Nixon tense, and the young cosmonaut says, "Sir, I spit on your ideological bigotry." He does, too. Directly on the lapel of the President's pinstriped jacket.

"Why, you filthy SOB!" the President snarls.

Pandemonium ensues. Vear can scarcely believe that such chaos has descended on the isolate little world of Von Braunville. What luck that the President's speech *isn't* being televised home. No healthy impact on global opinion could derive from a brawl between the Leader of the Free World and a youthful cosmonaut.

Even so, Nixon has decked Shikin with a badly telegraphed right cross. Shikin failed to duck it only because an irate 'dozer pilot—a staunch Nixonian—shoved him into it from behind.

Now, one of the President's bodyguards is holding Shikin to the floor. The other is wielding the butt of his pistol, yanked from a shoulder holster, to knock the outraged Nemov to his knees.

Gubarev and Romanenko are expostulating for calm, but the fever for fisticuffs has infected half the room, and finally the Soviets must fight to keep the surlies from knuckling them under, too.

Bishop Marlin has also jumped into the fray—not to add himself to its combatants, but to limit the mayhem. He grabs the berserkly flailing Nixon from behind, imposing a full nelson, and walks him away from the two standing cosmonauts. The agent with the pistol goes after the bishop, who is hopping along behind the President as the latter's rodeo-bronc antics demand. Cal Pickford slips forward to grab Robinson's arm and pry the pistol loose.

"Stop this nonsense!" Bishop Marlin cries. "Stop this nonsense immediately!" His powerful voice confounds some of the surlies, and when he shouts again, it quiets even the most implacable among them.

Vear, who has been standing on his chair, watches Bishop Marlin twist Nixon back to the podium and release him with a disgusted push. Then the bishop bumps Nixon away from the mike, orders the bellicose 'dozer jockey to help Shikin and Nemov up, and scolds everyone on the premises for their "puerile barbarism."

"This is what comes of beginning our meeting without a proper invocation," he declares.

Nixon, Vear notices, is standing at the bishop's right elbow, more or less in control of himself again. His eyes, however, have a hooded look, and his jaw seems bluer and carved to a crisper jut than it did upon his entrance.

"And so," says Bishop Marlin, "we end with a benediction." He blesses the abashed crowd. "Bury your animosities and go forth in peace."

The President shoots his cuffs with a robotic shoulder hunch, pivots, and leaves the hall by way of the galley. Commander Logan and the two Secret Service men follow him out.

"Congratulations," Dolly tells Vear.

"For what?"

"Being selected for the Mars mission. It's a high honor."

"It's a nightmare. A nightmare I've already had."

The plants festooning the hall sway in the perceptible wake of the late disturbance. Vear and Dolly, exiting ahead of thirty-five or forty others, bemusedly return to C dome.

* * *

Cal was lying in the web of the low-g hammock that he had hung in the chaplain's quarters, for Marlin had asked him to share this space and the two men were mulling the President's behavior.

"He lost it, didn't he, sir?"

"Some say he never had it. In truth, though, he's been going rapidly downhill ever since the '80 election."

Cal tried to prop himself up in the hammock; Marlin's reply was the first disparaging remark that he had heard this man utter about the President.

"What do you mean, 'rapidly'?"

"The imperial presidency came to full flower in his first term, and he was definitely beyond clear-eyed self-assessment even before the victory in Vietnam. But only within the last two years has he surrendered his soul to the Evil for which he has been an unwitting—but not unwilling—instrument for so long."

"The Evil? What do you mean? I don't get it."

Bishop Marlin was sitting at the former chaplain's desk with a Bible and a prayer book open beside him. He printed several words on a sheet of paper and carried it to Cal, who, taking it, read the following message: HE'S POSSESSED BY DEMONS. MAYBE SATAN HIMSELF.

Cal looked around. Obviously, the bishop feared that their pie wedge in B dome was bugged. Marlin printed several more words on his pad, tore off this sheet, and handed it to Cal, too. INSULTING SOVIETS, TAKING PUNCH AT ONE. THIS IS OVER-THE-EDGE BEHAVIOR.

Twisting, Cal managed to free his legs from the uncomfortable hammock. "I agree with you, sir, but—"

Another sheet: NOT ONLY EVIDENCE. BERTHELOT TOLD ME SOMETHING THAT CLINCHES IT.

"That clinches—" Cal wanted to say "possession," but the bishop shook his head and handed him this block-printed message: PRESIDENT PLANS PREEMPTIVE NUCLEAR STRIKE AGAINST SOVIET UNION & SATELLITE-BASED LASER ATTACK.

"When?" Cal blurted.

WITHIN NEXT 2 WEEKS.

"Why?"

SUPPOSEDLY BECAUSE OF BAD SOVIET BEHAVIOR IN CENTRAL AMERICA, AFGHANISTAN, POLAND. EVEN HE BELIEVES THIS. BUT

IN TRUTH BECAUSE HE'S IN THRALL TO DEMONS WHO WANT TO
SEDUCE WHOLE SPECIES & BRING ABOUT ARMAGEDDON.

Wait a minute, Cal thought. This guy is crazy. I've got
good cause to think our fourth-term president the evilest
bastard this side of Nazi Germany, but I don't for a minute
think that I've got to attribute his treacherous megalomania—
a word that Lia has even applied to me—to demonic possession.

They conversed in this same way—Cal talking guardedly
aloud, Bishop Marlin scribbling on his notepad—for several
more minutes, and Cal learned that Nixon had come to the
Moon not just to lift morale, etc., but also to ensure his own
safety when the preemptive nuclear strikes by SAC bombers
and silo-inhabiting ICBMs, as well as an attack by experimen-
tal satellite lasers, put planet Earth in jeopardy of outright
and total destruction. Still other signs of the President's
irreversible depravity were his complete abandonment of his
family and his desire to get the four Soviet cosmonauts home
to Russia in time for these annihilating fireworks.

There was a knock on the chaplain's door.

The two men started. Have we already given ourselves
away? Cal wondered. They began gathering up and crumpling
into balls all the bishop's incriminating notes.

"Coming," Marlin cried. "Just a minute."

"Why didn't you tell me this before?" Cal demanded.

"Where? At the NASA facilities in Houston? You
wouldn't have come. Aboard the *Clemency*, the *Checkers*, or
the *Daisy Duck*? That was impossible, too. The President was
practically sitting in our laps."

Another insistent knock.

"Coming!" the bishop cried again. He pushed the button
to open the door, and Cal saw in the B dome corridor (1) the
shuttle ferry pilot who had brought them down from lunar
orbit, (2) a tall blond man wearing a boyishly perplexed
frown, and (3) a familiar-looking woman with large eyes and
discolored teeth. "Major Vear," Bishop Marlin said. "Please
come in."

The trio entered. Vear made hasty introductions, and Cal
found himself hugging Erica Zola, the resident psychotherapist, not from any initiative of his own but because she had
sprung upon him as if she were a long-lost sister. It took a

minute or two to iron out the particulars of their previous acquaintance, but when he finally had it straight, Cal returned her hug, reflecting, This is it, this is the beginning. . . .

Erica stepped back and spoke to Bishop Marlin: "You've come to help us abreact our suppressed liberty, haven't you?"

Even if the chaplain's office were bugged, Cal thought, no one overhearing that remark would be able to deduce much from it. He knew what *abreact* meant, of course, but it didn't seem to have an immediate application to this perilous situation, a conspiracy of five motley, very nervous persons in the chaplain's quarters at the U.S. moonbase.

Even so, they arranged themselves about the pie wedge, Erica on the sofa opposite Marlin's desk, Peter Dahlquist on a chair, Cal back in his hammock, and Vear on the seat of the confessional that the last chaplain, Easson, had refused to use. Bishop Marlin gave out Magic Markers and notepads so that they could "talk" without tipping Big Brother to their plans.

"All we lack now," said Dahlquist aloud, turning a skeptical eye on his Magic Marker, "is our resurrected boss man, Kai."

"Who?" Cal exclaimed. "What did you say?"

"Shhhh," said Bishop Marlin. "Use your notepads. The walls have amplified telemetric auditory capabilities, and if we fail, our entire terrestrial ecosphere may die."

That's just the reminder we need, Cal thought, to work calmly and assuredly toward our goals.

"Actually," Dahlquist said, "I regularly check the chaplain's and Dr. Zola's offices to make sure they *aren't* bugged. But we'll use your silly Magic Markers if you like, sir."

"Oh," said Marlin, nonplussed, after which their plotting went forward aloud. Cal, meanwhile, put his hand into his jumpsuit and found Lia's fish pin: It was faintly warm, a soothing talisman.

At Brown Thrasher Barony, Lia showed up in blue jeans and one of Cal's western-cut shirts. The shirt had mother-of-pearl snaps and a blue satin yoke in front and back. The sky above the horse farm was clear, the air brisk, and the ground slightly marshy from a recent rain. A pretty good afternoon for riding.

Jeff Bonner said, "No news from Cal since he got to the Moon?"

The entire Bonner family was walking from the double-wide to the horse barn. The azaleas along the fence had already faded, but wild flowers—primroses and violets, mostly—still punctuated the meadows, pastel corks on a wide emerald lake. A bit farther down the road, a red-capped flicker was drilling a fence post.

"It's a pretty expensive long-distance call, Jeff."

"Yeah, but—"

"'Yeah, but,' 'Yeah, but,' 'Yeah, but,'" mocked Suzi. "Listen, Jeff. We got Lia out here to take her mind off that stuff, not to quiz her on it."

Bless you, thought Lia. Only the chief executive of the United States can call home from Censorinus and reverse the charges to the American taxpayer. And although you guys don't know it, none of us may *ever* hear from my hubby again—at least not in this historical continuum. And what our chances of encountering one another in the abreacted reality are, well, I honestly don't know. . . .

Abreacted reality? Where did you get that? Lia asked herself. The term had a strange, almost an ominous, ring, and yet she knew intellectually that Cal had gone to Von Braunville to help Bishop Joshua Marlin and presumably some unspecified others "engineer the redemptive shift." That King Richard had gone, too, was ominously significant, for although Cal was Kai's "lens," a glass that would focus the dead writer's stereographia, the President was the tinder that this purifying focus must ignite and burn out of existence to make room for the better, long-suppressed reality that their effort would . . . well, *abreact*.

Jeff said, "Hey, Suzi, I'm just making brotherly conversation."

"As usual, you're pick-pick-picking. Please stop it."

"Christ. Forgive me for breathing."

Martin and Carina, who were running ahead of the three adults, disappeared into the stable.

"You guys ever ride the thoroughbreds?" Lia asked. What would it be like to sit on one of those magnificent animals? she wondered. Most of the people who rode at Brown Thrasher Barony were given a quarter horse. The thoroughbreds, which Horsy Stout trained for the private tracks in Florida, Alabama, and Kentucky, were *verboten* to amateurs because of the huge sums invested in them—not so much for the racing purses that Wiedenhoedt pipe-dreamed they would win as for the tax write-off that they already represented. It seemed to Lia, in fact, that Divine Intervention, Radioactive, and the other thoroughbreds were living off the fat of the land. They got groomed, fed, and pampered, and they did virtually nothing—beyond exist—to justify their staples and stall.

"Not often," Suzi said. "They're persnickety creatures. We really don't want the kids on them."

"What if *I* rode a thoroughbred? I'd like to."

"Lia—" Jeff began, transparently annoyed.

They entered the high-ceilinged stable. Shafts of bourbon-hued brightness slanted in from the skylights, and Suzi said, "Come on, Jeffrey. Let her. It'd be good for the horse and fun for Lia."

"She'll break her neck."

"Then you'd be well rid of me, wouldn't you?"

"My luck, your lawyers would descend with thirty-six lawsuits."

But Suzi prevailed upon Jeff to give Lia one of the high-strung horses, and Horsy came down from his rafter room to help Carina and Martin saddle up. Again, the dwarf's crippled-seeming but bluntly powerful physique reminded Lia of a trash-compacted bodybuilder.

As soon as Horsy had the kids mounted, he swaggered over on his bandy legs to ask the adults which horses they wanted.

"Sophisticated Lady for Lia," Jeff directed. This was a sorrel filly with white stockings.

"But I want Ubiquity," Lia said.

"Christ."

"Let her have him, Jeff."

Lia had known that this choice would further upset her brother and that Suzi would probably jump to her defense. But why go out of her way to nettle Jeff and to energize Suzi? Well, because after returning to Georgia from the Cape, her days had alternated drudgery and disappointment.

Striving to rattle her brother was a cheap way of exorcising

her pique—first, that Cal was so far away and, second, that a
fickle actress had apparently dumped her as her psychotherapist. Not satisfied with merely blackmailing them, Grace
Rinehart was compounding Lia's sense of isolation by abandoning her.

But I'm going to ride away from my worries, Lia thought.
I'm going to arrest my melancholy on Ubiquity's back and
restore my capacity for wonder.

"Ubiquity's a good choice for what ails you," Horsy Stout
said, uncannily seconding her private reasoning.

Jeff said, "Yeah. He'll flip you over onto your head and
make your every ailment obsolete."

This sarcasm was his final objection, however, and Horsy
went into the blue-black stallion's stall to ready him for Lia's
ride. A saddle as delicate as a leather doily. A bit and bridle
as light as an oversized paper clip. Stirrups as stylish as
macramé swings. Lia mounted from the wooden ledge inside
the stall, whereupon Horsy led Ubiquity out onto the concrete floor of the stable to join Jeff and Suzi and the kids, all
of whom were astride easygoing quarter horses that looked
like spavined mules—in comparison, that is, to Lia's majestic
thoroughbred.

Still afoot, Horsy led the horseback Bonners through the
long building to the east pasture.

"Run 'em hard," he said. "But bring 'em back so's I can
rub 'em down and give 'em their mash."

"Ride with us," Lia said.

"Don't got any ponies here, ma'am, and the colts, besides
not bein' broke, ain't stout enough to hold this Stout."

"But you're just jockey size, Horsy."

"Only from head to toe. From shoulder to shoulder,
though, I'm a cannonball they don't fancy balancin'."

Lia and the others rode. The east pasture graded into a
stand of pines riven by a bridle path. They made this
pinecone-littered circuit in forty minutes and came back into
the pasture. Here, Jeff nudged his horse into an all-out trot.
Martin and Carina, whooping like Indians, followed suit. So
did Suzi, less gleefully than her kids. Ubiquity—whom Lia
had been handling with a taut rein and a stream of comforting
nonsense—snorted, reared, twisted, and leapt off after the
other galloping horses.

"Whoa!" Lia cried. "Damn you, Yubik, slow down!"

But the thoroughbred ran past Suzi's mount, split the kids' two horses, and overtook Jeff's laboring animal about a hundred yards from the eastern end of the stable. Ubiquity was flying, and Lia would have relaxed and enjoyed the wind scouring her eyes—except that she could sense through the stallion's flanks the marshiness of the pasture and her own utter lack of control in his headlong dash. As in a corny cowboy movie, she was aboard a runaway, and Cal, the hero any screenwriter would have named to save her, was a quarter of a million miles away.

"I told you!" Jeff was shouting at Suzi somewhere behind her. "I told you this would happen!"

Lia thought, But I'm all right. There may be peril here, but it isn't mine. Ubiquity's more likely to suffer than I am. He's generating terrific speed under adverse conditions, and I'm waiting to hear one of his ankles crack. If I'm thrown, well, the ground's going to receive me like a big benevolent catcher's mit. . . .

Unfortunately, everyone behind her was shouting—Jeff, Suzi, Martin, Carina. They were offering advice ("Rein him in, rein him in!"), expressing dismay ("Oh, my God!"), or cheering her on ("Go, Aunt Lia! Ride him!"). The sound of this uproar drew Horsy Stout from the east end of the stable. He ran bandy-legged into the pasture. Clearly fearful that Ubiquity would collide with one of the paddock fences, he began waving his arms.

"It's all right!" Lia yelled. "Just get out of his way!"

The horse was trying to spook her. This "out-of-control" jaunt was meant to panic the poor female astride him. Well, she'd ridden a meaner creature—not just high-strung but congenitally ornery—in one of the annual Pioneer Days rodeos in Snowy Falls, Colorado, and Ubiquity was a pussy-cat next to Buckshot. If only Horsy would jump aside. If only he wouldn't try to play the hero that he thinks I'm desperately worthy of. . . .

But the nearer Ubiquity and she approached the stable, the more agitated the dwarf became. Now he was running toward them, and as the thoroughbred ripped past the muscular little man, Horsy reached up, grabbed Lia's leg, and toppled her out of the saddle. Damn it all to hell! she thought, bruising her shoulder but simultaneously rolling to a sitting position. She fully expected to find Horsy on the sodden ground somewhere nearby. It would be pleasant to thank him for attempting a rescue but even more pleasant to tell him that his effort had been totally unnecessary.

Then she saw that Ubiquity was running south along the paddock fence dragging the stirrup-entangled dwarf and bouncing him off every primary support post along it. All she could really see of him was his lower body, the blur of his blue jeans rotating within the eggbeater blur of Ubiquity's limbs, and a shocking flash of white from the tail of his shirt. The way he was getting whipped around off those fence posts—a staff for scoring pain—it was hard to imagine him surviving.

Stupid, stupid, stupid.

Lia got to her feet and ran along the fence after both Ubiquity and Horsy Stout. Jeff came riding up, too, and, suddenly, after a breakneck run to the outside corner of the paddock, Ubiquity eased off, blew a mucous bubble from one flaring nostril, and nonchalantly began to nibble at the grass. The dwarf was a shapeless body bag, leaking blood, hung up in the left stirrup strap. Lia slowed to a walk, while Jeff turned his mount aside. The trip along the fence had torn nearly every button off Horsy's shirt and lacerated him as if with a cat-o'-nine-tails.

Lia approached and knelt. A simple twist of the stirrup freed him, and he slumped into the grass. Lia hit Ubiquity on the thigh to get the horse to move off, then stretched out beside the dwarf to study his pain-filled face.

"You didn't have to do that," she said.

"My pleasure," Horsy Stout managed.

"You've killed yourself for no reason."

"Ain't dead. Ain't dyin', either. What I am is"—a contorted smile—"goin' travelin', ma'am."

"Yeah? Traveling where, Horsy?"

"Don' always know. Mebbe the Moon."

Delirious, Lia thought. "Well, say hello to Cal for me."

"'S not me who'll be there. 'S my angel. My pilot."

"Get him to say hello, then."

"Ain't dressed to travel, ma'am. Look at me, all bloody like."

"You're fine, Horsy. You look just fine."

"Button my shirt, Miss Lia." Horsy peered down his nose at his lacerated chest. "To keep up the proprieties."

He may not be dying, Lia thought, but that sounds like a last request. She tugged his shirt out from under him and buttoned its sole remaining button. Then, tenderly, she took the fish pin off the yoke of her western shirt and used it to fasten Horsy's shirt just below its collar.

"Thank you, Miss Lia," he said. "Remember now: Cal loves you, gal, and somewhere, somehow, you all gonna see each other again in the happiest sort of way. I'm off."

Jeff came walking up. His shadow fell across both Lia and the prostrate dwarf. As it did, the air around Horsy began to tingle, a sensation both visual and tactile. Another face was hovering above the black man's: a clear Caucasian mask over the dwarf's Negroid visage. And the very air had changed, giving their May sky the fragile, fairy-tale color of muscadine wine.

"Holy shit," Jeff said, awed.

Lia, looking back toward Suzi and the kids, saw their horses frozen in midstride and a crow flapping over the woods behind them suspended there like a bizarre taxidermic illusion.

"Horsy's okay," said the man on the ground. "He's just off on a jaunt is all."

"Kai!"

"Hey, I don't have long. I've got to follow him before his glorified body gets there uninhabited."

"Censorinus?"

The laminate features masking Horsy's nodded. "I've got this thing I want you to do. It's okay with Horsy. He's come to see the two of us as symbionts, I think."

Jeff knelt beside Lia. Through clenched teeth, he said, "Would you tell me what the fuck is happening here, little sister?"

Kai ignored the intrusion. "There's an envelope with several twenty-dollar bills in it on the bedside table in Horsy's rafter room. It's already addressed. I want you to seal it, put a stamp on it, and mail it. Okay?"

"Sure, Kai. Of course."

"Fine. That's it, then. I'm off, too."

"*Lia!*" Jeff insisted.

Lia shook off her brother's touch and stood. Kai had followed Horsy; now the abandoned husk of the dwarf's body was lying in the grass breathing on automatic pilot, sustaining itself through mere habit until its animating spirit could return to reclaim it.

Meanwhile, the muscadine-tinted stasis surrounding Kai's pocket of out-of-time mobility was decaying and the sky's immemorial blue flooding back in. The horses belonging to the other three Bonners unthawed, and so did the crow briefly pinned to the muscadine sky above the woods.

"Is he dead?" Suzi cried, riding up. "Did he break any bones?"

"You talk to her," Lia told her brother. "I've got something to do." She kissed her dismounted sister-in-law, told her agitated nephew and niece that Horsy would be all right, and walked along the paddock rail to the horse barn.

A moment later, in Horsy's rafter room, Lia understood that Kai had addressed the envelope full of cash to the cab driver who had driven him to Warm Springs from the Atlanta airport. That's good, she thought. Maybe things are getting better already. At the same time, her innate practicality asserting itself, she realized that she would have to buy a money order at the post office. Only an utter idiot would send so much cash through the mails, and both Kai and Horsy would want her to do everything in her power to make sure that the wronged cabbie finally got his fare.

Another thing immensely cheered her: Horsy had promised that somewhere, somehow, she and Cal would be reunited. Of course, we will, Lia thought. Of course we will. How could our story end in any other way . . . ?

24

Eating dinner with Major Vear and the computer troubleshooter Peter Dahlquist, Cal had two disturbing insights.

"Bishop Marlin isn't eating," he announced. "He hasn't eaten since we got here. Three whole days."

"The Black Fast," Vear said. "He's readying himself."

Yes, Cal thought, for the exorcism. But his second insight was even more disturbing than the length of the bishop's fast. "What's happened to Easter?"

Vear and Dolly looked at each other.

"Easter," Cal repeated, annoyed. "Look, I'm not a churchgoer, but the calendar says May, and Easter hasn't happened yet."

Vear's face finally registered puzzlement and a discernible trace of worry. He found a small date-book calendar in one of his jumpsuit pockets and consulted it.

"Easter is always the Sunday after the first full moon after the vernal equinox," he said. He looked at Cal and Dolly. "This year, it should've been April the eleventh. But we didn't observe it. Easson took no special note of it at all. It was a Sunday like any other Sunday."

"A Sunday like any other Sunday *on the Moon*," Dolly qualified. "Maybe the chaplain didn't celebrate Easter on that Sunday because, up here, we don't *have* full moons. Or vernal equinoxes. Or enough rabid Christians to make the holiday worth getting hot and bothered about."

"Easter?" Vear said, outraged. "Even tepid believers observe Easter. How could Chaplain Easson utterly forget it? How could *we* forget it?"

Cal said, "It didn't happen back home, either. If it had, Lia would've dragged me to church."

"Hey, Gordon," Dolly said, "I'm not even tepid. I'm your basic agnostic-on-good-days, atheist-on-bad."

"What about Kai?" Vear attacked him. "How do you account for a phenomenon like Kai?"

Heads began to turn, and Cal realized that he had to shut these two guys up or risk losing something in addition to Easter, namely, any chance of abreacting a time line that would restore it.

"Let's go talk to the bishop," he said.

Vear ignored Cal. "If you're an agnostic, Dolly, why in God's name would you write an elegy for Kai that goes 'Philip K. Dick is dead, alas. / Let's all queue up and kick God's ass'? That's pretty fuckin' irreverent, I admit, but at least it acknowledges the fact that God exists."

"Hold it down," Dolly cautioned the major. The eyes of three quarters of the people in the hall were fixed on their table.

Just a minute, Cal thought. Just a damn minute. Dolly didn't write that "pretty fuckin' irreverent" elegy. *I* wrote it. I wrote it the afternoon of the day I learned of Dick's death. This guy—this *computer person*—can't run off with my poem just because he's been up here longer than I have. . . .

Angrily, Cal declared that authorship of the elegy in question belonged to him, not to the major's roommate, and that if Vear kept insisting otherwise, he was a liar.

"Watch it, Pickford," Dolly countered. "Gordon's no liar. I *did* write it. Maybe I shouldn't jump to confess myself the author of such doggerel, but honesty has its compulsions and so I'm being honest and taking you off the hook."

Very clever, Cal thought. You arrogant wiseacre. Aloud, he declared, "Listen, if you say you wrote *my* elegy, you're guilty of plagiarism."

Dolly feigned a look of abashed horror. "Oh, no. Please don't accuse me of plagiarizing that drecky couplet. I hereby abjure all claim to its authorship. It's yours, Pickford."

"You can't give me what's already mine."

"He can give you what's his, though. And Dolly wrote that poem not long after I saw Kai dancing around suitless outside."

"You're both—" Wait, Cal told himself. This is absurd. It's not the authorship of my elegy for Dick that's important; it's the evaporation of Easter from the April 1982 calendar. *That's* the issue. And Cal said so aloud.

"Maybe Phil Dick's resurrection in late March preempted Easter this year," Dolly conjectured. "Maybe it's a temporal law that you can only have one big resurrection event every spring."

But Vear roared, "Nothing's so goddamn big that it preempts the resurrection of the Son of God!"

A high-ranking officer at a nearby table got up and approached them. At least it isn't Commander Logan, Cal thought. Instead, it was Colonel Mick Hoffman, the ranking ferry-shuttle pilot, who had recently persuaded their leader to set aside Vear's "house arrest" so that he could return to full active status.

"Major," the colonel said, "would you gentlemen hold it down to a minor tumult, please?"

"Theological discussion," Cal said.

"No such thing as a discussion on that head, Pickford. They're *arguments*. Yours is ruining everybody's digestion."

"What happened to Easter?" Cal gave the colonel a challenging look. "That's what we've been trying to decide."

Hoffman's craggy face split into a grin. "Can't you goyim keep up with your own goddamn holy days anymore? No wonder the West's going to Sheol in a shopping cart." Now grinless, he scrutinized them as if they were the Von Braunvillian counterpart of the Three Stooges; then, almost disdainfully, he turned and left.

Larry, Curly, and Moe, Cal thought. That's exactly the crew we resemble, sitting here puzzling over the dimension, or the temporal singularity, into which Easter has vanished. Therefore, my earlier suggestion is the only one that makes any sense.

"Let's go talk to the bishop," Cal said again.

The three men strolled the circumferential corridor of B dome until they had come to the chapel and the chaplain's quarters. A glowing sign above the former indicated that

Bishop Marlin was busy confessing someone, and they remained in the hall until this sign was automatically extinguished by the penitent's departure from the confessional. Then they entered.

Cal was surprised to find that the man whom the bishop had just shriven was Robinson, one of President Nixon's two Secret Service bodyguards. About Cal's own age, he had a sinewy physique, a face like a youthful night watchman's, and long hands that he had often used aboard the *Checkers* to operate a portable videocam. Cal had always supposed him the more trusted of the President's two agents, and Vear and Dolly's cool reaction to his presence suggested that they, too, were troubled to see him here. As for Robinson, he was compulsively squeezing his beret, manipulating it like an exercise ball for arthritics.

"Major Vear, Mr. Dahlquist, allow me to introduce you to Tyler Robinson," said the bishop. "Cal already knows him."

Do I? wondered Cal. We voyaged across outer space together to reach Von Braunville, but during those four days he probably spoke two complete sentences to me. In my opinion, the only good thing about him is that he falls just a little shy of Griegs's glowering ogrehood. . . .

Added Bishop Marlin, "He's officially off duty, which he *never* was on our voyage out, and now I know that he's an Episcopalian."

"Congratulations," said Dahlquist.

"Thanks," mumbled Tyler Robinson, throttling the beret.

"And now I'm free to tell you," the bishop said, an avuncular hand on Robinson's shoulder, "that he's our seventh. Because he's joined us, we can proceed. And everything should be easier because of his involvement."

Am I supposed to laugh or cry? Cal wondered. Hurrah, on the one hand. On the other, what if this guy is a plant? What if the President's setting us up for a bun-busting tumble?

"Our seventh?" Dolly said. "Why do we need a seventh?"

Virtually simultaneously, Vear asked, "And what's happened to Easter, Bishop Marlin? Where did it go?"

"We need a seventh because it's a holy number, Mr. Dahlquist, and nothing's happened to Easter, Major Vear, except that it's been delayed—I have this, gentlemen, on divine authority—until we can do what we must do."

Cal said, "And when's that?"

"Today. This afternoon. As soon as possible." The bishop let Robinson out, assuring him that the penance he had prescribed would absolve him of his sins; then he walked past the confessional to the altar at the rear of the tiny chapel. "Come over here," he urged Cal. "You'll want to see this."

Cal joined him beside the low altar. Behind it, concealed from Vear and Dolly, sat one of the cavy cages that they had transported all the way from Earth. Looking down, Cal saw that the pregnant guinea pig inside this cage had given birth to at least four baby Brezhnev bears. They were minute, and naked except for the collars of colorful fur around their heads and shoulders. Despite himself, Cal grinned and reached down through the cage's open top to scratch the brindle mane of the mother. Except for the crucifix above the altar and the low gravity, it was like being back in Mr. K.'s Happy Puppy Pet Emporium.

"I'm finally getting fond of these stupid things," Cal said. "They're like crosses between a link sausage and a woolly bear."

"Don't get too fond of them," Bishop Marlin advised. "It's not too likely the little guys'll make the shift with us."

Erica Zola was sessioning with Major Romanenko, the cosmonaut whose technical specialty—materials science—was the same as the late Roland Nyby's. Romanenko had come in, literally begging for a consultation, during the psychotherapist's lunch break, and she had acceded to his request because he was so painfully distraught that to have refused him would have been a small crime against humanity, both his and hers.

"I want to kill him," he repeated for the ninth time.

"An illogical response to the insult of a deranged man, Kolya. Intellectually, you know this, don't you?"

Kolya Romanenko gave her a look hot enough to singe the potted hydrangea basking in the fluorescent panel behind her desk. "You cognitive therapists are all the same, doctor lady."

"A behaviorial therapist would advise you similarly. As

far as that goes, so would a family therapist, a psychodynam-
ist, probably even an interpersonalist. You've got a right to be
angry, but you have no right to kill President Nixon."

"I want to defect."

Another off-the-wall desire, Erica thought. Did Cal's
wife, Lia, ever have clients like this? Aloud she said, "To the
country whose leader insulted you?"

"No. To here. Your führer cried, 'I am a Von Braunvillian.' So let me defect to this moonbase. Forever."

"That's a political problem, Kolya, not a psychological or
an emotional one. I can only help you with it if you understand that your wish is at bottom an absurd one."

Besides, Erica reflected, after today this place may no
longer exist. And if you've defected to it, you'll be without a
country. Without a *community*, even. And what hyprocrisy—
my asserting it's wrong to want to kill Nixon when I myself
am part of a conspiracy to effect his overthrow by
parapsychotherapeutic means. . . .

"*I am a Von Braunvillian*," Romanenko insisted.

A knock on the door and an announcement from the
speaker unit next to it: "Erica, it's Cal Pickford. May I come
in?"

Erica said, "Just a mi—"

"I'm leaving," Major Kolya Romanenko said, standing
up. "But I promise you that I will *die* a Von Braunvillian." He
stormed to the door, jabbed the button unsheathing its panel,
and brushed past Cal Pickford into B dome's circumferential
corridor.

"Kolya!" Erica shouted. What did that mean, "I will *die* a
Von Braunvillian"? Probably a suicide threat. No idle one,
either. Romanenko will precipitate himself out of our community in the same desparate way that Nyby did. I need to go
after him. . . .

But Cal was entering, clutching a Brezhnev bear. "For
you," he said, setting the cavy on her blotter and casting a
puzzled look after the cosmonaut. "A feisty little male." The
panel whooshed shut again. "The 'bear,' I mean."

"I'm afraid Kolya needs it more than I do, Cal."

"Should I go after him?"

Erica could not say. The fluorescents in her office flick-
ered, bringing darkness but snapping back so quickly that

every cabinet, computer, and console was lit as if by a sustained nuclear flash. When the intensity of this light—oddly pink in color—at last fell off, the crippled body of the dwarf called Kai (alias Horsy Stout; alias Philip K. Dick) began to materialize in the chair that Kolya Romanenko had so abruptly vacated.

A spirit clothed in the glorified body of a black stable-hand, Erica thought. But it *looks* as if our homunculus has only barely escaped from a fistfight with his life. Torn shirt, lacerated chest, bunged-up face—all of him paradoxically spilling a sheen that bespeaks an incorruptible spiritual body. And never mind his perishable-appearing flesh and duds.

"Let him go," Kai said, nodding after the Soviet. "If we work fast enough, he won't have time to off himself."

"Now?" Erica asked.

"Yeah. The place is already prepared. You, Dr. Zola, are the secular specialist on our team. You'll help Biship Marlin and me direct a massive spiritual assault. Everyone else has a role, too, even if it's only assisting our abreactive exorcism by projecting love at the guy pinned down to the gurney."

"Projecting love at King Richard?" Cal said. "You've got to be joking. I'll be absolutely worthless to you."

"No. No, you won't. You'll be holding the joker to the table for us. And when you're not doing that, well, you'll be—this is the truth, even if it sounds dumb—you'll be radiating love at the invaded person you think you've got cause to hate. Broadcasting it like a radio tower. 'S true. Cross my heart."

Cal, Erica noticed, was shaking his head. Then he caught sight of something glittering on Kai's shirt front—a pin of some kind—and knelt to touch it. The homunculus warned him off by wagging a finger at him. So Cal pulled back and stared up at the enthroned dwarf with . . . well, what? Expectant awe, apparently.

"Yeah, you've got one, too. And Lia's going to find another one later tonight in her jewelry box. A trinity of fish pins."

"Why?"

"To keep us three lost crumbs in this vast perceptive omniverse from getting separated when the shift comes."

Lost, Erica reflected. I'm the one who's lost. None of this

adds up to diddlysquat. A trinity, Kai says, but to me it's all *koine* Greek. . . .

The dwarf looked directly at her. Then he said, "The spirit of evil is one of unreality, Dr. Zola, but it, itself, is real. It genuinely exists. To think otherwise is to err."

Erica stroked the mane of the animal on her desk. Then she put the "bear" in a cage that Cal had brought by earlier. What would happen to her pet when the abreaction came?

Kai said no more, and the three of them made their way from B dome to C and from C into the narrow underground tunnel to the converted slump-pit cavern where she, Vear, and Dahlquist had first "safely communed" with the homunculus. Erica knew that this time they would go farther than the warehouse/motor pool. In the musty lunacrete honeycombing beneath Censorinus, she could hear her heart beating beating beating. . . .

On the pretext of doing some selenological work that his house arrest had prevented, Vear suited up and exited C dome from an air lock near his and Dolly's pie wedge. Claiming that he wanted to gather two or three bags of breccias from the "impact gardening" on the crater floor and that he needed some help, Vear had convinced Logan to let him take Dolly. Dahlquist, he had argued, had already resolved every major computer problem at the base, and if he, Vear, had his roommate's help, he'd finish up faster and limit the loss of unrecyclable oxygen.

This ruse was necessary because Bishop Marlin believed that the seven should use at least three different routes to the slump-pit cavern chosen for their exorcism site. Suspicion would accrue—at the very least, questions would arise—if they all converged on the underground chamber en masse. Vear agreed with the bishop, and he was ready to do anything in his power, including pray, to frustrate prying eyes and expedite their mission.

Dolly seldom left the domes. He would have been content, Vear knew, to wear a space suit only on arriving at and departing from Von Braunville—if he'd had that option. Unfortunately for him, institutionalized safety procedures required everyone to suit up periodically and to bound around outside as if one of the domes had suffered a meteorite strike. Fortunately for Vear, Dolly therefore remembered how to comport himself on the surface. Still, he was overdeliberate in his movements and an inevitable brake on the more reckless major.

Moondozers were gouging out shovelsful of the crater floor, as well as parts of its slope, to feed the O_2 plant opposite the domes, and a pair of space-suited technicians were working in the near end of the solar-array field. They looked like tiny, articulate dolls, and Vear was amazed—as he always was—by the bootprints in the monochrome powder underfoot. These herringbone patterns would remain on the windless Moon forever—unless wiped out by a machine or a meteorite. It was therefore base policy to erase the prints occasionally, usually by rolling them with huge aluminum drums that attached to the rears of the 'dozers.

"All of this is going to disappear," Vear said. A closed radio band carried his words into Dolly's helmet, and Dolly turned to him a wide reflecting visor that concealed his expression. "After the exorcism, I mean." A pause. "How, Dolly? How?"

They mounted the lunacrete pad on which sat the *Daisy Duck* and a second ferry shuttle. Dolly moved with more assurance here, but he was fatigued. "Nixon's the focus. Tolstoy notwithstanding, the 'great man' theory of history has real validity." (Huff-puff, huff-puff.) "The moral and metaphysical makeup of persons in power counts. It counts heavily, Gordon."

Dolly halted near the *Daisy Duck*, an upright craft whose four spindly legs, terminating in platelike footpads, were each taller than a human adult. The ship's crew-and-cargo cabin resembled a two-story balloon gondola, except that it was made of metal and bore upon it a pair of engines like hair dryers in a beauty salon for Titans. Above the blocky cabin rested a spherical tank that could hold thirty tons of oxygen, and perched atop this sphere was an end-standing oval tank as tall as the cabin and the oxygen tank combined: It hauled hydrogen.

Waiting for Dolly to recover, Vear marveled at *Daisy*. Here on the Moon, she could soar. On Earth, however, she would never even achieve lift-off. And if Von Braunville were doomed to disappear in the wake of a suppressed time line's abreaction, well, his ability to pilot such an ungainly-looking flying machine would mean nothing at all. A poignant rime of regret added itself to the cold anxious lump in Vear's gut, and he clenched the fingers of his pressurized gloves into fat quasi-fists.

So what if piloting the ferry shuttle becomes obsolete? Vear asked himself. Aren't you the guy who wanted to go home and enter a monastery? Well, how much better for everybody if your monastery exists in a just rather than an unjust reality. And, if the Earth is again redeemed, how can you mourn the passing of *Daisy*?

Dolly had recovered his breath. "Kai says that by exorcising the President, the 'great man' who primarily shaped this time line, we'll halt the temporal flow altogether. Naturally, time will seek another channel to run into. If we've effected Nixon's healing in the right—I mean, a *loving*—way, we'll abreact a saner reality, and time will back up and flow into a channel in which his grossest crimes have no moorings and so can't occur. As for us, we'll find ourselves riding the new current at a point parallel to this moment in our unexorcised time line." Dolly was ready to go again. "And, more than likely, we'll be ignorant of the shift."

Crazy, Vear thought. Sci-fi gobbledygook for the credulous. It could only work in a storybook.

But he spoke into his helmet's radio unit: "Von Braunville dematerializes, and we're thrown back across the void like so many passive puppets?"

"*Dematerializes* is the wrong word. And we're not 'thrown back across the void,' Gordon, because, in our abreacted reality, we'll never've been here, anyway."

"Fuckin' A!"

"You don't like the scenario, my foul-mouthed friend?"

Actually, Vear thought, I don't follow it. On the other hand, Dolly, I cursed because of *that*. And in the black, black shadow of the ferry shuttle, the major turned Dolly about and pointed toward B dome so that he could see an unsuited human figure rush from the main air lock and come leaping across the surface as if his life were the prize in a deadly lunar footrace.

In truth, it was.

"My God," Dolly said. "It's Romanenko."

The Soviet materials scientist was fighting the effects of both anoxia and decompression. Unrecompressed, he would find his bodily fluids percolating within five minutes. Running across a surface with a temperature of two hundred degrees below zero Fahrenheit was making him cold-foot it even faster than he might otherwise have run, and his joints had surely already begun to burn with neurological fire.

Vear was fascinated and appalled. Both emotions grew in him as the cosmonaut sprinted straight at them, his head and hands bare and his eyes glittering like fractured rubies in the ruddy mask of his inhuman face. Kolya Romanenko's every driven stride lifted him balletically high, but when he reached the edge of the lunacrete pad, his limbs were already flailing out of control and he fell headlong, sprawling like a puppet, spasming with the gracelessness of a beheaded chicken.

"Holy shit!" Dolly said. "What'd the crazy bastard think he was going to accomplish?"

"A Nyby," Vear murmured. "A Nyby."

"We've got to get him inside. Maybe—"

"Maybe nothing. He's dead. He was dead the moment he decided to bleed the oxygen out of that air lock and make his run."

"But it's worth a shot, isn't it? I mean, if we ta—"

"If we take him back inside, we won't make it to our rendezvous with Marlin and the others. There'll be an uproar, a hubbub. We'd be prime candidates for a twelve-hour grilling."

Vear looked toward the polarized window on the hardened cap of A dome, Von Braunville's headquarters facility. No one stirred there. Nor had the 'dozer jockeys working at the oxygen plant seen Romanenko's dash, and the two technicians among the weird blossoms of the solar array had retreated deeper into it. Sheer luck. Now, though, Vear hoped that the dead man had told none of his Soviet comrades his plan to emulate the last run of Roland Nyby. But that seemed unlikely. You rarely advertised a suicide attempt unless you hoped that someone would foil it, and Romanenko had succeeded. Conspicuously.

"So what the hell do we do?" Dolly asked.

"Hide him. Come on. You can help me."

They returned to the dead Soviet—Vear had never seen a

sight like him before—and grasped his heavy arms. The whites of Kolya's eyes were bloodshot, the capillaries in his nose had burst, and the blood and mucus oozing from his mouth and nostrils were "boiling," turning into bubbles that broke as soon as they formed, splattering fluid on everything near him. Backtracking, Vear and Dolly pulled the decompressed cosmonaut up the beveled edge of the lunacrete pad and into *Daisy Duck*'s shadow.

"Okay," Vear said. "Let's meet the others." He pointed at a structure like a vitrafoamed telephone booth: the surface entrance to the slump-pit cavern. It was a hundred yards away.

"Yeah," Dolly said, audibly winded. "Great."

Robinson was jittery. He, a Vietnam veteran, an emeritus Green Beret, a Secret Service man, had decided to betray the President. No, not the President, actually—the man that so many malcontents and bleeding-heart liberals had dubbed, not wholly without reason, "King Richard."

Tyler Robinson still believed that he had fought in Indochina for a noble cause and that too many of the President's noisiest critics were jealous airheads, but over the past several months the Boss had slid down the psychological curve from *In Control* to *Off His Nut*. Taking a punch at that cosmonaut Shikin—whom Logan had confined to quarters until the next t-ship arrived—was only the latest sign of his deteriorating grip on himself.

Often, nowadays, Nixon would fly into towering rages, usually for petty or perplexing reasons: an aide's failure to remember his daughters' wedding anniversaries, someone's offhand reference to the charm and wit of the late JFK, etc., etc. Tyler had seen him boot his press secretary in the coccyx, throw a handful of pens at a congressman who had tried to amend a favorite bill, and roundly curse a nine-year-old boy who had climbed up on the statue of John Wayne near the marble frieze of helicopters, B-52s, and tanks that the President was dedicating as a late addition to the Vietnam War Memorial. Of course, all three networks deleted this part of his "address" from their evening news programs, but it had offended almost everyone present—the kid had only been trying to see him better—and later, of course, the President, realizing that he had made himself look bad, spent an hour excoriating the Secret Service corps for "a fuckin' goddamn lapse of security."

He's unbalanced, Tyler told himself, driving a battery-powered corridor cart to the President's suite to pick him up. Once upon a time, the federal legislature would've removed a fella like him in favor of the veep, but Nixon's got that entire bunch of D.C. pols buffaloed. They're scared to death of him. Me, too, truth to tell, but I'm finally in a position (maybe) to do something about him. Before he blows up the planet in a fit of presidential pique at Leonid, or Margaret, or another excited nine-year-old.

Because, as Tyler had already told the bishop, King Richard's little snits weren't just the tantrums of a spoiled toddler. They were scarier than that. They had global implications. Moreover, the expressions that Nixon's face acquired when he stormed were . . . well, inhuman. They suggested that the planet was his Nerf ball, a toy that he could squeeze, or rend, or bounce madly around with impunity.

And when Bishop Marlin told you that the Boss was possessed, Tyler reflected, you knew from your familiarity with his pop-eyed rages that the old cleric wasn't shittin' you. No, sir. He was dead on the money, and if he and his crew can exorcise the demons that've infested the Boss, well, you, Tyler, you'll've played an important role in . . . in saving the world.

Griegs came out into the corridor, checking to make sure that no would-be assassins were around. He also checked the rear of the battery cart for lunar terrorists who may've tried to hop a ride without Tyler's knowledge. Satisfied that no one had, Griegs came back around to talk to his partner.

"Where's Commander Logan? I thought he was going to escort us on this phase of our tour."

"He's going to meet us there," Tyler Robinson lied. "I've got the route right here." He tapped his temple.

"Okay, buddy-mine." But Griegs spoke with some suspiciousness, before going to get the President, and when Nixon emerged, he was wearing—for the first time since their arrival—sports clothes: cleatless golfing shoes, pleated slacks, and a short-sleeved banlon shirt (pale blue). With no word to Tyler, he climbed into the rear seat of the cart. Griegs leapt in beside Nixon even as Tyler hit the juice, and their ivory-enameled cart purred about the circular periphery of A dome to B, and around that of B to C, and around that of C to the entrance of the undergrounds connecting Von Braunville proper to its slump-pit facilities.

The President, Tyler noticed, spoke not a word. Griegs kept his hand inside his jacket as if willing to risk ricocheting a bullet or ten off the lunacrete walls if anyone tried to impede their progress.

"Sir," said Tyler, partly to hide his nervousness, partly to show off what he had learned, "most lunar slump pits are formed by the draining of loose surface material into subsurface cavities. A bit incongruously, there are several good-sized slump pits on the floor of Censorinus. NASA engineers integrated four of these pits into the 'architecture' of Von Braunville, knowing that 'basements' of this natural kind would be good storage areas, garages for lunar vehicles, and shelters from solar flares, meteorite showers, and possibly even deliberate bombardment by the Soviets or"—Tyler let an amused chuckle escape him—"hostile aliens. Remodeling these cavities wasn't as expensive as trying to dig—"

"Shut up, Robinson," said the President.

"Yes, sir." But this peremptory command stung. He had wanted to explain that for the President's tour the base commander had authorized the pressurization of a storage cavern ordinarily kept in vacuum. Therefore, the Boss wouldn't have to don a space suit to get a good look at it—but, obviously, at this point, King Richard was merely going through the motions. Hadn't he already regaled everyone with a speech, punched out a Russian, and inspected nearly every aboveground cranny of Von Braunville? Now, really, he didn't want to do anything but zap the Soviets, lie low on the Moon, and, sooner or later, go home to Earth, preferably Key Biscayne.

Faintly whining, Tyler's cart took them through the motor pool and past a warehouse for comestibles, the quartermaster's office, a storage bay for equipment parts, and seven or eight areas marked RESTRICTED ACCESS. Yellowish-green lights, reminiscent of those that Tyler's CO in 'Nam had powered off a gasoline generator in a bamboo-covered trench, cast a spooky murk and even spookier shadows over everything. And like popcorn or automatic rifle fire, Tyler's ears kept popping.

They purred down a ramp to another tight tunnel. Ahead of them in it walked a stocky figure. Griegs shifted on his seat, probably to grip the weapon in his shoulder holster, and Tyler, knowing that the pedestrian was Bishop Marlin, wondered if he would have to bump the old bird—gently—to prove to Griegs and the President that he was as unsympathetic to two-legged obstacles as they were. As they drew closer to him, the bishop, feigning deafness, deftly ignored their approach.

"Haven't you got a horn up there, Robinson?" Griegs asked.

Tyler pretended to search the uncluttered instrument panel for a horn. "I don't know."

"The middle of the steering wheel. Just like on an automobile, you hotdog."

"Oh, yeah. Here it is."

Exasperated, Griegs said, "Well, then, damn it, why don't you use it?"

"Yeah. Sure." Tyler hit the horn, which sounded like a duck quacking in an empty oil drum.

Bishop Marlin flattened his body against the right-hand wall of the tunnel. His paunch, however, would make navigating between him and the opposite wall a risky, threading-the-needle business. The only two-way traffic down here, Tyler understood, was foot traffic, and the drivers of corridor carts had to take care not to impale or steamroll pedestrians. For that, and at least one other reason, he slowed.

"Go on by him!" Griegs said.

"I'm afraid I'll hit him."

"Well, that'd be too damned bad for him, wouldn't it?" Griegs was on the same side of the tunnel as Bishop Marlin, and, glancing back, Tyler saw that the President was eyeing the overweight cleric with mild annoyance. Otherwise, Nixon was unperturbed, his knees together and his clasped hands on his knees. Suspecting nothing, but smoldering with resentment at anyone who got too obtrusively in their way. . . .

Griegs recognized the bishop, too. When Tyler edged their cart past the bishop so that the bishop and the agent in the back were virtually face to face, Griegs said, "What the hell're you doing down here, Your Right Reverendship?"

With no warning, his right reverendship grabbed Griegs by the lapels, stepped aside, and, tugging with all his strength, banged the agent's forehead into the wall. Griegs went limp. Witnessing this, the President instinctively leapt for freedom. Possibly, he hoped to run back into the labyrinth of bays in search of a hiding place.

Oh, no, you don't, thought Tyler. Despite the agility that the President had just shown, the agent hooked his trouser cuff with his forefinger and sent him sprawling. Tyler then hurled himself into the backseat to restore his boss to the cart and pinion him there. Bishop Marlin hurriedly assumed the wheel, accelerated, and drove them lickety-sputt-sputt-sputt toward the slump-pit cavern, where the others already awaited them.

Griegs lay unconscious behind them, but the President, to Tyler Robinson's dismay and astonishment, was struggling so ferociously that the agent kept expecting to hear a bone crack, either one of his own or one of the President's. Worse, the man had the strength of legions and the tongue of fifty smut-peddling blasphemers. If Bishop Marlin didn't get them to their destination soon, they might never reach it at all. . . .

Maybe I deserve this, Tyler thought, essaying a choke hold on his thrashing employer. After all, I'm a Quisling, aren't I? A Benedict Arnold? A . . . well, a Judas?

"Hang on!" the bishop cried. "For God's sake, Tyler, don't let go! We're almost there!"

25

In this slump-pit cavern, forty-nine coffins. Cal can't keep from looking at them—even though, for the past three subjective hours, his exorcism team has been busting its butt trying to evict the spirit of evil from the truculent President.

These forty-nine coffins, arranged about the frigid chamber in seven stacks seven coffins high, keep popping up in the corners of Cal's eyes. He knows with a dreadful certainty that if this combat goes on much longer, Nixon will go free, but all of them racking their bodies and souls to effect his "cure" will end up *inside* those friggin' boxes.

Maybe even Kai, who has already died once. Indeed, Kai may soon find Horsy Stout's glorified body—in which Philip K. Dick's resurrected essence has hitchhiked to the Moon—sapped of volition and rendered useless as a means of transport. That's how violent and dispiriting the struggle has so far been, and Kai is even yet blaming himself for Romanenko's suicide.

Over Bishop Marlin's angry protest, the chamber also contains (in addition to the forty-nine coffins; the gurney on which Nixon lies; and a small table set with candles, an aspergillum, several cruxifixes, a chalice for holy water, and the Sacrament), yes, an electric coffee urn.

An hour ago, Kai insisted on sending Tyler to fetch the machine from the galley in B dome. And Tyler was able to accomplish his assignment only because a colorful timelessness—a muscadine-tinted stasis—prevails at Von Braunville. "Meanwhile," the only persons immune to its

effects are the seven exhausted exorcists beneath its translucent umbrella.

At this exact subjective moment, the coffee urn gasps,
gurgles, and whoops, filling the slump-pit cavern with unsettling echoes. Cal, his hands on the President, hears these
noises as intimations of mortality, and he, like the bishop,
wonders why the hell Kai, himself practically a spook, wants
to subject them to the ghostly, godforsaken moans of a
percolator.

Haven't we got enough to sweat? he thinks. At the
moment, King Richard's lying here as quiet as a basking
snake, but ten minutes ago he was writhing, hissing, bucking,
and twisting.

Blaspheming everything beautiful and good, not excluding Bishop Marlin, Erica, Gordon, Dolly, Tyler, Kai, and
(even if I qualify only on sufferance) me, Cal Pickford. And
now, when we ought to be preparing for our next bout of wills
and obscene cant, we're gazing around zombie-eyed and
listening to the high electric keening of that stupid coffee
maker.

"Philip," the bishop says, "why in God's name did you
have to have *that* brought in here?"

Kai sits Buddha-fashion next to the coffee urn; the
urn itself rests on the cold floor beside the table with
the candles, the holy water, and the wafer and wine. He is
hugging himself and rocking imperceptibly from the waist;
the aura surrounding the homunculus flickers bluely, like
a gas flame on an old-fashioned stove, while the stack of
coffins behind him glints and glooms in rhythm to the
flickering.

"I'm beginning to feel psychotic. I need a cup of hot
coffee to keep me from evaporating and floating off the way
Easter did."

"Coffee?"

"Right. Coffee with chicory. Maybe that'll hold me here
long enough to evict the devil from our friend."

"Nonsense," murmurs the ecclesiastic.

Cal, behind the President, presses down on his shoulders.
The major and his roommate are each restraining a leg, and
Tyler stands opposite Erica and the bishop at the middle of
the gurney (they've removed its wheels, turning it into a

rickety examination platform) with one hand on Nixon's fabric belt. Tyler is ready to push down hard if the President resumes thrashing.

Nixon's pale blue shirt is indigo with sweat; sweat dots his face like beads of molten glass. He is staring upside down at Cal with an expression deceptively mild. Simultaneously, he emits a hellish body odor. Acrid. This smell commingles with the bitter fragrance of the coffee beans and chicory discoloring the water in the whoop-whoop-whooping urn.

Says the President to Cal, in a growly voice unlike any he has ever heard him use, "You're right to worry, Pickford. I *am* going to cram your scrawny ass into a coffin. You'd better believe I am, fuckbrain."

"How're you going to do that?" Cal asks him.

Bishop Marlin says, "Don't talk to him. How many times do I have to tell you people that it's dangerous to try to talk to the liars possessing this man."

The bishop looks done-in. Considering that he fasted for three days to purify himself for this encounter, no wonder. It's plainly a miracle that he hasn't already collapsed—an extension of God's grace into the Stop-Time Crimson beneath which Kai has mysteriously endomed them. Even so, Cal fears that if the exorcism goes on much longer, Bishop Marlin may not survive.

"Mr. President," Erica says. "Mr. President, if you're still in there, we'll talk to you. But *only* to you."

Whoop-whoop, whoop-whoop.

"I ate Easter," announces the entity living in Nixon's body. "It's gone because I ate it."

Bishop Marlin refuses to acknowledge this boast. Instead, for the second time, he begins to recite an Episcopal version of the *Rituale Romanum*; its purpose is to locate, scourge, and expel the demon or demons, up to and including Satan, occupying the body and suppressing the personality of the one possessed.

The reading of psalms constitutes nearly half the ritual, and the bishop is reciting, " 'Some sat in darkness and gloom, prisoners in affliction and in irons, for they had rebelled against the words of God, and spurned the counsel of the Most High. . . .' "

Whoop-whoop, whoop-whoop.

Cal shuts his mind to the psalm. Ritualistic formulas, unless they involve ranch work, bore the piss out of him, and once already today he has heard the modified Roman rite.

But the President's body, tensing, bridges between buttocks and shoulder blades, and Cal and the other men lean their full weight on him to keep him on the gurney.

Bishop Marlin's voice grows more authoritative: "'I cast thee out, you filthy spirit, along with the least encroachment of the enemy, and every phantom and diabolical legion! In the name of our Lord Jesus Christ, depart and vanish from this creature of God!'"

Erica Zola says, "Hang on to him, guys. Make it through this go-round and maybe the Richard Nixon core will assert itself, and we can proceed psychotherapeutically rather than ritually."

"Fuck you," blurts the spirit of evil, arching the President's back. "A python in your pumpkin, a rattler up your rufus."

Whoop-whoop, whoop-whoop . . .

This is no "creature of God" talking, Cal understands, and they are supposed to *love* the person possessed by the malevolent entity taunting Erica—but, so far, Cal has had real trouble mastering his outright revulsion. The growly curses escaping King Richard, along with the terrifying whoops of Kai's coffee pot and the disorienting effects of lunar gravity, have half convinced him that this entire experience has sprung from his subconscious mind.

Right. This is a dream of the id. A Freudian nightmare. If Lia were here, she'd wake me from it.

But the nightmare persists, and with Nixon's body straining under him, Cal knows that love is the last thing he's likely to shed on either the possessor or the possessed.

But at least I'm participating, he consoles himself. Kai, by contrast, hasn't gotten any closer to this gurney than a yard or two. His revulsion is that much greater than mine, and *he's* the anamnesiac who wanted us to "engineer the redemptive shift."

Whoop-whoop . . .

Coffee. Kai's sitting on his glorified buns brewing a pot of black-black, molasses-thick, swamp-water swill. Hoping the chicory and caffeine will put enough starch in his plasmic substance to get him *off* those buns.

As the bishop speaks, one of Nixon's legs kicks out and sends Dolly backward into a stack of coffins. Then he crosses the free leg over and hammers his foot into Vear's abdomen, loosening the major's grip. Now the President's head is trying to come off the gurney, too, and Cal must brace his own legs against the floor and flatten his chest against the man's brow. Whereupon the possessed man begins to bray, a continuous, ungodly braying that Cal can scarcely believe is issuing from a human throat.

"Dear God, we've got a case of nearly perfect possession here," Bishop Marlin cries. "Usually, my patients *want* to be healed. But this time we've undertaken the rite without Nixon's consent—the *real* Nixon's consent—and we may be in for a war a helluva lot longer than it's already been."

Great, thinks Cal, gritting his teeth and pressing down. Just great, Your Right Reverendship.

He remembers that three hours ago the exorcism procedure began with a brief outcasting ritual and a fifteen-minute waiting period as they sought to penetrate the occupying demons' identities. This was the stage of the ceremony called the Pretense, Bishop Marlin explained, and its sole function was to break through the sham that *no* possessing spirit inhabited the patient. This stage lasted only fifteen minutes primarily because Tyler's struggle with Nixon in the corridor has clearly disclosed what everyone already suspected, namely, that at some point during his presidency, perhaps the year after the U.S. win in Indochina, Richard Nixon's own evil cunning began to give way to the evil cunning of a greater malefactor, and he was eaten by it from the inside out with no *apparent* diminution of his own personality.

Whoop-whoop, whoop-whoop . . .

Cal recalls that the demonic liars inside Nixon began cursing them just as he was starting to think that all that would come of the whole boring business was their capture and a series of summary executions.

Suddenly, the patient's bray mutates into other animal noises—a wolf's howl, a boar's grunting, a rhino's rhonchus, a series of raucous cluck-cluck-cluckings.

As if, thinks Cal, someone has gassed a whole flock of turkeys with helium.

Meanwhile, Dolly has come back to pinion Nixon's belligerent leg, and Erica has rushed to help Tyler recinch the gurney straps on his forearms.

Shut your eyes, Cal advises himself. Don't look at him.

Earlier, when their silence broke the Pretense, Nixon's face flowed into such a corrupt mask that Cal could not imagine how mere human musculature could achieve so hateful a look. Now, the same hideous expression is back, and to gaze upon it—unmistakable sign of the Presence—may be to succumb to its iniquity.

It's *not* human, Cal reflects. Does that make it fiendish? I can't honestly say, but it's definitely something *other*. . . .

"Perfect possession," the bishop said. That's a case where the inhabiting entity has pushed the person's real human personality down so deep that the body becomes the unquestioned property of the occupier. In such cases, the chances of even *discovering* the fact of possession are remote.

Whoop-whoop, whoop-whoop, whoop-whoop . . .

Bishop Marlin has told them that the evil occupier works hard to disguise its presence from the suppressed human personality. It convinces this person that the occupier's goals exactly mirror the occupied's. That, in fact, the occupier and the occupied are one and the same being. In such cases, the occupied human personality becomes comfortable with the fact of possession; it never occurs to this person to seek healing. If it did, the possessor would hurry to squelch the notion. The bishop has also said that only persons with an innate, rather than an imposed, bent for evil ever become so self-extinguishingly occupied, and these persons seldom undergo exorcism because they do not present themselves for it.

But that's the kind of patient, Cal realizes, listening to the President's falsetto gobbling, that we're working with here. We've taken the man against his will, as well as against the will of his occupier or occupiers, and this is the result. . . .

Abruptly, the coffee urn ceases to whoop; the cessation of this noise stuns even the patient.

For a moment, no demented animal sounds escape the President's mouth; he lies perfectly still. His eyes flick from side to side. Cal, staring down at them, sees nothing reflected in their pupils but a dizzying blackness that spirals down to an absolute void. Unriven emptiness. Meanwhile, the walls of these unplumbable eye sockets radiate hatred, a blistering thermal energy.

Kai comes out of his Buddha posture and grabs a plastic bag of Styrofoam cups. "Anybody besides me want some of this brew?"

All but Dolly and Tyler say no, and Kai keys the spigot on the urn to fill three cups.

Cal can smell the hot coffee, see its rising steam, and hear it pitter-pattering into the Styrofoam. He'd drink a little of it if he weren't already sweating like a dockhand.

"Not a good idea, Philip," Bishop Marlin says.

"Maybe not for you, Your Right Reverendship, but I'm literally going to go up in steam myself if I don't have some."

He comes toward the gurney, extending cups to Dolly and Tyler. Even Cal agrees that this is a bad time to interrupt the process, but how can he rebuke the resurrected Kai?

Nixon's body begins to bridge, hump, thrash, flounce.

The fragile cups go flying, and coffee splashes Cal's neck and lower jaw. Cal yells. Erica Zola and the bishop jump back. The President has broken the straps on his forearms, and Cal, despite his pain, steels himself and covers the man's upper body.

Nixon's head goes crazy under his chest, bumping him, trying to find a nipple or a fold of skin to bite. His mouth slides from side to side like the bubble in a carpenter's level. It snaps like a piranha's. As it snaps, the President begins quacking like a duck. Like Daisy Duck.

"Kai," who returned to the coffee urn as soon as Nixon's body began flailing, shouts, "*The Dream Impeachment of Harper Mocton!* My God, it's coming true!"

He spigots a cup of chicory-doped coffee, down-gulps the stuff, and discards the cup. Then he comes to the gurney to tell everyone to let the possessed body of the President go. Cal refuses to obey him because this is so clearly a formula for siccing a galvanized Frankenstein monster on all of them. What in hell does Philip hope to accomplish? Their communal ruin?

"Don't let go of him!" Bishop Marlin cries, one hand on the purple stole at his neck. "Don't!"

"Do!" Philip urges. "This is a fucked-up situation, but it's going to be okay if you guys'll just trust me."

"Quackquackquackquacka . . . !"

Major Vear, Peter Dahlquist, and Tyler Robinson all step away from the gurney, and Cal finds himself restraining the quacking chief executive all by himself. One stupendous bridging of the presidential spine dislodges Cal; in fact, it sends him skidding toward the coffee urn on the seat of his jumpsuit. Whereupon the President flaps his arms, slides off the platform, and, growling his falsetto growl, confronts the seven of them from the crouch of a sumo wrestler.

"Get back," Philip K. Dick commands, waving everyone away with the stumpy black arms of Horsy Stout. "Get back."

With Gordon Vear's and Erica Zola's aid, Cal gets to his feet. The muscadine-tinted air in the slump-pit cavern seems to be losing a little of its color. Is Philip's psychospiritual support of the timelessness affecting the rest of the moonbase starting to decay? Cal's own lightheadedness suggests as much. So does the fact that his body wants to rise through the floor of the Censorinus crater and up into a celestial orbit similar to the dead writer's. Into what alternative continuum would such a flight carry him?

Well, thinks Cal, Philip has his wish. He and Richard Nixon have squared off to contest each other's possession, and all we can do is stand back and root for the home team. Crap.

"Satan," Philip says, circling the President's body, "why have you invested this man?"

Robotically, the Nixon body turns as Philip turns. " 'One can kill many,' " he says, the voice a sepulchral blur.

"And one *in a place of power* can kill many more, right?"

A stream of overlapping obscenities from the entity inhabiting the President. (That means yes, Cal tells himself.) In response, Bishop Marlin begins to recite psalms again, and to utter chants of expulsion, and to sprinkle holy water at the possessed from his aspergillum.

The muscadine color of the chamber's air has already decayed to plum, and from plum to pink, and from pink to a thin claret. . . .

"And why do you want to kill?" Erica Zola asks.

The President turns upon her his impossible face.

" 'Because I hate the many who hate me,' " he says, bassooning the blurred words and revealing a tongue as red as blood.

This pronouncement is followed by a verbal assault unlike any Cal has ever heard. The President's possessor blasphemes, taunts, and ridicules, facing each of its would-be exorcists in turn and telling on them intimate private shames. Rather than have such matters publicly revealed, Cal realizes, many people would commit suicide, and yet the seven of them must stand together amid seven stacks of coffins listening to this scandalmongering. The demon motivating the captured meat of King Richard recites seven litanies of past crimes and sins previously so well hidden that Cal wonders at its malign omniscience.

"Philip, you're right," Bishop Marlin says. "Only God or Satan could know such things about us, and only Satan would reveal them."

" 'O Satan, enemy of mankind and rebel against heaven,' " chants Philip, " 'tremble and be afraid!' "

And the bishop joins him in reciting, " 'Leave this man's body and go to your place of darkness!' "

Satan, incarnate in the body of the President, advances on the spirit in Horsy Stout's body and delivers a spastic haymaker to his nappy head. The punch flashes, sizzles, and knocks the Nixon thing into an astonishing backward stagger.

Get down, Cal thinks. And he draws Gordon Vear and Erica Zola into a self-protective huddle beside him. Tyler and Dolly scamper for cover, too, but the radiant homunculus leaps forward and grabs Nixon's Frankenstein-monstering body by the ankles. This contact produces another series of flashes and frying noises.

"Look," says Vear. "It's like Jacob wrestling the angel of God for a blessing. In reverse, I mean."

Cal knows that he would not have thought of this image himself, but it has a certain appropriateness. Horsy hanging heroically to the legs of Tricky Dick, noisily illuminating the coffin warehouse, does have weirdly biblical overtones, even in a lunar context, and it's undoubtedly the eschatological implications of their struggle that provide them.

Time itself may not be ending, but this time line (as the pale claret of the chamber's air decays into a crystalline translucency) is quickly reaching its terminus. Von Braunville trembles, and the ramparts of Censorinus quake like those of Jericho.

Nevertheless, the evil soul frog-marching Nixon about refuses to let him topple. Instead, it changes him. It subjects him to a series of transformations whose purpose is to shake Philip's dogged spirit and defeat their exorcism team. First, the President's body blisters as if burned in a fire. Second, it splits at the abdomen and evicts its salmon-hued internal organs, many of which balloon, grow hair, and emit a stench unlike any Cal has ever encountered. Third, with the dwarf still astride its ankles, the golem sucks its vitals back into its gut, peels away its face, and stares at each of them from the eye holes of a death's-head.

Fourth, again illusorily whole, the Nixon body sprouts horns, inflates to elephantine size, and trumpets deafeningly. Fifth, it dwindles, acquires a nauseating dermatosis of lesions and whelks, and begins to spin—first one way, then the other. Sixth, it stops spinning, levitates, and begins telekinetically hurling the stacked coffins. These collide, ricochet, smash, and clatter. Cal and his friends must scurry to escape being crushed.

And, seventh, when these several ploys have failed to dislodge the dwarf, the evil spirit inhabiting the President combines the tricks of levitation and inflation and floats above Bishop Marlin's team of exorcists like a blimp.

Cal cannot help thinking of Bugs Bunny, Popeye the Sailor, and Daisy Duck in a televised Thanksgiving Day parade. The Nixon thing is not so large as those friendly, vulcanized monsters, but large enough, with Horsy Stout dangling from its bloated feet like a man in danger of falling from a burning dirigible.

The room's ceiling is eighteen feet high, and Philip's boots—Horsy's boots—tick-tock about six feet above its floor. Bishop Marlin continues to recite the modified *Rituale Romanum*, and Cal can tell by the expressions on their faces that the major and the Secret Service agent are praying.

Dahlquist, on the other hand, seems to be searching the chamber for something—a slingshot, a bow and arrow, a pistol—with which to shoot the President down, while Erica scribbles frantically in a pocket notepad.

"Cal," Philip cries, "help me!"

By doing what? Cal wonders. What *can* I do? If this were *The Dream Impeachment of Harper Mocton*, I could lie down and dream a human monster to justice. But this isn't. Even if it were, where would I lie down? What would I dream?

Here, Philip, we've got the evil of an ancient demonic force on our hands—Satan itself, it seems—and its hold on the Nixon body will take more than wishful thinking to terminate. . . .

"Who the hell's thinking wishfully?" the homunculus calls down to him. "Move your butt, Pickford! I need you!"

Cal approaches the gurney over which the continuously inflating Nixon body and the dwarf are hovering. Because the President can go no higher, his expansion proceeds horizontally, spreading out under the ceiling like a thundercloud.

Riding the instep of the President's foot, which is now a kind of teat on the underside of the ballooning monster, the glorified body of Horsy Stout fights to unpin the intaglio fish holding its shirt together. With one hand, this is hard, but Philip is using Horsy's other hand to hang on for dear life.

"Climb up here!" he cries. "*Now*, you sorry cowboy!"

Glad for the weak lunar gravity, Cal climbs up on the gurney, takes one of the dwarf's legs, and hoists himself high enough to grab the President's other inflated foot. Frightening himself, he swings into its saddle the way a cowboy would mount a bronc in a rodeo chute. If the chute were upside down. If the bronc had the body of a huge rubber shoe with perforated wing tips.

Meanwhile, Bishop Marlin is holding a cruxifix up and reciting, "'Source of death! Root of evil! Seducer of men! Behold the Cross of the Most High God! I command thee: obey and begone!'"

Hunkered under its bloated posterior, Cal is surprised to hear the spirit of evil speak again. It does so from the vast pucker of King Richard's mouth, and its voice fills the chamber like that of a chorus of spoiled children: "'It is the essence of moral responsibility,'" it pontificates, "'to determine *beforehand* the consequences of our action.'"

But there is something pleading in the evil one's tone, a cold fearfulness. Cal looks at the dwarf for direction, and he makes an eloquent upward stabbing motion with his fish pin.

"Death is the absolute end!" cries Satan.

"Depart from this dwelling!" counters Bishop Marlin.

Philip and Cal stab the President from below, and a confounding explosion rocks everything in Von Braunville.

Blackness rushes in. Airlessness rushes in. The Moon asserts itself around these people like a great white mouth.

Cal's consciousness—his memories of Lia, Mr. K., Viking, the Bonners, Lone Boy, Miss Grace, the Brezhnev bears, and everything else—flies apart, dissipating into the void along with every other temporal or material trace of Von Braunville.

Into nothingness or plenitude . . .

CODA

Thi Boi Loan, night-shift foreman at Revolutionary NanoTech in Hanoi, United Republic of Vietnam, paused outside the main entrance of the industrial complex to study the Moon. It was pinwheeling through a series of ruby, emerald, sapphire, and amethyst strobes—as if on the verge of exploding and showering fragments of Choral rind and hidden lunar rock all over the sky. The windshields of nearby automobiles and the glass facades of government skyscrapers were reflecting this show in ways that dizzied Loan pleasantly. He blinked and entered the assembly plant.

"Sir, you're late," said Ngo Pham Lan, his assistant. "Our visitors have been here fifteen minutes already."

He checked his watch. "Then *they* were fourteen minutes early, Lan. My tardiness is negligible."

In his office, Loan found the Americans docilely biding their time. He knew the man, Harmon Bertholt, as President Jordan's national security advisor and the woman as Bertholt's wife, Grace Rennet, a former film actress who had once actively championed her country's illicit involvement in the conflict between Vietnamese nationalists and the toadies of Western colonialism. Apparently, her marriage to Bertholt, along with certain other historic events, had tempered both her xenophobia and her zealous anticommunism. A good thing, too. Such a person would be lost in a world under the joint rule of every legitimate state entity and the benevolent eye of the Choir from Mira Ceti.

With the couple were two burly Secret Service men. They

wore—tactlessly, Loan felt—the green berets that had identified their barbarous special unit in the ill-advised U.S. effort in the late war. A war that had concluded a decade ago.

Also in the room was the Bertholts' nine-year-old son, "Master Bryerly." Loan, himself a parent, looked twice at the boy. He was pale and hangdog, more like an abused urchin from a Dickens novel than a fun-loving Mississippi lad from a book by Twain. Clutched to Master Bryerly's chest was a canvas satchel that he appeared to value at least as much as his own life.

"Welcome, Mr. Security Advisor," Loan said in English, politely bowing. "Welcome, Miss Rennet." But, he knew, almost any greeting would have been wasted on the boy.

"My title's an anachronism," Bertholt said. "Nowadays, you'd do better to call me an advisor on technological progress than on state security. Unfortunately, old terminology dies hard."

Loan pointed his guests toward the plant's broad floor. But a problem immediately arose. Master Bryerly begged to be allowed to stay in Loan's office; he wanted to read. To meet this antisocial whim, one of the Secret Service men would have to remain with him. What a shame, thought Loan. The boy would learn so much more from this tour than from whatever trivial reading matter he has dragged over here from the States.

Only a moment later, Loan was walking Mr. and Mrs. Bertholt and their bodyguard past the window-riven stainless steel vats in which programmed molecular assemblers—machines invisible to the unaided eye—were "growing" lightweight tractor, car, jet, and even rocket engines in canny mixes of protein-rich fluid. Labyrinths of pipes carried needed materials into these vats, while water-cooled heat exchangers kept them from becoming untouchable furnaces. Loan conferred with the operators "feeding" the vats, then introduced his guests to one of the molecular programmers who had laid out the agenda for tonight's nanotechnological miracles.

Miss Rennet, Loan could tell, was amazed by the supple devices taking shape beyond the windows in the vats. She watched them forming as attentively as any wide-eyed movie fan would watch a favorite Hollywood star on a theater screen. And Thi Boi Loan, despite the fact that the Choir from Mira Ceti had bestowed this technology on his country as a free gift, felt a deep sense of pride and accomplishment.

"I don't understand the mechanics of this," the woman said.

Cao Thu, the nanoprogrammer, began an explanation in his native Vietnamese. Loan translated.

"In the middle of the base plate of each vat rests an invisible 'germ.' This is actually a molecule-sized computer containing the blueprints for whatever item the nanoconstructors in each vat will finally build. These molecular constructors—assemblers, you see—stick to the 'germ,' and the 'germ' gives their inbuilt computers the information they need to start 'generating' the item. Every single assembler in the chemical-rich fluid 'knows' where it is in relation to all others. After a time, from this liquid turmoil, a variety of 'assembler-crystal' emerges, which directs the further sculpting of the template—whether rocket engine or helicraft body or solar oven. Later, to shorten my explaining, we drain the milky fluid, leaving behind this template, which through the window will appear to be made of clear white plastic. The nanoconstructors yet in the vat are fed by fluid again and begin to build the very item represented by the see-through model hovering within. Eventually, again to be brief, the assemblers complete their work, the vat is a second time emptied, and the product itself—not the template—is hoisted out. To dry and soon enough to use."

"Incredible," Harmon Bertholt said. He reached out and shook Cao Thu's hand. Thu was embarrassed by the American's enthusiasm and dropped his chin to his chest. A humble posture that, somewhat surprisingly, reminded Loan of the Bertholts' son.

Loan glanced toward his office. Through its wide window, he could see Master Bryerly sitting at his desk poring over a book or magazine. Thought Loan, His parents should have *made* him come on my tour. But, like too many indulgent Westerners, they worry more about placating their children than about guiding them. Not even the Choir have been able to change that. . . .

Irritated, Loan led the Bertholts and their guard away from the assembler vats to show them some of the finished engines suspended over the floor in the drying area. He pointed out that they were seamless, resilient, durable, and so light that Miss Rennet could carry a nanoconstructed tractor engine all by herself. He had her reach up and tap one of the engines, an opalescent thing more like a large jewel than a piece of machinery. The engine, swaying in its harness, rang like a goblet of crystal. Loan explained that it was made of aluminum oxide and interthreaded fibers of carbon, all nanocomputer-designed to reduce mass and increase strength.

"Why did they give *you* this technology?" Miss Rennet blurted.

Loan recoiled from her question as if she had slapped him, and Bertholt said, "For God's sake, Grace, don't start in."

"I'm sorry," she said, not genuinely contrite. "I just don't understand the rationale behind the Choir's handouts. Why these people? Why not the Australians or the Filipinos or anybody else with some respect for human freedom and dignity?"

"Damn it, Grace!"

Loan stepped back toward the woman. "Each country has received different things from the Choir, Miss Rennet. Vietnam, because we lacked true industrial development, received the knowledge to begin Revolutionary NanoTech. The U.S. has received other boons—faster, cleaner, and less costly transportation, for example. And all of us have received the promise of brand-new spiritual knowledge." Not that it would do a tactless woman like you any good, he thought.

Aloud, Loan added, "And, of course, once we have perfected the gifts bestowed on us, we must pass them on to every other people on our planet. A gift from the Choir to one country is, ultimately, a gift to all countries."

"That's why we've come," Bertholt told Miss Rennet. "To claim our share in the technology that Mr. Loan and his compatriots have developed here in Hanoi."

These explanations silenced the former actress, but she walked through the remainder of the tour in a sour mood that was palpably oppressive. Loan had to struggle to remain courteous to her. Back in his office, however, the resentment that she felt toward him and every other Vietnamese was directed at her son: "Bryerly, pick up all your trash and come on. We're going back to the hotel."

Loan got in a final subtle dig: "Happy Easter, Miss Rennet and Master Bryerly." The hidden implication, which they had probably not even registered, was that professing Christians ought to behave in a more loving manner than Miss Rennet had just done. Tomorrow was the ostensible anniversary of her Savior's Resurrection, but she acted as if she had no deep belief in that debatable historical event. Possibly, in fact, she had none; consequently, his dig had failed to wound her.

She dragged the startled Bryerly from Loan's desk while the boy was still trying to stuff pamphlets into his satchel. Accompanied by Ngo Pham Lan and the larger Secret Service agent, mother and son flounced out of the plant, bound for the Ho Chi Minh Hilton.

Bertholt apologized for his wife's behavior ("She's badly jet-lagged"), thanked Loan profusely for the tour ("It was a genuine eye-opener"), and sat down to read a hard-copy macrofacsimile of a nanocomputer program for vat-assembling a communications satellite from the protein in rice hulls and water-buffalo dung ("This sort of pollution-free manufacture could well be the redemption of our planet"). The ebullience of the "security adviser" had a tonic effect on Loan, and he was feeling much better about the Americans' visit by the time Bertholt took his leave.

Alone again, Thi Boi Loan sat down at his desk to check which vats would be yielding product before dawn. His foot slid across something foreign. He stooped, retrieved the item, and found that it was a comic book.

A decadent capitalist fantasy for children. A superhero in a funny-looking suit. A series of action-packed panels of American street crime and its resolution through physical mayhem.

The Choir have been here eight years, Loan thought. Tomorrow they plan to reveal the names of the seven human families who will journey to their home world to meet God. So why do they yet allow this nauseating drivel—he struck the comic with the edge of his hand—to poison the minds of impressionable Western children like Master Bryerly?

Having no ready answer to this question, Loan knocked the comic into the trash can beside his desk.

Twenty-five minutes later, after checking to see if anyone were likely to see him, he lifted Master Bryerly's book from the trash can, opened his desk drawer, slid the pamphlet inside, and guiltily perused its pages.

Although in 1974 (two years after the defeat of the colonial puppets in the south) he had studied English in Ho Chi Minh City, much of the vocabulary in this comic was unfamiliar to Loan. He would have to take it home and study it.

My interest, he told himself, is academic. What is the allure of such trash for Western children? Is mere greed enough for grown men and women to involve themselves in the production of such power fantasies? And what will the Choir do to direct our species away from such lamentable enterprises and interests?

Mulling these questions, Loan went deeper and deeper into the adventures of the red-suited hero sprinting and karate-kicking his way through the pages of Bryerly Bertholt's comic. . . .

Leah heard the twins coming before Dolf had his eyes open. It was scarcely light, but she could see puffs of vapor escaping her nostrils in the cold room.

Ordinarily, the last Sunday in April—this year it fell on the thirty-seventh—marked the beginning of springlike weather for the people of Walsenburg, Gardner, and Snowy Falls. This winter had been a harsh one, though, and, weeks after the vernal equinox, snow was still sifting down on the Sangre de Cristo range and the towns huddled in or near it.

"Wake up, Mommy! Wake up, Daddy!"

"Wake up! Wake up!"

Eldred came bursting through their bedroom door first, closely pursued by his sister, Karina. They were clad in flannel pj's with cutesy-poo animal decals and sewn-in feet with reinforced soles. Dolf kept saying that five was too damn old for them to be running around in such tacky nursery-school garb, but the sewn-in feet were definitely winter necessities and Dolf's daddy, Reece, had picked out these pajamas himself. The elder Packards bought so many clothes for the twins that Leah sometimes thought they usurped her maternal prerogative. But, my God, it was a real financial help, she had to admit. . . .

"Get up, get up!" Eldred cried, tugging on Leah's autothermic blanket in hopes of exposing her to the cold.

"Yeah. Time to see about opening our presents." Karina began to work on Dolf, who turned to his belly and pulled a pillow over his head. "Come *on*, Daddy. After we open presents, the Choragus is gonna announce Lottery winners."

"All right, all right," Leah said. "We're coming."

"No, we're not," Dolf mumbled.

But, inevitably, even Daddy gave in, and the four of them—Dolf by far the least enthusiastic—bundled into robes and descended the A-frame's cedar stairs into the living room. The wall-sized window fronting Big Sheep Mountain revealed a grainy dawn full of drifting flakes and ghostly evergreens. A huge magpie was perched on the rearview mirror of the blanketed pickup truck that Dolf had driven home yesterday from Earl Rudd's ranch, and the monorail joining the towns of eastern Colorado to the high plains near the Great Divide flashed by in the dazzle like a coruscating beam of laser light. Leah shivered.

"Look," Dolf told the kids. "Your first white Easter."

The Packards' tree—a tall spruce decorated with polymer lilies and mirror-worked oyster shells—stood directly across the living room from the Resurrection rood that Dolf had built for Leah six years ago. Packages lay beneath both rood and tree. The rood sheltered gifts that a service commune in Denver would later hand out to the prisoners in Canyon City; the tree shaded gifts that the Packards would soon open themselves.

If, thought Leah, I can get the kids to hold out long enough to thank God for this delicious morning. And to let Dolf put a pot of coffee on in the kitchen.

Getting the kids to kneel at the rood wasn't hard, but keeping them there for more than a minute was impossible, and Dolf was no help at all. As soon as he had the Yubik perking, he found the master remote and clicked on the pool-table-sized tri-D screen that Earl Rudd had given him as a bonus for fieldmarshaling last fall's roundup in a record three days. This screen took up most of the brick wall under the upstairs bedrooms, and as soon as it began generating images, Eldred and Karina were off their knees, confused about which way to turn. The tri-D or the tree?

"It's Easter, Dolf. Can't you forgo your electronic fix?"

Dolf, still watching *The Today Show* over one shoulder, came out from under the dormitory overhang.

"The President's about to speak, Leah. Besides, I feel like I have to get . . . hell, I don't know, *reoriented*."

"Reoriented? What do you mean?" He was always exasperating on Easter morning. He had no patience with the kids' excitement, and if it weren't still snowing, and if the holiday didn't mean so much to her and the twins, he would've probably already driven back up to Earl's to babysit the spring calves.

Dolf pulled her to him and kissed her. Eldred and Karina sat down by the tree like tiny Buddhas. But God knows, thought Leah, they're too damned antsy to emulate Buddhahood convincingly.

The Today Show announcer yielded to a close-up of President Jordan. The twins scooted toward the screen, and Big Barbara began delivering her Easter message in her lilting female baritone. The sound of it seemed to warm the entire downstairs.

"O my fellow Americans," she said, "what an auspicious morning this is. If you're a Christian, we in the White House wish you all the most joyous blessings of the Savior's Resurrection. If you're of some other religious or metaphysical persuasion, the day *remains* an auspicious one.

"At one o'clock this afternoon, eastern standard time, but four hours from now, the Choragus of the seraphic Choir that homesteaded our Moon nearly eight years ago will announce the names of the seven Earth families chosen to visit their planet of origin in the Mira Ceti binary system. From that wonderful vantage, these lucky folks will witness the beautiful turmoil of Mira Ceti A in the last stages of its stellar evolution—only days before that star, whose diameter is more than four hundred times our own Sun's, blazes out in supernova.

"The Choragus assures me, and every other world leader, that our human representatives will have full protection from cosmic-ray bombardment. Further, they will return to Earth within a mere six months of their departure. Forget those relativistic effects that would bring them home hundreds of years after all of us who tell them good-bye have died. How the Choir proposes to accomplish this, we do not fully understand—but, it seems, our travelers will be taken to the eighth planet of Mira Ceti B by way of the same paradimensional tunnel that the Choir used to pop into sight near our Moon in 1976.

"Why has the Choragus chosen to announce these Lottery winners on Easter Sunday? Well, those selected to visit Mira Ceti B VIII, the Choir have repeatedly told us, will witness not only the death throes of their binary's larger sun, but also a tangible appearance of divinity. To be specific, a manifestation of the Holy One who ordained the entire physical cosmos and who sustains it even in the face of cataclysmic galactic violence. This is a boon vouchsafed the intelligent denizens of solar systems doomed to destruction by supernova, but the Choir wish to share it with humanity. Why? For permitting them to take up residence on our Moon and for so readily accepting their advanced technologies and their wise mediation of our many political, economic, and religious conflicts."

"As if we had any choice," Dolf says.

After President Jordan's Easter message, the *Today* newscaster recaps yesterday's news, ending with accounts of a joint British-Argentine satellite launch and the dedication of a fusion-power facility in the Golan Heights that has already begun to serve both Israel and Syria.

Leah stood by Dolf, an arm through his, only half her attention on the tri-D screen. She remembered the weird evening in '76 that the Choir—as most English speakers call the aliens—"popped" into view in Earth's sky. They arrived via a paradimensional realm that her friend Erica Gipp dubbed the "Id Grid." Often, one's mind can better solve problems through dreams or daydreams than through conscious logic. Similarly, star travelers can better cross vast distances by forsaking the physical plane of the universe than by skating its surface. Therefore, if Space, like Mind, has conscious and subconscious aspects, the shortest distance between Mira Ceti and the sun lies along Erica's Id Grid.

However one explains their advent, the Choir emerged from their paradimensional corridor aboard a transparent globe as large as the Moon. This globe, which had no measurable gravitational effects on the Earth or its seas, neared the Moon, opened a vertical seam, and engulfed the satellite. This process—alternately fascinating and horrifying—took exactly one week. Ever since, the Moon has been a chameleonic stranger. Sometimes it looks like a burnished hubcap, sometimes a bowl full of tropical fish and bioluminescent eels, and sometimes the lens of a giant projector showing surrealistic movies in kaleidoscopic Technicolor.

Things are going on up there, strange things. Now and again, the Choir floods the airways of Earth with eerie music, messages that synchronize with the pulsings of the Moon's alien skin. A few select human beings—the Choir have singled them out—are able to translate this "singing" into recommendations for implementing new technologies or for solving the various problems still dividing the people of Earth. And, so far, nearly all these recommendations have had an immediate influence for good. On the other hand, Lia thinks, you can no longer look at the Moon and find the features—craters, seas, and lakes—that NASA and the Soviets were mapping in earnest in the heyday of the East-West "space race."

"I'm tired of sittin' here on my butt waitin' for you guys," Eldred told his parents.

"Me, too," Karina seconded him.

Oh, no, thought Leah. Daddy's going to blister that butt you're tired of sittin' on. And our whole damn morning will be ruined.

But Dolf only laughed. "I *bet* you are, podnah," he said. "And you, too, Missy K." He turned off the tri-D with the master remote and led everyone over to the tree.

The Packards sat down near the frosty rectangle of the picture window and began opening presents.

The first two were for the kids, big boxes that Dolf told them to open together.

Package one contained a pair of foot-high plastic horses, with toy saddles, bridles, and riders.

Package two, which required no unwrapping, only the removal of the carton's top, held two more quirky creatures. But these were alive. A pair of guinea pigs, with fur the color of snow. Pet shops were calling them "snow babies" rather than guinea pigs, and that's what they looked like: snow babies. The kids needed to be a bit older to take care of them properly, Leah thought, but Dolf had insisted on buying them anyhow.

For Leah, the smallest box of all. It contained a gold pin, the intaglio profile of a fish. She was surprised and delighted, for Dolf was not usually the sort to give jewelry.

For Dolf, a book. He had recognized the item inside its paper as soon as he had seen her place it under the tree. Of course, he couldn't know *which* book she'd bought, and Leah watched intently as he pulled the wrappings off.

"Ah," he said. "Philip Kyle Dick. *The Three Desiderata of Calvin Deckard*." And he kissed her.

"I knew you liked his novels."

"This one's not a novel. It's what Dick calls his 'Exegesis,' a work of speculative theology. All that's novelistic about it, I think, is that he puts it in the mouth of a precognitive disciple of the Immortal One. The disciple's name is Calvino Deckard."

"The Immortal One? Christ?"

"Not exactly. Dick—I mean, the fictional Calvino Deckard—calls him a 'plasmate,' a form of living information, and he writes this about him." Dolf thumbed through the hardcover. " 'The Head Apollo is about to return.' He wrote that in '74, which makes it sound predictive of the Choir's arrival.

"Farther on, this: 'All creation is language and nothing but language, which for some inexplicable reason we can't read outside and can't hear inside. . . .' Of course, the Choir have begun to show us how to read and hear this 'language,' and when our Lottery winners go to Mira Ceti to behold God and to witness from ringside the events preceding their star's supernova, we'll know more about creation—and the language that formulated it—than anyone who ever lived before the Choir showed up here. It's just too bad that I resent them for hijacking our Moon and horning in on a search that we ought to be bright enough to conduct for ourselves."

"Maybe we *aren't* bright enough."

"They're millions of years older than the human species. Given that much time, we'd surely evolve an intelligence—and abilities—comparable to theirs. They're not giving us the chance."

"We're just as likely to blow ourselves up."

"I don't think that justifies their meddling."

Leah put her hand on Dolf's arm. "Enough for now, okay? Let's help the kids."

"Okay," he agreed, setting the book down. And they showed the twins how to prepare a box of cedar chips for the snow babies, how to put food pellets in jar lids nailed to small boards, and exactly how the babies' gravity-flow water bottles worked.

Bishop Jamie A. Parr of the Georgia diocese of the Protestant Episcopal Church stood by himself on a platform in the Mountain Convention Center in Gainesville, Georgia. He was waiting for the Choragus to speak to him through the two-hundred-member human choir standing on tiers to his immediate left. A tri-D camera was aimed at him from the control booth opposite his dais, perhaps a hundred yards away.

Spotlights fell on the bishop and on the robed choristers, whom he had personally selected from the choirs of forty of the largest churches in his diocese. Otherwise, the Convention Center, a great tiled hangar of a building, was ominously dark. Air conditioning had dropped Gainesville's springlike outside temperature to a nippy sixty-two degrees, but Bishop Parr was sweating.

When would the Choragus, who spoke for the alien Choir, reveal itself to him this time?

At exactly one o'clock, if its recent promise of today's modern Easter Event were trustworthy—for the Choragus had spoken to Parr two Sundays ago, while he was holding forth in the pulpit of Christ Episcopal Church in Savannah. It had ordered him to tell the world that seven human families would soon be given an audience with God, and it had urged him to gather a representative Episcopal choir to act as its mouthpiece. This command, this urging, had come to him as a kind of auditory hallucination in the midst of his sermon, and the congregation had had to tolerate a queer lapse in his delivery until he could sort out the matter.

The Choragus of the Choir from Mira Ceti B VIII wanted *a human choir* for a mouthpiece, Parr believed, not only for the spectacle that it would provide on the world's tri-D sets but also for the irony inherent in this arrangement. Over eight years, the aliens who had homesteaded the Moon had slowly developed something vaguely akin to a sense of humor. A human sense of what was both funny and fitting. . . .

In Parr's ear sounded the voice of a technician in the control booth: "You're on the air, Bishop."

Looking toward the camera, Parr managed an awkward hello and a few equally awkward prefatory words about today's Easter Event. As he spoke, the dark hall began to fill with a translucent mulberry light. A suffused glow like rippling silk.

A wind—nearly arctic in its chill—swept from one side of the Mountain Convention Center to the other, sighing past the bishop, billowing the indigo, saffron, maroon, or ivory robes of the choir members. Thus cued, the choir sang a major chord, a cappella. Then another, and then another. The alien wind corkscrewing through the hall inspirited every person singing.

Soon, the bishop was translating these powerful wordless carols as if they were all pieces of a lost text of which he was the sole reliable interpreter. The choir sang on and on, the silky crimson light in the hall waved rythmically, and Bishop Parr rendered into both English and graceful sign language the latest love message to humanity from the alien Choir on the Moon. Time ceased for him as he translated, and for the two hundred people singing, and for most of the world's people watching on their tri-D screens and listening to the magnificent accompanying chorale.

During the last minutes of the broadcast, Bishop Parr spoke the names of seven families worldwide. The fifth name spoken was that of the Dolf Packard family of Snowy Falls, Colorado.

Dolf held his breath. The last American astronauts to attempt to reach the Moon were the hapless crew of the Apollo 15 mission in 1971, and their deaths in lunar orbit—a drama played out over five excruciating days on live radio and television—had put an emphatic period to the American space program, wrapping it up at nearly the same time that the United States was pulling out of Vietnam at the direction of President Muskie.

Now, Dolf, Leah, Eldred, and Karina Packard—as un-

likely a crew of intersteller explorers as Dolf could imagine—
were flying to the Moon in a craft hurled into space by means
of a set of acceleration tracks on the flank of Mount Kilimanjaro in East Africa. The ship itself had been molecularly
assembled, three months ago, by Revolutionary NanoTech of
Hanoi. All around the Packards, on couches like their own,
sat the other passengers aboard the iridescent ship carrying
them heavenward.

A family from Leningrad, a family from Hong Kong, a
family from Zaire, a family from Saudi Arabia, a family from
Peru, and a family from Malaysia.

None of these families, Dolf had long since learned, spoke
the native tongue of any of the others; all communications to
date had consisted of nods, smiles, and bemused shrugs. The
fact that the vessel held thirty-five people added to this
confusion.

All that kept Dolf from panicking was the presence of his
loved ones and the knowledge that they would reach the
Moon in thirty-six hours. Then they would fly through the
multicolored rind encasing the Moon into a paradimensional
expressway linking humanity's solar system to the Mira Ceti
binary.

Or so, nearly nine weeks ago, Bishop Parr had told the
world, deciphering the alien Choir's message from the eerie
harmonies of their two-hundred human mouthpieces.

"I've told you guys before," Eldred whined, "I don't *want*
to meet God."

"Me, either," Karina said, squirming.

"Just hush and watch the Moon," Leah advised them, for
the Moon was visible as a huge bronze and verdigris
cantaloupe in the banks of windows at the forward end of
their craft.

When the twins continued to protest, Dolf leaned across
Leah's seat-belted body and shouted, *"Hush!"*

Much more quietly, he added, "You're damned well going
to meet God. And *like* it. Didn't we have a democratic vote to
see if we'd do this or not? And didn't you guys say over and
over again that you wanted to see a star explode?"

"Almost explode," Eldred corrected him.

"Okay, 'almost explode.' Well, ours is a free family, and
your votes counted, and I don't want to hear any more of this

guff about 'not wanting' to go. It's too late for second thoughts."

"I'm worried about our snow babies," Karina said.

"Gramby and Grandma Packard have them," Leah said. "They'll be fine. We've been all over that, too."

The argument continued, and Dolf wondered briefly if the Choir had ever considered supplying their Lottery winners with some kind of soporific for hyperactive five-year-old pilgrims. If the twins were this fidgety all the way to Mira Ceti, he'd be a nervous wreck long before entering the awesome presence of the Holy One. He and Leah both . . .

At last, though, the kids quieted, playing a made-up zero-g game with a red squeeze ball and a Dixie cup.

Leah laid her hand on Dolf's thigh. "It's too bad President Humphrey didn't live to see this," she said, nodding at the Moon. Its bronze and verdigris bands had turned pewter and platinum; now they were streaming in opposite directions across the glassy Choral rind. A remarkable, if disorienting, sight.

"Yeah, it is," Dolf agreed. Humphrey had died in a helicopter crash at Camp David the day after the Apollo 11 astronauts took off from Cape Kennedy for the first successful Moon landing. Muskie, freshly sworn in, had greeted Armstrong, Aldrin, and Collins on the aircraft carrier *U.S.S. Hornet* upon their return, but the nation's triumph had been tempered by a profound sadness. NASA dedicated its next four Apollo missions to the memory of the late President, but the shocking failure of the fifteenth was the entire program's death knell. The Soviets, by limiting their efforts in space to orbital flights, had virtually assured that men would not set foot on the Moon again before the year 2000.

And then, in the year of America's Bicentennial, the Choir had arrived. Initially, mass hysteria. Afterward, the growing global conviction that humanity would never venture to the Moon so long as these mysterious aliens occupied it.

Later in the year, Barbara Jordan, after taking the Democratic nomination for president from Muskie, defeated Ronald Reagan in the general election, and the Choir began bestowing both technology and advice on the shell-shocked human species.

Eight years of their largess had not inured Dolf to the

oddness—the down-and-dirty *perversity*—of the relationship between these impalpable energy beings and humankind, but here he was riding one of their ships to the most improbable sort of celestial rendezvous, and his foremost concern was not that the Packards all get back safely or that he make a good impression on God, but that the kids refrain from driving him and Leah crazy during the journey. He was on the verge of praying for their good behavior, and, if he did, he hoped to hell that the Holy One would hear him. . . .

In a monastery near Conyers, Georgia, Philip Kyle Dick sat in his cell writing.

God or the demiurge had a hand on his shoulder, giving him to understand that this oddball reality was still not the one that he wanted to live in.

He was fifty-three years old, and his literary career lay in ruins behind him.

Hence his retreat to this Trappist institution, a spin-off from the one in Kentucky to which Thomas Merton had belonged.

Hence his feverish cogitations long into the night, past all the canonical hours of monastic worship.

Hence his realization that he would have to write his and his compatriots' way out of bondage.

For this reality would hold them forever unless he lifted his pen and began to re-create the world. Once again, he must make a concerted effort to bring about the redemptive shift.

Therefore, Philip Kyle Dick put pen to paper and painstakingly altered the basic lineaments of the universe.